THE DISTANT EMPIRE

A Story of Early Louisiana

HENRY HOWELL

Bloomington, IN Milton Keynes, UK

authorHOUSE®

AuthorHouse™
1663 Liberty Drive, Suite 200
Bloomington, IN 47403
www.authorhouse.com
Phone: 1-800-839-8640

AuthorHouse™ UK Ltd.
500 Avebury Boulevard
Central Milton Keynes, MK9 2BE
www.authorhouse.co.uk
Phone: 08001974150

First published by AuthorHouse 5/3/2007

ISBN: 978-1-4259-8949-1 (sc)

Printed in the United States of America
Bloomington, Indiana

This book is printed on acid-free paper.

Foreword

The great struggle of the eighteenth century was between France and England for control of trade through empires that spanned the entire globe. The most important of these empires was in North America and its interior. For half a century these world powers fought for control of the Mississippi River Valley which stretched from the Appalachian Mountains to the Rocky Mountains and from the Gulf of Mexico to the Great Lakes.

The key to this vast empire unto itself was the mouth of the Mississippi River which the French claimed in 1684 and named the entire region Louisiana. In 1699, Pierre le Moyne, the Sieur D'Iberville, founded the colony along the Mississippi coast but war and death were the hallmark of the period and it was left to his younger brother, Jean Baptiste le Moyne, the Sieur de Bienville to build and protect the colony. He would serve as governor for thirty-three of the next forty-five years.

In 1717, Bienville founded New Orleans and made it the capital of the colony. From this small capital on the edge of the world he built settlements, dealt with natives, conducted trade with France and her colonies across the Atlantic ocean, and with Canada through the

Mississippi River and its tributaries that ran through the Illinois region to the great lakes.

The two great native tribes of the lower Mississippi River Valley were the Choctaw and the Chickasaw. Natural competitors and enemies, they made alliances with the Europeans who came into their lands. In the south, the Choctaws had more dealings with the French along the coast near the mouths of the Mississippi and the Mobile rivers. The Chickasaws allied themselves with the English traders who came over the lower Appalachian Mountains from the Carolina colonies on the Atlantic coast.

The French colonists that came to this new world were faced with many dangers. Supplies and tools were always in short supply. Ships from France were few and far between. The fear of Indian uprisings was constant. Political intrigue was a fixture in the colonial government. Rich men received royal grants of land and brought African slaves as they attempted to raise tobacco and sugar cane. The threat of a slave uprising added yet another fear. Greed and politics became the driving forces in relations with the Indians, the English, and in the division of land.

Despite these hardships settlers, from Germany as well as France, made their way to the colony in the hope of a better life. They came into a world of heat and humidity, of insects and reptiles, of fever and death.

Also, into the colony came the coureur de bois, the woods runners from Canada. These were hearty frontiersmen and trappers who plied the rivers of this vast wilderness in their pirogues, or canoes. These were men that knew the land and the natives. These men were the eyes and ears of Bienville as he tried to govern the ungovernable territory.

Bienville was replaced as governor in 1723 and six years later the worst fears of the colonists were realized. The Natchez Indians slaughtered all the colonists in their territory along the Mississippi River. Eventually the Natchez were defeated and went to live among the Chickasaw. From their base in what is today northeast Mississippi, and supplied by English agents, the Chickasaw and their Natchez guests harassed both the French settlements and the lands of the Choctaw.

Bienville was reappointed governor in 1733. He determined that the Chickasaw must be subdued for there to be peace in the lower Mississippi Valley. In 1736 he planned to defeat the Chickasaw and seal the interior from English influence forever.

It is in this world that our story takes place. The events in this story are based on historical events. Many of the characters in this book were actual persons while others are composites of the real colonists of early French Louisiana.

THE COLONY OF LOUISIANA
CA. 1740

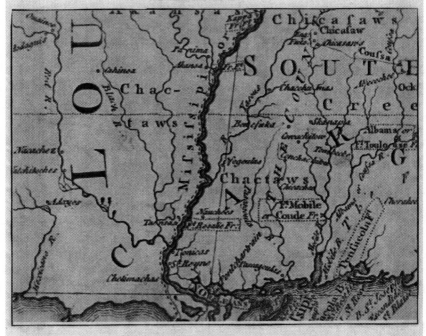

THE MISSISSIPPI RIVER NEAR
NEW ORLEANS CA. 1736

Chapter I

On an afternoon in late October, 1735, Evan MacDonald sat in Simon's public-house on the Quai de la Ferraille, getting drunk as thoroughly and as deliberately as he was able. A step down from the Seine quay-side, Simon's common room was long and low with a bar on the right-hand side behind which Simon himself sat, fat and greasy and frizzle-haired. Deal tables and benches stood down the middle, filled with river fishermen and quay hands laughing and drinking with Simon's girls. At the back of the large room a hearth-fire smoldered, curling up smoke which eddied in a thin, blue cloud the length of the windowless room. Quay-side was the Seine, flowing placid and dirty under the Paris bridges. The long rays of the sun reddened the water and, falling in a ruddy shaft through Simon's door, tinted the unswept floor.

Watching this light patch fade, Evan leaned on the table and croaked at Collette, the landlord's daughter, to bring more wine.

Evan was getting more drunk by the minute. He still had his hat on, and now he slid it rakishly over his eyes and peered out from under the brim at Rene Broussard across the table. Rene sat there easily in his patched trousers and heavy sabots and thin cotton shirt which was ripped half-way down the back between the shoulders. His lantern

1

jaw was loose in an approving grin because Evan had called for more liquor.

Evan grunted. "He's sober as a damned abbe," he thought irritably. It disgusted him to see a man who could drink wine down like water.

Collette, a short, slim girl of perhaps sixteen, with a tousled head and a round face which was a curious mixture of brightness and sullenness, swaggered up and slid a bottle of red wine between them.

"Thank you, mademoiselle," mumbled Evan fumbling for the bottle.

"Damn you, mademoiselle!" said Collette, plopping herself down beside Rene and giving Evan an impudent childish grin.

Her eyes above the grin were not childish. They watched on with a shrewd regard, "God pardon me, it's no business of mine," she said, twisting her full lips. "The more you guzzle the more metal for us. Maybe it's because I see men-swine enough every day that makes me hate to watch a good looking man lie down in the trough and wallow with the rest."

Evan eyed her owlishly while his hand crept away from the bottle. He was a tall youth, now humped over the table. His lean, tanned face had no superfluity of flesh. The bones of forehead and cheek jutted close beneath the skin. It might have been a dour face except for his mouth and his eyes. Now his lips were sullen from drink and his fine eyes, as brown as his hair, were clouded.

"I told you my father was dying," he said, with a thick tongue. "Can't a man take just one drink when his father is dying?" He looked down at his hands on the table and gulped faintly. "I expect he's dead by this time."

Collette narrowed her eyes. "Holy Mother! Have you no feeling? Dying, is he? Then the more reason for you to be with him, and sober.

What are you doing here?" She jumped up at a bellow from Simon but lingered, her eyes on the brown top of Evan's hat.

"You should be at his side, praying God for his soul, instead of drinking yourself blind."

"Let him alone," said Rene, with a black scowl. "The man's not drunk. Your wine's too thin to make a kitten drunk. The man's grieving. Wine is good for grief. Grief is good for nothing."

Collette squared to survey him scornfully, fists braced on immature hips. "You're full yourself." She flounced her shabby petticoat at him and walked on to the next table where two Seine fishermen, smelling of their trade, had just seated themselves.

Rene chuckled at her back and she looked over her shoulder giving him a derisive tongue. Rene's clumsy hand crossed the table and poured Evan's mug until the wine slopped on the board

"Maybe he's not dead," he suggested. "Maybe he'll be hale again. You never know. Now take my old father. When I was a child he had fits and used to go as stiff as a musket barrel. We thought he had died a dozen times, I guess, before he went for good."

"I know he's dead," said Evan querulously. "I know it. Didn't I see the priest coming up the stairs as I was coming down. With my own eyes. All in black. The color of death. He had a skull for a face. He was bringing death into the house. I sidled against the wall to keep him from touching me." He drew a deep, shuddering breath and stared wide-eyed past Rene's shoulder. "It made me cold. I couldn't stay there, I tell you."

Rene's blunt fingers plucked at his sleeve. "Easy, gars, easy," he muttered. "For sure, you'll feel bad to begin with. God knows I missed my old father." His grin was crooked. "particularly after dark. He used to beat me every night without fail."

Evan had not tasted his drink. He clutched the mug between moist palms and stared into it, his lips moving without sound.

"God!" he said, suddenly. "How could a man grow so old and change so much in eight years

Eight years, he thought, eight years since he had left his father's house in the Fauxbourg de Montmartre and gone away to his Uncle Jamie MacDonald's in the Scottish Highlands. Eight years in the Highlands, of forgetting Montmartre and Paris and France: and David, his father; and Raoul and Catherine, his brother and sister; even Antoinette, the adored playmate of his childhood, who had lived in the house next door. Memories! They were buried under the sands of eight years until he had come home two weeks ago to find his father an old and broken man. His mind which had been fogged with the wine and a swirling sense of terror came suddenly clear. He shut his eyes, blotting out the mug and the spilled wine on the deal table and Rene's hairy forearms at the rim of his vision.

It was as if he had opened a door and walked into a room crowded with memories, like people dancing. Fragments of memories which flickered away and others which stood as steadily as life. David MacDonald in stout steel-buckled shoes and rusty brown coat and breeches, walking so briskly through the open country outside Montmartre that Evan on his long colt-legs must fairly run to keep pace. And he could hear that vital, burring voice of David speaking the Gaelic which he had taught Evan, his youngest and most pampered child. Tales of the heather and the glens, of folk not human, the little people who were as much a part of Scotland as the hills themselves, of the raids on the lands and cattle of the MacKenzies and Campbells, and of the Sassenachs who had brought their English law into the Highlands. Evan had heard how his father had run away from home, over the North Sea to his land of Frenchies.

4

Tales, tales! He had been like an itinerant peddler pulling them from his pack: the same old ones, no doubt, in a new dress, but dazzling to a boy's eyes. France, and New France, and Hudson's Bay with Le Moyne d'Iberville where (good and rare memory!) they had whipped the English. He had been a salt of the Navy and had known not only D'Iberville but his brother De Bienville, and had seen the great muddy Mississippi River in far off Louisiana. It had been the great pride of Evan's childhood that he, too, had known that Sieur de Bienville who had then lived near Montmartre. He could still vividly picture the small, irascible man with his overlarge head and his quaint way of cursing, in the vernacular of the Canadian voyageurs, all things which displeased him. He had cursed particularly the Company of the Indies for having exiled him from Louisiana where he had been Governor, off and on, for more than twenty years. In his curses and his tales, that faraway province had become a boy's image of heart's desire. And Evan had dreamed of adventuring there and growing old, like David and De Bienville, with tales of his own to tell.

Yes, his father had been a virile man then, and happy in recollections and his adoration of Evan's mother though she, a birdlike, thoroughly frail Frenchwoman, was utterly unlike Highland David. It was probable that in all France there had been no more ill-assorted pair, yet when she died a part of David had died, too. The meaning and reality of life had been taken from him.

From that day he was a man in a fog which Evan, then in his thirteenth year, had been unable to penetrate. His affairs (never too competently managed, for business had been David's forte) had proceeded to the point of ruin before Raoul, then establishing himself in the practice of law, had retrieved them. Those were days not good to recall even now. Raoul had been head of the house and thirteen-year-old, pampered Evan had resented that as bitterly as he had resented his

5

father's sudden indifference. No doubt, he admitted ruefully, he had been a thorough pest to deal with in those days, but that had scarcely justified Raoul in packing him off to Uncle Jamie.

By this act, however, Raoul had unwittingly done him a good turn. In the Highlands he had found those things which a boy needed to become a man. That was a land of palpably frightening beauty and strength; whose people lived poorly and half-savagely by continental standards but they lived as they pleased. He had learned, at the hand of Uncle Jamie, to use the Highland weapons of the broadsword and dirk. He had learned to hate the British Sassenachs and the rule of their German King. But the freedom of the open Highlands, the moors and the braes, was intoxicating. He had become one of those folk and felt that was his land. He felt it so much so that when Raoul's letter had reached him in September with the news that David MacDonald was near to death, he had felt no emotion save annoyance at being disturbed. He would as soon have journeyed to London among the Sassenachs as to have returned to France.

It had been only a compelling sense of duty, not compassion for his father, which had brought him home. Certainly it had not been consideration for Raoul's wishes, although the comradely tone of Raoul's letter had puzzled him to no end. As to that, Raoul had not kept him long in the dark. And now as he thought of Raoul's schemes his temper flamed up again and his head had room for nothing else.

He snatched the mug between his two hands and drank it half-empty, like a lout swilling soup. The wine and his hot anger mingled making him giddy. For half a minute his head spun crazily. Then as it steadied he could feel himself puffing like a pigeon with self-confidence. He cracked his palm on the table.

"Damn him!" he said, so loudly that Simon drowsing behind the counter popped up his frizzled head; and a couple who were making for the side door which led to the bedrooms upstairs turned around to stare. "Why, damn his soul to hell! I won't do it!"

Collette, swaggering down the room, was behind him. He spoke. Her laughter bubbled as she dropped her bare arms across his shoulders, hooked her fingers beneath his chin and rubbed her smooth cheek on his. "Feeling better, little one. Good!" Before he could turn his head her fingers fell away, her body spun with a swirl of skirts and then dropped down beside Rene giggling and winking at him while he scowled blackly back at her. "Don't kill me with looks, you!" she cried merrily.

Her quick movements had upset Evan's precarious balance and made his head throb.

He muttered at her: "Stand still!"

She laughed at him. "What do you damn, then?"

"You maybe," Evan said, sullenly. His great feeling of confidence had evaporated. He felt sick and helpless and alone. "You know what my brother wants me to do?"

He looked from Rene to Collette craftily to ascertain if they might be in on Raoul's schemes. "He's trying to make me marry!"

Collette choked gleefully. "Holy Mary!" she said. "Is that a crime?"

"When you consider the circumstances, yes." Said Evan sourly. "Julie Duplessis. That's the woman. The daughter of old Duplessis, the farmer-general, you know."

Collette looked dumb but Rene twitched on eyebrow. "Julie Duplessis, a female turkey if I ever clapped my eyes on one." I'll grant you that old Duplessis has ears at court and manure enough to make Raoul's land and mine as rich as any in France." His voice went shrill. "God! Why can't they keep their money and their ears and let me be?"

7

Rene grunted. "Ears have a way of going deaf when they like," he said. "But money, by God! Money always gets an answer. Me, for a little money I would marry any woman." He prodded Collette so viciously in the ribs that she squealed out loud. "Even this one."

He could not catch her hand before she had hit him across the ear. Evan eyed the ensuing scuffle with disgust.

"You're hungry," he told Rene. "Your belly's empty. There's nothing you wouldn't do to fill your belly."

Rene took his hands off Collette. His eyes burned, angrily in deep sockets.

"Hungry?" he said, slowly. "For sure, I am hungry. Where I come from you don't know what a full belly is. Back there in Auvergne I used to grub my fingers into nubs, in dirt that wouldn't grow a respectable weed. So I got out of there and joined the army and fed on black as hard as a cobblestone, while the lice were feeding on me. I don't know who got the best of that bargain, but I expect the lice must have suffered from lack of nourishment, too."

His physical hunger was plain in his face; hollow cheeked, clean-shaven, with a bluish tinge where the beard showed through the skin. But for an instant a more subtle hunter peered intensely from his sunken eyes. He stood up none too steadily, hitching at his waistband.

"If I need food, now, I'll take it or steal it. I'm no beggar, see. You, with your fine clothes and your money, if you don't like what I say you can take your damned wine and drown yourself in it."

Collette pulled at his arm and shook her head. "Sit down, dindon. He meant no harm."

Evan waved his hand graciously. His eyes were beginning to blur again, which disconcerted him not a little. He knew what he wanted to say but his tongue was unmanageable.

"Friends," he said, thickly. "Me--you, good friends. What's mine, yours--friends."

Rene's harsh face softened. "You're feeling bad, mon vieux," he said, kindly. "You'd better go to bed."

"No," said Evan stubbornly. Rene had been telling that for hours. He felt a foggy annoyance. "No bed. No woman. You know what my father said?"

He was trying to remember it himself, but all he could think of was his father as he had last seen him; a face so formless it seemed to melt into the pillow, with eyelids like transparent waxen cups, tight-closed, hiding the eyes that had once been so alive.

He heard Rene saying as if from a vast distance: "Come on, gars. Come upstairs with us. We'll find you a bed and a good girl."

"Go away," said Evan. "I don't like this place. I'm going home. Home--long-way--Scotland. I don't like this place." He brushed his hand at them with clumsy petulance. "Go to bed."

He heard their footsteps dimly retreating and his head drooped closer to the table. He could still see that dreadful waxen face of his father and its lips move, framing words, "You do as Raoul says, my son. It is better. It is better. . ." Then words came from a healthy, well-remembered Gaelic face. His ears strained eagerly to hear this new face speak, yet it truly looked kindly at him. The words, when they came did not come from the face at all but from somewhere within his own consciousness.

"Sooner or later, my son, a man will find a woman who fits into life as naturally as the earth under his feet and the wind and the sun in his face. If he begins by sampling a little of every woman he meets he is bound in the end to be wearied of them all."

These were the words he had been trying to remember, and he felt strangely comforted, somehow protected against Raoul and Julie Duplessis. His head rested on his crossed forearms and he drowsed.

Rene, who had been waiting in the side door, came back, lifted him in his arms and carried him up the stairs outside.

Chapter II

David MacDonald had been dead for exactly one week. A week which to Evan seemed like a ghastly dragging year. On the fourth of November, which was chill and gray with a distinct threat of rain after two wet days, he spent the better part of the morning wandering disconsolately about the muddy streets of Montmartre and into the withered fields beyond the village. Still full of bitterness against Raoul and disgust for himself, he cursed the lethargy of mind which seemed to be causing him to drift with the tide. About noon, he supposed, without being sure, for the ashen waste of clouds entirely hid the sun, he returned to the village and, still rambling aimlessly, found himself at last before the old Church of St. Pierre de Montmartre. Looking up he saw the Gothic tower looming against the wintry sky. Without premeditation he turned past the church into the cemetery at the back of it.

He walked quickly to his father's grave in a rear corner of the cemetery, and some force outside himself sent him down like an automaton, resting on his right knee beside the truncated, oblong mound of yellow sandy earth. The rains of the past two days had begun to settle the loosened soil and had washed away the flowers which had been piled above the grave. There was something forlorn and naked and new about this new grave among the old ones all around. It stood apart, as Highland David MacDonald had always stood from the men of this French town.

Evan's finger fumbled his cocked hat against his chest, and dropped it in the mud, soiling the brown brim. Idly brushing away the stain he wondered why he had come at all or how to feel now that he was here.

As he gave the question conscious thought he felt embarrassed, an immense hypocrite, kneeling in an attitude of grief when there was little of grief in him. What sorrow he did feel was for those years when he had been away and David MacDonald's life had guttered like a dwindling candle. His boyhood memories made the beginning of that period so vivid that his father's actual passing seemed rather like something he might have dreamed . He had not seen him die, he had not seen him buried. On that night a week ago when David MacDonald's heart had stopped at last, Evan had been lying dead drunk in the untidy bed above Simon's tavern where Rene and Collette had dumped him. He had been so drunk that to this he could not remember if a girl had been with him. What he could remember was staggering home in the middle of the morning to a house in mourning; and how sick and sober he had turned at the look in his sister Catherine's face. He could still see those faces of the three who greeted him, as if they floated bodiless in the air: Catherine and Raoul and Monsieur de Villiers, his father's old friend of Navy days who had come up from the city for the funeral. Long before Catherine and Raoul had finished upbraiding him for his conduct he had been too sick of heart and body to care what they said.

He had turned to totter upstairs and would have fallen had not spry little Monsieur de Villiers caught his arm. It had been Monsieur de Villiers, too, not any of his ownblood, who had put him to bed with a damp cloth on his bursting head. And he had sat at the bedside and talked and talked upon all subjects, save that of David

MacDonald. Of his ship the, Gironde, which was filling at Le Havre to sail to Louisiana within a fortnight, of the difficulties he had been experiencing with the Comte de Maurepas, the Minister of the Marine, over the coming voyage. Talking and talking with all the kindness in the world in his weathered, mobile face, until Evan had fallen asleep. Evan had known the little ship's captain all life, but he had never felt closer to him than in that bleak hour.

Monsieur de Villiers had returned to Paris on the day after David MacDonald's funeral which Evan, still confined, had not attended. Evan had wished that he, too, were going to Le Havre and the ship that was bound away from France. Not only because he was fond of Monsieur de Villiers and sick of Paris, but because the Captain's tales of the sea and the colony of Louisiana had sent a brief, bright flash through the prevailing melancholy of his mood.

When he put down one hand, digging his fingers into the wet, cold earth of the grave he could fairly feel the loneliness of his father pushing up to match his own loneliness. His father, too, had been an alien among all these French people, and his aloneness after his wife had died had been more than he could bare. How desperately at times must he have longed for his native Highlands?

Evan closed his eyes visioning on the back of his eyelids the beauty of that land of rugged hills: a beauty that was deep and alive, bright and joyous or austere and terrible, ageless and adhering to no constant pattern, but forever changing. Year in and year out he had watched summer and the heather throw a purple shawl over the shoulders of the mountains; or as the seasons turned, seen winter come to drop its cold, hard hand upon the heart of the Highlands. The mountains throw off the purple shawl and draw a deep, white cloak about them, and frozen silence fill the woods where the great pines stooped white headed to the earth.

As the memory of the hills became too poignant he opened his eyes quickly. He stood up, looking out over Paris which was easily seen from the hill on which Montmartre was built. Under the pall of clouds Paris was only a waste of gray buildings fading to the westward into the gray sky. In the mid-distance the Seine flowed dully through the heart of the city, without a sparkle, like a river of lead. Seen from this perspective Paris seemed sober and peaceful, even clean; but Evan knew that it was filthy and churned a veritable volcano of life. A volcano which might one day erupt out of its own fermentation. There was nothing in it which he liked, not even the quays and low public-houses which he had frequented a great deal of late because there, at least, men did not wear wigs upon their heads and masks upon their souls.

His mind was made up, crystal-clear. He knew what he was going to do. His father, out of love for woman, had allowed himself to be imprisoned here. He was damned if he would make the same mistake! Not for money and a little property and an ear at Court.

As he walked out of the cemetery he saw the spire of the old church rising high and clean above the squalor of the town. He had played in its shadow as a little boy and for all his newfound determination he felt a pang that this was likely the last time he would ever see it.

It was with an air of almost giddy self-confidence that he wore his mud splattered shoes and hose to the dinner table and ate a hearty meal. The frigid displeasure of Catherine and Esther, Raoul's wife, did not disturb him at all. He felt himself the complete master of events and when Raoul, directly after the meal, retired to his office at the rear of the house, Evan lost no time in hurrying after him. His grin was crooked and defiant as he cracked his knuckles against Raoul's door and waited for an answer.

At the irritable response he stepped in and closed the door softly behind him.

The room was curtained and dim and smelled of Raoul's law books lining the wall. Raoul sat at his writing table, quill in hand, with a sizable stack of currency before him. A short squarish man, very neat in his blue coat and breeches, his face was as smooth and well ordered as his wig. All in all, he looked as calm and meticulous a man of law as one could have found in all Paris, but Evan knew the violence which trembled behind his impassive front. In that respect, and that alone, were he and Raoul brothers. Realizing that he was in for a bitter dispute, Evan's high spirits fell slightly. He hated disputes. He was too hot headed. They turned him tight and sick inside, filled him with a black turmoil and a desire to settle matters with his hands. He braced himself, remembering that his mind was made up. Here and now he would face Raoul down.

"I want--I want a word with you, Raoul." He had meant to speak evenly and despised himself for having blurted the words.

Raoul's sardonic eyebrows lifted. "Well? Out with it. I am a busy man." He dropped his quill and leaned back with his fingers upon the stacked notes. "These accounts must be settled. I have a brief to prepare." He smiled. "Your time may be of no worth, Evan, but I have few idle moments."

"I won't detain you," said Evan, shortly. "I'm going home."

"Home?" He saw the calculating change in Raoul's eyes. "Well, well, Evan. I must confess you mystify me. I thought this was your home."

"Don't play the donkey," said Evan angrily. "You know what I mean. I'm going back to Uncle Jamie's."

"Indeed." Raoul maintained his faint tone of sarcasm. "Then, I take it, you propose to return with Mademoiselle Duplessis to Scotland, rather than make your home here?"

Raoul's sarcasm infuriated Evan. His face paled. "I propose returning Mademoiselle Duplessis to the devil." He said, between his teeth, "I'm going home, and I'm going alone. If I had to look into Julie Duplessis's blue china eyes day and night, and listen--Good God! I'd be a drooling idiot within a week!"

"Indeed," murmured Raoul.

Evan doggedly stared back at him. "I will marry no woman for mere money."

Raoul said, patiently; "It's quite as simple to marry a rich girl as to marry a pauper."

Evan dropped his hands helplessly. "I don't want Julie Duplessis, Raoul," he said. "I don't want Paris or anything Paris can give me. I want to see what the world is made of. Some day I shall do exactly that. In meantime, I'm going back where I'll be at peace."

Raoul groaned, "Peace and adventure! They are not often bedfellows, brother. This is a matter of common sense. Duplessis is one the richest farmers-general in France. He is able to give you worthwhile things— almost anything within reason."

"Give me or give you?"

Evan had taunted him with deliberate malice and the satisfaction of seeing anger rub the smoothness from Raoul's well ordered face rewarded him. Raoul's nostrils and his lips thickened and curled.

"You ungrateful whelp!" Raoul slammed his chair back and stood up glaring. "After all I have done for you."

Evan knotted his hands, his restraint was dwindling, dwindling. . . He whirled from Raoul to the window of the house next door trying to deafen his ears against Raoul's words which lashed out at him, not so much like whips, but more like ropes intent upon binding him. He was not afraid of their sting. It was the power of Raoul's cleverness to hold him against his will that he feared.

He sought to make his mind a blank and succeeded in so far as Raoul was concerned, but it was queer how thoughts associated with the things he watched seeped in. On the wall of the opposing house the plaster had cracked and fallen away, leaving a bare spot roughly the shape of France. Years ago, when he was a boy, that bare spot had been in the shape of a gigantic cat's head, and a Madame Castilloux had lived in that house with her little granddaughter, Antoinette. When he was thirteen and she ten, she had been his little girl sweetheart. He had adored her to distraction. How she had used to laugh at that cat's head on the wall! People of another name lived next door these days. He wondered where Antoinette and her grandmother had gone. But that was all of the past, pretty memories, like the ones of his father, lost forever. It was the present which counted. He shrugged, turning back to that present with an urgent desire to end at once his interview with Raoul.

Raoul was standing, his arms folded in an attitude of great determination. His judicial air was more menacing than words, and to Evan the mustiness of the law books was suddenly stifling in the close room.

His voice trembled slightly with the restrain he put upon himself. "I'm going home, Raoul," he said carefully "That is final. But first I shall have my share of father's money. If I may."

Raoul stared back at him as if he had gone mad. "Your share? Then you have not the sense to know that there is no estate except that which I have redeemed. Whatever there is belongs to me. You have no share save what I allow you."

He stepped around the desk and came close to Evan, his smile broad across his face.

For an instant, as Raoul looked up, Evan looked down, and the black tide inside him surged higher. Without consciously realizing that it had moved at all, he found his hand on Raoul's shoulder, clamping like a vise. The shorter man winced perceptibly and Evan, grinning wickedly, spun Raoul off balance, shoved him stumbling against a chair which overturned with a ringing clatter. Before Raoul could recover, Evan took two strides to the desk and scooped up the stack of bank notes.

"I'll settle for this," he muttered, cramming the currency in a loose mass into the large pocket of his coat.

The blood went out of Raoul's face, leaving it dead white from fury. His voice shook.

"So! You are a common thief! Put down that money!"

Evan walked toward him slowly. While they both breathed hard, Evan towered over the short Raoul. His words came between his teeth: "Get out of my way."

Before the cold menace of Evan's voice Raoul shrank back a step, his face ludicrous with astonishment. Evan was at the door, his hand on the nob, before Raoul could find his tongue.

"You--you idiot! Where do you think you are going?"

Evan laughed crazily. "I'm going to get drunk first," He said. "Drunk as the drunkest fool that ever was. Then I'm going home."

CHAPTER III

Under the overcast sky, the light was already as dim as twilight when Evan turned out of an alley at the lower end of the Quai de la Ferraille. The wind whistled off the Seine, scattering rubbish along the waterfront and rattling and banging the blistered signboards above the public-houses and the dingy row of ironmongers' and sword makers' shops from which the quay got its name. Evan ambled moodily in the direction of Simon's watching his toes as they stepped, his chin in the collar of his coat and his hands bulging his pockets. So sunk was he in introspection which ranged from the extremes of vastly pleasing schemes for pickling Raoul in brine to fits of shame over the whole sorry situation, that the sudden banging of a drum and squealing of a fife almost shook his shoulders out of his coat. He pulled his chin out of his collar and looked around.

Halfway between him and Simon's place, as much in the lee of the buildings as was possible, a pavillion had been thrown up, gaily decked out in pennants and bunting, trembling in the wind. Evan's eyes brightened. It had been years since he had seen such a sight, but he recognized it at once for the portable bureau of Army enlisting agents.

19

A young officer presided over the bureau. Probably a lieutenant, Evan thought, but he was ignorant of the insignia of rank as well as of what regiment the shining white uniform represented. The officer was scarcely more than a boy, but he stood like a mapling with his beautifully powdered head high, trying to straighten his girlish lips into a proper military line. Beside him was an old, leather-faced sergeant with a halberd.

The sergeant was speaking, holding forth in a great, gusty bass upon the beauties of army life. His audience was a thin crowd, mostly countrymen and beggars and quayside ragtags, dead faced in the premature twilight, shivering in the biting wind. They cocked ears at the blaring music, looked now at the shining officer and now at the bunting, but for the most part they seemed not to pay much attention to the sergeant's harangue. Now and then, upon a wave of ribald comment and laughter, one in the crowd would be shoved forward by a couple of his companions, but he always squirmed free and his identity lost in the rabble. Evan hesitated, watching them curiously.

"Good men," roared the sergeant above their heads. "But think of it! You don't need to starve any more. You, there! And you, and you! You've had to toil for your bread, maybe you've had to steal it, God forbid! Now the King wants you! Ease. Plenty. The King's bread, the King's wine! Want more? Why, the King's coat, to be sure! Look at mine. None like it for prettiness. Warm? Well, you don't see me shaking in the cold. Pockets—pockets you can put your heart's desire in. Why, the women will kick their heels for a man in the King's coat. You wouldn't like that, eh?" He let his great voice drone. "And you are paid--paid for all these!"

"His sharp eyes caught Evan edging past and his forefinger, pointed like a pistol, singled him out. "You, there!," he bellowed. his lusty voice raveling the wind "You're a pretty cock, now, strutting on the walk.

The length and the breadth and image of what the King is looking for. Step up here, my friend. The King's proud to have you. And by God you're proud to serve the King!"

His words were like a halter dropping over Evan's head. He swung one step in the direction of the pavillion. Then he remembered Rene Broussard, and Rene's tales of the ten years he had spent in a provincial garrison. He scowled viciously at the sergeant and turned back towards Simon's, leaving the man bellowing and beckoning with his beefy hand. As he came under the perilously flapping signboard which announced without shame that Simon's old good wine inside, two ragged men stampeded through the doorway, one of them shouldering him off balance as he went plunging by. Behind them, a tousle-headed whirlwind, came Collette, shrieking. The men scuttled for the crowd, with their hands protectively over their heads. But the missiles which Collette hurled after them were nothing but words, loaded with implication and bedaubed with filth.

Evan grinned in spite of himself, watching her straight and sturdy figure in her coarse blouse and petticoat. Beneath the blouse her chest was a flat as a boy's; she might have been a boy in a woman's clothing, he thought.

"So that's the way you speed your parting guests?" he teased her.

Collette shrugged. "Guests? That scum! They come to roost and not spend a sou. Out they go!"

"The weather's bad," observed Evan. "Perhaps they only wanted a fire to stand by."

"The devil that got them can build them a fire to stand by! We earn our living here. Let me be fool enough to give one food or drink and I'd have a mob from one end of the quays to the other kicking the legs off the tables and lapping up all the wine." She pointed at the enlisting-agents and gave them an obscene name.

"The fine feathers yonder have all my trade today Still, maybe they'll bring in one or two before the day's over." She added in softer voice, "Poor devils!"

They stepped down into the common room which was deserted except for two fishermen dicing half-heartedly across a table near the front, and Rene Broussard, far in the back, beside the fire morosely contemplating the empty table before him.

"There's a man not drinking," said Evan. "Why don't you run him out?"

Collette said, tartly: "I ought to."

Rene looked up at them and rubbed his long jaw. "Bon jour," he greeted Evan. "I'm glad you came. I need a drink."

Evan kicked back the other bench and sat down "Red wine," he told Collette, and laughed at Rene.

"Where's your way with the ladies, my friend? Can't you wheedle a drink from little Collette here?"

"If my tongue was black from thirst she wouldn't give me a drink," said Rene sourly, "Unless I had a dirty sol to clap on the board."

Collette trotted up with the wine. "No, no, "she said. "He wheedles no wine from me. He's too far down in the dumps." She put her lips close to Evan's ear and whispered piercingly, "I think his mind is on Sophie, who lives upstairs."

Rene grunted disgustedly. "Don't show your jealously," he said pouring himself a drink

Collette leaned on the table, cupping her palms beneath her chin as she gazed intently into Rene's face.

"Me jealous?" she cried. "For sure, it's you that is jealous. Jealous because Sophie's with somebody else this minute. Why," she shrugged and twisted her lips in an imitation of commiseration, "Sophie must earn her living some way. Don't look so glum, it may not be serious, this man she has business with now." She fell to laughing so hard at herself that she choked and caught both hands on the table's edge for support. Evan pounded her between the shoulders and she sat down weakly on the bench, gasping for breath.

She pushed her hair back from her hot, flushed face and watched Rene narrowly. He studied a dirty fingernail which seemed to goad her on. She whirled saucily to Evan "You don't know Sophie?" Her was voice high and rapid. "No, or Rene would have had your heart out. She's from the Ile de St. Louis, but the good people over there don't approve of Sophie. Oh, no. They are too bigoted to understand Sophie. No man in that quarter would have married her. So she came on this side, and now Rene wants to make an honest woman of her."

The color had been mounting into Rene's face as if the wine instead of going down were spreading out beneath his skin. He slammed down his mug, making a splash on the table.

"Baste!" he said savagely. "I spent last night with the woman, yes, if that's what you're harping on. I spent the night before with you, so you might as well say I want to marry you."

He made a harsh sound of derision. "Don't talk so fast, little one. Simon will have you upstairs, before you know it, doing business, too."

His contempt, like fingers pinching a candle flame, snuffed the jeering from Collette's face. Her mouth drooped like a whipped child's, then turned hard and bitter. She leaned across the table, thrusting her face almost against Rene's.

"Yes, yes, yes!" she whispered fiercely. "But I don't want it. Holy Mary, preserve me! I don't want it!" Her voice dropped very low. Evan could scarcely catch the words. "You could stop it! You could--"

Rene avoided the dark appeal in her eyes, staring away from her at the tavern door. The fingers of his hand beside him the wine glass

23

opened and closed, opened an closed, and he seemed unconscious of it.

"Much you care," said Collette, bitterly. When he still said nothing she reached with a swift gesture past his left arm, snatched up his wine mug and drained it without taking breath.

Rene roused. "That wine's been paid for," he told her as if he were relieved to be again on bickering terms with her.

"Not by you," responded Collette tartly. "Not a dram would pass over the counter if you had to pay for it. You had your wine too long at the King's expense."

She said it to hurt him, but he took it calmly. "Ten years," he said, soberly. "Long enough."

He lifted his hand and as they stopped talking they heard the squealing fife outside.

"Hear that? I was eighteen the first time I heard it, a dindon of a peasant boy out of Auvergne. What would happen, you suppose, if one of those lice should walk in here?"

"Nothing," said Collette, perversely.

"I'm not so sure," muttered Rene. "I've thought about it many a time." He mouthed the last of his drink and poured more. Evan hefted the wine bottle. It was all but empty, though, in spite of what he had told Raoul, he had filled his mug but once. He nudged Collette and told her to bring another bottle.

"Where is the good Simon?" he asked when she came back.

"God knows," she said. "Half the time I have it alone--morning to midnight."

Rene's mind was still occupied with the enlisting agents. "This is a hell of a country," he mumbled, "with carrion like that at the top and me at the bottom."

Evan pulled at his lip. "I'm leaving it," he said

"Tell me a way to get out," said Rene. "and a place to go where a man can get a good meal at least once a day, and I'm with you."

"I'm going to Scotland," said Evan.

"That's England," objected Rene, shaking his head.

"Too cold, too wet. Too damn much fog, and ice, and snow."

He was so serious with his objections that Evan grinned. "Why don't you go to the colonies? New France?"

"Still too cold. I talked to a man once who had lived there. He said the only reason the savage people had no tails was because they froze off in the cold."

"Louisiana, then?"

"Louisiana? That's the place with the big river.

Jean L'as' land." Evan nodded, watching Rene's long face brighten a little. "It ought to be hot enough for you."

"Maybe," said Rene, turning glum again. "Why don't you tell me about the moon? One's as close as the other."

Evan shoved his hat back so that it covered his queue.

"There's a ship sailing for Louisiana from Le Havre," he said thoughtfully. "In a week."

"What ship? How do you know?"

"The Gironde. I talked to Captain de Villiers last week in my father's house. In the old days my father sailed with him."

"Why don't you?"

Evan glanced at him sharply while the seed of an idea sprouted. He wondered why he kept considering all these alternatives to returning to Scotland. "Why don't I?" he mused slowly. Then he shook his head. "No. I'm going home."

Rene was rubbing his forefinger in the puddle of spilled wine. "When I was in the army, I use to talk with soldiers who had lost everything in Jean L' as' scheme. They said there were rivers full of pearls and mountains of gold and diamonds and rubies, and God knows what, in Louisiana. Only no one ever found them."

"What do you think?" asked Evan.

"I don't know," said Rene. "I'd like to look. I'd like to get out of this country." He marked absently on the table top with his damp finger tip. Collette leaned across his shoulder and cried out with unrestrained delight.

Evan peered closer. With no better materials than his finger and the wine Rene had sketched a fair likeness of Collette on the rough surface of the table. He looked up again at Rene, unfeigned astonishment on his face

"I like to make pictures," Rene muttered with a shame faced smile. "All my life I've liked to make them. I can see them in my head." Again Evan saw the subtle hunger which he had noticed before flash in the man's deep-set eyes. "Do you suppose a man could do that in Louisiana?" "Any man?"

Then the brief intensity drained from his eyes because the front door of Simon's slammed open and the burly sergeant of the enlisting bureau lurched in, herding a clumsy, juling boy before him. Evan knew the stumbling boy was a peasant. He had all the docility of a domesticated brute and from him there seemed to exude a faint odor of earth and manure.

Rene put his hand hard on Evan's arm, never taking his eyes from the advancing sergeant. "Don't let him cross me," he said tensely. "I don't think I could stand it. I keep remembering too much."

"Watch yourself," said Evan sharply, "it doesn't pay to molest the King's coat."

The sergeant came between the tables straight down the room to the fire, rubbing his hands together to get the chill out of them. His eyes were small and red, and he narrowed the lids speculatively when he saw Evan and Rene. Collette jumped off the bench.

The sergeant shoved the peasant boy down at the next table. "This is good," he said, unbuttoning his coat. He looked first at the fire, then at Collette, slowly, from her tousled head to her ankles under the hem of her skirt. "Bring us wine, girl. Two bottles, and none of your thin slop for me, or I won't like your looks." He chuckled and throwing his arm around her waist pinched her sharply on the buttock. "When I'm done here, ma petite, we'll run upstairs for a little, eh?"

Collette's mouth opened but she had no chance to speak. Rene leaped to his feet and stood swaying. His bench overturned with a crash.

"Charaogne! he roared. "Keep your paws to yourself!"

The sergeant wheeled, face flaming, whipping his arm free of Collette. Rene had his wine in his hand. He flung the contents straight into the soldiers face, and as an after thought followed the mug itself. Collette yelped like a startled puppy. At the front of the tavern the two fishermen pocketed their dice and slid quietly out through the door. The sergeant with his hand over his eyes where the heavy mug had struck him, yelled profanely for help, and the wide-eyed peasant jumped up from the table like a dog at his master's command. Evan kicked his own bench against the peasant's long legs and the boy's feet caught together. Before he could stop himself he pitched headlong into the bar. Evan, feeling his blood going hot in his chest and a cold lump in his belly, leap-frogged the table after him. He saw Rene and the sergeant lock together, arm to back and chin to shoulder, and go down to the floor with the soldier beneath, taking the full shock on the back of his skull.

Evan quickly found he was no match for the burly peasant. His first lunge pinned the lad's arms, but then he was spun around by the

27

sheer strength of the other's shoulders and slung bodily along the bar. The countryman got his forearm like a bar under Evan's chin and bent him backwards across the counter. The breath wheezed between Evan's lips. He felt the pain in his back like a maul mangling it. He struggled desperately; the peasant's forearm was crushing his Adam's-apple, crushing the breath out of him. His head began to whirl. There was a shattering sound almost in his face and before his blurring eyes the face of the peasant boy fell away and vanished.

Wincing with pain he straightened his back. He stood tottering, pressing one hand on his back like a decrepit old man, while he held tight to the bar with the other. At his side was Collette, her breath coming and going hard, her face savage and exuberant. She had in her hand the jagged neck of a wine bottle and under foot lay the limp body of the peasant boy. The blood from his lacerated scalp mixed with the spilled wine and stained the floor in a widening pool.

It all had the substance of a nightmare. Evan labored to grasp it. In front of the fire Rene was snarling, his knees astride the sergeant's chest. Rene's powerful hands were on the man's throat. He looked dead, his tongue lolling and his face turning black and mottled. The exultation faded out Collette's face, she went white as paper. She caught Rene's shoulder, his shirt.

"Mother of God!" she moaned, "You've killed him."

Rene staggered to his feet, shaking his head savagely His wild eyes swung from the sergeant to the peasant. Soberness and sanity came back in to them.

His voice labored. "Dead. They're both dead."

They all stood numbly, their hands hanging.

Evan said, trying to keep his voice from trembling: "Those other soldiers! We've got to get out of here!"

The music had stopped on the quay outside the silence beating on their straining ears was more ominous than thunder. It was broken by the sound of running feet and at the same time a rising blast of wind and the swift, hard patter of the rain. The crowd on the quay was going pall mall to look for shelter.

"Here they come." yelled Rene. "Run for it. Vite! We can get away in the rain."

Wrenching open the tavern's rear door he plunged with Evan and Collette at his heels into a narrow, tortuous alley. Night had fallen. In a moment they were swallowed up by the darkness and the alley and the cold, gray wilderness of the rain.

Chapter IV

A gray mist seeped upward from the surface of the level flowing Seine and spun a web of obscurity between the Quai des Celestines and the black bulk of the Ile de St. Louis. Silence prevailed upon the quay. It was yet too early for the boats to commence traffic upon the river; those which were tied up at the quay lay like denser shadows in the shadow of the river wall. On only one, moored to the foot of a flight of steps which led to the water's edge, was there any sign of life. A dim lantern swung on the bows of the craft and there was a sound of movement upon it, soft and lonely in the hollow dawn. That and the measured lapping of the ripples at the base of the quay were the only sounds on the river.

At the northeast corner of the quay a little alley ran back from it like a rat hole into a wall. Huddled in the darkness of this alley Evan and Collette waited for the day. They also waited for Rene who had been gone two hours on a mission which he had not seen fit to divulge. Evan was in no good humor. His clothes clung to him in a disagreeable fashion like a rumpled and waded second-skin, and he was impatient that Rene had been gone so long. Then too, his thoughts were yet behind him, traversing the nightmare of pitch black, rain swept alleys by which they had gained the Quai de Celestines.

They had reached here an hour after nightfall, now many hours ago, when the rain had abated and the wind had begun to drive swift gray clouds which scattered like smoke across a sky of slate. But before that they had halted for breath in the shelter of the Church of St. Louis in the Rue St. Antoine. Then, and only then, had they found leisure to consider their predicament.

It was Rene who had spoken first, trying to be optimistic. "I doubt that that sergeant's dead. His neck was like a pig's, so thick I could not get my fingers well around it. The peasant had only a cut head."

"At any rate," said Evan, "They're seriously hurt. C'est pourquoi, we must get out of Paris."

"And after that is done," asked Rene. "Where to then?"

"I know where I'm bound," declared Evan. "The ship Gironde sails from Le Havre for Louisiana in four days. The captain of her is my friend. If I can get there I sail with him." Having made his decision his heart felt lighter.

"Louisiana," Rene said softly, "I have heard of it. A new land. France is old and set her ways, bad ways. Perhaps in Louisiana a man might walk upon his two legs and not be an owned brute. Is it no? Do you know?"

Collette broke in, her voice shaky with impatience, "Then, that's settled let's not waste time. The sooner we're out of Paris the better for all of us."

Rene peered at her through the darkness. "Where do you go?"

"Where you go, I'll go," she said simply.

Rene ventured dubiously: "What do we do for money for the ship's passage?"

Evan was none too sure of that himself, but he spoke with confidence. "Leave that to me. The captain, as I said, is my friend.

But we'll need money to get to Le Havre before the boat sails." He held up his own wallet: The coins rattled "This is not enough."

"So," observed Rene, "What money we get we must conserve." He struck his fist in his palm. "The water coach of Jules Jacot leaves the Quai des Celestines for Rouen at sunrise. We'll go aboard it. It is cheaper and safer than the diligence." He took stock as best he could in the gloom of their bedraggled appearance. "We would draw attention on the diligence. On the water coach we can go unnoticed among the peasants and poor folk who commonly travel by way of it." He stood up suddenly. "Let's get on to the quay. I have some business to attend to before the dawn." They had followed him then to this alley off the Quai des Celestines where he waited with them until past the hour of midnight. Then without explanation he had slid off into the darkness.

Now as they awaited his return Collette, her teeth chattering from cold and fright, crowded against Evan. He could feel the shape of her wet body through the wet cloth, but it held no warmth, no comfort against the reflections which tumbled in his brain. To the north, behind them, in the black corridor of the Rue St. Antoine, stood the great Bastille with its eight massive towers, dank cells and torture chambers, the imposing mausoleum of unnumbered and forever nameless political prisoners. To their right down the river in a labyrinth of narrow squalid streets lay the sinister Place de Greve, the place of public executions His taut nerves screamed to him that these two were the jaws of a vice which were closing upon him. He gripped himself upon the edge of panic. In him at that moment was a trace of the instinctive dread of the law which always daunted the Gael. The girl's body trembled against him. Somehow it was reassuring. His own fears lessened as his mind dwelt upon those which she must be enduring.

Minutes dripped away like the water from invisible eaves behind them. A shadow slipped down the alley. It was Rene coming back.

He crouched down by Evan without a word. To the east the night was lifting, the sky was streaked with pearl.

"Where have you been?" whispered Evan irritably Rene grinned in the half-light. "You said we hadn't enough money to get to Le Havre, non?"

"What do you mean by that?"

Rene hefted a dark object in his hand. "I made up the deficiency," he said dryly and passed the object to Evan.

As soon as he touched it Evan knew what it was without looking closer. It was a wallet and by the feel quite full. Suspicion flashed into Evan's mind.

"Where did you get this?" he demanded.

Rene stretched himself, pulling at his wet shirt where it clung to his back.

"Don't let curiosity make your nose grow long, my friend. There are ways of getting money in Paris, if a man knows them.

"Where did you get it?" repeated Evan. "You stole it."

Rene said hotly, "I did not steal it! I took it a fat pig who was on his way home from a rout. It was easy because he was drunk. But I didn't steal it. Let me tell you, he made it from the sweat of men like me. So it was no more his by right than it was mine. Am I right, hein?"

Evan shrugged resignedly. "Without doubt," he said. "Eh bien, there's nothing gained by arguing the matter. Since we've committed murder I suppose we've no right to be squeamish over a little thievery. This will come in handy." And he pocketed the wallet.

Dawn had broken clearly into the sky by this time and the gray light fingered its way into the alley. The quay came to life. There were men hurrying to and fro upon it, with lanterns and without. A clock mellowly tolled from the isle. Voices bawled orders and curses from the boats on the river. The waterfront was awakening to another day Evan got stiffly to his feet and Rene and Collette followed suit. Collette held to Rene's shirt for support, though he tried to break away.

"I've a notion to take off my skirt," she said wriggling he cramped legs. "It must be lined with lead the way it bears down on my hips. I'm wearied out with dragging it."

Rene's fingers almost unconsciously touched the wet garment, lingered where it was molded to her thigh.

Collette's breath came in sharply between her teeth and Rene, startled, jerked his hand away. Loosening her grip upon his shirt he pulled away and walked out upon the quay. "Where is the water coach?" asked Evan joining him and peering toward the river.

Rene indicated the craft which was moored to the steps. In the light of dawn it took shape as a squat, broad beamed vessel, curiously like an inverted turtle shell upon the water. It's upright mast and cross-arm were silhouetted above the level of the quay.

"That is the coach of Jules Jacot," explained Rene He studied the activity on the deck, the water coach and the number of persons, prospective passengers apparently, who were grouped at the head of the boarding steps.

"He'll have a full load, it seems. Some of the countrymen spent the night aboard, like as not. We had better go on now. He'll cast off as soon as the sun is up or his hull is filled."

He walked to the edge of the quay; "Eh, Jules!" he called. "Is there room for three more?"

A squat, bearded man rose up near the helm of the turtle shell.

"Aye," he said, removing his pipe only for the length of time it took him to say the one word. He was about to disappear into the cabin but Rene stopped him.

"Good." he said, "what time do you go?"

"When the sun comes up." Skipper Jacot pointed to the eastward where the sky held a pink glow. Shivering a little in the cold, transparent light which comes between dawn and the sunrise they waited at the head of the steps for the earlier arrivals to descend to the water coach. Then they went down in single file with Evan ahead and Rene bringing up the rear.

They picked up their way across the deck which was a litter of ropes and rigging upon which, if one were not careful, he was likely to trip and fall, and found the bearded skipper at the helm. As Evan paid over the money for their passage, Skipper Jacot gave them a cursory glance. He removed his pipe as he counted out their change audibly, in order to make sure, then he dismissed them, thumbing them to the cabin while he bawled an order to the mate forward.

As he ducked behind the other into the cabin, Evan could see plainly that the coach had never been constructed with an eye to the comfort or convenience of its passengers. The cabin was dark, musty as an ancient cellar, and so low that a man above medium height bumped his head when he stood upright. The passengers fitted together almost as closely as pieces in a mosaic. A diversified lot they were, but all humbly born; countrymen, laborers, small tradesmen, men of no trade, and a pair of monks.

Evan found room beside a pious faced peasant. He nudged the man with his elbow.

"Move over, friend, and let this lady sit."

As he and Collette squeezed into the space thus provided he saw that Rene had obtained a seat against the opposite wall. The peasant looked approvingly at Collette. "Your wife perhaps? Or your sister?"

Evan shook his head.

The peasant grinned knowingly, dissipating his pious mien. "She is young."

"The peasant, his eyes still on Collette, grew more friendly. He produced a bottle from beneath his coat. "Wine," he confided. "A man needs to fortify himself against a voyage down the Seine. Old Jacot has bad food on board and not much of that. If you brought none of your own you will go fasting. But he has good wine. He knows there is money in wine, the old fox. Drink with me friend. Where do you go?"

"Rouen," said Evan, drinking and handing the bottle at the peasant's behest to Collette. She drank and then drowsed against Evan's shoulder.

He watched other passengers come into the cabin and probe among its occupants until they could find space to sit.

"Are there always so many?" he asked the peasant.

"Eh? Often there are more, for soldiers travel this way. I see none this trip."

The thought of soldiers gave Evan a bad moment. He looked carefully around the cabin and was relieved to find that the peasant was right.

The vessel gave a sudden lurch, surging the packed passengers about and to the accompaniment of the skipper's.

profane bawling cast off into the stream. Slowly she floated down the Seine and Evan could feel a thrill inside him that he was on his way into world unknown, although he could see drifting behind only a strip of the river and the stones which held it in confinement.

The river ran out beyond the walls of Paris. The cabin was silent, full of sleepy people who had nothing to say. Collette was now deep in slumber, worn out from their sleepless vigil of the night. Beside Evan the peasant had fallen asleep over his bottle and across the cabin Rene snored. Evan remained awake thinking and watching the river. He rose cautiously so as not to disturb Collette and then made his way to the deck.

Here, beyond Paris, the Seine had flown into a tantrum. Flowing without reason first to one point of the compass then to that point most opposed, spinning in a great loop from Sevres southwest of the city to St. Denis on the north. Turning south again it threw out loop after loop folding back upon itself like an enormous intestine until Evan, first with sun at his back, then in his eyes, began to wonder if all their motion would ever resolve itself into an atom of progress.

His eyes on the changing shore, Evan had ample time now to take careful stock of his situation. Up to this time he had been forced to go ahead without much reflection. Now he began to check back over his course, wondering if there might have been an alternative way. On the whole he had to admit, except for the possibility that the two men in the tavern had died of their injuries, he was well satisfied with the way things were working out. Yet there were a few things to regret. Quite likely he would never know whether the men had lived or died and that would trouble his conscience. No, it was past. Regretting would bring no change. Certainly he was overjoyed to be leaving Paris behind. He smiled to himself thinking what a joke it was on Raoul. The complacent, self-centered fool! He would have the very devil setting things right with Monsieur Duplessis, of whom he had said never forgot a slight. Eh well, though he got no pleasure gloating over Raoul's misfortune, he felt no sorrow. After all, Raoul had only himself to blame.

Beyond the broad Atlantic, lay the things upon which he had long set his heart. Adventure! Things that happened in a man's life in the far, strange corners of the world. A vast country at once dim but enchanting in his imagination. The land of promise, of battle and honor for which his Gaelic blood yearned. The land of queer savage

37

races and untold wealth. Why look back on sordid things? The past was disillusionment and the future, hope. He remembered a Latin phrase from his schooldays. Fortes ortuna juvat. Fortune favors the brave. It was a great truth, he concluded. The small soul whose adventuring lay between hearth and threshold lived out his dull existence without a smile from fortune. It was the brave man, the conqueror, whom fortune provided should build the world. It was to Aenaeas, the survivor of Troy and founder of Rome to whom the ancient poet had ascribed this motto. Alexander the Great had read the same passage and taken it for himself. Now Evan saw himself, in his own way, helping to carve a vast new empire in America.

Entranced by the chimera which his mind had wrought he stood staring at the river without seeing it, forgetting his clothes which hung to him sodden and wrinkled like some scarecrow's attire.

Perched on a rock sheer above the Seine the Chateau Gaillard looked down through the cold dawn upon the water coach drifting between the twin villages of Les Andelys. Evan was again on deck shivering in the chill air, but thankful to be out after a night spent in the cabin. His muscles felt quite as rigid as the bones in his body as he paced about the deck in an effort to bestir some life in them. He felt groggy from sleeplessness. Little wonder, for he had caught no more than fitful winks wedged upright in the cabin as he had been through the night. Moreover, his mouth had a putrid taste.

Cocking his eye at the weather he perceived that it was bad, with no sign of improvement. Gray clouds skimmed above the river, drifting a ghost of rain behind them. He swore at the prospect of storm, for it prevented his spending the day on deck. There was rebellion in his stomach against the ripe atmosphere and close quarters of the cabin, yet it was twelve hours and more before they should reach Rouen.

He looked at the skipper and the mate oblivious of his presence, puffing their pipes in the lee of a stretched tarpaulin. They were to be envied. They could enjoy the clean breath of the storm and yet be sheltered from it.

He continued to pace the deck until the storm broke with howling flurries of rain from stem to stern of the water coach. Then he dived into the cabin. His peasant friend of the day before had been put ashore and Rene now occupied his place, with Collette huddling miserably at his side.

The three of them were companions in misery. They were ravenously hungry, but there was nothing to eat. The skipper had complacently announced that bilge-water had gotten in the provisions; therefore, those who had not provided themselves with food before embarking would have to go fasting, as the peasant had warned Evan, until they reached Rouen. But they soon forgot their hunger as the water coach wallowed in the force of the storm. The wind swept great sheets of rain and spray along the deck and in at the cabin door, drenching the passengers. There was nothing to do but endure it and brace to the lurching of the boat.

Evan could feel his empty stomach turning inside out with every heave of the craft. At his side Collette, her eyes rolling, wretched with her mouth hanging open. He and Rene, hard put to maintain their own equilibrium, supported her from either side lest she pitch to the cabin floor. He saw Rene's throat work as if he were trying to scream something, but with the roar of the wind and the spinning of his head like a Catherine wheel he could hear no intelligible words.

All through the morning the storm continued to buffet them. Now it would subside briefly, lulling their shocked brains into false security. Now it would leap up suddenly to lash them with redoubled vigor until their bones seemed to splinter and their bowels strained against their nostrils. By noon, however, it commenced abating, leaving them to recover from their misery as they floated nearer Rouen.

For minutes after the rocking of the vessel had ceased Evan remained as stupefied as any of the passengers, then the circles in which his head had been swimming began to lessen in their circumferences, grew smaller and smaller until he was aware of his surroundings. He was still deathly conscious of his stomach which seemed to surge about inside him as soft and formless as a bag of mush but he was able to look around. The cabin floor was an inch deep in black water which swelled from side to side of the cabin with the motion of the boat. On it floated the vomit of the passengers, the sight of which brought Evan's stomach again into his mouth. Had it not been empty he would have added to the burden of the water. The stench of the cabin had increased, which seemed incredible considering its former proportions.

He looked dully at Collette who lay like a discarded rag across Rene's lap. There was not the slightest suggestion of femininity in her now, he reflected. Yet she was a woman, and for the past two days and a night his body had pressed almost as closely against hers as if the had been the mistress who shared his bed. A water coach was surely no place for the tender nuances of sex. He had seen in the course of their journey manifestations of her physical being which would not have been his privilege to witness even in the privacy of a conjugal boudoir. But in this case it had been forced by expediency. However, it had not given him a feeling of disgust. She smelled terribly foul now, it was true, but in happier and more clean circumstances he might yet be tempted to claim her body for want of a better one. Now even the contemplation of such action sickened him.

Groggily his brain asked what was Rene thinking, anything? Rene, who with such ostentation named her a slut, but whose eyes in an unguarded moment would watch her with more than casual regard.

His brain refused to ponder the question. Mists seemed to rise up in it and after a moment his chin drooped on his chest. It was good to sleep and in his dream he could feel himself sinking slowly down, down into a bottomless pit of unconsciousness.

It was Rene shaking him savagely which brought him back to life. For minutes he could do nothing but yawn until he began to fear that his jaw would drop off. At length his blurred vision began to focus, objects shed their fuzzy coverings and became real. He was on his feet and Rene was propelling him without ceremony through the cabin door. He could see it was night. Darkness lay on the river and men with lanterns upon the deck bawled to men with lanterns upon the quay. This must be Rouen. Rene left him and plunged back through the door to get Collette.

When they had mounted the quay Collette clung to the arm of each man.

She laughed, a pitiful sound, "My legs are like water They won't hold me up."

Rene's voice might have been a crow's. "No more than mine. We must get some food, and quickly."

Collette gagged and Evan rubbed his stomach.

"I don't know if I can keep it down," he confessed.

"We must eat," persisted Rene. He made as if to move off but Evan caught his arm.

"Tiens, we must look more respectable before we board the boat for Le Havre tomorrow morning. Mon Dieu, look at us! They are likely to throw us into prison just upon our appearances!"

"Oui", agreed Rene, "I hadn't thought of that. How much money do you have?"

"Perhaps enough to buy clothes and fare to Le Havre. No more," said Evan. "But here is something else." He looked speculatively at Collette. "What do we do with Collette here, upon the ship for Louisiana? Monsieur de Villiers tells me that he is taking a cargo of recruits this passage. You, then, if you go, will go below wit them. But what of Collette? She can't ship in the hold. One woman and half a hundred men."

Rene looked uncomfortable. It was Collette who spoke.

"Mon Dieu, it is simple!" she exclaimed. "I will dress as a man."

"She looks like a boy, at that, except for her clothing," Evan said. He ran his eye over her. "Enfin, she shall go as a boy. We'll buy her male clothing when we buy our own."

Rene said doubtfully, "If she ships in the hold, sooner or later the men will find out she's a woman."

Evan sighed. "It will be difficult, I know. We must attend to that matter when we reach it. Perhaps, if I sail as a cabin passenger, she might pose as my valet. That, at the least, would keep her out of the hold."

He saw the hot flash of suspicion in Rene's eyes and grinned disarmingly, which seemed to reassure Rene.

"Now," said Evan, "some of her hair must come off so that we can tie it into a queue. We must find a barber for that, and then a shop to buy clothing and a place to eat and sleep."

They found the barber after a short search, in a by street, the appearance of which something less that prepossessing. No more the appearance of the barber. He was a scrawny Norman with a bedraggled brush of a moustache. Perched upon a stool in his deserted shop the only interest which he displayed upon their entrance was to slide from his seat. Evan pushed Collette forward in the direction of the stool. The barber scratched his greasy head in perplexity.

"A woman," he said at last, in the manner of one chancing upon a great discovery. "What does she want? I see no hurt which I can cleanse and bandage."

"It is not to be doctored that she is here." Evan told him. "She wants her hair cut. Cut it like a young boy's."

"Pouf" cried the barber. "I have never sheared a female. The sailors will laugh at me and shun my shop. It might bring them ill luck, the will say, like a woman on board ship."

A glint of suspicion came into his little eyes. "Why does she want it cut? Are you fleeing from the law and seeking to disguise yourselves?" He threw up his hands. "My shop is a respectable shop, as any will tell you."

From its appearance Even had his doubts about this.

The barber went on, "I give no aid to those who break the just laws of His Majesty the King!" Thus he ended a picture of righteousness, with his eyes cast up to heaven, which was, unhappily removed from his vision by the grimy ceiling of the shop.

Evan waited patiently by until he had lowered his eyes. Then drawing out his wallet, he filled his cupped palm with a coin. It was more than he liked to spare for a simple hair cut.

"Your incorruptible honesty moves me deeply, friend," he said feelingly. "A man of such integrity should not go unrewarded. Therefore, I offer you this silver merely as a token of respect. How soon can you have mademoiselle's hair trimmed?"

The barber's beady eyes turned genial at the sight of the money. "It will take but a moment," he rejoined "And since we are strangers in the city," went on Evan as Collette took her seat. "Where can we find one who will sell us clothes, and where can we find food and lodging for the night?"

The barber's fingers moved nimbly about Collette's head. "It is a pleasure to be of service to a gentleman such as you. Upon this very quay you will find Bernard the Jew, who has a fine stock of clothes which have been worn. And one square from here upon the north is the house of Madame Lacoq, who lodges sailor men. She will give you beds and food and will not rob you in the bargain."

The sun drowned in the heaving channel leaving a bloody trail between that point where it had gone down and the boat from Rouen as it steered into the harbor of Le Havre. The masts and spars of all manner of craft, from seagoing vessels to river boats, fishermen to ships of war, stood up within the harbor like pins in a lady's pincushion. The pilot brought the Rouen boat in slowly through the busy harbor and they were tied up to the quay.

Before leaving the vessel Evan inquired of the skipper about the possible whereabouts of Monsieur de Villiers. The skipper who said that he knew De Villiers by sight could not, because of the darkness which had now descended upon the harbor, vouchsafe where his ship might be, but he tendered the information that were he not on board he would in all likelihood be found at the Hotel de la Marine. Evan gathered their belongings into a bundle and stepped on to the quay to follow the directions given by the skipper.As they stood in the gloom among the piled bales and boxes and casks, the swaying lanterns and shouts of the harbor crew, they felt of considerably better estate than they had the night before.

The clothes which they purchased after prolonged haggling from Bernard the Jew were neat and respectable. Well they might be, reflected Evan ruefully, for together with the food and lodging from Madame Lacoq they had emptied his purse of all save that which he had held out for boat passage from Rouen to Le Havre. Now he had not one sol to his name. His thoughts turned upon a pessimistic trend. Suppose, now they should be unable to find Monsieur de Villiers? That would leave them at a pretty pass, indeed. Turning his head he watched Collette standing beside Rene, straight and slim with a juvenile masculinity in her clothing and short hair. She seemed quite free from worry now, as if she glimpsed more pleasant things ahead.

He drew a deep breath. "By the grace of lying and thieving we have come this far. But danger is far from past. We'd best mind our manners!"

Rene grinned. "A beau mentir qui vient de loin."

"We've not come so far that if we're caught in a lie we'll not rue it." said Evan. "Eh bien, time's flying. We must find Monsieur de Villiers."

They proceeded through the sailor's quarter, a pig sty of narrow streets and tumbledown houses, redolent of tar and tide water. At length the dark quarter opened out into the broad Place de L'Arsenal upon the left hand extremity of which they made out a graceful little building which Evan took to be the Hotel de la Marine.

They had no sooner reached this building than a man burst out of it with a great show of hurry and all but collided with them. At the sight of the spry, small figure in the great blue coat Evan cried out with relief. In response to his hail Monsieur de Villiers gave an exclamation which might have been an echo of Evan's and hastening forward swept him into an enthusiastic embrace. "Dieu me pardonne! It is Evan, if I can believe my eyes! Welcome, lad! Were you looking for me?"

Evan laughed with him. "I was looking for no other, monsieur! To come to the point, I have made up my mind to sail with you to Louisiana."

"Bravo!" cried the captain heartily. He peered closer at Evan. "I'll wager Raoul had no liking for that decision."

"He had no say in it, for I came away without consulting him," said Evan dryly. "So, you see, sir, I have no money to pay for passage."

Captain de Villiers gripped him impulsively by both shoulders. "Upon my soul, lad, what does that matter? Leave such affairs to me. I will arrange for it. I shall convince the authorities that I could not sail without you! So you came off without Raoul's permission, eh? Well, as a naval officer I'm not a man ordinarily to encourage mutiny against the voice of authority. But," he chuckled delightedly, "but I'll shut my eyes to it this time. Enfin, I'm pleased to take you lad. I sail this time with a full cargo. Gunpowder, lead and salt provisions for Monsieur de Bienville's troops but little in the way of passengers, unless you include the human cattle in the sainte-barbe. They could scarcely be called passengers of free will, poor devils, impressed for service in Bienville's garrisons. God help the settlements, I say, which must depend for protection upon the like of those!"

"You have no cabin passengers at all?" asked Evan.

"Eh?" said the captain, "but yes, though few. I have the party of Monsieur Castilloux: himself, his daughter, and the Baron de Laval." He shrugged suggestively. "Monsieur Castilloux is a bad odor."

Then, peering into the gloom, he made out Rene and Collette at Evan's back.

"Those two?" he asked, pointing, "Are they with you?"

"Yes, monsieur. They wish also to go to Louisiana. The boy, if it is possible, I shall make use of as my valet." He saw Monsieur de Villiers smile at this conceit. "The man is merely seeking a place for himself in the colony. I thought perhaps he might join the recruits you have. Will it trouble you greatly, monsieur?"

Monsieur de Villiers rested his eyes upon Rene's stalwart figure. "Trouble? Mon Dieu, after the hundreds I have seen seized and thrown aboard without writ or warrant! This fellow shall go in the sainte-barbe

46

with the recruits for Bienville. He looks the worth of any three of them. They're not fit to clean a musket, much less shoulder one."

He waved away Evan's thanks.

"Come with me," he said, "I do not sail until tomorrow afternoon, but you can spend the night aboard."

He looked closely then at Evan's clothing and shook his head. "You departed in a hurry, non? No matter. We shall go into the city tomorrow and buy you some presentable garments."

The four of them set off thought darkness in the direction of the quay. The night around all at once seemed not so dark, the stars more benign.

Rene, striding beside Collette, murmured, "So. We're going to Louisiana, after all. All I ask is that it give me a chance to work for my own. It's not work a man's afraid of. It's being robbed of the fruits of his work, of forever laboring as we do here, burning out our lives to fill the pockets of some fat landlord."

Collette looked up at him. Her eyes dilated and quickly, protectively, her fingers pressed his hand. For once he did not draw it away.

CHAPTER V

The Gironde rocked gently on the swell of the bay, yet protected by the last cape of Normandy from the full blow of the seaward westerly winds. She had sailed in the early afternoon and by the time darkness had fallen the shores of France were still discernible on the horizon. It was a clear darkness with the stars looking down.

Evan MacDonald stood at the shipside watching the sea and listening for the steward's call to supper. He was hungry. The salt air had keened his appetite and the sea was not yet so rough as to blunt it. It was good to be no longer harassed; to be thoughtful of his stomach and not of his life. His quarrel with Raoul and his flight from Paris seemed already unreal and far away.

His sense of well being fitted him as neatly as did the clothing with which Monsieur de Villiers had munificently provided him. He let his eyes drop and run down the length of him; the light blue of full skirted coat and the breeches, dim shadowed in the star shine, the dull silver button holes, silver garters at his knees. At least he need not be ashamed before his fellow passengers. There were but a few, he remembered, Monsieur de Villiers had said. He had not yet met them for, worn out from his travels, he had slept all morning why they, in turn, had remained in their cabins since coming aboard. The party

48

of Monsieur Castilloux, that was the name, had a strangely familiar ring. He puzzled with it a moment before remembrance came. To be sure, the little girl who had lived once in Montmartre, Antoinette Castilloux. That had been long ago, before he had gone to Scotland. But she had lived with her grandmother. He could recall no father. No Monsieur Castilloux. No doubt this man and his daughter were another family. At any rate he hoped they proved agreeable company, since he must live in proximity to them for the next three months.

He heard the bugle call to eat. A little spoonful of sound dripping into the vast void of the sea. Walking aft he entered the great main cabin where the paid passengers and the ship's officers took their meals. A lamp swung in gimbals from the ceiling making a shine on the glazed ports. The company was gathered, but not yet seated, about the heavy fixed table in the center of the cabin. Evan observed the uniforms of the officers, the captain's short figure and, as he came into their midst, a girl. He stopped short. He stood silent for a moment with his eyes opening wide.

Monsieur de Villiers touched his arm as he stared.

"Mademoiselle Castilloux," he said, "I present Monsieur MacDonald."

The girl's face was pale but delicately colored like the flush of late sunlight on an alabaster wall. Her hair was sun-gold, worn low without covering with curls which fell to her shoulders.

Evan bowed above her hand. His eyes passing it lingered upon the slender body of the girl, upon her rose colored gown. The skirt, bloom shaped, flounced about in the form of petals of a rose. Flower like, it swayed from the stem of her hips. He drew his breath. It was incredible, but this was Antoinette Castilloux, his little playmate from long ago, now grown up.

He raised his head, looking into her eyes. They were as blue, he thought romantically, as any loch in Scotland but what he did not perceive was that they were also as deep, unfathomable and coolly reflective of all which looked therein. Just now they held a little puzzlement which cleared as he watched.

"Why you must be Evan MacDonald." She let the syllables of his name drop like notes in music.

"Antoinette," he said, laughing a little, feeling a wholly inordinate pleasure that she had not forgotten.

She took his hand in both of hers. She seemed quite delighted.

"Evan, she exclaimed. "I am so pleased to see you again! How long has it been, my dear? We were mere children. You went away and I was heartbroken." She released one slim hand to shake a finger at him.

"Oh," she rattled on, turning him about. "I must present my father. You have never met him, I believe."

That about Monsieur Castilloux which struck Evan most forcefully was his belly. It pushed so far forward that his waistcoat and his waist band had the very devil to meet across it. His entire aspect was one of heaviness. His eyes heavily lidded above, heavily pouched below. His lips were heavy, also, and it seemed to require a muscular effort to prevent the lower one from drooping down upon his threefold tier of chins. His words as he acknowledged Evan's introduction fell fatly from his lips. It was quite shockingly preposterous that this obese monstrosity should have sired the vision of loveliness which was Antoinette.

While Evan was trying to digest this paradox Antoinette's insistent fingers had turned him again until he found himself facing a small, pallid man attired faultlessly in claret cloth, immaculate lace at the throat and wrists. The Baron de Laval, Antoinette's voice had said. Evan categorized him in a single glance from the arduous hauteur of his eyes to the heels on his slippers. His face was quite narrow and almost chinless. His age would have been hard to determine. In a manner of speaking he might have been newly born, so innocent was his face of any line of character, yet upon the other hand, the looseness of the skin about his jowls and beneath his eyes were not a sign of youth.

"Monsieur MacDonald?" he said making a delicate arch of his eyebrows, "Ah, it is a Scotch name is it not? How interesting."

They then were all seated about the great ship's table. The meal passed this first night afloat without discomfort, for the roll of the ship was scarcely enough to put ripples in their soup. Talk and laughter traveled back and forth across the board. The three midshipmen, young lads all of them, who had the privilege of dining at the captain's table, seldom removed their eyes from Antoinette's animated face. Evan did not blame them, for his own part he was as much enchanted as they. His preoccupation with her left him unmindful of the sounds of her father applying himself assiduously to his soup. To his delight she paid more attention to him than to anyone else at the table.

"It is strange, is it not, this meeting you here," she said. "Almost as if we were children again. Both of us on a voyage to Louisiana. It is my first voyage, Evan. Is it yours?"

Replying, he missed the scowl which Monsieur Castilloux bent upon his daughter.

"I am eager to get there!" she exclaimed, "It must be a strange land, so different from France, I cannot imagine it . What will you be there, Evan? A soldier, I suppose, since all men love to fight."

He shook his head, smiling. "I'm merely a traveler." He had a sudden startling impulse to tell her his dreams. Speaking to her, he was possessed with a sense of his own importance. "I--I-- it is that I want to see the world before I die. This Louisiana, this America, it is so vast, so overwhelming. It must be the new land of Canada. I feel

51

that God has ordained it should be the making of a new world. And I must be there to see it, to tell of it, to write of it so that other people may know." He paused, all at once conscious of his audience, while the blood mantled his face. "I suppose to you it seems a foolish dream," he finished stammering.

"It is a worthy ambition," said Monsieur de Villiers.

Antoinette smiled but said nothing.

Monsieur Castilloux was amused. "Youth, it is magnificent," he observed. "Now, my chief desire at the moment is that we have a smooth and a swift crossing. I remember the Dromedaire some fifteen years ago, that would be 1720, I think. It had bad weather, bad accommodations and bad food. Ma foi, the filthy cattle which cluttered that ship caused us all to suffer!"

"They were, in part, your people, monsieur," said the captain with grave malice. "Settlers for your concessions. They died like flies at Biloxi."

Castilloux said callously, "I lost heavily on that flock, but I learned my lesson. There is no profit in white concessionaires. No, monsieur, I will take Negro slaves."

"It is a matter of opinion," returned the captain. "But at lest you will not be overly inconvenienced aboard the Gironde, Monsieur Castilloux. I have but a scant half-hundred recruits in the sainte-barbe."

Monsieur Castilloux's fleshy eyelids drooped. "Soldiers, hein?"

"Of a sort. A very poor sort."

Castilloux said with a fat smile, "Monsieur de Bienville has an excellent opinion of himself as a leader of men. Surely he will be able to work miracles with them."

"If it is within the power of any man, he will do so." said the captain shortly, "It is a miracle that the colony exists at all. A miracle, monsieur, of Bienville's working.

"Nonsense!" exclaimed Castilloux. "That sorry little martinet! Dictating that everything shall be thus and so, to his desiring. The colony is a madhouse, I tell you, sir. The savages are utterly without fear of Bienville. He has coddled them too long. His Indian policy which he prates of so--what did it ever consist of, save allowing French soldiers to live with the Indian women?"

The Baron de Laval looked up with a smile. "These native women." he inquired, "Are they quite lovely wild things?"

Castilloux was now amused. He shook his fat finger at the captain. "I am, in truth, afraid to return, monsieur. The province was placid and prospering! Yet Bienville must needs stir up a witch's cauldron."

It was plain that a sore spot of the captain's had been touched. His disgust exploded in a snort. "Witch's cauldron, indeed! It was not of Bienville's brewing! Mon Dieu, when I think of the shameless exploitations, the arrant treacheries, which have been played in the name of self interest."

Monsieur Castilloux grew livid. "Do you insinuate--"

"I insinuate nothing, monsieur. You know the facts as well as I do!"

They glared at each other like a pair of angry cats.

Antoinette broke the tension. She rose, the slenderness of her body springing upright in her swirling skirt.

"Messieurs, I beg your leave," she said, laughing "Father, I am sure that you and Monsieur de Villiers will be in disagreement all night. In the meantime I believe I will stroll upon the deck before I retire. Would you care to accompany me, Evan? I will not disturb the rest of you in your argument."

Her father shot her a disturbed glance.

Evan was already upon his feet, while the other gentlemen stood up about the table bowing as Antoinette took his arm. The Baron de Laval's eyebrows went up in his white face, but he said nothing. Castilloux, for his part glowered openly at Evan's retreating back

Antoinette shivered delicately in the light breeze. The moon was rising beyond the coast of France and the ocean moved restlessly below them in the moonlight like a black silver etching. Evan did not look at it, he stared at the girl. The moonlight watched her in subtle light and shadow. Evan saw her with a power beyond that of his eyesight. The power of emotion, which is unlimited in its potentiality for distortion. His heart felt strangely in pain and he found himself stammering.

"Antoinette. Antoinette you have changed."

She gave him a fleeting side long glance and laughed gently. "Is it so strange? I was ten years old, was I not? Now I am eighteen. A woman changes so much from moment to moment, Evan, that in eight years no amount of change should be surprising."

Evan did not speak. This was little Antoinette, yet now that he was alone with her she awed him. He had had little experience with women. None at all with a woman of such overwhelming femininity. He was not used to the emotions which swelled within him. He thought involuntarily of Collette; the feeling which he had had upon occasion for her had been a world removed from this sensation. He had at times desired Collette, it was true, but in the natural manner of a man for female flesh. There would be no more adventure or romance in using Collette's body than in eating a leg of mutton; although, to pursue the parallel it would be quite pleasant to eat the mutton if hunger pressed hard enough. But his emotion for Antoinette Castilloux had the substance of a dream. It was deliciously inviting, filled with romantic implications; it was idealism of the same pattern as his dreams of adventure and glory in Louisiana. His heart swelled as the thought flashed into his mind that he would gain trophies there to lay at her feet. He, with the image of her before him, would climb to the pinnacle beyond them all -- even the great Bienville.

Her broad skirt rustled against his knee; the perfume of her hair so near to his shoulder all but intoxicated him. Desires clashed within him, left him trembling in indecision. One instant his muscles strained to seize her to crush the slender warmth of her body against his own; but she was too fragile, (or his conception of her was too fragile, too fairy-like,) for any such crude approach. It would be almost sacrilege to think of her physical being with desire. If he should touch her thus in desire she might be forever lost. To him in that moment she seemed not human but a divinity; not as a mortal woman, constructed to accept a man's passion and to return those passions, but to be adored. He did not attempt to make reason of his swift emotion. With him, as with his father, another Highland man, love was an affair of the heart and not of the brain.

She broke into his reverie.

"You went to Scotland when you left Paris, did you not, Evan?"

"Yes," he managed, stiff-lipped.

She was in a reminiscent mood, sensing his agitation. "We, my grandmother and I, remained in Montmartre a year or so after that. Then we moved into the city so that I might be better educated, as my grandmother said." She laughed, quickening his pulse. "I trust that I have fulfilled her hopes and my father's."

"You are going now to live with your father in Louisiana?" he asked.

"Oh, la, no!" she exclaimed. "He is taking me for the pleasure, whatever that may be, and to show me the wealth he has accumulated in the colony. He brings Edouard, the Baron de Laval, I mean, for that same purpose, I suspect. My father has been in Louisiana so long that he and I are not well acquainted. But we understand each other, nevertheless."

Her lighthearted disrespect for her father perplexed Evan, and he felt a stab of jealously at the mention of de Laval.

Her quick voice went on gaily, "Yet if life in will not be too pleased with it."

Suddenly, startling them, a thick call came across the deck. "Antoinette!"

It was Antoine Castilloux, the huge bulk of him shadowed in the moonlight. He waddled across toward them.

"Antoinette," he said, gruffly, "too much of this sea air will do you no good. It is time you retired to your cabin. Bonne nuit, Monsieur MacDonald."

The abruptness with which he whisked Antoinette away left Evan staring. She went obediently, but her eyes which Evan had thought like deep pools now filmed over with cold, blue ice. She listened without comment to Antoine Castilloux's upbraiding when they had passed Evan's hearing.

"Are you a fool, my girl? Flirting with every nameless nobody! De Laval will not stand neglect."

Evan, left alone, walked slowly toward his own cabin. It was a small place as he entered, scarcely wide enough to accommodate the two shelf like berths upon which he and Collette slept. He stood in the dark, listening to the girl's slumberous breathing.

Thinking now of Antoinette, a returning surge of emotion flooded him, and this time, with the hypnotic quality of beauty out of his sight, it was a purely physical passion which contended mightily with his unfleshly adoration and seemed almost to overcome it. Torn by an impulse to go after her and seek her out, he repressed it and, furiously jerking off his clothes, sought his bed for comfort. But he could not sleep, made restless with desire.

Once he sat upright in his berth peering through the darkness at the berth where Collette peacefully slumbered For a moment, stirred as he was by his unsatisfied longing he considered relief in that direction. But his vision of Antoinette rushed back to him so pure and beautiful, that he was filled with disgust at the turn of his thoughts Cursing Collette he lay down again to toss among his pillows until dawn.

Rene Broussard spat into the sea.

He said, "God! How long will this voyage last?"

"We've only been at sea three weeks," said Evan, who stood beside him. "Monsieur de Villiers says the voyage will take three months, at least, possibly longer if the weather is unfavorable."

Rene looked over his shoulder and cursed. Behind them the sainte-barbe had disgorged its offal upon the deck as it did nightly when the weather permitted. The recruits lay all about, heaped in attitudes of leaden slumber, peacefully distorted, in the light of the half moon.

"Behold, the little animals," said Rene in deep contempt. "Are they soldiers, I ask you? Lying, thieving. They would steal the bread from one another's mouths. Filthy, stinking. But, so am I."

He looked disgustedly at his own apparel which was in a malodorous state. "Every day I have rotted in that infernal powder room, save one, when they called me up to take the place of a sailor who was ailing. At nights when the weather is rough I must stifle there below or sleep here on the open deck at the mercy of the storm. The devil take this sleeping nights with my head in a laundry basket to keep off the spray!"

Evan nodded in sympathy. So far, he suspected, it was Rene's belief that he had exchanged his lot in Paris for one no better. Nor could he find it in his heart to blame him. Not subjected to the acute discomforts of the sainte-barbe as was Rene, nevertheless, he was growing thoroughly weary of the voyage.

Part of his disquietude might be rightly attributed to the monotony of the days at sea. But the remainder of his unrest, he reflected ruefully, could be traced to Antoinette Castilloux. What he termed her capriciousness tormented him. That first night at sea she had been graciousness itself, seemingly delighted to see him again. Since then she had been friendly, indeed, but in a way which was baffling, suggesting to him in his overwrought state that she considered him not as a man but as the youth she had known long ago. It enraged him that she was never alone with him, but so often with the Baron de Laval as they promenaded the Gironde's quarterdeck. He cursed Monsieur Castilloux, wondering if he were behind it all From Monsieur de Villiers he had learned many things about Antoine Castilloux which he had not known. His fortune, which was considerable, the captain told, had been acquired mainly in the speculation over John Law's Mississippi bubble. At that time, about the year 1719, he had gone personally to Louisiana to take over his grants. By shrewd and unscrupulous manipulations he had greatly increased his wealth. Evan knew that Monsieur de Villiers was intensely prejudiced against Castilloux, but the more he saw of the man, the greater became his own dislike.

Rene, who had been brooding also, broke the silence.

"Tell me, he began, clearing his throat with embarrassment. "How is Collette?"

"Eh?" said Evan absently. "She's doing very well, I think."

Perhaps Rene mistook his inattention for a guilty conscience.

He said, his voice thick with suspicion, "You've been treating her well?"

"Of course I've been treating her well! What's wrong with you?"

Rene, turning sullen said no more, and after a minute moved off among the sleeping recruits. Evan watched him until he had found a place on the deck, then restless himself, he left the shipside.

As he walked aft he passed Antoinette and the Baron de Laval watching the moonlight on the sea. He bowed and spoke stiffly but did not tarry. The sight of the girl footsteps to hurry him away. He did not hear the Baron make comment after he had passed.

"Monsieur MacDonald keeps strange company." He observed. Did you see him just now in the most amicable conversation with one of those foul wretches from below decks?"

Antoinette said, "He is different from us, Edouard."

"So he is," said do Laval with a smirk. "A most ingenuous young man, with his talk of Indians and deeds of bravery in Louisiana. I wonder if all Scotsmen are like that, seeing only a vision, never the practical side of life?"

Antoinette gave him a sidelong glance. "It is a fault is it not?" Her blue eyes looked away to sea. "I am afraid for him. He seeks so many things where he will never find them."

"The mirages of Louisiana, or ... " de Laval asked slyly.

She did not smile in return. "Perhaps. Perhaps not." She said as an after thought, "I cannot say of Louisiana. He may be right as to that. I do not know Louisiana."

The baron's eyes were amused. "You know life, mademoiselle, of that I am sure."

"Without doubt," she said dryly. "Sometimes it is a knowledge which pays."

Although de Laval went on speaking she forgot him as she stared across the heaving waste of water. She had not intended deliberately to hurt Evan MacDonald. She had been genuinely glad to see him again;

to recall in a moment her own childhood. But, as her father had said, it was not profitable to let matters grow more serious.

Almost involuntarily she compared the two men, Evan MacDonald and the Baron de Laval. The one a clean, idealistic youth who would be faithful to her; who, if it were her soul which desired, could make her sublimely happy by his adoration. The other, a palpable wastrel and profligate who would never observe a moment of faithfulness to her, once he had his hands upon the money which she would bring him in dowry in marriage. Yet Evan could offer her no more than devotion. The Baron de Laval could provide her with the title and prestige which she desired. He was quite an impecunious nobleman, to be sure, seeking only to recoup his fortunes and rehabilitate his estates.

But as the Baronne de Laval she would be a part of the Court at Versailles The Baron might intend using her as a steppingstone, but she, in turn could make the same use of him. She breathed hard at that image of Versailles. It was the center of the world and she was a very beautiful young woman. It was not mere vanity which told her so. Who could say, but that even the King's eyes might not fall with favor upon her among his Court? His Majesty Louis XV was but a man. A man, indeed, whom it was whispered was not averse to feminine charm.

Meanwhile, Evan had reached his cabin. The sight of Antoinette in such propinquity to De Laval had let loose within him forces which bayed like a hunting pack upon the track of his faltering self control. As rational judgment deserted him, he was possessed by two desires; to catch de Laval by the seat of his pretty breeches and heave him into the Atlantic, and, having done that, to take Antoinette in his arms and carry her here to his cabin. No longer did he think of her body as inviolate. Nights of stifled passion had bred in him a passion which transcended such fragile dreams. He stepped into the darkness of the cabin, his body trembling as he fought to control his desire.

There was a restless rustle from Collette's berth, telling him that she had retired. That moment, as she turned in bed, sent thoughts tumbling through his mind. In two swift, unpremeditated strides he had crossed the tiny cabin and was groping her among the bedclothes. His hand closed upon her arm. Roughly he dragged her from the berth. He could scarcely make her out in the darkness. She did not protest, but asked a question. "Did you see Rene?"

He did not answer, but shoved her into his own berth while he fumbled in the dark to undress. By the time he had divested himself of his clothing, reason had begun to come back to him, and he was ashamed. He had been about to violate a girl who had never been anything but his friend; simply because his passion for another girl could not be satisfied.

"Collette, I'm sorry," he said. "I don't know why--" She looked steadily into his face. "Don't worry. I know how you feel. God knows."

Still, trying to fight his desire, he argued with her. "But why don't you deny me? Collette, why should you be willing to prostitute yourself to me? You said once--" Her voice was unsteady. "I'm lonely. It isn't that I'm cheapening myself. You have done a great deal for me. I'm not ungrateful. I know that I can never repay you, but I can try. Anything that I can do to help you, I will do. Why should I not give my body if you need it? There is no one else to give it to."

For a moment, digesting what she said he could not speak. "But you don't love me," he said at last. "Non. No more than you love me. I'm glad you don't because I'm not good enough for you." She caught his shoulders roughly. "But neither is she good enough! Oh, I can see through her kind. She's playing with you. Don't break your heart over her. She'll throw you way. She has thrown you away already. For God's sake, don't let her hurt you!"

All his sympathy for her vanished in a wave of anger "Hush, damn you!" he said fiercely. "What do you know of her? Don't let me ever hear you say anything against her. I'll--I'll..."

For an instant the impulse held him to throw her bodily from his bed. But the stimulation of anger and her talk of Antoinette had aroused his passion to fever heat. His desire for a woman, any woman, was too strong to be denied. Roughly he settled his arms about her.

The moon rose higher, casting an arrow of silver through the cabin portal. Evan, his passion spent, rested his weight upon her. He looked out through the portal at the waves which raced shadowed under the moon, barred with silver where their crests broke beneath its light. Turning his eyes down upon Collette he saw that she had twisted her head around, that she too, was watching the waves. As well as if she had spoken them he knew the trend of her thoughts. It was ironically amusing. If he could have looked on, instead of being a part of this he would have laughed.

She, he knew, was wishing that Rene lay above, as he was wishing that it were Antoinette below.

CHAPTER VI

Evan MacDonald stood on the quarterdeck of the Gironde, the sea wind blowing in his face from the southeast as he looked out across the green waters of the Gulf of Mexico. There were a few birds in the sky. He knew that they were the first harbingers that land was within sailing distance. The birds had seen the Gironde from the north and were now trailing her for whatever debris on which they could feed.

Evan noticed that the green water was now being streaked with brown.

"Are we very near to land, monsieur," he asked Monsieur de Villiers.

"Not for several leagues," responded the old captain. "What you see is the muddy water of the great Mississippi river. It pours its burden of earth at some leagues out into the sea from the mouth of the river. But we are now reaching the end of our voyage."

With this the ship turned more to the northwest. Evan took a deeper breath as he felt that a part of his adventure was about to end and an unknown future begin. It had been nearly three months since his encounter with Collette. They had not repeated the encounter and he felt somewhat ashamed. Had she been like Sophie back at Simon's he would not have felt as he did. But Collette had fled with them partially to escape the life that she knew her father would force upon her. For this, as other things, Evan had a respect for her that did not extend to most women of her station. It was also true that she had given herself to him. But to use her body given from gratitude was even worse to Evan.

He did not wish to see himself in the same company as the Baron de Laval. This was the natural station of the people to the nobility and to the aspiring businessmen of France. To use the cattle as they wished and only to fulfill some need or desire.

Evan had learned to feel differently in the free air of the Highlands. The crofters and common folk there had been his friends and companions. They owed allegiance to their chief but each had an air of independence about him. If they were imposed upon it was their chiefs duty to support or avenge them but they were not shy in defending themselves first. Evan refused to see himself as an abuser of station as the French aristocrats did. Finally, he was aware of her feelings toward Rene who, despite his recriminations, obviously had strong feelings toward Collette.

Evan felt a bit of betrayal to both of them. Collette, for her part, had not mentioned the affair. He knew that she felt an obligation to him but he would not allow himself to sink so far as to ask of such again. Indeed, he had not spoken with her much in these past weeks. She kept had kept to the cabin most of the voyage, acting the part of a valet.

Rene was a different matter. He had been somber the entire voyage. He knew too well the wants of men and women and was quietly jealous of Evan and suspicious of his relationship with Collette. When they had moored on Saint Domingue he had not returned from the taverns in the town with the recruits. The recruits, such as they were, were watched closely for desertion which was almost a certainty if they were allowed any freedom. Monsieur de Villiers was ever uneasy about this cargo and much more so as the Gironde lay in port for two weeks longer than he planned as they made repairs. Just as they were to make sail again a storm hit the island, not only delaying them, but doing damage to the rigging and causing another week's delay.

Rene had managed to evade Evan and the officers that escorted the recruits into the town one day. Evan feared that he would desert the company and remain on the island but after several days he returned. Monsieur de Villiers did not lash him as he was not a conscript but Rene would not speak of where he had been or what he had done. Apparently he found the island not to his liking. More likely he would not leave Collette.

Collette cursed him for a fool while he replied he had no need to listen to a slut. For the remainder of the voyage he would speak little and, while not hostile to him, did not share his thoughts with Evan.

Monsieur Castilloux had kept Antoinette close by him. As the voyage progressed the coolness between himself and Monsieur de Villiers had increased. They had seldom shared meals at the captain's table. When they did there was little polite conversation. Antoinette would speak but only of matters that concerned her father and De Laval or asking questions of the conditions of Nouvelle Orleans or the shops in the colony. There was no more talk of the past or their childhood days in Montmartre.

Occasionally, Evan would see Antoinette on the deck of the ship but always in the company of her father or the Baron. He exchanged pleasantries but there was never a prolonged conversation between just the two.

Evan still had not stopped thinking that her reserve could not come from her own wishes. Her father must be keeping her from speaking her mind to him. He could see the jealousy in De Laval at every meeting. He could see how she guarded herself in her conversation with him. He was certain that she could not have feelings for De Laval and he consoled himself with this.

The voyage seemed to last forever. Evan had busied himself in learning much of sailing. He had worked with the sailors when he could. Monsieur de Villiers and the pilot had shown him how to read maps and the stars. He had learned about the Gironde itself, its construction and its rigging. In these pursuits had he filled his days. In the evenings he had talked with Monsieur de Villiers. Often they had supped with only the ships officers and then talked alone in the captains cabin with only Collette acting as valet.

Monsieur de Villiers had regaled him with tales of his youth with Evan's father, David MacDonald. Many of these tales he had heard before but was happy to hear yet again. He told of Canada and Hudson's Bay and of the Le Moyne brothers who they followed. The eldest Le Moyne, Pierre, was the Sieur D'Iberville. Forty years earlier he had led them in the wars against the English with such success as few Frenchmen had ever had. Evan listened with envy at the exploits that Monsieur de Villiers and his father had been a part. He listened of how they had come on this same ship, the Gironde, to help place the first settlement in Louisiana at Fort Maurepas. Bienville had been no older than Evan was now. Several years later they had come again to Louisiana, this time to follow a younger Le Moyne, Jean Baptiste, the Sieur de Bienville who had become Governor of the infant colony upon the untimely death of his brother D'Iberville. They had been with Bienville when he had bluffed an English warship into leaving the Mississippi River when his own fleet consisted only of the canoe they were in. David MacDonald had returned to France where he settled in Montmartre while Monsieur de Villiers had become a ship owner and captain.

Monsieur de Villiers had made many voyages to Louisiana in the past twenty years. He had brought colonists, supplies, and soldiers to the struggling colony. He had first come to Fort Maurepas on the shores of the Gulf of Mexico in the lands of the Biloxi Indians. Now his voyages terminated in Nouvelle Orleans on the great river itself. Bienville had founded the town seventeen years earlier and made it the capital of the colony.

"Ah bien, Bienville has given his life to this colony," the captain had said. "For thirty years he has kept the colony alive, through many adversities and many heartbreaks. But he has built settlements and outposts which connect New France with the Gulf of Mexico. It has been hard work and he has made enemies, as well as friends, in France and the Americas."

"My friend, Louisiana is a poor colony but it is very important to France. Bienville sees this but there are too many who only see an opportunity to make themselves rich at the expense of others. Your fellow passenger Castilloux is one of these."

"There is no secret of your dislike of him, monsieur," Evan had responded. "I must admit that I do not like the look of the man but what is the cause of your distaste for him."

"Evan, you do not know of the people who came to the colony on the promises of John Law and his company. Some were villains. I should know for I brought my share over. But most were farmers and men with a skill. They came, with their wives in many cases, to build a strong colony and a new life for themselves. Most of them died within three years of reaching the colony and were no better off than they were in Europe for the trial. But those like Castilloux, the merchants from France who were to supply these people with the goods necessary for survival, were only interested in inflated profits. They did not make the shipments promised on time and then at inflated prices."

"Is that not the way fortunes are made?" responded Evan.

"Not by honorable men, my young friend. It is also not the way to build a strong, prosperous colony. That is what the Sieur de Bienville has worked so hard to do. To build a colony that can pay for itself and be a strong citadel against the Spanish and the English. But others have their own nests in mind. Just six years ago Castilloux was in league with the commandant at Fort Rosalie in the country of the Natchez upriver from New Orleans. They conspired to drive the Indians from their land and open it to settlers who would be dependent upon them. A great plan for profit. The land for free and they sell it to people who have to pay them for all their supplies and protection. But the Natchez attacked and killed nearly every settler in the fort and in the district. Bienville had to subdue these proud people before the war spread to the entire colony. He destroyed the Natchez people."

"I cannot forgive these men, ever. For in their greed they caused the deaths of hundreds of Frenchmen. They cost us an important ally who now aid our enemies, for the surviving Natchez have joined the Chickasaw in the Illinois country. These Indians are allied with the English and are causing trouble even now. There is much you will learn when you reach the colony."

Evan had learned much on the voyage and now was eager for it to end.

Within a few hours the ship's lookout spied land. Not the rocks and beaches of Normandy or Brittany or the cliffs of England but a flat marshy land that seemed to grow out of the sea rather than rise from it. As they came nearer Evan could see a grassy marshland broken by rivulets running into the sea. The sea was shallow with a sandy bottom that crept from the shoreline so gradually that the Gironde must keep a safe distance or run aground.

"This is the delta of the the great river." Monsieur de Villiers told him. We must find the deepest pass before we can enter it. It is not always an easy thing to do. The Sieur de La Salle, the great explorer who claimed this land for France and gave it its name, could not find the pass and was lost".

They sailed on along the coast for several hours when a call came from aloft and the Gironde turned toward the north and the west toward a large stream of brown water flowing from the delta. The ship sailed up the channel in the midst of the marsh first toward the the northeast, then north and finally into a the widest river that Evan ever seen. It was truly a river and not a bay or a firth that was a part of the sea.

As the channel bent to the northwest a small boat came down the river towards them. It was a boat like none that Evan had ever seen, one large piece of wood, the trunk of a tree hollowed out into a canoe. Three men were in the boat and as it came along side the Gironde a ladder of rope was lowered and a large barrel chested man climbed aboard. His face was weathered as no man that Evan had ever seen before but he was not old and he was strong and robust. He wore clothes of both leather and cloth.

"Lazac!" shouted Monsieur de Villiers. "This is a surprise! How could you have known that we were just coming into the river?"

"Mon Captain de Villiers, I have been waiting two weeks along the river for you. Before that I have been making trips down here for two months awaiting your return." The burly voice fit the man "Come to my quarters," De Villiers said. "I see that you must have news. Will you journey to Nouvelle Orleans with us?

"Yes, if I may" he replied and before an answer was made he called over the rail to his companions, who turned the canoe and headed up river to their camp, then he turned to follow the captain.

"Will you join us?" Monsieur de Villiers said to Evan as he turned toward his cabin and Evan followed without saying a word As Evan closed the cabin door Monsieur de Villiers was handing Lazac a glass of brandy.

"What is the news, my old friend?"

"There is trouble in the Chickasaw country. The governor is gathering an expedition to make war with the Chickasaw. Very soon we will go north. I have been waiting for news of you and the new troops that you bring." "The Chickasaw," said Monsieur de Villiers slowly. "I wish that I could bring better news. Do not look for much help from the vermin that come on this ship. I hope that the Governor has others that can provide some real help."

The man he called Lazac nodded slowly as though he had expected such an answer. "You will learn more when we reach La Nouvelle Orleans," he replied. "I am also here to help you navigate up the river. I have seen the river bottom change and can help lead you over the sandbars."

"I thank you," said the Captain, "and may I introduce my young friend, Evan MacDonald, the son of and old friend of both the governor and myself. I think that you will find a liking to this young man."

Evan bowed to the man.

"This, Evan, is Gaston Lazac, who knows the woods and rivers of this country as well as any man alive. He is a man after the heart of your father."

With a contagious laugh Lazac grabbed Evan by the shoulders, "The son of David MacDonald?" he grinned. "If you are then like the tales I have heard of your father, we shall be good friends."

The Gironde steered slowly, her masts and canvas towering above the marsh. Rene Broussard stared outward from the bulwark seeing as much the dreary circling of his own thoughts as the expanse of wasteland now rendered more forlorn by a heavy overcast sky which threatened rain at any moment. He should be satisfied to be out of the filth of the sainte-barbe, even for a day. And he was satisfied, so far as it went, but the moment's ratification did not blind him to the probabilities of the future. The more he saw of this land of promise the more he was assailed wit doubts. Collette's babbling at his shoulder did not move him to respond. When a flock of wildfowl, startled by the ship, took wing with a sound like thunder, he shook his head like a man waking from sleep and watched their numbers freckling the sky. Then he felt Collette's sharp nails pinching his arm and heard her voice, for once making sense instead of just noise.

"Look at him," she whispered tartly. "Rubbing and purring against her like an old cat. And all the time her mind is on the big one."

Rene glanced aft where she nodded and saw that Evan was strolling with Antoinette. The big woodsman, Gaston Lazac, was with them. Lounging at the shipside he pointed toward the flying birds with some comment which made the other two laugh.

Rene shrugged. "What is it to you? Is it because he leaves you for her? Is it because he no longer cares to sleep with you?"

"Who said he slept with me?"

"Who needs to say it? You're a little slut and the daughter of an old slut. But what does it matter to me."

"Then shut up, damn you!"

Feeling her anger almost as sharply as if she had slapped him, and seeing it in the curious intensity of her chubby features, he decided to say no more than that. After all there was no use getting serious over her, nor yet of denying himself pleasure because she had trafficked with other men. Still, as he gazed intently into her angry face, the fact to which he had resolved to reconcile himself became harder and harder to swallow. There was something about this child of the Paris gutter which made him wish to be ignorant of her shortcomings. He turned his eyes away, hoping that desire would follow and this would be forgotten.

"I'm sick of this cursed marsh," he said, to be saying something. "Marsh, marsh, marsh! We have come leagues and still nothing but marsh. I don't believe there is a town or a decent place for a town on the damned desolate river."

But Collette was not pacified by the change of subject. "He keeps calling me a slut," she thought furiously, "If he keeps calling me a slut I shall be what he calls me, and worse. Mother of God! If all this country is no better than what can be seen, it must take even a hard slut to survive."

"The green heads are called French duck," said Gaston Lazac." The little ones, the swift fliers, are cercelle."

Antoinette had again shown attention to Evan from the moment he had emerged from Lazac's meeting in Captain de Villier's cabin. Evan had been elated that she wished to speak to him and be with him but he was sorely annoyed that it seemed Lazac was there at the very time she wanted to talk with him.

"But, monsieur, how can you possibly distinguish them all? So many, and the swiftness of their flight!"

Lazac laughed the slow, easy laugh he had for women, not the loud one he had for men. "How do you tell men apart, ma'm'selle? Because that is your business. Ducks and wild dindon on the wing, fish in the water, those are my business. And on the dry land deer , bear, coon, Indians. Yes, and women. It is my business to tell them apart and to know what to do when I find them. Compris, ma'm'selle?"

"Truly, when you make it so plain," murmured Antoinette, watching him slantwise. Evan looked glumly at the flying fowl. By this time he was used enough to Gaston Lazac not to be shocked when the woods runner took conversational liberties with Antoinette. But he did not pretend to like it.

He remained moody and monosyllabic while Antoinette plied Lazac with eager questions. The clouds over the river stooped lower, and in answer to his wishes a slow rain began to wash down the deck. Maliciously pleased to have the talking done, he escorted Antoinette to her cabin and bowed her out of the weather. He was damned sick of playing second fiddle, first to De Laval then to Gaston Lazac. It infuriated him. Yet, as he and Lazac walked to his own cabin he had sufficient sense of the ridiculous to consider wryly that if he desired Antoinette for his wife he had certainly got the spirit of French matrimony, if not the substance. Most of the wives he knew assumed a casualness toward their husbands which well matched Antoinette's attitude toward him.

Gaston Lazac annoyed him with a sudden chuckle. "That Castilloux! Europe and the Big Water left his belly as big as ever. But that daughter, now! By God, I would never have thought old Castilloux could get a slim doe like that one."

Evan tensed with his hand at the cabin door. Lazac's sharp black eyes missed nothing.

"You like her, eh" he said softly. "I've been watching you."

Evan flung open the door and went in without speaking. Lazac followed.

"You like her," he said again. "And I like you. Don't mind old Gaston Lazac. The woods are full of women. One don't mean a thing to me."

Collette was stirring on the edge of her bunk swinging her feet, and hearing every word. "He likes her?" She choked, tumbled upon her back and shook convulsively.

"He thinks it's funny," said Lazac, staring curiously at Collette's knees.

Evan turned from his own bunk. His fingers were wrapped tightly around a bottle of brandy.

"Stop your infernal sniggering," he snarled. But his anger merely inspired another spasm of mirth.

"He don't mind you very well," Lazac took the bottle and tilted it. "I believe if I had a lackey I'd make him jum'."

Collette laughed even harder at this.

Evan sat heavily on the side of his bunk and slapped it for Lazac to do likewise. "I'll make him jump in the river if he doesn't watch his step," he muttered wrathfully.

"You treat him too easy," said Lazac. "You have some strange ways for a Frenchman. Come to think of it, that

name you have there." As he mouthed it he made it anything but "MacDonald." "A damned queer name for a Frenchman."

"I'm no Frenchman." said Evan, stiffly. "The name is Scots."

"Bien, sure. I know a Scotchman. There's one up the Coosa with the Creeks." He came out with a word as strange as his rendition of MacDonald.

Evan's irritation ebbed as half-reluctant interest was aroused. "McQueen?"

Lazac nodded. "That's it. The Scotch and the Irish names are all the same," he observed sagely. "There are some Irishmen at Nouvelle Orleans. Bienville's aide-major is one. Macarty-Mactigue. A good man, he is, that don't think too much of his rank. I have got drunk with him many a time. But Scotch or Irish, as I said, it's all the same. Anything, so long as you're no damned Frenchman."

Evan goggled at him. "You're a Frenchman."

"By God, no! I'm a Canadian."

Evan continued to stare. "Canadian? That's New France, eh? What's a Canadian if not a Frenchman?"

The big man eyed him with pity. "You don't look like you just broke out of the egg," he said. "But I reckon all you people from Paris are like a goose, wake up in a new world every morning. A Frenchman is like the little jaybird that takes so sick from this country that he has to lay on his backside in his cabin. The Baron, whatever it is? Falbala? Yes, that is a Frenchman. The Governor, Bienville, is a Canadian. Like me. I thought a Scotchman might be a man of sense too, till I heard some of your talk."

Evan felt thoroughly put in his place. "Maybe it's the French coming out," he said humbly, My mother was French."

"That Scotch country? asked Lazac, "what kind of country is it?"

"Not like this. Mountains. Broken country, heather and gorse, and many rocks."

"Bien, sur." said Lazac. "Mountains. I like the flat lands better."

Evan, reflecting upon the illimitable flatness of the marshes stretching in all directions around the Gironde wondered aloud what Lazac knew of mountains.

"Know mountains?" said Lazac. "You think all this country is flat like the marsh out there? You've got a lot to learn. I could show you mountains north of the Chickasaws. I could take you through mountains running east from our posts on the Ohio, into the English country. I've seen a whole sky full of mountains, just hanging in the sky. You felt like it wasn't real mountains you were looking at. Like--like--"his thumb scratched his beard as he groped for an expression.

"Like a picture," Evan supplied with a trace of irony "Perhaps so," agreed Lazac. "I never saw many pictures. Only Indian pictures."

Evan grinned inwardly. He knew as well as anyone that Indians were wild, uncultured brutes with no knowledge of art. "Savages don't paint pictures," he said positively. Lazac's bearded jaw dropped. "You're trying to tell me what Indians do?" He asked incredulously. "Me that has seen all of them? Forty years, since I was a child in Canada. Indians along the St. Lawrence River and all down the Mississippi. Boy, I've been with the tribes to the east as far as British Carolina, and west to the springs of the Arkansas. Chickasaw, Tunica, Choctaw." He rolled off the tribes and grinned in satisfaction at Evan's complete bewilderment. "Seminoles in Spanish Florida, Missouri, and Caddo, and Natchitoches west of the River. Illinois, Cahokia, Oubache, Weas, Chippewa. I could name you a hundred more. By God, I've been so far I've bedded with Dakotah women."

Evan's head whirled with the outlandish names. "But they are all Indians. They are all alike. What's the difference?"

Lazac's snort expressed this contempt he reserved for such ignorance. "What's the difference between me and the Baron Falbala? The look different, dress different, talk different, build their lodges different. The don't make the same medicine and they don't make the same war. Take the Chickasaws, now, that we're going to fight. There's a creek, the Oktibbeha, running between their hunting grounds and the Choctaw country.

They hunt the north bank, the Choctaws hunt the south bank, but they don't cross over. There's an old tale in the lodges that both tribes sprang from two brothers who came from west of the Mississippi a long time ago. Maybe they did, but there's more difference between a Choctaw and a Chickasaw than between a Frenchman and a French cat. A Choctaw stays dirty from smoking himself over his lightwood fires and has a mortal fear of water. It's a damned seldom Choctaw that can swim a stroke. That don't go for a Chickasaw. He's clean for an Indian, almost as clean as I am, and he takes to the water like a loggerhead turtle. He's a hunter and fighter and he leaves the work

76

to his women the way it ought to be. I've seen Choctaw men get out in the fields with their squaws .And for fighting, a Choctaw's courage don't go far out of sight of a Choctaw town."

"But the Choctaws," Evan was a little in doubt, "they are with us?"

"Soit!" Lazac pulled at the bottle to console himself. "And don't I wish it was the other way round. Bienville is leaning on them, and God Almighty Himself couldn't promise that a Choctaw would carry war north of the Oktibbeha among Chickasaw towns. I think the General is looking for trouble this time, but he has got to do it. British agents are all over the Chickasaw country and they don't keep their eyes shut. I went trading in their Carolina once. The man that beats Gaston Lazac in trade don't keep his eyes shut. Compris?"

"You're going when the Commandant-General Marches?"

"Me?" Lazac wagged his head unbelievingly. "When did anyone take an army off and leave Lazac behind? You've got a lot to learn."

Evan admitted ruefully: "I suppose I do."

"Va, and I'm the man to show you. If I feel like it." He lifted the bottle. "Understand I don't waste my time on everybody."

Now, as the Gironde steered further up the vast river Evan had to adapt himself to changes in the geography, fauna and flora of the a country unlike any he had ever seen. While the weather alternated between gray and bright, the marsh disappeared and was replaced by cypress swamps flanking the stream. In some of the bends the land of the timber was so thick as to form a windbreak. With the canvas hanging idle the Gironde must put a hawser ashore, take a turn about a big cypress and work her way through the bend by the capstan. Progress slowed in the timbered swamps, which Evan found as gray and depressing as the marshland they had left behind.

By the afternoon of the seventh of February, when they were, in Lazac's estimation, some three leagues from Nouvelle Orleans, boredom had become an intolerable weight.

In the cabin, games of bezique with Lazac languished. Disgusted, Evan hurled the cards into the corner. He had not a word to say now, not to Lazac or Collette or anybody. Incredibly, even Lazac was talked out. The cabin was oppressive. Evan, fleeing from it walked the deck alone in the twilight. The sky was gray and cold as a stone, rain was falling over the river.

He looked listlessly at the swamp; a dead world, the gray rain wrapping in it a winding sheet. Gray cypress, rising like the masts and spars of long dead ships. Queer gray moss, which Lazac called Barbe Espagnol, drooped tattered sails around them. He had thought of this as a bright new world, but all of it had taken on the monotony of dull wet gray, like the ashes of a burned out fire. He felt as desolate as the swamp.

As he looked over the trees the blue chimney smoke of Nouvelle Orleans appeared, rising in several score thin ribbons against the wet background of cypress tops. Coming around a bend, through the slanting rain, he made his first view of the colonial capital.

Although they were two hours short of sundown the gray of twilight hung over the settlement. Rain, steadily falling, obscured the irregular contours of the cypress swamp which upon three sides shut in the clustered buildings. On the fourth side, the river bent sharply and elbowed the settlement back into the swamp where it huddled dripping, flat and gray as the low, gray ground upon which it stood.

The Gironde steered slowly into the bend. The cannon boomed a salute to the town. Smoke made a cloud which settled broadly on the yellow river. From the settlement, as if in reply, came the sound of a bell pealing, forlorn and hollow through the shifting sheets of rain. The wind which had favored the ship on her voyage upriver was bearing steadily to the north. It leaped high, whining through the Gironde's rigging.

The deck became a hustle and bustle as the ship moved sluggishly to shore. Her anchor went down, gurgling in the muddy stream. She swung upon the hawser, steadying to the slow flow of the current. A hundred feet off her starboard side lay the levee which protected the town from the high water, bare and brown, turned soggy under the steady beat of the rain. The yellow level of the river licked high against it. Evan crowded the rail staring. Collette pushed against his shoulder, her round face alive with excitement.

A crowd thickened upon the levee. People, not minding the rain, swarmed to the water's edge. People in homespun and cheap French cloth and wooden shoes. Faces used to poverty and the rigors of a harsh climate, but faces lightened by the sight of the ship. Evan gazed at these Caucasian faces, at the few blacks among them like the ones he had seen at Cape Francois, at the one Indian in a colored blanket.

He thought, "A vessel to these people at this end of creation must be manna from heaven."

Beside him Collette cried out in quick dismay. "Mere de Dieu! Is that the town?"

Gaston Lazac spat in the river. "Is Paris better?"

Evan and Collette stared together beyond the mud dike into the town which sprang from the mirey ground like a part of its natural growth. One, seemingly, with willows and weeds and dwarf palmettos. Streets ran through the brakes, stark ribbons of morass cutting into regular squares, like a chessboard, a hodge-podge of huts and shanties and unpretentious brick-and-timber houses. Behind the square with the flagpole, the Place d'Armes, was the church. Its flimsy steeple, in which the bell continued to ring, overtopped the town.

A white coated file of soldiers, muskets aslant, marched in to the Place d'Armes. Beneath cocked hats their faces drooped, splashed by the rain. Like figures in a dreary pantomime they shuffled into ranks before the flagstaff, grounded their firelocks, and stood at melancholy attention.

The first yawl was down, rocking gently on the river. Evan continued to gaze at the town. Gaston Lazac bit a Fresh chew from his black twist of tobacco and surveyed the deck.

"There's Castilloux," he remarked. "Watch him hog the first boat."

Evan turned quickly. Castilloux, shaking a raindrop from his fat nose, seemed angry. De Laval huddled in his cloak. Staring out through the slanting fall of rain at the primitive houses in the muddy jungle, Antoinette's face, nun like in her hood, and still as a cameo, seemed to withdraw into itself. Evan's heart lurched painfully. He wanted desperately to comfort her, but was conscious of his utter inadequacy.

"What an abominable place!" murmured De Laval, raising his smelling bottle with the affectation that, even at this distance, the odor was overpowering. "It is as filthy as a peasant's byre."

Antoine Castilloux, moving to the shipside as a sailor stood upright in the yawl to steady the ladder, did not bother to reply. As Antoinette hesitated, Evan roused from his trance. Too late. Castilloux swung his bulging middle over the side of the ship. His arm supported Antoinette on the ladder as if she were a child. Evan's hands hung empty, his emotions balanced between chagrin and incredulity as he watched Castilloux's progress. That fat, indolent man, to whom the simplest movement had seemed an effort, was going down, slowly it was true, but securely. Collette giggled nervously. "Blessed Virgin, perhaps The rope will break!"

She spat in disappointment when it did not. Castilloux was seating Antoinette as comfortably as possible. The standing sailor assisted De Laval into the boat. The oars moved, the yawl slid across the narrow interval of yellow water. Evan's heart followed until the craft slid against the levee, envying the sailor who carried Antoinette ashore. .Castilloux and the Baron struggled for themselves, arriving mired to the knees at the levee top. Below the levee, a berline drawn by a well fed team of four, had stopped in the muddy street. A lady with a high coiffure leaned out, somewhat puzzled of countenance. Her expression cleared as the spied Castillo. She made a motion with her hand and called out. Castilloux plunged down the levee, skidding in the mud. In a moment the sailor had handed Antoinette, dry shod, into the berline. The others clambered after. The closing door seemed like the end of a chapter in Evan's life. The Negro coachman cracked his whip, the horses stirred ,and the berline rolled through the watching people.

Mud whirled from the wheels, spattering the crowd. A few yells followed the berline as it gathered speed.

Gaston Lazac's rumbling voice returned Evan to the Gironde.

"Look" he said and pointed. "There's Major de Noyan and Monsieur Salmon on the levee. And the Irishman I was telling you about, Macarty-Mactigue. We better hurry. The captain's going down now."

Already Monsieur de Villiers and his officers, wrapped in their naval cloaks, were dropping down to the second yawl. Evan hurried, unmindful that Collette had not followed, and took his place beside Lazac as the boat filled. The sailors pulled strongly. In a moment the party was splashing ashore to join the cluster of bright cloaks waiting for them on the levee.

The Chevalier de Noyan, Bienville's nephew and Commandant of the military at Nouvelle Orleans, was slight, sallow and nervous.

He looked like a man who had known the ravages of fever. Macarty-Mactigue, Bienville's aide-major, burly and ruddy faced, had a visible web of veins across his nose and cheekbones. Monsieur Salmon, the Commissaire-Ordonnateur, showed pinched, preoccupied features sunk deeply in his cloak. His thin shoulders, stooped under the rain, seemed dutifully bent upon enduing the weather. All of them hailed Monsieur de Villiers as an old friend, and when Evan had been presented to them, greeted him cordially.

"My uncle, the Sieur de Bienville, thought most highly

Of your father, monsieur," De Noyan assured Evan in his high, nervous voice. "I am expecting him from Mobile almost any day now. Meanwhile, you and Monsieur le Capitaine shall accord me the honor of your presence in my house, such as it is."

The Captain smiled. "Evan shall indeed. But I, with exceeding regret, must decline. Of nights I must sleep with the Gironde, my only mistress. Regulations, my dear Chevalier."

De Noyan snapped his fingers. "So you must, Monsieur. But night is not yet come, and regulations say nothing against a glass or two to drive the chill from our bones. I'll go aboard tomorrow and look over the recruits." He smiled thinly. "Tonight will be cold. No doubt they will keep until morning."

Monsieur de Villiers responded lightly to his badinage, "Don't be too sure. An hour ago, when I put my head through the hatchway, they seemed near to spoiling,."

As they all laughed, Evan remembered Collette, and realized that she had not come ashore. He thought of fetching her then shrugged the matter off. Let her stay, she was probably with Rene, and enjoying herself more than she would in Major de Noyan's house. He would get her tomorrow. He turned with the others as they moved single-file in the mud of the levee.

On the right he could look down into the Place d'Armes. Inside its stockade of little pickets it was a plot of wet grass swiftly darkening in the shadows. Two paths cut it diagonally like a soldier's cross belts. From a marsh pool near its center a frog began to croak.

Chapter VII

With a slow gurgle the river slid under the Gironde's stern and vanished into the misty darkness. Collette, hanging on the after bulwarks, half listened to the water. Her chubby face screwed in concentration. It was well into the night now and Evan had not returned with Monsieur de Villiers. She could still see him jumping to carry Antoinette Castilloux down the ship's ladder. Grinning to herself, she recalled her impulse to send uncouth noises after Antoine Castilloux and his trollop of a daughter. Now they were safely ashore and Evan was ashore but she was still on this stinking ship. Not that she cared much about Evan leaving her. She would soon be on her own. But being on her own in this weed patch that passed for a town was not likely to be a frolic. The hatch head to the sainte-barbe had been made fast so she could not seek Rene for advice. The recruits had no chance to swim ashore and escape, if any of them had the nerve, into the jungle. But she had the nerve to swim, not into the jungle of course but into the town. It would be better to risk the town than to be exposed publicly, perhaps to be whipped in the town square, or subjected to whatever punishment these people reserved for loose women.

It was not far from the Gironde to the dim levee. She had swum many times in the Seine. This would be easy. Shivering in the chill she stripped herself bare and making a tight bundle together with her shoes she bound them to her back with her belt. She hoped to keep from getting soaked before she reached the bank. She crept over the bulwark and slid down the rope into the river. The sudden rush of chill and the river's current hit her at the same time. She held on to the rope tightly as the current bumped her soft skin against the rough timbers of the ship's hull. She pushed off the hull as forcefully as she could. The current swept her down as she tried to swim to the levee. Such a short way and already she could feel the knotting of her muscles. Her legs were like stones and her feet dropped down. She felt soft sand and mud between her toes. Her body upright, dull silver in the moonless night and cold as ice, she turned slowly toward the shore.

It seemed that her feet would never carry her to that mass of mud which marked the levee top. She skidded in the yellow mud and went to her knees at the water's edge, pulled forward by the weight of the bundle which was now under her breasts. Scrambling on hands and knees she made her way up the dike. Already a tingling after warmth suffused her body.

She did not pause at the top but plunged down, brushing through the willows and dead weeds at the foot. Beyond the fringe of brush she saw the loom of buildings in the town. As she unbuckled her bundle she wondered how far down the current had taken her, and realized that it made no difference. All parts of the town were equally unfamiliar to her. Her numb fingers fumbled to open the bundle. She was freezing once more. As she stooped she heard a man laugh. So close it seemed almost in her ear.

Her breath sucked in as she wheeled quickly "Hey little one," said the man softly. "Where did you come from?"

She saw him then, materializing from the shadow of the willows. She saw him not much more than a shadow himself but smelled him strongly. Her first impulse was to run. But his fingers wrapped tightly around her wrist and held her. She stood stiffly with her clothes scattered in he mud around her bare feet.

"Not so fast." When he put his whiskers close to her face his breath was stale with rum. "Pretty, pretty," he clucked with his tongue. "And out of the river, too."

As the sandpaper fingers of his left hand touched her body she became a small wildcat, scratching with her free hand at this eyes and trying to drive her knee into his groin. But he pressed her too closely and his thighs held her legs down. In an instant he had her clawing hand as well and twisted both of them behind her back. They stood for a heartbeat immobile, face to face, breast to breast. Her head twisted sideways, her strong teeth snapped in the loose flesh around his jawbone. He squalled with pain and slung her sprawling among the weeds. Immediately his lean body pitched upon her. She flipped like a crawfish. He got both hands and most of his weight upon her and held her still. They lay panting, in a momentary truce.

"Damn you, she-cat," He muttered.

She scoured her brain for the last dreg of filth and poured it on him. When he tried to cover her mouth she bit his fingers and clawed him with the hand he had freed. Repaying her vilification with interest, he rescued his fingers and dug her nails from his cheek. They lay still again, at a deadlock, while Collette's teeth snapped in futility in empty air.

"Let me up! Let me up!" she raged. "I'll have you to know, you donkey's bastard, that I am a respectable woman!"

"Respectable woman?" he scoffed, "With the language you use? And as naked as a day old muskrat! You swam from the ship. I heard you in the water. You're Salpetriere."

"Damn you, you lie!" she cried furiously. "I'm no correction girl. Nobody shipped me to satisfy the likes of you. I came of my own fee will."

He chuckled. "For sure, you did. With a lash on your behind to make your will even freer."

"Let me up or I'll bite you again."

"Venere Saine Gris, she-cat, we can't lie here all night."

"We can lie here until we rot if you don't let me up."

She said obstinately. "Listen, you, I came here to find a home and a place, and to earn my living like any honest woman. Now get away."

She was beginning to enjoy the sensation of having him, in a sense, where she could call the tune. But the mud on her bare flesh was like ice. Her whole body trembled, she could not lie here naked much longer.

He seized hope from her remarks. "You have no place to go?"

"If you think for that reason I will go with you--"

He eased his weight without, however, giving her sufficient margin to squirm free.

"I'll bargain with you, little one," he suggested. "I'll find you a home. A good home. You'll not find one otherwise. You will go loose on the town, for sure. The streets are full of girls like you."

The ague in her body sapped her resolution. Her throat was raw. Her breasts ached. Knowing that he was not lying, she began to whimper. "Holy Mary, I can't go on now. It is so cold. I'm freezing. I'm sick, so sick. I'm hungry. Oh, let me go! Let me go! Let me put my clothes on and I will see about later."

He lay upon her for a minute longer but her sobbing had moved him. When he stood up his hands, still tight on her wrists, pulled her after him

"Don't cry, pretty," he soothed. "I know you're cold. You're slippery as an oyster. By God, look at the mud on your back! Vite! Get into your clothes, girl. I will take you to Jacqueline Martin's."

Groping in the weeds she found her clothes and painfully go into her breeches first.

"Who is Jacqueline Martin?" she mumbled. My brother's wife. I am Henri Martin. Remember that name, jeune fille." He fastened her blouse for her and chucked her under the chin. "I would take you to my own shanty but my partner would have other plans for you. You're one woman I'll keep out of the reach of Gaston Lazac."

Her jaw dropped. "Gaston Lazac! You know him?"

"We have the same cabin," he told her. "You saw him on the ship? Then maybe already you know what kind of men we are?"

She had felt the man's body and smelled him. Now, for the first time, she was seeing him as clearly as the gloom permitted. He was not like Gaston Lazac though he wore the same stinking garments of deerskin. This man was lean, with a hatchet face, and a twisted smile. She stared at him until he pulled her by the arm and led her out of the willows. They crossed the muddy street and headed into the town.

Jacqueline Martin thought that a lump in the corn shuck pallet had awakened her. She was trying to locate it with her fingers when she heard the rasp of knuckles at the door. Her bare feet made no sound on the puncheon floor. Resting both hands against the door she listened intently, wondering if she might not have imagined the sound. Then the knock came again, gentle but persistent.

"Who?" Her voice was low. She was taking no chances of awakening Etienne.

"Henri."

She knew it was true. She recognized Henri Martin's voice.

"Henri. Holy Mother! What is it that you want? At this hour."

"I have a sick child here." She fancied that she could detect the thickness of rum on his tongue. Coming here in the middle of the night with such a preposterous lie. It outraged her so much that she threw open the door and stepped out in her nightdress bent upon giving him a piece of her mind.

"Henri, you fool! You're drunk. You're--" Then her eyes made out in the gloom the bedraggled, shivering figure beside him. "Good God! Who, eh, what is that?"

The cabin was raised above the marsh ground on cypress piling three feet high. Henri and a crying stripling stood at the bottom of the steps looking up.

"A sick child," said Henri, with his twisted, mocking grin.

"A young boy," whispered Jacqueline. "Why in God's name did you bring him here?"

"All that's male about this one are the rags on its back," said Henri. "It is a female kitten I picked up by the river. Sick and looking for shelter. Will you leave it out in the cold, belle soeur?"

Jacqueline Martin stood with her hands locked in the folds of her nightdress. "Henri, you know you are drunk and lying," she whispered fiercely. "You think it is a joke! If that is a girl, it is one you picked up in the street."

Collette had remained silent, almost too full of chill now to even think, watching wide-eyed the tall, raven haired woman whose loose nightdress concealed an individuality of figure. Now terrified that she might be turned out into the cold again, she forced her stiff lips to open.

"No, No, madame! He is telling the truth. I am sick. I am--" As her voice trailed off she saw the dark haired woman bit her lip.

"But..but Etienne," Jacqueline Martin murmured uncertainly.

Henri grinned. "I can hear Etienne snoring now. Keep his gun and his knife from him and I'm not afraid to look my good brother in the eye."

Jacqueline stepped back through the door and nodded her head. No good could come of taking in a strange girl who was probably off the streets, and with Etienne, probably only harm. But Jacqueline could only wonder at herself as Collette crumpled on the steps and Henri scooped her up and entered the door as Jacqueline stepped aside.

"Where will she sleep?" he whispered.

"In the loft. Put her down and go, before Etienne hears."

"Let him. She is too sick to climb the ladder and you can't carry her. Make a light, Jacqueline."

"And wake Etienne?"

But there was no need to wake Etienne. His snoring had stopped. His querulous voice reached out from the bunk across the room.

"Jacqueline! Jacqueline! What is it?"

"Go back to sleep, Etienne. It's only me, Henri," said his brother. "Make a light Jacqueline."

The man on the bed began to curse horribly.

Jacqueline, knowing that the more light thrown on the situation, now the better, fumbled above the fireplace for a candle and lit it. The feeble flicker populated the room with shadows among which her anxious eyes found Henri, a few steps inside the door with the pasty-faced, mud bedaubed girl in his arms. Against the far wall under the window was her husband Etienne Martin. He had pulled himself into a sitting position, awkwardly because of paralyzed legs that lay under a bearskin robe. The candle played strange tricks with his harshly

90

angular features, at once lighting them with malevolence and scarring them with cruel shadows.

His black eyes, blinking in the light, slid from Jacqueline to Henri.

"It's a sick girl," said Jacqueline swiftly. "I promised I would take her in."

There was something obscene in Etienne's laughter. "A sick girl," he mimicked, "So you gather all your trulls together under one roof, Henri.?"

The tall woman stiffened with fury which edged her voice. "Hold your tongue, Etienne," she said. "Henri, take the girl to the loft and put her on the petit-lit. Then go. I'll quiet Etienne."

"If I had my knife," said Etienne, fumbling at the bed clothes. "If I had my gun."

"A trull is it?" Jacqueline's voice was quite low now as the stood over the bed her dark hair falling cascading over the shoulders of her nightdress. "A trull who has worked flesh to bone and soul to shadow to care for you! A trull has more self respect than I do. Body and purse, she gets what she wants. I get nothing but the vileness of your tongue. Is it your knife you want? You're lucky I do not stick it between your ribs!"

Henri alit from the loft.

"Go now. I will attend to her," she said gently.

He shrugged, looked once to Etienne, and let himself out of the door. Etienne was entirely speechless, but his breathing came so harshly that he might have been strangling. In the loft she heard the girl whimpering.

Collette's ears were filled with voices. She thought she heard Evan's voice but she was only half awake and could make out no words only a sound like a fly buzzing.

"Where am I?" she could see a roof angle above her. The flies below her were buzzing without saying anything intelligible. She was tired and so very weak. Her eyelids closed and her drowsing deepened.

Evan held his hat in his hands, and looked around the single room of the cabin. Both windows were closed making the interior as dim as twilight even though it was full morning. Two stools and a plank table stood before the fireplace. A log split down the middle and set upon pegs made a bench in one corner. The man who lay on the bunk built into the rear of wall under the window looked steadily back at him. His face under the lank gray hair reminded Evan a gargoyle on the Cathedral of Notre Dame in Paris.

"Etienne," said the woman, "This is Monsieur MacDonald from Paris." Evan liked the way her soft voice slurred his name. She went on hurriedly to him, "You must pardon Etienne, that he does not rise. You see he cannot walk."

"Nor run, m'sieu'. Nor leap nor dance, nor stand on my head. There's a musket ball next to my spine." He was so sardonic, it seemed he almost cherished the things that he could not do.

"Hush Etienne," warned his wife.

His caustic voice mocked her. "Hush, Etienne! Hold your tongue Etienne. You talk too much. Somebody might hear you! My tongue is the only thing left to me that I can use and I will use it as I please, madame, by your leave or without it!"

Evan's embarrassed eyes returned to the woman. Her finely molded, uniform features had stiffened a little, the suggestion of lines was a little more perceptible at the corners of her thoughtful mouth. That was all. There was no other sign of anger at the man's words. Her large eyes, as black and lustrous as the braids which wrapped her head, were perfectly clear. But she looked terribly tired, and he had the sensation that the

92

face was merely a mask and that the real woman was somewhere deep behind it.

As he faced the woman he was turning in his mind what he would say. How would he say that this morning Lazac had learned from Henri Martin of the girl he had brought in. To this woman it would appear that Collette was his doxy. He was not even sure that this girl was Collette. His first instinct upon hearing was to come immediately but now, as he squirmed, he thought that he should not have come at all. He just stood like a tongue-tied fool before the disconcerting calm of Jacqueline Martin.

While he fumbled for words Gaston Lazac came to his rescue.

"He wants the girl that you have in your loft, Jacqueline."

Jacqueline Marin's black eyebrows arched. "Yes, m'sieu'?"

Etienne uttered a triumphant, "Hah! Then the little trull is yours? Do you know how she got here? My damned petticoat chasing brother, Henri, dragged here in last night." His sly eyes slid sideways at Jacqueline. "It pays to watch him, m'sieu'. He will have your women before you know it. You know, he and my wife are such friends Such close, close friends." He began to snicker in a sort of spasm.

Evan felt like taking to his heels. What kind of madhouse had he gotten into, where a man talked so to his wife before strangers? He shuffled his feet and grew red in the face while Lazac, leaning in the doorway, whistled. Jacqueline Martin's shoulders twitched but she did not lose here composure.

"Etienne is sick, m'sieu'. Don't mind him," she said evenly. "Now, about the girl."

Evan stammered. "Didn't, didn't Gaston tell you? I brought her from France dressed as a boy that she might not be molested. I feel that I am responsible for her. That is all, madame. Truly." Why did he hope so earnestly that she would believe him?

Her dark eyes revealed no flicker of interest. "The girl is on a petit-lit in the loft," she said. "She has had a chill and a little fever. It is nothing serious. You may see her, m'sieu'. But she cannot leave here now." Her husband, pressing his sardonic face close to the pillow, snickered until his body shook, while she followed Evan up the ladder. Pulling himself through the trapdoor Evan looked round the loft. Collette lay under the eaves on a little pallet stuffed with corn shucks. Her eyes opened at the noise of his entrance.

He stood over her. "Collette, you little fool! Why didn't you stay on the Gironde?

Her eyes were big and glittering in her flushed face "Let me alone," she mumbled. "I'm all right here. I'm going to live here."

"Live here? Are you out of your head?"

When she propped herself on her elbow her hair fell down in her face.

"I shall live here! Damn you, I shall!" Tears filled her eyes and streaked her flushed cheeks.

Evan gaped at her. Jacqueline moved him aside and dropped down by the sobbing girl. Her vital brown fingers combed Collette's matted hair. "Don't cry little one. For sure you stall stay with me."

"As you will madame," he said. He did not admit, aloud, his relief at having Collette disposed of. "I hope it won't work a hardship on you. I will help in any way I am able. She will need clothing and such things. I am sure, madame, that she will be better off with you to mind her."

Rolling on her side, Collette brushed her hair from her eyes and grinned at him wickedly.

"He could not help laughing. "You little she-devil," he said. Keep and eye on her, madame or she will be the ruin of you."

94

At that moment Gaston Lazac called up to them, "Evan, come on, vite! I have just got word that the Governor is back in the city. We must go and meet him."

"Yes. Run to the Sieur de Bienville, even before he calls," called out Etienne. "My old comrade Gaston. Run like a dog. I will lie here and wait on my ever faithful wife to keep me while you do his bidding for a bone."

Gaston Lazac did not answer as Evan descended and they hurried from the cabin and across the town with the scarred faced woods runner, Claude Dubuisson, who brought word from De Noyen that the Commandant General had returned. For all his eagerness to see Bienville, Evan could not free his mind from the encounter with Jacqueline Martin and her singular husband.

Evan, feeling the Sieur de Bienville's wire-strong fingers bite into his shoulders, knew that every eye in the alon was on them. He had the uneasy feeling that he looked flustered with his hot face and his short breath from the pace of his walk through the town. But he quickly dismissed that in the eagerness of the meeting as Bienville lifted his hands and stepped back.

This elderly gentleman in the rumpled blue coat and brown breeches was the same Bienville of Montmartre days, yet there was a subtle difference. He was shorter than average but not small in his thigh high boots. His face was older but not old for a man past his middle fifties, and his lips made a pale pucker from a scar across them. As he set his eyes upon Evan they seemed weary but were piercing and active. The eyes of a man who missed very little and was wary, almost harried Monsieur Villiers has brought me the sad news that your father, my old friend David, is dead."

Evan nodded, thinking that Bienville must be half ill. His eyes looked fevered and his voice was harsh.

"Yes, monsieur, he died scarcely two weeks before I left France."

"I am indeed grieved." Bienville watched the window and the pale light which fell through the fine linen panes "Montmartre," he said, softly. "The walks in the country. Do you remember Evan? I suppose not, but I recall more. Long before you were born, the old days. He was my true friend. There are not so many of them left in these times. Eh bien, it is God's will I suppose. We all grow old. I, too, and the time comes before we expect it." He turned his head looking directly into Evan's eyes, and said simply, "You are welcome in my house, Evan, as David would be welcome."

With a gesture to the standing men to be seated he moved behind his table and, coughing as he did so, lowered himself stiffly into a rolled armchair with the carved fleur-de-lis on the back of it. As he folded his arms across the litter of papers he looked at the nine facing him. Evan covered a grin at the sight of Gaston Lazac settling himself gingerly upon one of the frail gilt chairs, his legs flexed under him as if he meant to spring up in case the thing broke beneath his weight. But the chair held and Evan felt a little disappointed.

Bienville turned his eyes on Evan again. "With Monsieur de Noyen's approval, why don't you go now and get your belongings from his house and bring them here? There servants will find a room for you and we will speak more tomorrow." It was more a command than an invitation.

Without waiting for a reply from either Evan or Monsieur de Noyen, he turned and addressed the council of men, "Gentlemen we must discuss this business now at hand. I will not keep you long. I am very tired. I will meet with you all again tomorrow."

Evan excused himself without a word and returned to the house of Monsieur de Noyen.

In Meunier's common room the lantern burned late, throwing its ruddy light over a persistently convivial company. It was not every day that a ship from France put down her anchor off the levee-front and the habitants of Nouvelle Orleans took such an event as license for celebration. Liquor and talk ran freely. Woods runners and shop keepers, sailors from the Gironde and white-coated soldiers from the garrison, all found a common meeting ground within the walls of Meunier's Inn.

Evan and Gaston Lazac had dumped Henri Marin, like a sack of flour at the shanty of Clementine Billiot on the levee-front, disregarding the obscene protests of the buxom Clementine. They found there the same group of men who had shared Lazac's table earlier in the evening. The first of these was Claude Dubuisson, a coureur de bois like Lazac. A lank fellow in fringed, beaded deerskin, with a most peculiar scar running whitely across his swarthy cheek to corner of his mouth so that his lips seem twisted into a perceptual smirk. Next to him sat moon faced Marc Aufrere, who made tar and pitch in the pine woods across lake Pontchartrain, in coat and breeches of shabby blue, with his long-queued hair falling over his shoulder. The third was Camille Billiot, the husband of Clementine, seemingly no more substantial inside his patched blouse of hand spun wool than a broom straw, with not enough hair to be queued at all, who fished in season in the river and the lakes and sold his catch to the gentry.

All being well down in the bottle, they received Evan with open arms, taking advantage of the opportunity when they learned that he had come straightway from Paris. "Hein? Paris?" said Claude Dubuisson, turning his smirk into a grin. "What is he looking for?" He asked Lazac, "Mountains of rubies? Or is he just digging for man-roots?"

Camille Billiot snickered. The lantern's light gleamed on his bare head.

"It may be he's looking for a woman-root," he ventured. He ducked his head as Lazac swung a playful paw in his direction and almost tumbled backward off his stool. "Baste!" Lazac admonished him, "This man is no fool."

Claude Dubuisson still maintained a doubting expression. "I never yet saw one from Paris but was looking for something of that sort." He fixed Evan with a thoughtful eye. "Look here, let's have it straight. Did you never hear of the man-root?"

Evan returned his stare blankly. He was not yet at all certain if they were serious or having fun at his expense.

Dubuisson's face was perfectly sober except for the involuntary smirk. He tapped the table top with a judicious forefinger.

"You know nothing of the man-root? Well, let me tell you, friend, you must be as stupid as a donkey. The man-root is the greatest gift God ever gave to this country." He pushed his empty mug toward Lazac whose hand was nearest the bottle. "Au vrai, friend, and I was the man who found it."

Lazac's hand twitched pouring the brandy and it spilled. He smothered a grin in his beard.

Dubuisson cleared his throat with a draught of the brandy.

"That was when I was digging the fosse around the town," he went on, carelessly. "I uncovered a colony of man-roots, male and female. Oui, all sexes and sizes. All white, they were, made like pomme de terre, but the man never lived that saw one so large. The negro slaves took fit of terror and attacked them, yes, massacred then right down to the lone female. She was une petite, that one. I saved her from them."

He paused with great significance and Evan could not resist asking, "What then?"

Dubuisson wept into his brandy. "I married her. Think, mon vieux, think of the children we might have had. Nothing like them in the world before, half man and half root. But one day she wandered from the house and a pig, mistaking her for a pomme de terre - ah, I cannot think of it!" He buried his face in his hands, then lifted it to say miserably, "The beast devoured her!"

Lazac bellowed, beating the table with his fist, and the others joined him, leaving Evan to nurse a sheepish grin. "Va donc, Claude! roared Lazac, wiping the tears from his eyes. "Get along with your lies! This man did not come here to listen to goblin stories. He wants to tie Chickasaw scalps to his belt, like you and me." scalp tied to a Chickasaw belt."

Marc Aufrere rubbed his palms together uneasily. "On the north shore of the lake and along the sound there is more fear of the Choctaws," he said. "There's talk that they're coming down on us."

Lazac round eyes stared at him. "What's that?"

Aufrere shifted upon his stool. "It may be true, it may not. Here is the news as I had it from Pierre Dandonneau, of the River of the Pascagoulas. The tale is about in the town now. Bienville knows it. Eh bien, Monsieur D'Artaguette at Mobile has ordered the militia captain at the Pascagoulas to keep on guard against the Choctaws. The English have bribed them, says Monsieur D'Artaguette. They are with the English and will be down upon us. The habitants, says Pierre, are out of their wits with fear of the savages, they will leave their homes and run here."

Lazac's mouth stayed open. Then his lips began to move and curses poured out like water over a millrace. His fluency amazed Evan. When he had exhausted this supply of profanity Lazac spat upon the floor and rubbed it in with his toe. "That for Monsieur Diron D'Artaguette," he sneered. "Yes, that will be his talk. When it comes to knowing Indians

99

he is like an old woman, always taking bladders for lanterns and going off into a panic." He glared at Aufrere as if holding him responsible. "What did Bienville do?"

"To begin with, he cursed D'Artaguette, even as you did. Then he sent Pierre back with the word that the habitants had nothing to fear from the Choctaws, and at no cost to leave their homes."

Lazac solemnly nodded his approval of this action. "So the habitants of Pascagoulas would run here?" he said, scathingly. "They should have better sense, knowing D'Artaguette's loose tongue. Didn't he go among the Choctaws last year when they were ready to march with Jean Paul Lesueur against the Chickasaws? Went among them, by God with a canard of a dream he had had. He swore until his belly was blue that the spirit of their fathers had caught him by the foot while he slept and told him that since the Choctaws were leaving the French for the English he should go to them and warn them that unless they all made war against the Chickasaws it would all be over with them."

Again Lazac fell into a lurid fit of cursing and mauled his fist upon the table until the mugs jumped. You know, Claude, what a dream means to a Choctaw. It makes him stink with fear. Lesueur said that he persuaded them to march almost in sight of the Chickasaw village. When they heard the war songs of the Chickasaw women they began to remember D'Artaguette's dream. It meant bad luck , they said, and they ran so fast they left their guns. Lesueur says they ran for twenty leagues." He revolved his mug slowly between his palms, peering at it while he meditated upon the folly of Diron D'Artaguette. "The trouble with D'Artaguette is that he hates Indians just because they are Indians. There's no sense in that. There are plenty of good points about Indians."

"Females in particular?" suggested Dubuisson, slyly.

Lazac gave him a foul name.

"Still," said Dubuisson, "they are treacherous, those

Choctaws. You can't trust one. There's Soulier Rouge, it is fact that he went to the English at Kaapa."

Lazac nodded gloomily. "Va, that is the way it goes now. Ten years ago, before Bienville went back to France, there was no such damned foolery. That's what comes of having men like D'Artaguette and Perrier dealing with the Indians."

He was looking at Evan, talking for his for his own benefit. "Listen to me, there is a snake in this country that makes a noise like seeds rattling in a dried gourd, when it shakes its tail. If it bites you, it kills you. Still, if you know what you're about, you can get a forked stick behind its head and take it alive. But once you have your hand on it you can't let it go. It's the same with Indians. Bienville caught the tribes and tamed them, then Perrier let them get away. Now it's for Bienville to catch them back." His fingers tugged at his beard. "It's much to ask, even to that little bastard."

Dubuisson's eyes popped at him. He had drunk enough to feel belligerent.

"Bastard?" he demanded thickly. "Listen, Gaston Lazac, I have scouted for Bienville almost as long as you."

Lazac bellowed, laughing. "Va donc! I call him the same sort of bastard I call you. It is a compliment, compris?"

Dubuisson grumbled, not mollified. "You, Gaston, think that Bienville's bowels couldn't move without you. You're the best scout, you say, you know the country better than any man living."

Lazac agreed with him profanely. "I do," he declared. "I know my beard, by God, every hair and whisker. I know this country, every bush and tree."

Dubuission improved upon Lazac's profanity, but broke off to grin as he slapped the bosom of his hunting shirt. "Me," he said, "I go to

Fort Chartres with Captain Leblanc! Not you, my friend." His laughter was high pitched and shrill.

Lazac blinked. "When?"

Dubuisson leaned across the table and patted Lazac's shoulder with commiseration

"Tomorrow," he said. "Dispatches it is. Yes. Most important dispatches." his head wagged wisely, "To Pierre D'Artaguette at Fort Chartres."

Lazac had recovered his balance. He grunted. "It's no secret, and that is to the good, since your tongue would make it common gossip." He was still plucking at his beard.

"I'm glad it's you will be with Leblanc, Claude, you know the river. Keep him away from the east shore, for the love of God. That's where the Chickasaws caught Ducoder."

"I'll tend Leblanc like a wet nurse," Dubuisson vowed thickly.

He reached for the bottle and made as if to throw it when he found it empty, Lazac grabbed him and they tussled almost upsetting the table, while Lazac kept up a bellow for Meunier to fetch a new bottle. His bull voice carried above the sound of other voices beginning to be raised in song.

Dubuisson got possession of the empty bottle and thumped it against the table. He started, as if a thought had suddenly struck him.

"Look here, Gaston," he said. "I won't be able to get back before Bienville marches. You'll be with Bienville and I'll be with the Illinois army." That seemed to make him sad almost to the point of tears. "God! I hope D'Artaguette is a better man than his brother, Diron. Suppose something happens and D'Artaguette can't make his rendezvous in the Chickasaw country with Bienville?"

Lazac's voice was heavy with iron. "Then may the good God get us all out of it."

Marc Aufrere crossed himself. "He may need to," he said darkly. "Bienville is having more than Indian trouble. If he goes by the River of the Chickasaws he needs boats. I, for one, know that Antoine Castilloux's saw-pits are behind on the bateaux they contracted for. I talked today with Gerard Mallot, Castilloux's director. He contracted with me for pitch for caulking at sixteen livers a quarter. Now he tries to pay but twelve! I sent him to the devil."

Camille Billiot cut in with his shrill pipe. "Where do they get their airs, these chats puantes, those Malots, those Castillouxs, those de Pradels? They would pay me less for my fish than my fish are worth. My wife, Clementine, they do the same with the bread she bakes."

"Why they're gentry," said Lazac, with an air of mock sagaciousness. "They're not people like you and me. I hear that de Pradel and his wife don't even sleep in the same bed. Now that is gentry for you."

Camille agreed, smirking. "De Pradel's wife sleeps in another bed, yes. In another house, too, on most nights."

"Hein?" said Lazac. "Like Clementine?" He grinned broadly. "That reminds me. I left a man tonight for Clementine."

Camille winked. "Who?"

"Henri Martin."

"Bah! He was drunk."

Lazac nodded. "Clementine didn't want me to leave him. It may be she was expecting somebody else."

Camille's beady eyes gleamed defensively. "You say she does. I say I have not caught her at it. Wait until I catch her at it!"

This declaration set Lazac and Dubuisson laughing until they choked and their eyes streamed. Plump Aubergiste Meunier saved them from strangulation by waddling up with their brandy. At his heel stepped one of the sailors from the Gironde.

Lazac gave the bottle a critical appraisal. "This is eau de vie?" he asked. "It looks like slop from the latrines."

Meunier shrugged and smiled and went away. When he had gone the sailor touched Lazac's shoulder.

"Pardon, mate," he said, in a tone of apology, "I used to see you aboard the Gironde. Can you tell a poor sailor man who has not had a woman to himself since St. Domingue where he can find one in this town?"

Dubuisson's mirth made itself apparent in a whoop. "He is the man for it! Make him tell! Draw the worms out of his nose!"

"Friend," said Lazac to the sailor, "you've come to the wrong man. I don't know one woman in this town from another."

The sailor eyed him for a moment with profound disbelief, then, as Lazac turned away he trudged resignedly back to rejoin his companion at the bar.

"The only reason you don't know one from another," observed Dubuisson, "is that you can't tell them apart in the dark." He waited until the laughter had died down. "Did you hear about the one they call La Libre, Gaston?"

"No," said Lazac warily, "What about her?"

"She went up before the Registrar two days ago. She is five months gone with child and she had to declare whose it was." Dubuisson leaned back on his stool and watched Lazac. "She claimed it was yours."

Lazac burst out in great indignation. "She lies! She furrows as often as a sow. I have not been near her since last January."

Camille Billiot was delighted. He could not control his giggling. His Adam's apple jerked up and down.

Lazac glared at him. "I would laugh, too" he said contemptuously, "if I had a woman like Clementine."

Camille would not be squelched. His tittering became infectious.

They all howled merrily and senselessly, even Lazac. A sound of blundering footsteps interrupted them and a man lurched against Lazac's broad back, then reeled and clung to his shoulders.

"Ah, messieurs!" cried the newcomer in a high pitched voice, "you have some cause for levity, no doubt?"

It was a young man of medium build who thrust himself between Lazac and Evan. He placed his palms carefully wide apart upon the table and with his shoulders weaving above this support looked around with a foolish smile. His face was narrow, of high color, for which his breath gave the reason. He wore a coat and breeches of green velvet, but no waistcoat, so that his shirt of fine linen was visible. His apparel had the appearance of having been slept in, his small wig hung precariously upon the back of his head.

"Am I welcome, Messieurs?" he babbled. "I, who push the humble goose wing, am I welcome among so many brave coureurs de bois? It is so, Monsieur Lazac."

"Sit down, M'sieu' Hebert," said Lazac.

The new-comer lowered himself with great care upon the proffered stool. By the time he had got himself seated Evan realized that this must be Charles Hebert, Bienville's secretary, whom the Governor had reported unaccountably missing. He began to perceive the reason for Monsieur Hebert's absence.

Charles Hebert blithely appropriated the bottle.

"Monsieur Lazac," he said, when he had satisfied his thirst, "you are a trapper, are you not?"

Lazac admitted that he trapped at times.

"You know the worth of hides, then?"

Lazac said that also was true.

"Well, then, Monsieur Lazac, perhaps you can tell me what the worth of mine may be when Monsieur de Bienville next lays his eyes on me."

The matter touched Monsieur Hebert so deeply that he must needs take once more to the bottle not, however, allowing the liquor which flooded into his mouth to impede the talk which flooded out of it.

"I trust that some of you gentlemen will take my part with the Governor and tell him that I was unavoidably detained from the performance of my duties." He turned appealing eyes upon each in turn.

"I shall explain. It was last night, messieurs, and the wife of a good friend, Jerome Allain, the voyageur. A pretty wench she is to have such a lout for a husband. It is God's pity. But there was I--" he hiccoughed, "there was I in that pigsty which is his bed. Mon Dieu! Why cannot the man provide his wife with a decent bed to entertain her friends? There I was, I say, and there came a rattle at the door latch which could only be the good Jerome coming home. Sacre nom! What to do? You gentlemen know that I would have the brute out, but the wench was in a fit of terror, so to please her I crawled beneath the bed. Le bon Dieu preserve me from such beds henceforth! It was so low to the floor that I bumped my backside smartly getting under. In stamped the good Jerome and down upon the bed like a sack of grain without bothering to get of his clothing."

He paused to snicker tipsily. "You gentlemen, you are gentlemen I pray, and will not use ill my confidence, you gentlemen, as I say, can appreciate the position I was in. Cramped there beneath that atrocity of a bed with the great ox Jerome snoring away above my head. In a cold fear, messieurs, lest the bed give way and I be smothered beneath Jerome and his foul bedding. Oh, mon Dieu! What a horrible night! I could not remain there until dawn, since he would be sure to discover me then. Nor was it safe to attempt to steal out for the reason that he might waken. Still, that was the least of two evils. At last, making up my mind, I took my shoes in my teeth and crept out to safety. That was near the dawn. I have been apprehensive since then of confronting Monsieur de Bienville."

He paused, thoughtfully. "Do you know my friends I have a sneaking feeling that I have left something behind me? Ah, what can it be?" He shook his head as he clutched Lazac's shoulder affectionately. "Eh, bien, but here I am messieurs!"

Behind him a voice growled. "And here am I, also, Monsieur Seducer!"

At his immediate rear a man loomed. A low man built like a hogshead and fiercely mustached, who brandished aloft in his left hand a waist coat of fine flowered silk, while in his right the naked blade of his hunting knife caught a gleam from the lantern.

Charles Hebert crouched low above the table as if petrified. His mouth gaped fish like, muttering incredulously, "Jerome!"

"Is this your garment, Monsieur Seducer?" roared Jerome.

Charles Hebert's head turned slowly until one of his terrified eyes fixed upon Jerome Allain. With a single blood curdling shriek he burst from his pretrification and dived under the table Jerome lunged in pursuit, his short, powerful arm lifted and struck. Lazac sprang up from the table so suddenly that his stool bounced with a clatter upon the floor. Flinging wide his arms he hugged Jerome to his breast, but not quickly enough to prevent the keen-bladed hunting knife from inflicting one neat slice across the skin tight seat of Charles Hebert's green velvet breeches as they disappeared beneath the table.

Aubergiste Meunier came with his arms upraised to heaven screaming that such goings on would have his placed closed by the Governor, but Monsieur Hebert remained in the security of the table, holding his backside and howling mournfully like a lonesome dog.

Chapter VIII

Evan sat up in bed, his knees a sharp peak beneath the bed clothes, heartily wishing that he could go back to sleep. His mouth tasted like a piece of cowhide, long dead, uncured, with the hair still on. An intolerable weight filled the inside of his skull, concentrating in particular immediately behind his eyeballs. He let his head hang, it was less uncomfortable than holding his head up.

As he sat there, his mind quite blank, a knock fell upon the door. It opened to his grunt and a coffee tray appeared, supported by a pair of black hands. Behind the tray a was face like a black cherub preserving a serious man. It was Bon Temps, Bienville's house-slave. He poured the coffee and stood by attentively while Evan drank off the scalding liquid, even blacker than the negro's face. "Master say you come, 'Sieu'" Bon Temps said when Evan had finished. "You see him downstairs." As soon as he relaxed his lips they opened in a grin.

Evan wagged his head and watched the negro go. The coffee made him feel better. He hitched himself out of bed beginning to remember the last night, and getting into his clothes, he could not restrain a chuckle, recalling how he and Gaston Lazac and Claude Dubuisson had brought Charles Hebert home after his melee with the outraged Jerome Allain. Monsieur Hebert, thought Evan, was a fortunate man to have got off with nothing worse than a nicked bottom. He would be unable to sit for some days but that was all. It occurred to him that he had spent a good part of his night escorting drunken men hither and yon about the town. Not only Charles Hebert, but the woodsman, Henri Martin. That set him to thinking of Jacqueline Martin. He must not forget her kindness to Collette, for Collette was yet his responsibility. He must remember to provide some feminine garments for her. Above all, he must not allow her to become a burden upon Jacqueline. It pleased him to think of Madame Martin as simply Jacqueline, and wondered why it was faintly annoying to recall that she was Madame Etienne Martin, the wife of that half-mad cripple.

Poor devil. He was sorry for him. But he was also sorry for her. Those two and the drunken, Henri, Etienne's brother, had aroused his curiosity, but Lazac had told him little. Only that Jacqueline had come to Nouvelle Orleans after the great massacre at the settlement at Fort Rosalie by the Natchez six years before.

Etienne and Henri, both woods runners, had been with Jean Paul Lesueur and his Choctaws when they had rescued half a hundred women and children whom the Natchez held prisoners after the massacre. Jacqueline, then fifteen years of age, had been one of those. In Nouvelle Orleans she had lived a year with the Ursuline sisters and then had married Etienne before he marched off with Perrier's avenging army. From that campaign Etienne had come back to his bride with a bullet in his left hip. That, said Lazac, was the reason he lay in bed all the time, his body, from the hips down, was paralyzed. His legs were like two cylinders of stone.

It was a strange business, he thought. Was there something between Henri and Jacqueline to make Etienne hate his brother so? In spite of her worn, weary look there was a quality about the woman that would undoubtedly attract men. He could not define it but he recalled the glint of the firelight upon her blue-black hair and the level look of larger dark eyes, and found them fascinating. Without meaning to do so he mentally matched her against Antoinette's fair, carefree beauty. As always, the thought of Antoinette hurt him. It sent Jacqueline out of his mind. Today he must go to see Antoinette. Yet he was afraid to do it. Nervously he walked to the window, throwing it wide open

The sky was a clear, pale blue, the air flowing into the open window crispy cold. He saw the sunlight tracing distinct dark shadows across the ground. In secluded places there were lingering traces of frost. He got the fresh air into his lungs and turned back into the room, making ready to go downstairs and join Bienville. Again, of its own volition, came a fleeting, fragmentary recollection of Jacqueline Martin. Her soft voice slurring his name, "Magdenok."

In the salon downstairs he found Bienville in conversation with three other men. He recognized the hawk face of Major de Noyan and Claude Dubuisson, in his faded hunting shirt, gazing up at the portrait of the Grand Monarque. The third man, short, dark, with beetling brows and a prominent jaw, wore a white uniform with the shoulder-knot of a captain. Bienville introduced him as Captain Leblanc, with whose party Claude Dubuisson was going to Fort Chartres in the Illinois country.

"You sent for me?" Evan asked Bienville.

"Aye," said Bienville. "I have seen Monsieur Hebert this morning and I wish to thank you for returning him safely to the fold, but -- " his lips twisted in a tight, dry smile, "I greatly fear that particular indisposition may well prevent him from being seated at his desk for some little while." He stared at Evan and snapped with a suddenness that was a little disconcerting. "What manner of hand do you write?"

"Of tolerable legibility, sir, I hope," said Evan. "Bien. Then you shall substitute for Monsieur Hebert until his wound permits him to return to his work." Evan recognized the tone as no request, but a command. "You may breakfast now, then come immediately to my office. Compris, monsieur?"

"Perfectly, sir. I am your servant." Evan bowed as he withdrew.

After he had breakfasted, drinking copiously of the coffee to clear the last vestiges of cobwebs from his brain, Evan hurried to rejoin Bienville. This prospect of working with the Governor, of becoming already a part by which the vast province functioned, fired him with elation. In his haste he ran full tilt into the rear of the two men who were just entering the salon. The broad, ruddy face of Monsieur Macarty-Mactigue swung round, then seemed to split as he roared with laughter. His companion, as tall as Evan, but heavier, speared Evan with cold eyes before letting his sensual lips relax in a smile at the adjutant's mirth. He was dressed like woodsman, in hunting shirt, leggings and moccasins, and wore a growth of short, bristling beard upon his face. Monsieur Macarty-Mactigue seized his shoulder and Evan's and made them known to each other. This gentleman in buckskin, he told Evan, was Jean-Paul Lesueur, kinsman of the Governor and Indian fighter extraordinary. Monsieur Lesueur had not had time to change to formal attire; he had run his pirogue ashore below the levee less than an hour ago, after having been three days on the river coming from the post at Natchez.

They went together into Bienville's office, a smaller room which opened off the salon. The room was cold in spite of the fire; the linen-covered window threw a bar of heatless light across the floor. Claude Dubuisson faced the fire, teetering on the balls of his feet. Behind him, Bienville's large head bent over the long writing table as he fumbled among his papers. De Noyan and Leblanc stood by the window, talking. All of them turned as the door opened.

Bienville and Lesueur greeted each other gravely, but with a manifest mutual regard. When those formalities were over, Bienville motioned Evan to the small writing table in the light of the east window. "Well, monsieur," said Bienville, turning back to Lesueur, "I have been expecting you. What news do you bring?"

Lesueur spread his muscular hands in the fire. "Little enough!" he said. "I left the Small Nation of the Choctaw nearly a month ago. These past two weeks I have been at the Natchez post with Monsieur Petit Deviliers." He gently fingered his growth of whiskers. "I had the use of his razor there three days ago. I ask your pardon, monsieur, for the fact that I have need for another now."

Bienville made and impatient gesture. "You have been through the Choctaw towns," he said, coming back to the point. He advanced his large head and waited impatiently. "You have talked, without doubt, with Pere Beaudouin and Monsieur de Lery. Did you see, or did they tell you of any unrest among the Choctaw?"

Lesueur thrust out his lower lip in a speculative manner, but shook his head slowly. "No, monsieur," he said. "Not more than is their habit. They mutter, they grumble that our trade is not to their liking, that we do not pay enough for the scalps they bring. It is true that Alibamon Mingo of Concha and Soulier Rouge of Cushtusha, have both been to the English at Kaapa during the past year. But you have had word of that, monsieur. Pere Beaudouin told me, when I saw him at Chickasawhay, that Alibamon Mingo was greatly offended when young de Lery took the English trader who had come to his lodge. Beyond that, I do not think there is any disposition to quit us." He full lips smiled derisively. "No, I should say not, in spite of the fact that from what Monsieur Macarty-Mactigue has told me this morning, that Monsieur D'Artaguette is once more being frightened by his shadow."

Bienville's eyes held no flint of answering amusement. "The man must be mad," he said coldly. "The inhabitants of the coast are in an uproar. Whatever his game may be, by God, I shall put an end to it when I go out to Mobile."

"Speaking of his madness," said Lesuer, "there is no doubt that many among the Choctaws think him mad, or bewitched, with his damned dreams and his threats against them. Worse, monsieur, he has spread tales which caused them to mistrust others among us. He has tarred Pere Beaudouin and me with the same foul brush, confound him, swearing that both of us have been seducing the Choctaw women."

Jean-Paul Lesueur laughed suddenly, shaking his powerful shoulders until the fringe of his hunting shirt danced. "Since you refused his request and gave me the command of the Choctaw raiding parties against the Chickasaws, he has held a black grudge against me."

Bienville took his seat behind his writing table and looked over at Lesueur. "You have led them. You know their spirit," he said, "Have the Choctaws the stomach for fighting?"

"They are not so sanguine as one might wish," returned Lesueur. "They will fight with great bravery upon their own hunting-grounds, but they become timorous when they venture beyond them. Mingo Chitto, the Great Chief of Cowah Chitto, lost a son last year before the Chickasaw town of Chukafalaya. He is crying for Chickasaw blood, but the other chiefs would be well content to leave the Chickasaws to their devices. The English have greatly encouraged Alibamon Mingo and Soulier Rouge in this attitude. There is no danger of their fighting us, monsieur, as Monsieur D'Artaguette imagines, but there is danger that they may let us fight alone against the common foe."

Bienville propelled his wiry body upright and began to pace the room, walking rapidly and almost without noise It had been years since he had been in the woods but the lightness was still in his step.

"So! I have feared it," he said, vehemently. "The time has passed for talking." He seemed oblivious of the others, as if he spoke to himself. "The English poison is already in the veins of the Choctaw Nation, and the vaporings of Monsieur D'Ataguette has done the English cause no harm. If these were ordinary times, God help me I could cry a plague upon the capriciousness of the chiefs! I need only refuse them presents and withdraw our traders from the Nation to bring the rascals to their senses. The damned English are so far removed that they are able to bring goods in only by horseback and through terribly difficult country. It is this infernal Chickasaw war which drags on and on."

He whirled upon Lesueur. "You know, monsieur, that I had thought to end it by means of the Choctaws alone. Now, there is no hope of that, nor of our ending it without the Choctaws." He returned to his chair and sat heavily in it. "At every turn I am balked by ill luck. But for the attack upon Monsieur Ducoder's party I might have negotiated peace with the Chickasaws."

Lesueur thumbed tobacco into the bowl of his pipe, which was long stemmed like an Indian calumet. He stooped to the hearth skillfully plucking out a live coal with which he contrived a light.

"Your letter to Ducoder passed through the Large Nation while I was there. Pere Beaudouin sent it by a Choctaw runner who carried it within a league of the Chickasaw council house where he hid in the bushes until a Chickasaw brave passed. The Chickasaw killed him and fastened the letter to his belly with an arrow through it. Pere Beaudouin thinks it likely that the letter was delivered to Ducoder, since the Chickasaws wanted him ransomed."

He puffed, having difficulty making his pipe draw. "It was said among the Choctaws that the Chickasaw chief, Ymayatabe, had come to you at Mobile with offers of peace." "I talked with Ymayatabe this past spring," said Bienville. "He was not alone in his desire for peace, having brought several other chiefs. I made demands that they no longer harbor the Natchez, our enemies, and also that they expel the English from their territory. They agreed. Mon Dieu! It was simpler than I had thought. If Ducoder had not blundered into a Chickasaw party, my plan might not have miscarried."

He swore with a sudden expulsion of breath. "When the chiefs returned to their villages they learned that Frenchmen had been killed in the attack upon Ducoder. I have knowledge that this made them fear our vengeance and left them defenseless against the council of their own hotheads and the English traders." His face seemed suddenly old. "God knows, I have done my best to win over the Chickasaws. With them as our allies we might build a chain of forts like a wall connecting Louisiana with Canada and keep the accursed English pinned beyond the eastern mountains. As our enemies, they are like a wedge being driven between us and the northern settlements, splitting us farther apart."

Lesueur took his pipe from his mouth. "They should be taught a lesson," he said.

"One which they will not soon forget."

"My orders from the King are to annihilate the Natchez!" He snorted in disgust. "The Natchez be damned! They were never more than a trifling part of the conspiracy which the English and the Chickasaws hatched against us. If that great fool Perrier had continued my policy they would never have risen. Monsieur," he shook his finger in Lesueur's face, "I say to you and you know that it is true, that the English, through the Chickasaws, have made an effort to establish all the tribes of the Mississippi in a confederation which would spell doom for us. We face a dark hour, indeed. It is the strength of our arms now, or we shall perish."

"Soit!" murmured Lesueur, "It is so."

Evan, listening, stared into the fire on the hearth. The leaping flames became Indians, changed, mingling with red coated English and white coated French. The roar and crackle became the rattle of musketry and the banging of drums. In the midst of it himself, musket in hand, dressed in buckskin like Lesueur, there, marching off to war, and behind it all the bright picture of Antoinette and her tearful face as she threw him kisses in farewell.

"You speak of lessons," said Bienville, "I shall teach them a lesson." He held his hands before him, hooked like a hawk's talons, then locked the fingers and ground the palms together. "I shall catch them thus, those Natchez and Chickasaws, between an army which marches from Mobile and an army which marches from the Illinois. The bird shall not fly out of the snare this time as the Natchez did at the Flour Fort and at the Black River. While my army from Mobile strikes them from the east the Chevalier D'Artaguette shall strike them from the west with his army from the Illinois. We shall time our marches so that we shall strike them at the same time. I am sending Monsieur Leblanc to Fort Chartres with my orders to the Chevalier D'Artaguette to be at the Prud'homme Bluffs no later than the tenth or the fifteenth of March."

He fumbled upon the papers strewn untidily upon his writing table and found several leaves, closely written in his careful, upright hand, with many blots and marginal annotations, These he shuffled through, peering at them intently. He seemed satisfied and passed them to Evan. "Make a transcription of these letters," he said, brusquely, "Direct them to the Chevalier D'Artaguette, Commandant at Fort Chartres. And do not dawdle over it." Bienville swung back to Lesueur. "Well, what do you think of my plan, monsieur?"

Lesueur rapped his pipe stem thoughtfully against his knuckles. "I will say this, monsieur," he said at last. "It is the one play which might have an outstanding chance of success. The Chickasaw towns are scattered upon separate prairies covering a considerable extent of territory. They were well fortified the last time I saw them. One army operating in the hostile country so far from its base might court disaster. It is more than one hundred leagues from Mobile to the Chickasaw prairies. But two armies, if they were able to strike together, and were well led, should prove too much for the Chickasaw." He leaned forward. "How do you propose moving the army from Mobile, monsieur? By boat?"

Bienville nodded jerkily. "By way of the Mobile River and the river of the Chickasaws'" he answered. "I shall use both pirogues and bateaux which I am having built. I had thought once, as you know, to march overland through the Choctaw country. But it is impossible, the distance is too great. I have no soldiers capable of withstanding the fatigues of such a march. These soldiers which they sent me from France, you know of their worth as well as I do, monsieur. It will be the responsibility of Monsieur Salmon to make sure we have enough boats."

"Sang Dieu!" he added with great feeling. "If I had enough Canadians, men who know bateaux, men who know the woods."

Major de Noyan, who had been standing quietly, exchanging a word now and then with Captain Leblanc, turned from the window.

He said, "I have inspected the recruits who came in on the Gironde" His swarthy aquiline features seemed to grow sharper with anger. "I all but overlooked them mistaking them for rats which had escaped the ship; Nom de Dieu! This is the most scurvy lot they have yet sent us. One man among them, just one, was as much as five feet tall!"

Bienville's lips were so tightly compressed that a knife blade could scarcely have been inserted between them. "I had hoped," he started, "but I really expected no better."

117

He took up a rolled map and spread it flat upon the table. "Now to return to my play, messieurs. This is the map which Monsieur Danville made of the Choctaw country three years ago. It ends at Scanapa, the northernmost town of the Choctaw Nation, and takes me upon my route only so far as the mouth of the Oaknoxube. I wish to le bon Dieu that I had an accurate map of the Chickasaw country. But, here, I mark my course." His bony finger traced it out. "By pirogues and bateaux up the River Mobile and the River of the Chickasaws past the mouth of the Tascaloosas, where I shall establish a post." He looked up. "I shall leave my boats at the Chickasaw portage and proceed thence on foot against the easternmost towns while the Chevalier D'Artaguette advances from the west. Monsieur Lesueur, you have scouted the River of the Chickasaws above the mouth of the Tascaloosas. Will there be sufficient depth by early spring to float my bateaux?"

"Monsieur," said Lesueur confidently, "by April there will be forty feet of water above the great gravel shoals at the mouth of the Tascaloosas, enough to float a frigate."

"But in March," persisted Bienville, "or February?"

The confident look disappeared from Lesueur's face. "I cannot say, monsieur," he said slowly. "The winter was as yet scarcely upon the upper reaches of the river, but before I left the Choctaws there was talk among the shamans that the signs foretold a severe winter to the north. If that be the case, the thaw will be delayed and the river will be slow in rising."

Bienville, rolled the map carefully and laid it aside. "So. It is in the lap of fortune," he said. "Well, I have given you my plan complete, for better or worse, subject only to such changes as ill fortune may dictate." He turned his head as Evan rose from the small table and brought him the letters for the Chevalier D'Artaguette. When he had signed them and marked them with the seal of his office he looked up again.

"Monsieur Leblanc," he said.

Leblanc stepped quickly before the table and came to a stiff salute.

"Your pirogue is ready, monsieur?"

Leblanc stood like a statue, his large jaw thrusting out. "Yes, Monsieur le Commandant-General."

"Mark you, monsieur," said Bienville, handing him the sealed packet. "These dispatches must not fail to reach the Chevalier D'Artaguette's hand. Everything depends upon our forces acting together. If we do not, if we are divided and met separately by the enemy--" he paused. "I shall leave that to your imagination, monsieur You must not, at all hazards, make the error which Monsieur Ducoder made. That is all. God be with you."

Leblanc came again to salute, then turned and hurried from the room. Claude Dubuisson grinned at Evan, ducked his head to Bienville, and went rapidly after Leblanc's departing heels.

Chapter IX

Jacqueline Martin turned the wooden spoon, scraping it around the bottom of the little glazed pottery bowl and fed the last of the sagamity to Etienne. His mouth opened like a fledgling bird's. He was as helpless as one, thought Jacqueline, standing up with the bowl in her hands. Slowly he mouthed his food. His throat worked as he swallowed, his hand came up feeling the cut place upon his head and he groaned, turning his face away from her toward the wall. Her dark eyes watched him with pity but not with compassion.

"So many times I have fed him," she thought. "When he was sick and helpless as he is now and, also, when he was only feigning helplessness. So many times I have bathed him and made his bed. Only the le bon Dieu knows how many times in five years."

Overhead from the loft she heard the creek of the floorboards. Her face turned upwards. Something was moving up there; footsteps. Ah, she drew her breath in relief, it was the girl, Collette, of course. The girl in the blouse and breaches who had come with Monsieur MacDonald. Where was her mind this morning, to have forgotten that? She, herself, had sent the girl to sleep in the loft last night upon a little mattress made of husks of Indian corn.

She watched Collette's feet thrust through the open trap, feeling their way upon the ladder. The girl came down with her back to Jacqueline and turned at the cot, scrubbing away at her sleepy eyes while she tucked her blouse into her waistband with the other hand. Her grin in response to Jacqueline's greeting was quick and warm. "Ventre Sainte Gris," she said cheerfully, "but I slept! That mattress had a lump here and a lump there to tickle my spine, but it was a good bed. There was no damned waves of the sea to throw me out on my derriere as soon as I had shut my eyes." She looked eagerly around the room. "Tell me, what must I do? You have been so kind. So kind."

Jacqueline was startled to see the tears spring into the girl's eyes. "I will pay you. I will work. Pardi, I will pay you with work."

Jacqueline smiled at her. "You can pay me easily, if you will," she said, "but you will never be idle. Once there was no more work here than I could do myself." Her eyes shifted to the apparently sleeping Etienne and her voice lowered. "Now, for months I have had no peace for Etienne. Always he wants me. Always I must be where I can hear him call. There is no rest between working and waiting on Etienne. Enfin, I am not so unselfish as you believed." She thought of all that must be done; getting firewood, fetching drinking water from the river, and taking clothes there for washing; cooking, sweeping, scrubbing. She looked down at the floor. "There is a start for you. This floor, it is filth!"

She pointed at the muddy footprints which wove across it, and laughed. "Those big ones there, like the tracks of a bear. They are Gaston's. But, come now, let's eat first."

She filled two bowls with sagamity from the pot on the fire and gave one to the girl, keeping the other for herself. The sagamity was almost tasteless, since she had cooked it with only a sparing drop of bear's oil. The jug was almost empty, and at its price it must not be wasted. It had

121

cost Gaston Lazac two good beaver skins when he made her a present of it. Four piasters! Le bon Dieu! It was more than Etienne's pension for a month! When they had finished eating she sent Collette out to get water for scrubbing from the ditch at the street corner.

By the time the girl returned Etienne had roused and was fretful. Jacqueline sat upon the edge of the bed stroking his head and watching Collette, on hands and knees, working across the splintery floor.

Collette looked up at her. "You think I am soft, because I came from Paris," she declared. "But this work; it is nothing to me. It is honest work, non? What more do I ask? Mon Dieu," she said suddenly, "It may be that Rene will think better of me, now."

"Who," asked Jacqueline, curiously, "is Rene?"

"Hein,? Rene?" echoed Collette. "That is so. You do not know Rene. He came with us, with Monsieur MacDonald and me, upon the ship. Rene, he shipped in the sainte-barbe, that damned pigs' house. He is a soldier, one of the recruits. When I left the ship with Monsieur MacDonald, I did not see Rene, but by this time he must be lodged in the barracks. Ah, ciel," she said frankly, "but I love Rene. My body is hot for him. My heart hurts me."

The passion in her voice gave Jacqueline a queer turn. It shook her own calm, a swift tumult of recollection poured through her mind. She saw herself as she had not in years, a girl of sixteen, timid but ardent in her single night with Etienne. That had been madness, that night, made doubly so by the fear that they may never be together again, by the stark fact that when morning came he would march with Governor Perrier's army against the Natchez on the Black River. It had been like a prophecy, that fear, not for one hour since he had been brought home crippled had she and Etienne lived as man and wife. As far as passion or desire were concerned Etienne had passed from the land of the living.

Five years and she had been a nurse to him, a sister, a mother, but never anything more. That first year, as she remembered she had been all sympathy, buoyed up by her love to the never ending task of tending the sick man. Then, gradually, like a starved plant, love had died beneath indifference and the bitter scorpions of his tongue. Helplessness had made him querulous, and querulousness had made him snap at the hand that fed him and the voice which sang him to sleep. He had become a tyrant, no longer desiring her, merely wishing to keep her beside him that he might enjoy the sense of his own power when she obeyed him. She sat beside him quietly, letting her fingers run through his hair, thinking, "He has treated me shamefully, yet why should I hate him? I am sorry for him, terribly sorry, so that sometimes I cannot blame him. He loved the woods so, and now his life is spent upon a bed as narrow as a coffin. He is my man, I married him. He needs me. He could not live without me. He is my man. There is no other."

It was true. There was no other man. No passion. No children for her; she was a woman dried up and gone to seed at twenty-one years. She would have laughed, but that would have roused Etienne. Sometimes she wished that a man were all that she wanted. If that were all, it would be simple to satisfy her with Henri. Poor Henri, who worshiped her like a dog when he was sober and chased her like a rutting buck when he was full of liquor. But Henri would never do. Almost without realizing it she thought of Evan

McDonald, seeing his face, lean and grave with its clear dark eyes. He had been so polite to her, so gentle; so embarrassed, too, by the exposure of his entanglement with Collette. Ah, she was glad that she had been wrong in thinking that there might be something between them. This soldier, Rene, was by the girl's own admission, her lover.

Suddenly, she said, not aloud, "But why am I glad? What is he to me? This is my man, here." Evan MacDonald's Face became fearfully clear in her eyes. Her throat ached her. She felt, startlingly, like crying. Like leaning her head against someone's shoulder and sobbing her heart out. She did not cry easily. It had been years since she had cried, many years, for the last time had been in her mother's arms.

Sainte Marie, Mere de Dieu! There was no mother now to whom she might go. No father, no sister, no brother. They were all dead six years ago. Butchered by the devilish Natchez, all of them. She could hear their cries. She had heard them many times. Their voices were like phantoms bringing only despair. She was alone in the vast loneliness which was life with Etienne.

She closed her eyes, hearing the dreary sweep of the scrubbing rag across the floor.

Antoine Castilloux had built his maison so that it had no superior for comfort or elegance in Nouvelle Orleans. It was built on the Rue Royale, facing towards the river, which was southeast. A long house, the ground floor of brick, plastered over, flush with the banquette. A wide port-cochere in the center of it admitted Monsieur Castilloux's carriage to the carriage-house in the court. The upper floor, which comprised the living quarters, had a wide gallery with seven white posts shaped like ninepins, and was reached by a railed stair at the west end of the house. There were three doors opening upon this gallery, also three windows with green batten shutters. Behind the window at the eastern end of the house, Antoinette slept late upon her first morning in Nouvelle Orleans. When her blue eyes opened drowsily it was to a sense of strangeness that her bed did not sway, sway in a manner which never ceased to be sickening, to the pendulum motion of the waves. In a moment she realized that she was no longer upon the Gironde, that this was her father's house.

Stretching up a slender hand to part the bed curtains she looked curiously about the room. It was cool and dim, with the windows shuttered against the light. Yet it struck her more pleasantly than when she had gone to bed. She had been weary then, too weary and chilled after the drive through the rain from the river. Indeed, she remembered with a smile, she been barely able to greet with civility Gerard Mallot, director of her father's plantations above the town, and his wife, plump, dowdy like a peasant woman in fine clothes. Sleep had been uppermost in her mind, and she had dropped off almost immediately when she had touched her bed.

Now she noted details of the room for the first time. The walls were plastered, the floor milled planks carpeted by soft, fine furs. A crystal chandelier hung from the ceiling, a pair of candlesticks of like design and a bronze clock stood upon the mantle. The bedstead upon which she lay was an oak piece, curtained with damask as were the windows. Someone, surely, had been in this morning while she slept, for a fire blazed upon the hearth.

She thought of her grandmother's shabby old house in Paris and felt an instant yearning for it, remembering this house as she had first seen it in the rainy twilight. It had struck her as so indescribably forlorn; the slanting, shingled roof, black under the rain. And behind it and before it, and upon either side, the marsh and the wilderness. No wonder poor Madame Malot, who must live here, looked careworn.

She sat upright among the tumbled bedclothes, stretching her lovely body in a supple feline movement. The silk of her nightdress rippled against her soft skin like the barest caress of gentle fingers. She swung her legs over the side of the bed, untied the ribbons at her throat and stood up, letting the nightdress fall with a sibilant swish about her feet.

Her breasts arched, her finger tips moved to them, lingered then traced slowly down her white body as far as her arms could reach while she yet stood straight. Turning, she admired the loveliness of herself in the large gilt-framed mirror which hung upon the wall. She reached to her table and took from it a golden chain with a golden fleur-de-lis hanging from it. She hung it around her neck and admired the beauty of the gold as it lay between her breasts. Her laugh bubbled from her throat, full and rich. What a pity that foolish convention prohibited her from showing this nude marvel of beauty to others!

She caught up the small hand bell from the bedside table and set it clamoring. That would bring her maid. Before the echoes of the bell had died away she remembered that it would not be Lucie this morning. Poor Lucie who had accompanied her with such martyrdom across the turbulent seas. She had been taken with a fever of the chest two days ago upon the river. It would be a new maid this morning, a young negress which Madame Malot had promised to send.

The door opened suddenly and the negro girl came into the room, startling Antoinette because she had heard no sound of footsteps. An angular, long-legged wench of perhaps sixteen years, but mature, with full high breasts beneath her plain bodice of limbourg cloth. Her face was brown colored with high cheek bones, broad nostrils, and a flat mouth. The jungle was not far from her, Antoinette thought. She was like an animal, stealthy in her walk. "Ma'm'selle, I come," she said. "What you want, Ma'm'selle?"

Her voice was of a strange timbre, full of sultry vitality, not like a European's.

Antoinette stared at her, little cold needles of Uneasiness prickling her bare skin.

"You are my new maid?" she asked. "What is your name?"

"Yes, Ma'm'selle. My name, it is Fanchon."

"Good," said Antoinette. "Now, Fanchon, you may bring me a sponge and a bowl with water and bowl with warm water. I wish to bathe."

When Fanchon had brought her bath water in a great bowl of hammered copper, Antoinette allowed the girl to bathe her before the fire. She was remarkably deft with her hands. Plainly, Madame Malot had trained her well. Antoinette found her fascinating, like a creature of another species, almost. Her first feeling of disquiet had passed entirely. She was fairly bursting with eagerness to learn the habits, the everything concerning this travesty of a woman. She plied Fanchon with questions until the not-quick-witted negress's brain spun.

"Have you always lived here?" asked Antoinette.

"I was on the island --long way off -- "Fanchon waved her hand in no particular direction. "San Domingue."

"Then how did you come here?"

"Master buy my mother, ma'm'selle," said Fanchon, speaking behind Antoinette's shoulder as she worked the sponge along her mistress's spine. "Master buy many brutes from San Domingue."

"Brutes?"

"Yes, ma'm'selle. Like me."

You chose your words well, thought Antoinette. She said, "You have lived here in Nouvelle Orleans since then?"

"No, ma'm'selle. I live long time in Master's house at Cannes Brulees, Master's plantation. My mother, she die. Madame she keep Master's house. She take me."

"You mean Madame Mallot?"

"Yes, ma'm'selle. Madame, she good to me. She teach me to wait on her. She say only good brute woman can wait on pretty lady."

Antoinette smiled, picturing the plain face of Madame Malot. She breathed deeply, so that her whole body lifted lightly under Fanchon's hands.

"Do you think that I am pretty, Fanchon?"

"So pretty, ma'm'selle." Fanchon looked down upon her and upon the golden flower she had hanging from her neck and sighed.

"Are black girls pretty, Fanchon?"

She sighed. "Not me, ma'm'selle."

Antoinette laughed lightly. "How, then, do you make men love you?"

Fanchon's lips moved but no words came out.

"Do you have a lover, Fanchon?"

The black girl whispered, "Yes, ma'm'selle. One time."

Antoinette clapped her hands. "Who is he, Fanchon? Tell me."

"No, ma'm'selle."

Antoinette's voice held command. "Tell me!"

"Yes, ma'm'selle," said Fanchon resignedly. "But I do not see him now. He at Cannes Brulees."

Antoinette was impatient. "What is his name?"

"He is called Ulysses. Long time Madame keep him house-boy. He grow too big, too strong. Master send him to work in the saw-pits. I see Ulysses sometime, then, ma'm'selle. Now, Madame bring me here, I don't see Ulysses at all."

She gulped audibly, surprising Antoinette. What possible difference could one male or another make to a female animal like this?

"Don't cry, Fanchon," she soothed. "There must be many other black men here."

Fanchon shook her head. "Not for me, ma'm'selle."

She had finished bathing Antoinette by this time and was drying her with a large towel when a knock sounded upon the door and Antoine Castilloux's thick voice came through the panes asking admittance.

"One moment, mon pere," called Antoinette. "One moment until I have finished my toilette."

She smiled, hearing the grunt of impatience, but kept him waiting until Fanchon was quite finished. Then drawing her dressing robe around her, she told the negress to let him in.

He watched her sourly as she lay upon the bed cradling her bright head upon her locked hands.

"Good morning, my child." He settled his fat rump upon a cushioned chair. "Did you sleep well?"

"As if I were dead," she said. "I was so exhausted that I could have slept in a pigsty."

He scowled. She could not be sure if he were amused or angry.

"You imply no similarity?" he asked.

She pouted at him. "I am not sure," she said. Then laughing, "This room is delightful, truly. You did not design it, I dare say?"

Castilloux's laughter gurgled up thickly. "Right you are, my dear. I am no connoisseur of boudoirs. I am too fat!"

There were times when Antoinette wished he would be less uncouth. She waited until his big body ceased shaking from his mirth.

"So it pleases you, eh?" He said, "That is good. But here is what I came to tell you. I have word from Madame de Pradel that she and a number of ladies and gentlemen will call this afternoon to welcome you to Nouvelle Orleans."

"Indeed?" said Antoinette with faint interest.

Castilloux smiled. "Don't be so haughty, my girl. They are excellent people, to be sure. More important, they are friendly to me, and friends are as useful here as elsewhere. Be courteous to them. Compris?"

"Of course, papa mignon," said Antoinette, demurely. "Is it possible they might impress the Baron de Laval?"

Castilloux said dryly, "It is possible."

"Has the Baron risen yet?"

Castilloux shook his head. Something in his mind seemed to disturb him, and after a moment he came out with it.

"I think the climate has left him indisposed. Also, I am afraid he has not fallen in love with our land at first sight. The tales of this country which I spun were, perhaps, a trifle, ah, exaggerated. At any rate, he seemed depressed last night, almost, one might say, resentful." He rubbed his palms together. "Eh, bein, my wealth will improve his spirits, I think."

Antoinette said coolly, "He is an insufferable creature. Thank God I need not endure him long, once I have his name! It is a convenience, is it not, mon pere, that he does not desire me either, but my money only?"

"Don't complain," Castilloux said cheerfully. "We are fortunate in persuading him to inspect my affluence at first hand. If you had it in your head that he might marry you for your face or your figure, then you are more simpleminded than a daughter of mine has any right to be. You desire his name, I desire the ears which his name commands at Court, he desires my money. But for that, he would never have looked at you, my dear." He leered at her. "What would you have done them, eh?"

She did not reply, for she was thinking of Evan MacDonald. She was yet young enough that the thought of youthful passion was more than a little enticing to her. It annoyed her, this threat of emotion. She was almost afraid as she mentally balanced Evan against the Baron de Laval. But she did not balance long. Her thoughts went the life she would have a court once she returned to France with the title of

Baronne. The doors of Versailles would open and without either her father or her new husband around to interfere with a life that neither could possibly match.

Charles Hebert hunched his shoulder against the pillows, rolling himself gingerly half over upon his side so he could see Evan clearly.

"Try it on, now," he said. "See how it fits you."

Evan turned the hat in his hands admiringly. It was of dark, felt adorned with a rakish plume.

"But I tell you again," he protested, laughing, "It was not I who saved you from Jerome Allain. It was Gaston Lazac."

Charles Hebert scoffed, "Nonsense! I may have been drunk, monsieur, but don't tell me, pray, that I was so drunk I could not tell you from Gaston Lazac! Impossible! The hat is yours, as a token of my eternal gratitude. You can see plainly, at any rate, that I have no use for a hat just now."

Evan grinned at him. There was something in that, in his present position, which was rear-uppermost, Charles certainly required no hat. He set the hat upon his head, adjusting it to the proper angle, watching his reflection in Charles' mirror. Ah, there now, he looked very well! It was amazing how a hat transformed a man's appearance. The suit which he had on was the same light blue one in which he has sailed from Le Havre. Aboard the ship no matter how painstakingly he might have dressed himself in this or his other suit, he had always felt untidy, unclean, crusted over with the endless salt of the sea. Now, topped by this hat instead of his shabby tricorne, even this oft worn suit attained a splendor of its own. Surely, the hat itself could not fail to bedazzle Antoinette. If he had a sword, now, he would be a beau, indeed. But he must content himself with a polished oak stick.

Hebert maintained his head in its awkward position, inspecting Evan. "You see, my friend, it fits perfectly. Our heads in size are identical." He laughed. "I only hope yours has more wit than mine."

Evan, removing the hat, felt a twinge of embarrassment. He wondered if Charles knew that he, at Bienville's' request, had for the time being taken over Charles' function as secretary to the Governor. He was racking his brain to find a means of bringing up the matter when Charles anticipated him.

"Ciel, I had forgotten," he said as if it had just popped into is head. "Accept my congratulations, or condolences, perhaps I should say. Monsieur Bienville told me that you were doing the work I should be doing but for my damned impertinence in trifling where I have no business to trifle." He could not restrain a chuckle. "Those are Monsieur de Bienville's words, not mine!"

Evan said, hastily, "Don't feel that I am trying to replace you. It is only temporary, until you are up and about again."

"Certainment!" exclaimed Charles Hebert cheerfully, "I don't resent it. Mon Dieu, non" "I welcome your assistance. I have seen draught horses in Limousine where I was born which did less than half the work I have been accustomed to do."

He groaned, for in shifting his body upon the bed his hand had come into contact with his tender backside. "What a spot in which to be wounded! But to return to what I was saying. Indeed help. This plague of a war campaign has buried me in work. It will require at least two men to burrow me out of it."

Evan was glad that he took it with such good grace. "Monsieur, de Bienville said he would retain me to assist you after you were recovered." he told Charles. "To me he seemed generous beyond all reason. He told me he would undertake to pay me out of his own pocket until such time as my position might be made official. I could find no words to thank him."

"That is Bienville," Hebert replied with decision. "If you are his friend he will tear the sun from the heavens and give it to you for a lantern. But if you are his enemy, there is scarcely any means he will not use to discomfort you." He added, with a wry smile, "It is a good thing for me that he likes me in spite of what he calls my 'escapades'! Otherwise, I would be seeking employment elsewhere and you, my friend would be buried alone beneath the work that I have left undone."

Evan was smiling lightheartedly when he left Charles Hebert and went downstairs. Besides his pleasure at joining Bienville's official family and the exhilaration which possessed him at the prospect of calling upon Antoinette he had one other reason to feel free from care. Collette was no longer a problem. With some considerable embarrassment he had explained the affair to Bienville. He had been most pleasantly surprised when Bienville had laughed, saying that women in Louisiana were a rare commodity and much sought after. One seldom came of her own free will, but casket girls and corrections girls had been sent by the King to supply the demand and none of them had gone begging. No, said, Bienville, when a woman came to Louisiana, not much was asked whence she came, nor why, nor by what means. He had then, with his dry, baffling smile asked Evan how he proposed to make out without the services of a valet. That had been all and to Evan's immense relief.

Proceeding through the hallway from the rear of the house to the front Evan found Monsieur Macarty-Mactigue sitting in the portico with an empty wine glass in his hand and an empty wine bottle at his elbow. He was looking disconsolately from one to the other, but brightened somewhat when he saw Evan.

"Hold there!" he said. "'Tis my young friend Monsieur MacDonald, upon my soul! The name MacDonald makes me weep, it sounds like my own. They're a good race monsieur, the Gaels, whether they're your kind or my kind."

"That they are," said Evan with an eye on the bottle. "If you had left a drop there, sir, we might have drunk to them."

"Helas!" cried Macarty-Mactigue, shaking the futile thing disgustedly. "There is but enough in one of these accursed bottles to make me sorrow for things I have never seen. What do I know of Ireland save what I have heard? I am a Frenchman. There is a corporal, by name of Muldoon, in the garrison here, who was born in the isle itself. I have heard him curse the black Protestant English and my blood boils until I hate them as he hates them. Why do I do that, my friend?" Still fingering the bottle he looked up at Evan. "By God, that hat you're wearing! It looks familiar."

"It was Monsieur Hebert's," said Evan by way of explanation. "He made a present of it to me."

The adjutant's red face wreathed in a smile. "Be sure it takes you into more fitting places than it took Monsieur Hebert. But it will not. You are off to see some woman now."

"Don't you approve of women, monsieur?"

Macarty-Mactigue cocked a quizzical eye at him. "What else is there to approve of here? Women and drink. Drink and women. The same old refrain. A man takes to one or the other to relieve his mind of the damnable weather or the damnable wilderness, or the damnable fact that he is ill and starving." He waved his hand. "Monsieur Hebert takes to both, with what results you are able to see for yourself."

He patted the bottle. "I take to this. This is my woman. My good dame blanche."

Evan looked down at him, marveling. He was certainly half drunk, yet he held himself with military erectness in his white uniform, his scarlet cloak flung nonchalantly upon the back of his chair. His prominent eyes stared up at Evan as if he read his mind.

"You think I am drunk," he challenged. "You are mistaken. I have never been drunk in my life. Monsieur Perrier, the past Governor, said I was drunk when I tossed him out on his arse, but I was as sober as a magistrate." He laughed boisterously. "I'll tell you that tale one day It is worth hearing. That was in a year ago, when Bienville came back from France and took over Perrier's office. Now, that was a good day."

Evan, not caring to be detained by a long-winded story, however interesting, made hasty excuses.

"I must go now," he said. "Perhaps you could direct me to the house of Antoine Castilloux?"

Monsieur Macarty-Mactigue's eyes bulged more than ever. "Antoine Castilloux? Nom de Dieu! What possesses you to call upon Antoine Castilloux?" All at once the light seemed to dawn upon him. "Ah! It is the blond baggage! The one which landed yesterday on the Gironde."

Evan could have throttled him with the greatest of pleasure, "I asked you a question, monsieur," he said, coldly.

Macarty-Mactigue put on a droll expression. "Don't be so hotheaded, my young friend," he admonished. "I'll grant she's a pretty wench, if you will. But if you are wise, you'll stay away from that vicinity. Monsieur Castilloux does not like Monsieur Bienville. Neither does Monsieur Bienville like Monsieur Castilloux."

Evan, stiff with anger, stalked away before Macarty-Mactigue could finish speaking. Whereupon, laughing heartily, the ruddy-faced adjutant called after him the directions which he had sought in the first place.

Evan walked on through the brisk sunlit afternoon, turning into the various rues as he followed the course which Macarty-Mactigue had given him. His anger had passed by the time he saw a white house which he took to be that of Antoine Castilloux.

Directly in front of him, as he reached the house, was a green painted door. At the foot of a stair which led up to the white pillared gallery. The door was barred against him. He lost no time in pounding heavily upon it. In a moment it opened and a negro's black face peered out. The negro was stumpily built, dressed in steward's livery.

When Evan had given his name the negro admitted him. He seemed quite proud of himself and the establishment Which he represented.

"You call on Ma'm'selle Antoinette?" he asked Evan as they climbed the stair. "Madame, madame and monsieur call on Ma'm'selle Antoinette."

This disturbed Evan, who had wanted to see Antoinette alone and caused him to conceive a distaste of the butler for being so pompous, and Castilloux for his ostentation in possessing a steward in this wilderness.

He passed into the salon and heard the negro making a travesty of his name as he cried it in announcement. Then all his mounting irritation was swept away by the sight of Antoinette, in a gown of golden damask which clothed her lithe figure like a lambent flame, rising and calling his name with every evidence of pleasure. He was like schoolboy before his first love. His mind for an instant was a trembling blank, he did not even marvel that her greeting, so warm now, had been that way in times past only to change incalculably to utter indifference.

Coming out of the fog in which this first sight of her had left him lost, he saw a circle of faces that was the company. He cursed them beneath his breath, responding without enthusiasm as Antoinette presented them to him. The room seemed full of them, all talking in unison. They were, a he came to them: Madame Dalcour, past middle age but endeavoring to conceal it; her husband Etienne Dalcour, a colorless man younger than she; Madame Dubruil, whose husband was not present, young, quite beautiful with black curls and sparkling black eyes: Madame de Pradel, a tall woman with a high, white forehead and a predatory nose: her husband, the Chevalier de Pradel, shorter than his wife, reminding Evan vaguely of a ferret; plump Madame Malot; and the Chevalier de Louboey, with a dark, arrogant face, wearing a captain's shoulder knot upon his white uniform.

Of these, Evan was to learn, Madame de Pradel and Madame Dubreil, were sisters, the daughters of Madame Dalcour by her first husband, the late Monsieur de la Chaise, Commissaire-Ordonnateur of the province in the time of Perrier.

The Baron de Laval was not present, and of that Evan was glad. He thought, contemptuously, that the sight of Nouvelle Orleans must have been too much for the Baron's sensibilities.

Evan found a chair in some discomfiture. His stocking all at once seemed to tight, the back of his neck commenced itching, he wondered if his hair, greased and queued, but for all that his work, looked proper among these bewigged people. All of them, ladies and gentlemen, inspected him with an impersonal curiosity which fell barely upon the cultured side of rudeness. But their interest was fleeting; almost immediately they returned to their discourse. Being content to watch Antoinette without taking part in the conversation, it was soon brought home to Evan that they were a singularly discontented gaggle; talking of nothing but the hardships which they must endure, the slights which they received from Bienville and his friends, and how everything was so much better in the days of Perrier and de la Chaise.

The ladies chatted to Antoinette of the prices which they must pay, and the difficulties of getting goods from France. Madame Dalcour complained that some goods which she had ordered had not been put aboard the Gironde.

"Monsieur de Villiers gives some nonsensical explanation that his ship was strictly upon business of state, and could not delay for private consignments," she said. "Now I suppose I must wait for the next vessel, which may not be here before next summer. What shall I do in the meantime. Mon Dieu, it is like being buried!"

"Indeed," said Antoinette politely "it must be annoying."

"Monsieur Dalcour scolds me eternally to be economical," cried Madame Dalcour.

"Ah, dear Alexandrine," she added to her daughter, Madame de Pradel, "one grows so weary of that word 'economy', does one not?"

Madame de Pradel lifted her eyebrows and cast a look at Monsieur de Pradel as if to say: "I am never scolded for extravagance." Monsieur de Pradel hugged himself within his folded arms like some small, bright eyed bird fluffing its feathers against the cold.

"My own expenses are high enough," she said. "But in spite of all one's efforts it seems quite hopeless. This is such an abominably primitive place, I often wonder how I endure it. We try hard enough to create an atmosphere of civilized life here, but the obstacles are more the one can imagine. The clods, of course, get much pleasure from their uncouth amusements. But there is such a little opportunity for cultured gaiety, my dear, such a little opportunity for diversion."

Monsieur de Pradel hugged himself a trifle closer, with an unhappy eye upon his wife. Watching him, Evan was reminded of the comments upon the de Pradels which Gaston Lazac and his friend had made, and wondered if he were thinking of the sort of diversion in which Madame de Pradel was wont to indulge.

"La, we have had enough of unpleasant things," cried Madame Dalcour. "Do you play the harpsichord?" She saw Antoinette's nod. "My dear, play for us, please! I love music so!"

Antoinette smiled. "Of course, if you like."

She took her seat at the harpsichord while Evan sat like stone, oblivious of the others, his eyes upon her. Her playing was rapid, with fingers skimming like swallows above the keys. The room was filled with a slender, quivering melody, and Evan's head was filled with a golden dream.

Antoinette struck a final chord which lingered in the air after the instrument itself had grown silent. There was a spirited ripple of applause. Evan's dream dissolved like wind blown smoke. Antoinette rose and dropped a curtsy in acknowledgment of the applause. She had a trick of pirouetting on her toes as she turned which caused her skirt to swirl about her like a live thing. It brought Evan's heart into his throat. He felt unutterably sad, as if he yearned for something that was forever lost, and that he would go on seeking without finding through a lifetime of adventuring and emptiness of heart. His resentment of the others grew until he was afraid he could not conceal it, and because there was no prospect of their departing he made up his mind to go.

He had risen to his feet when the door of the salon swung open and stocky man with a shrewd, oily face came quickly in. He was a stranger to Evan, who noticed that the man seemed in some agitation as he made a general bow to the room.

"Monsieur Malot!" said Castilloux, also noticing the newcomer's perturbation. "Is something wrong?"

Gerard Malot came up to him. "It may not be," he said, lowering his voice, "but I am worried. A boy has just come from the Cannes Brulees saying that another slave has fled into the swamp. It is the second within two weeks, monsieur."

"Hein?" ejaculated Castilloux.

"The other was a brute, Basile by name, who worked in the saw-pits," Malot continued. "I had him flogged and he fled. I think to join the renegades." His voice tightened.

"Some of the black brutes who escaped from Natchez to the Chickasaws are at large among the plantations preaching sedition."

"Again?" cried Castilloux, plainly startled. "But it cannot be true! Monsieur Perrier stamped out their uprising three years ago and beheaded the leaders. Their heads were set on posts at the upper and lower ends of the city."

"Just the same," persisted Malot, "the smoke is rising again, and there must be embers somewhere smoldering. I know it. I have no word of it in plain language, but I hear the whispers. I feel the breath of it moving among the slaves. As was the case three years ago some will remain loyal, some will not. Already there is an increase in insolence. The floggings have doubled in the past two months."

The Chevalier de Pradel murmured, "I have had that same trouble, also."

This news seemed to induce a physical illness in Antoine Castilloux. "But Monsieur Perrier had crushed them!" he insisted. "All was calm when I sailed for France. What could have set them scheming again?"

"I think," said Gerard Malot, "that it may be the knowledge that most of our soldiers will be on campaign in the Indian country and that our settlements will be thereby stripped of defenders. They will strike when they are strongest and we are weakest."

There was a perceptible sweat upon Antoine Castilloux's forehead. "It is the work of the devil!" he groaned. "I wonder how I ever came to prefer those brutes to white concessionaires? They are even more of a menace than the red savages!" His hands moved nervously. Evan had never seen him more perturbed.

140

"How can I be sure they will not burn my buildings, my own servants, in my own house will not murder me in my bed?"

"You cannot, monsieur," said the Chevalier de Pradel, sadly. "Neither can I. There are so many among us. In our very homes, in Nouvelle Orleans, and out upon the plantations, so many whose skins are not white."

When he stopped speaking silence fell and to Evan it was plain that here was something they all greatly feared; an uprising of these black people they held in bondage, an uprising beside which the inhumanity of the Indians paled by comparison. He saw the thought of it tighten the faces of all those present. When startled apprehension began to dawn in the lovely eyes of Antoinette the terror communicated itself to him.

He leaned to her. At that instant the company burst again into a torrent of talk as if the dispel their fears. He bowed stiffly to them, and muttered his respects as he sidled toward the door. But the fear in the eyes of Antoinette followed him into the street.

CHAPTER X

For the next two weeks Evan was busied with the work that Governor Bienville had for him. He prepared messages to be sent to the different settlements around Nouvelle Orleans as well as official documents for the commandants at Fort Jean Batiste and Fort Maurepas. There must also be copies made of each and there was no one else to do this but Evan. In addition there were the notes of the council meetings to take and copies to make and, perhaps more importantly, there were the records of arms, munitions, and all supplies needed for the impending expedition to record and duplicate. Charles Hebert had not exaggerated the amount of work that his office entailed and Evan was overjoyed when his wound had healed well enough for him to resume his duties so that they shared the burden of paperwork.

The entire time was not spent in work as Evan went hunting fowl with Gaston Lazac on more than one occasion. There was also the evenings at Meunier's or the occasional visit to check on Collette at the house of Jacqueline Martin. It was there that Evan found himself one evening as a late winter rainstorm came once again upon the town.

The wind struck the small house with a flat sound and shook its flimsily walls. They heard the first fall of raindrops, slow and scattered. The atmosphere which the fire warmed had not changed, but they could sense the cold in the sound of the rain. Evan watched faces of the people gathered round the fire, intent, listening. Gustave Lambert, the cobbler from the Rue St. Pierre, blocky and bull-necked, with his empty eye socket turned toward Therese, his plump bland wife. Papa Jules Froissart, the old, old man who lived by himself on the Bayou St. Jean, and had no business to be out on a night like this. Rene and Collette sat side by side on the bench. Jacqueline Martin bent over her spindle and distaff with Etienne watching darkly from the shadows

Collette was admiring Rene openly. "You look like a soldier," she said, "but Holy Mary, that coat! Your wrists stick out and it is drawing your shoulder-blades over your backbone. Don't breathe now, or it will pop like a barley husk." She covered her mouth with her hand and began to giggle through her fingers.

Rene grinned one sidedly. He was in many ways a new man since the Gironde had docked in Nouvelle Orleans. On reviewing the new recruits the Major de Noyen had made him a corporal and housed him with the garrison. He had fit in easily with the other veterans and made gaming friends with corporal Muldoon. It was not an easy life with a harsh sergeant and grueling duties in the mud and rain of a Louisiana winter and the hard garrison bunk but it gave Rene a renewed sense of worth and the hope that in time he could have his own land in this new place, although he would be loathe to show his emotions to anyone.

It was Evan who had brought him here this evening finally to see Collette.

"I have brought the tardy swain," said Evan as he had propelled Rene through the cabin door.

"A la!" Jacqueline Martin had replied. "So you are Collette's Rene. It is time that you came. She has talked of little else."

Now Rene looked at Collette and answered her teasing. "The man who last owned this coat was nearer to your size than mine, but he was the biggest of the lot." "What happened to him?"

"He died in it before we got here, as luck would have it. They had sent no coats with us but we found thirty empty ones at the barracks. They tried to get them all on me, but only this one would go. Now I can't get out of it." He rubbed his blue chin and winked at Collette.

"Fortunately, there were no breeches at all so although we soldiers look alike with our coats we have all sorts of pants beneath. But at least this way my legs do not stick out the way my arms do."

Collette rocked with glee. "You great silly!"

Papa Jules Froissart's eyes were staring like a heron's in his old furrowed face. "You are a soldier," he told Rene. "I have been a soldier. I have been many things. I was studying for the priesthood when the great Louis crossed the Rhine. This is good land. Do you think so?"

"There's damned little of it I've seen," said Rene. "leaving out the mud on the esplanade and the rum in the tavern. Army's army the world around, I suppose. But maybe I'll be out before long." He faced Collette and seemed to explain himself for her benefit. "They have a rule, I hear, about giving land to soldiers. Every year two men from each company get a furlough and a tract of land. If a man works, he'll make the land his own.

Collette's eyes were like saucers, dark and luminous. "Land for us," she whispered.

Rene nodded soberly.

"Land!" burst out Etienne Martin bitterly, "Land is for those who are able to walk upon it. I would trade all of it -- if I had any instead of debts -- for one good swallow of rum."

144

Papa Jules clucked sympathetically. Apparently he had forgotten the others were present. "Now, now, Etienne, do not fret. Old Jules will not fail you."

"Papa Jules!" cried Jacqueline. "You haven't—you know how many times I have told you! Its not good for Etienne."

The old man started. With all his priestly face and neatly queued white hair he seemed like a child caught at mischief. "No, no, no," he muttered. That was all he could say. He put his head down and continued to mumble stroking his hand rapidly over his mouth.

Etienne lapsed into sullen silence, staring up where the firelight played among the rafters. Jacqueline spread her hands helplessly and exchanged a weary glance with Therese Lambert.

The wind raised ominously and the rain beat harder against the house. Now it had begun to trickle down the the chimney and sputter upon the fire.

"A plague upon this rain," said Gustave Lambert in his thick voice.

"Dindon," chided Therese placidly. "The rain is good for you. Bad weather means bad shoes. Bad shoes mean work for you. Praise the good Lord for it."

"Praise the good Lord for the knots in my joints which the wet puts there and the shoes do not tread out," said Gustave sourly.

Etienne stirred on his bunk. "The rain," he said in his queer halting voice, "do you remember it Gustave?" The night it rained on the Black River, and the camp was full of water, and we slept in the water in our wet blankets under the rain?"

Gustave said, "I remember, Etienne."

"Do not speak of it now, Etienne." Jacqueline said with a hint of alarm in her voice and eyes.

"That was the night the chiefs slipped out and we went forward in the morning to take the fort." He was acting it out. Reliving it all again. His face was tense and vibrant.

"They were shipping from the high ground." His voice trailed, then rose with shocking clarity. "That was when one hit me here next to my spine. I thought at first I had stumbled when I found myself on the ground." His voice trailed, then rose with shocking clarity. "Must I lie here until I die? God! For one hour to walk in the woods!"

The man's intensity spun a web of speechlessness around their tongues. They sat still, avoiding one another's eyes. Jacqueline dropped her spinning and walked toward the bunk, but Etienne waved her back pettishly. "Sit down," he commanded. "Don't snivel over me."

Gustave Lambert found his rumbling voice. "I remember, Etienne. The Natchez and the Black River. It seems long ago." He stabbed a stubby finger at his empty eye-socket.

"I left this old eye of mine there. Now they want me to go again. Jean Paul Lesueur, he comes to me: 'You are an old soldier, Gustave. You fought under me on the Black River.' That's what he says. Yes, but not again. In one fight I lose one eye. I go this time--who knows, I may lose the other, maybe my life. I cannot make a new eye as I make a new shoe. 'No, M'sieu' Lesueur,' that is what I say. I have this one eye, the King has the other. Let the Chickasaw and the Natchez come here and I will fight them."

Evan said impulsively, "But then it would be too late."

"What do you know about it?" cried Etienne with a fierceness which even stunned Evan. "Of the cold and the wet and the way savages fight? It's you Frenchmen, knowing nothing, but talking much, who have ruined us."

Gustave's good eye cut from Etienne to Evan. He spoke quickly into the interval of silence as Evan flushed darkly. "Without doubt,

M'sieu' Bienville knows best. Perhaps as he says, we will go hungry for want of grain and meat if the Chickasaws cut us off from the Illinois. But our rations will be scantier this year anyway, because the army is taking so much. It is hard, my friend," he went on, "for those of us who work for what we eat to go fight two hundred leagues away."

Already angered by Etienne's animosity Evan felt his wrath mounting at their stolidity, or stupidity, he could not decide which.

"Then the limits of your gardens is all you would defend?" He looked not at Gustave but directly at Jacqueline and did not know why.

She returned his gaze and answered gravely, "I do not want to see them here. I have seen enough of their savagery at Fort Rosalie, God knows. Do you think that I do not hate them, those devils out of hell, who butchered my mother and my father? But there is better work to be done than following them to the end of the earth."

He watched her vital hands on the spindle. Odd how such a humdrum occupation demanded and reflected so much skill and patience. Skillful patience, it was in this woman's hands, in her character, a waiting courage in the face of adversity which was greater than rash bravery. "You were at Fort Rosalie?" His voice was gentle, not so much asking a question as making a statement which he knew to be true.

Her reply was brief, almost short. "Yes."

In her silence his active imagination pictured the horror of the massacre. She must have been little more than a child then. Remembrance must come at times across the interval of years, sweeping like a nightmare wave. The hobgoblins of his own childhood suddenly seemed foolish futile wretches by comparison. He felt startled and disturbed. Until that moment Jacqueline Martin had been in his consciousness the withdrawn shadow of a person. Now she was a human being, with a depth of meaning. Moreover, she was not another man's wife, but a woman.

Etienne Martin cleared his throat harshly. Evan had the uncanny thought that the man read what passed in his mind.

"Jacqueline," said Etienne. "Jacqueline, bring me my fiddle."

She rose without a word and fetched the fiddle from the high shelf in the chimney corner. It was a tiny kit-fiddle wrapped carefully in a piece of doeskin. Etienne drew it out, the gargoyle lines of his face softened, he touched the instrument hesitantly with his fingertips and then cradled it beneath his chin. The bow moved, but the brightness in his eyes quickly dulled. He let the bow hang slackly silent on the strings.

"What is wrong, Etienne?" asked Jacqueline.

"You know I cannot play," he said quickly. "You know I cannot play unless I am alone."

Gustave Lambert looked for his hat as if Etienne's words were a signal for dismissal. So did Jules Froissart, still rubbing his mouth and grumbling to himself. Evan took a startled glance around the room and caught the inference. He got up quickly and punched Rene who had his feet stretched out comfortably to the fire. Everybody seemed to be moving toward the door at once. Etienne lay back on his pillow with his eyes closed, feigning sleep or exhaustion. To Jacqueline it was an old story. She felt no embarrassment as far as Gustave and Therese and Papa Jules were concerned. They all understood Etienne. But Evan MacDonald was different. He did not understand and she had a swift, almost desperate wish that he could understand. She felt upset and said good night to all of them more abruptly than she had intended.

Gustave and Therese had gone on ahead. Evan could barely see them through the gloom and the rain, but he could hear the paddle of their sabots in the slush. Old Jules Froissart stuck with Evan and Rene. He seemed not to notice the rain at all.

"She should have given him the rum, instead of blaming me," he grumbled. "That would have quieted him. I would not bring it to him if it did not do him good. It eases his pain, you know."

Neither Evan nor Rene spoke, so he nudged Evan slyly in the ribs. When Evan peered at him he was pulling at his lip.

"You are young and hale and hearty," he said in his oddly pontifical voice. "He is only half a man," he chuckled. "Old Jules is wise. She is a young girl yet. A virgin almost though she has a husband. What can a half-man do for a young girl?" He nudged Evan again. "You are young, too. I saw the way she looked at you."

Evan could have throttled the old man because what he said was so close to that which ran through his own mind. He did not want her, of course. He wanted Antoinette, or nobody. But, by God, she was an attractive woman and deserved better than that browbeating cripple.

When Evan returned to the house of the Commandant General he found Gaston Lazac coming down the stairs.

"The Sieur de Bienville is looking for you," Lazac said, quickly as he started out the door.

Evan looked at him. He had a leather pouch hanging across his shoulder. "What about you? Where are you off to?"

"I am going upriver to run messages for the Governor as far as the Tunica town," he replied. "A bien tot, my friend." With that he went out into the rain.

After Gaston Lazac had gone Evan went up the stairs to Bienville's room. Bienville lay quietly under the quilt, half-propped against his pillows, with his eyes closed. Evan sat at the foot of the heavy oaken bedstead. He thought he had fallen asleep. He covertly watched Bienville's face, calm now under the nightcap which made him look oddly like a graying woman. As he watched, Bienville opened his eyes very quickly. He might have been studying Evan under his lashes all the time.

"Have you considered what your plans to do here are?" The bluntness of the question disconcerted Evan.

"I, I don't really know," he stammered.

"No plans! No plans!" Bienville muttered fretfully. "Too many people with nothing in their heads but this minute and their dinner-- and a wench. Is that why you came?"

"No!" said Evan more sharply than he intended. "The truth is, I was unsettled after my father died. I don't like Paris, and I wanted to see the strange places of the world."

What had happened at Simon's was the affair of Rene and Collette, not his alone, and certainly not Bienville's. He laughed a little to cover his momentary hesitation.

"The botanical histories were Monsieur Villiers' famous idea. I don't know one plant from another, beyond those we have in the Highlands.

"Strange corners and strange sights, like nuts for a squirrel to nibble at," said Bienville sourly. "Too many young men, like squirrels, run here and run back. I'd be pleased to think you were differently inclined."

Evan said nothing. He saw the lifting emotion in Bienville's eyes. They fairly gleamed. He had turned his thin body on the bed, leaning toward Evan.

"This is land. Land without limit," he said almost harshly. "And land is wealth and power, the only wealth and power, because men come out of it, as I have. It's ours or England's, curse them. But I'll match them yet. When I've broken the savages it will be for the young men, not for me, to build an empire here to dwarf Europe."

Evan thought, "I am a young man." He stared past Bienville at the window and seemed to see his own fancies pass in a procession across the linen squares. Savages leaping and writhing with nightmare rapidity; the wind outside the window carried their voices and banging of drums. Then it all changed in a wink into a white city with broad streets and Antoinette, walking with the wind in her hair, like a queen. When Bienville spoke and he turned his eyes back, the man on the bed seemed to be a long way off and distorted as if seen through rolled water. He scarcely understood what he said.

Bienville's voice was considered, almost judicial.

"You must take care, Evan, of whom make your friends here. There are people, God help me, bent upon doing good for themselves alone. They are my enemies, of my willing and their willing. They can never be friends of yours." He hesitated, and Evan, who was fully listening at last, sensed his point even before he continued. "You have been to the house of the Monsieur Mallot, have you not?"

Evan nodded carefully.

Bienville's lips tightened. "That house and the house of Monsieur de Pradel are nests and gathering places of those who make it their business to undermine me. You will not go there again."

Evan felt the blood spreading in his face. He meant to hold his tongue until he could speak evenly, but while he was determining upon it, his voice came out loudly, sharp and impatient, almost an echo of Bienville's.

"The De Pradel's mean nothing to me, I scarcely know them. I went because I wished to see Mademoiselle Castilloux."

Evan was not prepared for Bienville's reaction. He sat bolt upright among the bedclothes, his eyes angry and disbelieving.

"Castilloux! An offspring of Antoine Castilloux!"

"We were children together," said Evan, and felt the angrier because he had spoke defensively.

Bienville continued to stare at him, shaking his head slowly with an air which infuriated Evan.

"A liaison with Castilloux! Good God!"

Evan sprang to his feet, white and stiff lipped.

"You forget yourself, monsieur," he said in cold fury, "Mademoiselle Castilloux is a--a most respected friend.

I'll hear nothing against her."

Bienville shook a bony finger at his eyes. "You'll hear what I am pleased to have you hear. It is you who, as a guest in my house, forget yourself. Courtesy, if nothing else, demands that you accede to my wishes."

"What are your wishes, monsieur?"

"You will see no more of any of Castilloux's breed. He is worse, ten times over, than De Pradel or Mallot."

Evan looked down at his hands and saw they were trembling. He cleared his throat. "With your leave then, I will go, sir," he said evenly. He felt sick and hurt. This was his hero denouncing the girl he adored. "I can't accept your hospitality under such conditions."

"Sit down," said Bienville, out of patience.

Evan backed steadily toward the door. "If you have need of me, I shall be at the cabin of Gaston Lazac." He hesitated with his hand on the latch as an inspiration struck him.

"Monsieur," he said, almost eagerly, in spite of his anger. "Give me permission to go with Gaston Lazac."

Bienville swore in surprise. "Have you taken leave of your senses? What do you know of woods running?"

His attitude annoyed Evan. "The Highlands are wild enough."

Bienville pursed his lips. He thought it might do the boy good, and get him away from bad influences, away from the Castilloux baggage. The wild country might clear his head. At the least, it could do him no harm.

He said with feign reluctance, "Go then, if you're determined upon it. Gaston Lazac can mind you and teach you the rudiments of woodcraft. Good night."

He continued to watch the door after Evan had closed it. The boy reminded him so much of the father. Thirty years before he had been hotheaded and would not listen to his friends about a woman either.

The argument then had gone much the same as this one. The quarrel just past had depressed him out of all proportion to its importance. It made his head ache and the constriction grew tighter in his chest. He was getting old ahead of his time. No longer was he able to control persons and events. The small affairs tied in with the large. His failure to influence Evan to his way of thinking seemed to him to reflect his progressive failings in all his projects. Most notably in Indian affairs. Once he had held the strings by which the tribes moved. Now he must bludgeon his way, and the bludgeon was a feeble reed.

He fumbled among the papers upon his bedside table and found the last sheet of paper to the Comte de Maurepas. Holding it close before his eyes, he read over the final lines.

". . .This. . . confirms me in my determination to march, myself, against them at the head of all the Frenchmen whom I can gather in a position to make the campaign without greatly disturbing their business. . . by assembling in this war all the forces of the lower part of the colony, with the exception of the settlers, I shall have hardly five hundred Frenchmen, a feeble army to carry a war at a distance of two hundred leagues with a nation equal in numbers to our force. It is true that I expect my presence will increase the courage of our

Indians, and it is only in this hope that I am undertaking, at my age, a campaign as laborious as this one. If I am able to obtain junction with the Illinois forces, I should be able to promise myself complete success in this enterprise. . .

His head ached worse than ever, a dull, throbbing pain like an embodiment of frustration. The premonition which had oppressed him all evening did not lessen. He had been a part of this colony, in flesh and in spirit, for nearly forty years. He wondered how many more he had left.

Chapter XI

Dawn was a gray promise over the cypress tops toward Chef Menteur when Gaston Lazac and Evan went up the river road at an easy trot. By the time the sun was an hour high shining over the river, the overcast had broken into gray columns of clouds marching away to the southwest. The sunshine drove the rawness out of the air and made it crisp. Evan, with the sun on his right cheek, felt his muscles loosening pleasantly as they jogged. He had been too long housebound. Not since he had left the Highlands had he been on a long jaunt. Then his body had been hard from rambling the hills. Now his muscles were soft, he knew he must ache before this scout was over.

His firelock swung, level, dragging on his right shoulder. The firelock belonged to Jean Paul Lesueur. So did the hunting shirt he wore, a gray woolsey one with thrums around the shoulders, and the leggings and moccasins. The garments fit well enough, except that he was thicker through the body than Lesueur. Lazac made the pace, chanting under his breath, "Vive la Canadienne--"over and over until Evan tired of hearing it.

Lazac did not stay long on the river road. A mile above Nouvelle Orleans he swung off on a track which ran west through the swamps, cutting across the loops of the river. He began to lengthen his stride.

155

He wanted to make his first camp on the Amite River where it ran into Lake Maurepas. He could do that easily and make the Tunica town on the third day. He told Evan that he was glad he had come along because Bienville had given him two letters, one for Pierre D'Artaguette and one for Petit Deliviliers at the Natchez. Since Lazac couldn't read he was afraid that he might give Chiki the wrong one.

After a while he stopped his chanting.

"It looks bad, like I told you," he said over his shoulder to Evan. "D'Artaguette can't hold his Indians the way Bienville says he's got to."

"That's what the Chevalier de Louboey said."

Lazac grunted. "Just because De Louboey said it don't make it right. But it is this time. And Bienville knows it. But he's got to do something." He trotted fifty strides before he spoke again. "That's why I'm taking my time. It don't make any difference where D'Artaguette gets this letter. Once he starts moving, he's got to keep moving or his Indians will all go home."

"If the Chickasaws don't fight any better than you think our Indians will, they ought to be easy," said Evan.

"They'll fight," said Lazac, "and they'll be ready. Jerome Allain, he was captain of Bienville's pirogue, saw Lieutenant Ducoder at Mobile. Ducoder had a tale about the Chief Ymayatabe giving him meat and corn, and putting him on the road to the Choctaws. But he didn't know much about the Chickasaw towns, Jerome says, because they kept him in a lodge all the time. He said there was another man, a sergeant under him, but he couldn't come because the Chickasaws had put out his eyes."

Evan asked, "Why didn't they put our Ducoder's eyes?"

"God knows. Maybe the sergeant took his eyes into the wrong lodges."

Lazac kept talking as they jogged along, but Evan lapsed into a gloomy silence. He was preoccupied with his own misfortunes. His quarrel with Bienville overshadowed everything else. He was sick of this country already, one way or the other he would get back to the Highlands as soon as he could.

In the afternoon they came out of the timber and saw the river. On the opposite shore the church of the German settlement struck by the sun, made a white wedge against the dark shadow of the forest. The sky was almost clear now and the air was sharp. Evan blew on his fingers as they rested a minute, looking out across the water. Then they went on to the northwest away from the river as Lazac followed a track that was little more than a deer run. They had covered eight leagues; it was four more, Lazac said, to the Amite River. Evan felt the calves of his legs begin to tighten and ache.

Three hours later after the crescent moon had gone down and they moved through a shadowless land, Evan and Lazac came to the banks of the Amite River and made camp on a spot of high ground a league from its mouth. They hunted dry driftwood which the last high water had left on a slope of the high ground, and got a small fire going. For awhile they squatted over the fire talking aimlessly and chewing salt beef and biscuit. The fire felt better when they listened to the north wind blowing off the open water and striking the timber which stood between them and the bend in the river.

Then they stopped talking and Lazac rolled in his blanket and lay like an Indian with his feet pointed to the fire. For all Evan knew he went directly to sleep. But Evan stayed awake, feeling his day's running in his feet. They burned but he did not touch them for fear he would find them blistered. He lay there looking up through the black boughs at the sky, listening to the hiss of the fire as it died down. The tops of the trees pointed to the cold, hard stars. He heard the wind sighing in the canes by the creek, the misty rippling of the water, and the splash of some small creature diving. Antoinette was constantly on his mind but the peacefulness of the night had blunted his bitterness. She seemed a long way off, and as he drowsed, moving closer, an embodiment of happiness. When he slept he dreamed that he had built a cabin in the middle of the forest and that Antoinette had left the Baron and her friends in Nouvelle Orleans and come to him.

In the morning they swam the icy river and struck out to the northward. At first, matching Lazac's pace, Evan felt his aches in every bone, but after he had labored along painfully for a while, his muscles began to loosen and he felt better in the crisp morning air. He began to realize that he was not as soft as he had expected. As he remembered his dreams he was already eager to have this scout over, to get back to Nouvelle Orleans.

All that day they ran for some sixteen leagues through a forest of hard wood and pine. The woods were full of game. Cat squirrels and fox squirrels frolicked overhead or humped themselves in flight over the pine needles as Evan and Lazac approached.

They saw a few white tailed dear, and those were gaunt for the forage through the months of a January and February were poor. Once Evan heard the sound of baying off to the north. A pack of hunting timber wolves, said Lazac. There would be one lean deer less in the woods before long.

Almost at dark of that day they came out of the woods and looked across a low valley clear of timber, with only scattered clumps of willow and red birch bordering a stream which turned like a snake from side to side of the valley. The sun stood up in the paling west, half an hour high. Through the leafless branches of the trees Evan could see long rays of the sun reddening the water. On the far side of the valley the bluff beneath which the stream curled was not high and seemed flat on top, a stretch of natural prairie rolling back into the timbered hills. The side of the bluff where the willows clumped was obscured in a wool gray haze, but the flat summit was marked by a fall of dusky sunlight. On a headland where the creek swung, three pine trees stood out, black and two dimensional against the red ball of the sun. Beyond them the farther hills faded, swelling with smooth formlessness into the dim vast distance behind the sun.

The sun plunged down, the valley lay in shadow, and Evan and Lazac picked their way through the jungle of blackberry briers which had overgrown the bottom. They made their camp by the water. The sky was clear and the stars reflected coldly from the stream. Lazac said before he went to sleep that there would be frost in the morning. Evan slept that night without dreaming.

When he awoke a white mist hung over the frosty bottom. The thin smoke of his own breath mingled with it. He saw that the leaves of the low briar's were fringed with frost and the flat stretches of grass glittered like silver. The frost was soft underfoot as they went down to the creek and startled a great blue heron that was fishing in the shallows. He gave one cry like a hoarse throated pig and flew off heavily, his bluff breast almost skimming the surface of the water.

In the woods beyond the creek there was no sign of frost. The sun was a great white fire seen through the trees above the rim of the ridge. The air was cold and so still that not even a dry leaf or twig so much as trembled Yet all around him Evan could hear a steady rustling as of raindrops, the dry leaves breaking away from the trees and drifting down to earth. They lay under foot, all hues and shapes. The fallen maple leaves turned up their dull gray undersides among the red and brown and yellow from other trees. A squirrel scattered the dry leaves, bounced like a ball of gray fur upon a log and vanished up the side of a tree. Somewhere back in the timber Evan heard the harsh screaming of a blue jay. By that time the sun was well up and the limbs of the trees glinted coldly in the light as if they were encased in thin sheaths of ice.

They traveled more slowly through the bluff country west of the creek. The ridges, in too small a space, shouldered one another for room. Their sides slipped into sheer hollows, sixty feet down, a matted jungle of canes and vines. A faint Indian path ran on the ridges and Lazac followed its windings

In the afternoon the hills rose higher, colored of brick dust, blood, and vermilion. Lazac told Evan that they were nearing the Tunica village.

Used as he was to hill travel, Evan was ready to drop when they reached a point where the bluffs ran out to the river and they sighted the Tunica town. The sun was low beyond the river and the shadows of the lodges stretched long to the eastward like an array of blunted spearheads. The round, vaulted cabins were yellow-brown like a cluster of weathered hay cocks on the leveling land, and beyond them the river turned to the west in a great bow and into the setting sun.

Evan stood quietly beside Lazac, looking down at the village and the vast river. He knew now what he should have known before. This was the land, as Bienville had said. This was his land. This was his fortune. If it took a brave man to attain it, that was his incentive to courage.

A swirl of children of mingled ages and sexes engulfed them as they trotted into the town. In all the crowd of children there was not one shred of cloth. They were as naked as the day they were born, male and female, and the growing chill of the air seemed to make no impression on their mahogany hides. Evan, with his own fingers stiff with the cold, marveled at them. They pranced alongside, forming two files, with the long rays of the sun burnishing their bodies into copper.

Behind the cloud of children, the squaws watched the white men. They stood and squatted in front of the lodges, grinding corn and minding kettles hung over the fires. Their bodies below the hips were covered by a kind of homespun skirt and some of them had skin coverings across their shoulders.

An old man, wearing a mantle of turkey feathers on his sloping shoulders, walked toward Evan and Lazac.

Lazac lifted his voice above the clamor of the children. "Nokuctawitcin! Imayo! It is I! Gaston Lazac!"

Nokuctawitcin's face was deeply lined. The flesh hung in leathery folds beneath his jowls and chin. Brandishing his hickory club he sent the children scattering before he took Lazac's hand, and then Evan's, when Lazac had made him known.

"Little brother of the Great French Chief, my father," he said solemnly. "Nokuctawitcin's lodge is yours." He spoke in the Tunica language, which Evan did not understand, and Lazac had to interpret.

"Where is Chiki?" Lazac asked Nokuctawitcin. "The Great French Chief has sent me with a message for him." Nokuctawitcin swung his arm toward the river and said that Chiki had gone dear hunting in the River Rouge bottoms and had promised him a piece of the leg.

Lazac looked where the old Indian pointed. "He is coming now," he said.

Evan saw nothing but the sun upon the water. The Mississippi had become a red river. The water was blood. The two white men and the Indian stood watching the gory splotch fade. Then they could see the boat on the river. It looked like a black log moving across the current.

It was Chiki. Evan, Lazac and Nokuctawitcin went down to the river and waited while he ran his pirogue on the bar. He came ashore shouldering the hind quarters of a young doe. A stocky Indian with a powerful chest and built for running, he could do twenty leagues through woods between sunrise and noon as good as any runner between LaBelise and Fort Chartres. He signaled Nokuctawitcin that the fore quarter was in the pirogue. But he would not receive the letter from Lazac until he had carried the venison into the lodge.

When he came out again he had on a tricorne hat and a full skirted French coat of scarlet velour. The hat had gold braid and the drooping remains of a rosette. It sat like a capsizing ship upon Chiki's black hair. The coat had been folded many times, on every crease ancient grease was black and stiff. The cuffs, the collar and the skirts were frayed almost to tatters. The skirts caught him at the bend of his knees, his leggings showed beneath. To Evan he looked like a spindle shanked beldame in pantellettes with the petticoat pulled high. Chiki touched his hat lovingly, setting it straight before he squatted down, and asked Lazac for the letter. Lazac took the two letters from his pouch and asked Evan which was for Pierre D'Artaguette. He handed that one to Chiki.

Chiki tucked the letter under the skirt of his coat into his pouch which was made of a raccoon's skin with the ringed tail dangling down his thigh. He grinned to himself. The white man's talking papers fascinated him. He wished one would talk to him sometime, but they never did.

"I sleep good tonight," he said. "Go at dawn."

Evan watched them while he endeavored to find a comfortable position for his feet. They ached and throbbed and burned. Below the knee his legs were petrified from weariness. The distance to Natchez -- sixteen leagues, Lazac said -- loomed like a nightmare. But a stubborn pride kept him from resting here at the Tunicas while Lazac went on with Chiki.

He moved his feet again and groaned inside. The old Indian, Nokuctawitcin, squatted like a toad, half asleep, waiting patiently for his piece of the leg

Chapter XII

The cold rain which kept the people of Nouvelle Orleans housebound this night, and made even Gaston Lazac look for shelter, fell as monotonously in the swamp which curved between the lake shore and the river northwest of the settlement. All that country which ran in wooded marsh clear against the lake, with its back to the plantations flanking the river, was a lost land full of cypress, willow and black gum small growth, with live oaks on the ridges sluggish bayous and sloughs which ran nowhere scarred its surface. The sleet rustled in the branches and dead leaves, spreading out into a pale fan in the darkness when the wind sliced down an aisle between the buttressed cypress trunks.

It was an hour past dark when Ulysses, the giant negro runaway from Castilloux's plantation at Cannes Brulees, crawled out of his covert branches of a downed tree. He stood up with his hands resting on the log; slope shouldered, his ears cocked as if he sought some alien sound above the lisp of the sleet. His dress was pitiful against the intense cold. He had added a tattered woolen cloak with a kind of hood to his breeches, but his feet were bare on the marshy ground. He stood shivering in the wind, but it was not the cold entirely which made him shake. Again and again he seemed to strain his ears as he listened to the wind.

There was no sound but the wind and the sleet. At length he seemed satisfied and began to walk, picking his way along the dry ridges and among the trees which were hard to make out in the dark. His direction, allowing for deviations, was generally southwest, always toward the river. But he went like a man who sought less to reach some destination than to leave some place behind. He had the look of a terrified animal; and now and again as the wind whooped on a louder note through the branches he was at the point of breaking into blind, panic stricken flight. His mind moved sluggishly, circling around and around like a slow eddy with its cumbersome burden of thought. It had been an hour ago, when dusk and the sleet had come together like a ghost into the swamp, that he had seen the big white man with the black beard pass his hiding place.

It had not occurred to him that the man had been headed toward Nouvelle Orleans, and had appeared to have no more on his mind than getting out of the bad weather. Into Ulysses numb brain had leaped the conviction that after this week of freedom the white men were closing in on him. It had been a devil's dance of freedom. A week of enduring the wet and cold, of grubbing for roots for food, or trying with sticks to knock down the agile small animals, of drinking bad water until his belly cramped and he thought he would die.

He would have died had not the animal in him always risen up to tell him that anything was better than dying. Anything was better than letting the white men catch him, because when they got him again they would kill him. He was sure of that. They would break every bone in his body before they would let him die. It was the one thought that kept his weak legs moving, that kept his frozen feet hobbling painfully one step after another. All other instincts were submerged in him but that of self-preservation. He wanted to get to the river, he wanted to get across the river. Anywhere across the river, just so he could get the river between himself and the horrible man with the black beard.

Into his consciousness came a slow penetrating recollection of Leon. He fumbled with this which was off the beaten track that his mind had been following. What had become of Leon? Leon was dead, he decided at last. Yes, he was beginning to remember, Leon had given out from weakness and the effect of his flogging. Leon had never been strong like Ulysses anyway, and the beating had sapped him. He remembered it all now. Leon had given out, unable to go further. He had waited with Leon two whole nights and days. If there had been any place of safety he would have left him, but they had been wandering aimlessly in the swamp. That place where Leon gave out was as safe as any other. He knew Leon was going to die, and he had been afraid.

He wanted to run away, but something had kept him there. Once he had heard a sound of something crashing through the brush and he had bolted. It had been no more than a white-tailed buck, and he had crept back. A little later Leon had died. Ulysses had seen death in the form of a streamer of swamp mist creep over Leon's face. When it had passed Leon was dead. Ulysses had not dared to touch him. He had gotten up hurriedly and gone out into the swamp just as the dawn light was fingering its way thought the dry coppery cypress tops.

Now, remembering, a kind of panic began to stir in him. For a moment the fear of the black bearded man was forgotten. He saw the ghostly mist rising from the coffee colored slough upon his left. With a shock of terror he imagined that it was coiling itself around his heart, as it had done to Leon. He could fairly feel the clammy touch of it. He broke into a shambling run, not heeding the pain to his bruised feet. The wet, cold branches whipped his face and he ducked his head, throwing high his arms to ward them off. His foot struck numbly against a root and he fell headlong, rolling down the side of a dry knoll into the edge of the slough. He scrambled up as quickly as he could, panting like a spent hound, and plunged on through the brush.

Suddenly, before he could realize it, the feel and rustle of wet leaves were gone from beneath his feet: the sleet, unimpeded, slapped harder against his head and hunching shoulders. He was in the open, stampeding across a piece of cleared land. Beyond him a half mile, a vague glimmer of gray light, ran the river. Like a thirsty horse scenting water his head came up. He began to slacken his frantic pace and, puffing and blowing, went trotting on to the river.

He waded into the sucking mud to the water's edge, and flopped, drinking. He gulped the muddy water, filling his mouth too full, choking. It was like tafia in comparison to the stagnant water of the swamp. He crawled back onto the batture and squatted, humped against the tattoo of the sleet, staring out across the broad, gray ribbon of water. The other shore was lost in dimness. He began to study in his mind how he was going to get over. He was too weak to swim it and it was too cold, the cramps would take him under before he had well started. It was hard to think, he felt more like sprawling out on the batture and going to sleep.

After a while he got up and started walking slowly along the edge of the mud flats. Pretty soon he found what he was looking for. It was a willow log lodged in the mud, half in and half out of the water. He bogged out to it and began to claw at it and work at it, trying to make it float again.

He began to realize then just how weak he was. A minute or two of struggling with the log and he was exhausted. He had to drop across it and rest. Apparently, however, it had not been long grounded. It was not stuck fast. All at once, as he pried, it slid out on the water and idled there in the outer current while he frantically sloshed out to it and laid hold of it with trembling hands. He began to shove it then, feeling the clutch of the mud at every cumbersome step.

The log floated free. He felt it rise higher against his body. He got it against his chest and shoved harder. It went out faster, feeling with its upstream end for the current and his feet jerked off the bottom. The lower half of his body had gone numb from the chill of the water. He hitched himself up and hung across the log. The log went out into the river, found the current, turned end for end, almost snatching him free. He clutched it, moving his lips. He knew he would sink like a stone if he lost hold of the log.

It was going straight down the current now. Dimly he was aware that he hadn't the strength to push it across the current. He would never reach the other side. He felt the cramps take hold of him agonizingly. His eyes began to pop out with the torture of it and his slipping fingers started to bite into the slimy surface of the log. His brain was going black and his fingers could not find a hold.

Like something a long way off, or in a dream, he heard the dip of an oar. It might have been white men who would capture him, but that possibility no longer terrified him. The sound had no attribute of reality. There was no space in his spinning brain for fear.

The men in the pirogue heard the man splashing water, or they might have hit the log directly and been swamped. They were paddling without a light and the mist on the river made clear vision impossible. As they back watered the pirogue bumped lightly against the logs and the man in the bow saw the black head of the man in the river sliding beneath the water. Instinctively, before he thought what he was doing he reached out and caught the swimmer's collar.

The man next to him struck at his arm with his fist.

"Fool!" he whispered fiercely. "Let him drown."

The other man pulled Ulysses' head above the gunwale of the pirogue.

"Black man." he said.

All three men in the pirogue were negroes. They hesitated, staring at Ulysses. The log floated past and was lost upon the misty surface of the river.

The second negro lifted his oar, the drip of water from its blade made a dull shine in the darkness as if it drew to itself all that meager half light which sifted down with the rain from the sky.

"Knock his head," muttered the second man. He looked at the third who nodded.

"Wait," said the man who held Ulysses. "Me know him. This man Ulysses."

They spoke in whispers as if any louder sound might drift across the quiet water to hostile ears.

"Pull him in, Basile," said the third man, with the authoritative air of a leader. "Man must have reason to swim river tonight.

Basile grunted and hauled Ulysses aboard. The dissenting member of the party continued to grumble as the tree oars worked the pirogue across the current toward the opposite shore. Before they made it, the cramps had begun to loosen their grip upon Ulysses. A semblance of rationality seemed to creep back into his eyes, staring into the vacuity of the sky. For a little while he did not think at all. Then he began to remember first the things which had happened latest; the log and the river and his fingers slipping.

He decided he must be dead. Lying upon his back, staring straight up, he was not yet conscious of the other men in the pirogue. If he were dead this must be the heaven of the Christian God, or maybe it was that of the Mohammedan Allah he had known in Senegal as a child. He felt no conviction that it was either. It might as as well be the after world of the ancient Senegalese tribal gods about which his toothless grandmother had told him.

For a reason he could not explain the thought of heaven made him think of Fanchon. It was the first time he had thought of Fanchon in a good many hours, or was it days. It made him remember that he didn't want to die until he had seen Fanchon again. It made him feel sad, so that he could not enjoy the feeling of being dead and not having to worry about anything.

Presently his illusion of heaven was dissipated as his physical senses returned. His first sensation was the sting of the sleet in his face. He knew by then he was still concerned with earthly affairs, and he had a momentary sinking of heart. He had been quite peaceful thinking of himself in the hereafter. He was pretty sure he wouldn't find much peace in the world he had known. Now he heard the gurgling strokes of the oars and, turning his head, saw the bulky shadows of his companions in the boat.

His eyes and his nose told him they were negroes. He was a trifle reassured. The man nearest him noticed his movement and spoke.

"Be still," he admonished.

Ulysses lay like a corpse, his muscles rigid until the boat grounded in the mud of the western shore. Then he tried to struggle up and the other man pulled him out of the boat and dumped him in the mud at the water's edge. They left him there while they shoved the pirogue well out into the stream and let it go spinning off in the current. They came back where he had managed to sit up flat on his buttocks. He felt a dizziness in his head and the three men seemed to gyrate as they passed him. Two of them got him under the arms, jerked him upright, and started to walk him away from the water toward the shadow of the woods beyond the batture.

He tried to twist his head to look at them. The two who held him were lanky, but not tall as himself. The third, who walked behind the others, was squat and bowlegged with arms which dangled to his knees.

Ulysses' head was practically clear when they halted in the edge of the woods. He looked hard at the man on his left and recognized him.

"Basile," he mumbled, remembering that Basile had run away from Castilloux's plantation more than a month before He had thought Basile was dead.

The short man faced him, his lower lip thrusting out.

"Who are you, big man?"

Ulysses was afraid of him, but he found his tongue.

"Ulysses. Basile know. Basile tell you. He master, my master."

Basile nodded nervously. "He say true, Toutou."

The way he said it told Ulysses that the small man, Toutou, was the leader, and the others feared him.

"What you do in river?" demanded Toutou.

Ulysses stared dully at him. It was in his mind to lie, but is was too hard to think up a lie.

"They be for whip me." he said. "Me run in swamp. Me get away."

"Whip you?" said the small man savagely. "Show me your back."

Obediently Ulysses turned and Basile stripped down his cloak, exposing the wounds where they had cut, festering against the dark skin.

Toutou nodded, much pleased. "Good," he said. "You hate them. You kill them for whip you?"

Ulysses lips slackened. He had not thought of that. He nodded jerkily.

"Good," said Toutou again. His face was tense with suppressed excitement. "You will. Soon. Their army go fight the Chickasaws. We kill all here, man, woman, all. We master then."

Ulysses did not believe him. It was a thing which had never entered his head. Which could not happen. Yet it was good to think of. As they walked on into the cold, wet woods he whispered to Basile about it. Basile told him that Toutou had come from the Chickasaws to free the slaves. For four days they had been on the east bank of the river getting the word among the slaves on the concessions on that side. Now they were headed for the backwoods above Montplasir, where they could camp safe from interference.

For hours it seemed that they blundered through the darkness. Then on the wooded ridge which ran north and south, Toutou halted. They scrambled in the dark for dry twigs and moss on the lee side of the ridge, and presently Toutou struck a light with his flint. It was a feeble flame and they huddled above it, teeth chattering. But Ulysses' heart was warm again. He was among friends now, safe, and it came into his mind that he would like to have Fanchon here with him.

Antoine Castilloux was considerably perturbed by the latest news which Gerard Malot brought him. To be sure, the slave, Leon, had been found dead in the swamp which circumstance was merely a loss in Castilloux's pocket. This did not, however, gainsay the fact that three other brutes had fled within little more than a month, Scot-free. More menacing, Malot had told him, was the perceptible uneasiness which had increased alarmingly among the remaining slaves within the last week. Malot was positive that the grapevine which carried intelligence among them had warned them to be on the alert.

To Castilloux all this meant one thing. Sooner or later, while the army was a hundred leagues and more away in the Chickasaw country, the slaves would rise. It caused him to hasten his plans for Antoinette and De Laval. When the slaves rose, if they did, Antoinette must be on her way back to France. He sought De Laval in interview and raised the subject.

As soon as he saw Castilloux's point De Laval's pale face grew resentful. It was a matter upon which he had yet to make up his mind.

"What you wish, monsieur," he said to Castilloux, "is that I should marry your daughter."

Castilloux did not equivocate. "I do," he said gruffly. The baron assumed a pensive attitude. "That is a proposition which will require some consideration," he murmured.

Castilloux was too canny to show his impatience. "I think you do not like this country, Monsieur le Baron?" he said dryly.

"Like it?" cried De Laval, showing animation for the first time. "I detest it! I loathe it! This beast of a country! The horrible place!"

"Then without doubt it would please you to return to France as soon as possible."

"Mon Dieu! But you greatly understate the case. I assure you, I can scarcely wait the day."

Castilloux's smooth voice droned. "But how, Monsieur le Baron, do you propose returning without money?"

De Laval's languid eyes opened wide. "Ha! my friend! So that is the game you play!"

"It is no game," said Castilloux. "It is a statement of fact."

De Laval drummed his pale fingers upon the arm of his chair. "You have misled me, monsieur," he said petulantly. "You informed me that this foul morass was a thriving city. You exaggerated your own wealth. You have lured me here with false promises, now you take advantage of me. Monsieur, you should hang your head in shame."

De Laval sighed. "Eh bien, she is a lovely creature, and though you beguiled me with tales of your great wealth, monsieur, still you are not actually a pauper. I will consider marriage to your daughter."

Castilloux smiled grimly, "Pere Raphael could marry you here."

"Monsieur, I will consider the proposition," De Laval hesitated. "Please, do not ask me to make such a decision at this moment. We can discuss this again soon."

"Very well," answered Castilloux and nodded a bow as he left the room. His plan was working as he envisioned. He would give the Baron a little time. There was only one conclusion that he could reach.

De Laval stood there for a few moments contemplating the situation. In certain respects it would not be a bad bargain, he had to admit. Of course, in France he might send Castilloux to the devil and seek a better dowry elsewhere. But in this foul wilderness Castilloux held the whip hand. That was what galled him, that he, a monseigneur, should be dictated to by this gueux revetu –this beggar grown rich. The man had lied most shamelessly. He had made out this country to be a paradise in which even the sands in the streams were gold. Otherwise, he, Edouard Sarrout, Baron de Laval, would never have set foot out of France.

He was so highly annoyed with his host that he had a servant obtain his coat and went out into the fresh air. Two days of sunshine following a day and a night of rain and sleet had partly dried out the streets. He walked aimlessly through a number of squares until he found himself passing the house of the Chevalier de Pradel. He decided to go in.

Monsieur de Pradel was busy in his office writing letters to Paris in which he complained of everything from the ill treatment which Bienville accorded him to the extravagance of his wife, Alexandrine. He was not overjoyed to see De Laval, who came in with an air of privilege, but he dissembled and greeted him with civility. While De

Laval was seating himself, Monsieur de Pradel fell to fiddling with his cuffs. He had business to attend to, and he was a fidgety little man who could not keep still when he had something on his mind. To make matters worse, Alexandrine had gone off with an ensign of the garrison whom the good God knew was years younger than herself. She was on business of her own, but he hoped that she would return that night. Yes, especially tonight since Monsieur George Auguste Vanderech of the German Village was visiting him, and for his sake he would like to keep up appearances. He knew that De Laval, as usual, was in a pettish humor.

"Do you know, monsieur, I have been here a month," he said, "and I find each day worse than the one which proceeded it."

"What is wrong now?" asked De Pradel, not meaning to seem ill mannered.

"Wrong?" complained De Laval. "What is not wrong? When it rains one is seized by the ague, when the sun shines one is devoured by insects." He scratched a welt upon his wrist.

"You will become used to it," said De Pradel indulgently. "It is not so bad, then. There are many things here our of which one may profit. I have been here for twenty years. I have made money."

De Laval's voice was thin with sarcasm. "Money? Of what use is money in this God forsaken wilderness?"

De Pradel felt like saying, it is money you seek when you marry Antoinette Castilloux. But he was not the kind of man who liked to dabble in unpleasantries.

Instead he said, mildly, "I find it useful, even here."

He was thinking that with Alexandrine he needed it Her extravagance sometimes tried his long-suffering soul.

"You are welcome to it," said De Laval sourly. "As for becoming used to this damnable place, I shall not stay here long enough for that. I shall sail on the Gironde and I shall not return."

De Pradel found himself wishing silently that the Gironde might be weighing anchor at that moment, but he was not soon rid of De Laval, who lingered complaining of everything he could think of until almost dark.

He might have remained longer, but a slave who had rowed across the river from the King's Plantation at Montplaisir came with a letter to De Pradel from the director of the plantation. The letter concerned wooden shoes for the King's slaves, as De Pradel knew without opening it. As he escorted De Laval to the door he spoke of the matter.

"The brutes wear out leather too fast, so they give them sabots to wear," he said. "In truth, they should use the footwear nature has given them, it is good enough. They are treacherous animals. See that one," he pointed to the messenger who was disappearing in the general direction of the levee. "He would carve out your heart, if he had the chance."

Well pleased with himself, he smiled slyly at the nervousness which De Laval evidenced as he hurried off into the gloom.

The slave from the King's Plantation was raw boned, with eyes that grew close together and large lips. Because his gums were as dark as the back of a catfish he was called Pierre le Bleu. He wore a gray woolen cloak, very dirty, and breeches which were gathered around his waist with a length of rope. His feet shuffled in sabots.

The instructions which he had from his master were to deliver the letter to Monsieur de Pradel and return directly to Montplaisir. However, he had business of his own which must be attended to first. For this reason, when he left De Pradel's house, he went only a little way toward the river, turned the corner and walked directly in the direction of Antoine Castilloux's. He had been there before, so he did not tarry upon his way.

It was dark when he arrived there and he skirted the house, keeping in the shelter of the hedge until he was opposite the kitchen at the rear on the side of the court. He vaulted the hedge and the low fence and found Michel, the stumpy steward, seated morosely on the kitchen steps. Michel merely grunted when Pierre le Bleu greeted him.

"Girl here named Fanchon," said Pierre. "Fetch her."

Michel regarded him with profound suspicion.

"She work," he muttered. "Master catch you here, he whip you!"

Pierre fumbled beneath his cloak and brought out a snuffbox which he had carved with his own hands from red cedar wood. The aroma of cedar and snuff blended temptingly. Michel eyed the box greedily.

"You fetch her," Pierre repeated, holding the box at a safe distance from Michel's itching fingers.

Michel licked his lips and rolled his eyes until they seemed all white. "No good for you le Bleu," he said. "Me know. She be for Ulysses. Say Ulysses all day."

He was surprised when this information seemed to please the slave from across the river.

"Good," said Pierre le Bleu. "You go." He balanced the snuff box in his palm.

Michel grunted and trudged off toward the main house while Pierre le Bleu withdrew into the shadows beside the kitchen and waited. Presently he saw them through the gloom, the squat steward and the tall girl. He peered out at her, liking the shape of her hips and her long legs beneath the cotton dress.

"Man for you," said Michel and stood by expectantly.

Fanchon's eyes as round as the owl's never left Pierre's face. "Me not know you," she mumbled.

Pierre nodded toward the darkness beyond the hedge. "We go outside."

Fanchon began to back away from him. "No!" Her voice quavered.

He said in a hissing whisper, "Ulysses!"

She began to shake all over and stopped dead. When he turned toward the hedge she stumbled after him

Michel cried out in quick dismay, "Snuff!"

Pierre swung back, muttering, tipped the snuff box above Michel's cupped palm, snapped the lid shut, and like a snake glided over the hedge.

He heard Fanchon scrambling in the hedge and cursed her clumsiness.

She panted up to him and clutched at his cloak. "Ulysses," she babbled. "You say Ulysses!"

He shoved a horny palm over her mouth. "He sent me. He hide. He want you."

He thought she had the ague the way she trembled. She was sputtering through his fingers and he took his hand away.

"Me go," she gasped.

"Not now," said Pierre. "You love Ulysses? You die for Ulysses?"

She nodded dumbly, her lips shaking.

"Good," he whispered. "You do this. When me come, say word. You kill this house. All. White man. White woman. You be free. Ulysses be free. All be free. You see Ulysses. He be happy. You do?"

Her terrified eyes startled in her face. "Me do," she breathed.

"Good," he said. "You wait. Me come. You see

Ulysses." He lowered his face close to hers. "You tell You die. Ulysses die."

While she still stood as if hypnotized, her heart pounding, he was gone, swallowed by the darkness. He went fast, back to his pirogue. He was thinking what he would tell Ulysses when he saw him. Ulysses had said to bring Fanchon back. But she was more use here, where she could kill the people of the house. He would tell Ulysses that the white master watched too well, he could not get Fanchon away. Ulysses would know no better.

Chapter XIII

Fanchon did not have to wait very long before Pierre le Bleu contacted her again. Shortly before dusk two days later, as she was shaking out the tablecloth following supper of the Castillouxs and De Laval, she heard a whistle from the bushes beyond the hedge that marked the extent of Monsieur Castilloux's lots in the town. With her heart pounding with trepidation she forced her way through the hedge. The long thorns clutched at her shirt and she had to snatch it loose. One of them dug into the calf of her leg. She could feel warm blood begin to run. But she shoved at the branches with her arms and sidled between them through the hedge. Humped in a clump of weeds on the other side of the street squatting back on his heels, she found Pierre le Bleu. His lips drew back from his gums as he watched her.

She stood over him. Her knees were shaking.

"You whistle. You want me go?" she suggested hopefully. "Me ready to go."

"No," he said, rising up out of the weeds, a lank shadow in the gloom. He thrust something into her hand. "You use this," he muttered. "When me tell, you do. Cut throat. Cut heart out."

179

She felt the cold thing in her fingers and, looking down, saw a bone handled skinning knife, whetted to a razor edge. She could not take her eyes off it. When she did Pierre le Bleu had vanished.

Her throat felt dry and scaly. In her agitation the knife slipped from her fingers and she had to stoop, groping for it in the deepening dark.

When she straightened her back she remembered what it was she had wanted. She had wanted to ask Pierre about Ulysses. But now he was gone. She slipped the knife into the fold of her apron.

"Fanchon!" It was old Michel calling her from the kitchen door. "What you do out here? Young mistress call for you. Hurry! If you do slow she mad at you and me, too!"

She hurried to the front of he house but her thoughts were still filled with what Pierre Bleu had said.

"Fanchon! Help me with this cloak!" Antoinette Castilloux snapped at her. Antoine Castilloux was standing at the door and in the street the Baron de Laval was beside the berline irritably waiting on the two of them.

Where they were going she did not know or care. She held the cloak on Antoinette's shoulders as she clasped it together at her neck and stepped away to allow her mistress to leave.

"Take this to my bedroom, I will not wear it after all," said Antoinette, placing something in her hand. "Place it on my small chest. Make sure that nothing happens to it or you will be punished."

Fanchon opened her hand and looked into it. It was the golden flower that Madame had worn that first morning in her bath. When she looked up they were outside. She closed it and turned to the stairs but her mind was filled with worry about Ulysses. She must catch Pierre.

Before she knew what she was about, she was stumbling down the street in the direction of the river. She had to find Pierre before he got to his boat. Yes, and she would make him let her cross the river where Ulysses was But when she reached the landing place it was dark on the river and there was no sign of Pierre or his boat. In a panic she began to run along the levee. She did not know what to do. She did not want to be a slave but she could not kill for it. She wanted to be with Ulysses, that was all she knew.

Jacqueline Martin jumped when Henri slid out of the tall weeds at the corner of the square. He was like an Indian the way he did it, and her heart kept hammering until it hurt her.

"Jacqueline," he said softly but with a grin. "I did not mean to scare you."

She had her breath back now. "No?" she said dryly. "I am sure."

She saw that he was entirely sober. His face was shaven and his hunting shirt was clean. He was staring at the heavy wooden bucket which she carried.

"Jacqueline," he said again. "Let me help you with that bucket. Let me get the water for you."

She shook her head, remembering that once before she had let him go to the river for water. That time he had stopped at Camille Billiot's and had returned hours later blind drunk, without the bucket. The clamor he had made had wakened Etienne and thrown him into a tantrum.

"It's late. It's dark." There was a pathetic kind of insistence in his voice. "You don't belong on the river at night. Let me help you Jacqueline."

She smiled wanly. "I had better go alone, Henri. You know it is so."

"Why didn't you go while it was light?"

"Etienne was ailing. He is asleep now. Don't stop me, Henri, I must hurry."

He blocked her way, crying angrily, "Then why didn't you send that little bitch who lives with you?"

"Hush!" she snapped. "Collette has a bad cold. Besides, she is too young. No one would bother me." He scuffed his moccasin in the dirt. "I sold some skins today," he said, and added meaningfully, "I'm going to Meunier's."

Jacqueline put here hand on his arm. "Don't do it, Henri. It does you no good."

He kept his eyes on the ground. "Hein? Why not? You will not look at me, drunk or sober." His voice quickened and rose. "You are a married woman, that is what you say. I must not come near you. Christ Jesus, it was bad enough when I thought you were telling the truth! But now there is MacDonald."

The color went out of her face and her eyes blazed at his tucked head. "Henri," she said between her teeth, "You had better go, now."

Her anger seemed to terrify him and he mumbled without articulation. Then, with the strangled sounds still going on in his throat, he wheeled from her and bolted.

She stood motionless listening to his footsteps until they had died away. She thought that her breast was empty as if she had no heart to feel. Everything which she touched, it seemed, was claimed by misery and frustration. Henri, Etienne, herself. The bail of the bucket screeched as her hand moved. She walked on slowly toward the river.

Darkness had fallen when she scrambled down the slimy side of the levee to the edge of the river. She could hear the gurgling of the water among the willow trunks at the foot of the levee where the rising river lapped higher and higher. Out upon the stream which flowed smoothly with a misty murmur there was yet a gray suggestion of light, but beneath the willows of the inundated batture night had already fallen. She went down the levee side cautiously, and knew that she was at the brink when her extended foot splashed water.

She drew back a little then, squatting upon her heels in the mud, and shifted the heavy bucket to her right hand. She heard the slap of its lip as she dipped it into the river, stretching out as far she could so that she would not scrape the muddy bottom. When she pulled it in the water was like thick soup in the bucket and yellow; but if she let it set for twenty-four hours the sediment would sink to the bottom of bucket and the water would be fit to drink. She was long used to it, and it was seldom now that she even thought of the good wells of the Natchez. There were no wells in Nouvelle Orleans, only crawfish holes.She steadied the bucket against her knee and rested. Her nerves were stretched taut. Henri, of course, was right.

It was downright dangerous for a lone woman to be there after dark. Behind her on the other side of the levee was a row of the trapper's shanties. One was not fifteen yards at her back. It was unlighted, which made her less uneasy. The owner must be away, but not far, because she could make out his pirogue, tied to a willow, rocking idly in the shallow water.

Overhead the stars had come out, glittering ice crystals upon the soft black sweep of the night. She tilted her head back, seeing the arch and expanse of the sky as an inverted bowl. She felt a breeze which set the bare willow twigs trembling, fingering at her hair. It was all utterly peaceful, with the whisper of the river and the dim cacophony of frogs from the pools behind the levee. She was not apprehensive any more, but glad that she had come. If only for a moment, she was outside the imprisoning walls of duty, away from the stark, soul killing task of administering to Etienne's needs and whims.

She thought: "Ciel, but I have always loved the open air in my face, and the smell of bark and the leaves. The smell and feel of the land out of which things grow." Her people had always lived and worked on the land until the salt of the earth was in their blood. But here in Nouvelle Orleans, there was no land. Only a piece of ground which was not hers nor Etienne's but the Western Company's, owed for, never to be paid for. From which they may be dispossessed any day or night. Only a weed patch and a tiny space called a garden where she had tried to make things grow in this soggy earth.

Always, these days, when she thought in that vein, she thought also of Evan MacDonald. Thinking of him, the warm blood stirred in her body and feeling it she became afraid. Her face set hard and she swung the bucket up. She must get home. If Etienne should waken he would be in a fret.

Up to the levee top she climbed with the bucket braced on her hip. Then she stood stock still. Someone was running headlong down the levee path. She could not move quickly enough, they collided and a great slop of water from the bucket drenched her petticoat. She clutched the bucket and managed to keep from falling. The runner, who had gone spinning and staggering, wheeled and leaped upon her. She could hear them gibbering in a kind of frenzy as they tore at her clothes, shoving her off balance so that she pitched full length to the ground. Looking up then, she saw silhouetted against the sky a woman, a lanky negress. Seeing a woman her relief was so great that it hurt in her breast.

The black woman stood panting. It was Fanchon, but to Jacqueline she was a total stranger. Fanchon's whole body was rigid. Her lips worked before they could form words. "White woman," she said, "What you do here?"

Jacqueline caught the terror in her voice, and her own subsided. She pushed herself up on her elbow, watching Fanchon.

"I was drawing water," she said. "I will not harm you if you are afraid of that."

Fanchon seemed to digest that.

"Get up," she said.

Jacqueline rose gingerly. Her clothing was drenched and muddy. She could feel mud on the side of her face. She saw Fanchon two yards away with the knife clutched in her hand. She might be dangerous, like a cornered animal thought Jacqueline. She would have to calm the woman's fears.

She heard the negress saying, "White woman, me want boat. Me want to cross river."

Jacqueline felt giddy. Now she would be rid of this savage. She pointed eagerly toward the boat tied among the willows.

"There is a pirogue. Take it"

Fanchon turned toward the boat. Then she stopped, a cunning light in her eyes. This white woman, if she let her go free would tell the others that she had gone. Then they might catch her before she found Ulysses.

She threatened Jacqueline with the knife. "You go. Me follow."

Jacqueline knew better than to argue with her. In a moment they were beside the pirogue.

"See," said Jacqueline, "I was telling the truth. Now, let me go. My husband is ill. I must go."

But Fanchon was no longer afraid of this white woman. Instead she found a strange exhilaration that the white woman must do as she commanded.

"No, white woman," she said, with conscious slyness, "You go tell. You get in boat."

Jacqueline opened her mouth to protest but a prodding motion of the knife made her hold her tongue. She stepped into the pirogue and began to loosen the rope. Fanchon splashed in the shallow water, and when the boat floated free scrambled in. She sat in the stern and directed Jacqueline to take a paddle and work the boat out of the willows. Jacqueline looked at the water but thought if she tried to jump now the knife would cut her spine. She pushed the paddle into the water and the pirogue slid through the sparse stand of willows toward the deeper stream.

Then they were out where the stars looked down on the murky river, and the wake of the pirogue made diverging ripples, half seen in the gloom. The pirogue still idled in the slow eddy of the counter current, but a short stone's throw beyond them the main current of the of the Mississippi fled past with a savage surge. The burden of the flood, chunks of wood, whole trunks of trees, mere phantoms in the dark, bobbed like corks on the torrent. Fanchon worked the second oar rudder fashion, at the rear of the boat, bringing the awkward craft about until they faced directly across the stream.

"Mother of God!" said Jacqueline, "You can't go straight across! It will carry us down for miles, if we ever get there at all." She peered at Fanchon. "Where is it you want to go!"

Fanchon held her arm in the direction of the point of land, invisible now, which marked the King's Plantation. Ulysses must be there, since that was where Pierre le Bleu lived, and Pierre had seen Ulysses.

Jacqueline stared at her. "There? But they'll catch you. You're a runaway slave? Hein?"

Then she wished she had held her tongue. The girl would be on guard now. It would have been better to let her go to the King's Plantation. Only God knew where the girl would take her now.

Fanchon eyed her. "Me say. You do, white woman. You row. Not, me kill."

She gloated in the fact that she was mistress of this pirogue. She pulled her oar again swinging the boat this time upstream.

"Row, white woman," she said.

Jacqueline looked at the river and knew that if the boat overturned she would drown, for she could not swim. She worked the paddle.

The shadow of the river shore slipped steadily past them as they moved farther and farther above the settlement and into the great crescent bend of the Mississippi. How far they had gone Jacqueline had no notion, but her back beneath the shoulders was already filled with a vast aching, when she heard Fanchon exclaim and stop paddling. Jacqueline raised her head.

Fanchon was pointing across the river. There on the opposite shore a fire made a fan shaped glow against the dark. It was not a large fire, because it lighted up nothing around it, nor cast any reflection which they could make out upon the river. There was nothing but the small patch of light above the dark line that was the level of the river. Obviously it was a campfire.

"Ulysses!" breathed Fanchon.

She knew that fire must mean Ulysses because Ulysses was on that side of the river. Go to the fire and she would find Ulysses.

Jacqueline relaxed, resting her weary arms upon the oar.

"Row!" Fanchon cried wildly. "We cross."

Once more she made as if to swing the pirogue into the stream.

"If you want to reach that campfire," said Jacqueline wearily, "we'll need to go up higher. Miles higher."

Fanchon seemed to know that what she said was the truth. She snatched savagely upon her oar so that the pirogue lunged upstream.

Jacqueline's oar steadied the boat. The dark shore upon their right began to slide past.

Presently they were abreast of the dim glare of the campfire and then, by slow degrees it commenced to fall astern. Later, after an eternity of rowing, Jacqueline looked wearily over her shoulder. The fire had now dimmed to an almost imperceptible glow, but whether that was because it had burned to embers or because of the distance, she could not tell.

It had disappeared entirely when they finally decided to cross the river.

The main current laid hold of the boat like a giant's hand pushing them down the stream. Jacqueline rowed until she could feel the muscles in her shoulders cracking. But the nose of the boat kept swinging downstream. She gripped her oar so tightly and worked it so desperately that her whole body took part in the struggle. She could feel her stomach growing smaller, tightening like and iron ring around the middle of her. It hurt her with a searing pain. Behind her she could hear Fanchon grunting and gasping with the exertion. The pirogue still held its course across the river, but they were being swept downstream rapidly. For many minutes she had forgotten their goal, and once, when she had cast a quick glance, there had been only the night and the river. The campfire had gone out or was invisible.

Then followed another agony of pulling the oar until she marveled that her racked body could still force itself in to stroke after stroke. She wanted only to drop the oar and stretch out in the bottom of the boat while the river carried her down to the sea. Her mind was too spent to tell why she did not yield, but somehow she was aware that it was not entirely the fear of the slave girl's knife that kept her fighting the river. It was a stubbornness which would not admit that even the Mississippi could When next she lifted her eyes from the river

Jacqueline saw the glow of the campfire. It was perhaps a quarter of a mile below her, and much dimmer, as if it had burned down after the builders had fallen asleep. But the reflections, as it flickered against the dark background of the forest, was as heartening as the fires of home. It was late, for the field of stars overhead had pivoted far to the west. Fanchon saw the glow and cried out, and they both set to rowing with might and made for the dark line of the shore which loomed suddenly not two hundred feet way, and the current of the river was already slackening its grip upon the pirogue.

Dark fell on the yellow flood of the river and turned it gray, the shore paling against the sky. A flock of herons passed overhead winging to the southward, the cry of one drifted down, muted by the height. Evan looked backward past the stern of the long bateau watching the shores of the river converging until they were lost in the deepening gloom.

The bateau belonged to a voyageur from the Illinois named Francois Petit, who was floating a load of salt beef down to Nouvelle Orleans. This was the fourth day out from the Natchez post where Evan and Gaston Lazac had boarded the bateau.

Francois Petit was a heavily muscled Canadian with an unkempt beard and a few snags of yellow teeth. The first day out Lazac had asked him if had seen any sign of Captain Leblanc's pirogue on the river.

Petit took a pinch of snuff first and worked his upper lip rapidly, wrinkling his nose like a rabbit. "He came to the fort the day before I left."

"By God he was fast," said Lazac. "Did you have any trouble coming down?"

Petit said no, the river had been quiet. No Indian sign, which he thought was perhaps because they knew D'Artaguette was coming down. Lazac asked why he thought that.

Petit shrugged. "No reason in particular. But, remember, gars, news travels fast in the woods. The Illinois didn't go against the Chickasaws last fall. Neither did the Weas. They gave a reason and that's as may be. But all the tribes from the Ouabache to Fort Charles have been knowing that it was likely a French army would march into Chickasaw country. They'll march, too, because they're our Indians. But, and I'm not blaming them, it's a way Indians have, when two tribes are fighting each other, only the good God knows how much traffic and talk goes on between them."

Lazac rubbed his big nose. "How long before D'Artaguette will be ready to move?"

"Not long," said Petit. "He had thirty soldiers from the garrison and was going to call in the woods runners and settlers. Monchervaux was going to the Cahokias and the Michigamias, and De Vincennes had word to bring in the tribes of the Ouabache. I think he'll march inside of two weeks, whether his Indians have come or not." He regarded Lazac in some surprise. "Listen, if Bienville is going to rendezvous with D'Artaguette in March he must be on his way. What are you doing here? Did he leave you behind?"

"Leave me behind?" Lazac roared, "Jesus, Bienville is still in Nouvelle Orleans. He'll be lucky if he's in Chickasaw country until the first of May. He sent a runner to D'Artaguette to delay his march."

Petit looked perturbed. "He'll likely catch him at Prudhomme Bluffs. Listen, Gaston, how in God's name can D'Artaguette keep two hundred Indians in camp at the bluffs for two months? They'll be breaking into parties and leaving him long before Bienville gets there. I think Bienville is crazy."

"No," said Lazac stubbornly. "He's had bad luck, that's all."

"I still think he's a fool," said Petit unimpressed. "I won't be joining him. Francois Petit won't be having his tail shot off just to burn some Natchez Indian town."

On the third day they had struck a snag off the German settlement and had to put in there for the night. In the morning they left late, having mended the leak, and had taken on board another passenger, a husky blond German youth, named Otto Schneider, who wanted to join Bienville's army. Petit had planned to reach Nouvelle Orleans that afternoon. But when dusk caught them two miles above the point at Montplaisir, he decided to tie up on the western shore rather than risk working the boat across river in the dark. As he watched a huge pine tree, double the bateau's length, lurched past them in the current.

Petit picked his spot and the bateau veered into the slack water along the wooded shore. There was a stand of willows in the shallows and the hump of a sand bar not yet covered. When the bateau began to scrape bottom two of the boatmen went over the side thigh high deep in the water and got a line around the big willow. The bateau scarcely drew three feet of water loaded. She came in steadily over the sandy bottom.

"Merde," said Petit when they had a fire going, "I had my mind made up to sleep in Nouvelle Orleans tonight. Those German women are too small."

Lazac grinned. "You like them big?"

Petit nodded. "Listen, the last time I was in Nouvelle Orleans, two years ago, there was one I liked. Clementine, they called her."

"I know," said Lazac, laughing as he winked at Evan. "She is married to Camille Billiot now."

Petit looked his disgust. "Baste!" he muttered. "That little excrement!"

Then he wrapped himself in his blanket and went to sleep. Soon they were all asleep except Lazac. From force of habit more than anything else, he made a circuit of the camp, watching the woods. But there was nothing and he came back and lay down with the others.

Ulysses was hungry. The sight of that bateau loaded with salt meat opened the saliva openings in his mouth. He bellied down behind the bushy little hump of a ridge which separated him from the river and watched the white men wading in the water. They had a line around the willow tree and were warping the boat in against the willows at the head of a narrow sandbar which was still dry ground above the river level.

Ulysses looked at Toutou who was flattened out beside him. Toutou nodded his head. Both of them took another look and then slid away into the woods before the white men had finished tying the boat. The woods were still and filled with the approach of night. Ulysses stumbled a little, feeling the water in his knee joints, and Toutou cursed him.

When they were out of earshot of the white men, Toutou clutched Ulysses' shoulder.

"You scared?" he said.

Toutou's eyes were savage. "Meat!" he said. "Meat! We starve. They have meat."

He thumped his belly like a drum, then reached out and thumped Ulysses'. "You want meat?"

"Me--want--meat," he said, terrifying himself with his own words.

Toutou said nothing, but he went fast through the woods and Ulysses followed. They had covered a league when they came into a glade where there was a small hut built of boughs and bark. Three black men were in the glade, Basile and the other man who had picked Ulysses up in the river, and a skinny boy of perhaps sixteen years.

The boy was trying to build a fire in a dug cavity, but Toutou rushed forward and kicked it to pieces. The boy flopped back on his buttocks yelping in terror.

"No fire!" snarled Toutou. "White men on river!"

The dull faces of the two men grew animated with fear. The boy went over on his hands and knees.

"O, le Bon Dieu!" he prayed. "O, le.."

Toutou slapped him sprawling. "White man's god. Do nothing for you."

The boy whimpered. "Only God I know. I born here."

Toutou lifted his long arm and shook his fist in the direction of the river. "Meat!" he cried, hoarsely. "You live on roots. You live on nothing. Your belly shrinks. White man's boat has meat. You eat."

He was gratified to see that hunger overcame their fear. Basile and the other man edged closer to him. Only the boy still whined.

"Soon they sleep," said Toutou. "We kill."

They squatted down, waiting in the dark. It had been a long time since their bellies had been full. They had almost forgotten how it felt, but now as they waited they began to imagine it.

In his sleep Lazac heard the sound in the woods and was awake instantly. The wind had shifted to the west and it brought him the sound again, a footfall back in the woods. He had his hand on his firelock and his other hand jerked the shoulder of Evan MacDonald, who was next to him. Evan rolled, muttering, and Lazac's hard palm silenced him when he awoke.

"Wake up the rest of them," whispered Lazac.

"Something is in the woods."

While Evan blinked at him Lazac slid off, crawling low toward the little ridge behind the bar. Still groggy from sleep Evan watched his butt end receding from him and suddenly comprehended what Lazac had said. He clutched his firelock, snapping open the pan to see that the priming was good.

There was no sound while he woke Petit. The fire had ebbed to a flush of coals in the dark. Lazac had been lost in the shadow of the ridge. As Petit sat up in his blanket, a grunting barrel of a man, Evan clearly heard water splash on the silent river. His eyes went that way beyond the dying fire. At first he saw nothing. Then it was there, materializing from the gloom, a boat not a hundred yards from shore with two figures in it.As he strained to make it out the men around him began to stir, cursing, from their blankets. Then bedlam erupted in the woods at their backs. A whoop, clear, and then broken off, a clamor of voices and the roar of a gun That would be Lazac. Evan wheeled away from the river, forgetting the boat. The boatmen were up with guns in yelled at them and they took cover on the sand in a ragged line facing the ridge. A line of shadows sprang up on the ridge, shadows of men. One man was screaming continuously. Then they came. Evan could make them out in the dark. Four or five dark figures. He saw the flash from his firelock and felt the recoil in his arms before he knew he had pulled the trigger. A wavering fringe of flashes came from the boatmen like a cluster of fireflies in the dark. One negro tumbled forward on his knees, struck by a ball, and began clawing at the sand like a dog gone mad.

Then, as suddenly as they had come, they had vanished, except for a huge black brute who came straight ahead in a perfect frenzy of fear, leaping full at Evan who was fumbling to reload. The man's body hurled him to the sand and the man went charging over him and plunged splashing into the river.

Evan rolled over, groping for the gun he let fall, and his attention was riveted on the river. The negro was swimming powerfully directly toward the boat which had drifted in. Evan began to fumble at his powder horn. There were two figures in the boat. They came almost upright, struggling with each other. Evan cursed spilling the powder.

Women, one of them white and one black. He was on his feet, running. The negro swimmer had reached the boat. His hands clutched the gun whale tilting it down. The struggling women tottered. One of them fell outward and the other pulled free, saving herself. It was the white woman who pitched into the river, crying out once as she fell. She went under at once and the cries stopped.

With all his clothes on, Evan went into the stream. The bank sheered off almost immediately. The water was chilly as he swam, weighted down by his clothes. The white woman's head came above the surface and she thrashed helplessly in the water. He was almost in reach of her. Already the big negro had scrambled into the pirogue and was pulling out into the river. Evan did not look at him. There was a shot from shore and water splashed as the ball went wide of the boat which was rapidly being swallowed by the gloom.

Evan's left arm went around the woman as she was going down. Her struggles became a frenzy. He twisted her about and got his fingers in her long, dark hair. He swam in towing her slowly, and saw Lazac wading out to help him. He let his feet down and found the bottom and Lazac eased him of his burden.

"Jesus!" said Lazac. "It's Jacqueline!"

Evan stood shivering, his clothes a soggy mass. He could only look at the woman's face, white as death, and her closed eyes.

Lazac muttered, "She's got a bellyful of the river," and rolled her over a willow snag to get the water out of her. Evan watched him, conscious of his own empty hands hanging idle. They seemed as heavy as his head. When Lazac turned her over and he saw that she breathed, he sat flat down in the sand and put his head on his knees.

Terror added to Ulysses' giant strength. He drove the pirogue through the darkness so swiftly that the shots from shore were wide of the mark. He was out of range when he heard a man swimming and the sound made his shoulders lurch into another effort.

The man treaded water and cried out. It was Toutou. Even then Ulysses was of a mind to go on. He did not know why he stopped and let the squat man pull himself aboard.

"Me cut off in woods," muttered Toutou. "See boat. Swim out." He looked back down the river. "No good here. We get away."

Ulysses let his arm spread for him as they propelled the pirogue mightily through the darkness. He felt that he could row forever if every stroke took him farther from the sound of the white men's guns. Now that their firing had long since ceased, the remembered horror had made his insides cold.

Toutou took the second oar from Fanchon and the girl turned, crouching, to look at Ulysses. For a long time she simply kept her eyes on him, and his presence seemed to comfort her as her presence comforted him.

"Where we go, Ulysses?" she said, at last.

Ulysses shook his head, it was Toutou who replied.

"Chickasaws," he replied.

It meant nothing to Fanchon. "Chickasaws?" she repeated. "Where?"

Toutou pointed to the north. "Long way. Maybe two hundred leagues. We get there. Hide in day, travel in night. You be free."

It was enough for Fanchon. She was with her man. That was all she wanted.

"We get there, Ulysses," she said.

Ulysses looked up and his fear fell away and he grinned. He heard the smash of his oar in the river and the yellow water fleeing behind.

Chapter XIV

The woods were quiet and filled with the long russet shadows of the sun, though the sun itself was yet invisible. Gaston Lazac let his musket-butt rustle in the dead leaves and looked at the deserted bark hut. Francois Petit squatted above the little fire pit and scratched at the dead ashes.

"Old fire," he said, looking around at Lazac. "This is where they'd been camping. But they didn't stop here last night."

Lazac grunted. "This ought to satisfy Salmon and Mallot and Castilloux. They and their slave plots! We got two, that I know of, but no telling how many there were."

Petit sifted the dead ashes through his fingers while Lazac walked the edge of the camp site.

"I'll bet ten sols they're running yet," he grinned. "When you scare one of those brutes he stays scared for a couple of years. I remember once at Old Fort Rosalie I took a shot at one who had been stealing off my boat. He didn't stop running until he crossed the Pearl River." He stood up and wiped his hands against his thighs. "Are you going chasing after them?"

Lazac was walking away from the camp and into the woods upriver. "One of them will not run too far. There is blood over here." He leaped into the trees with the others following.

Gaston Lazac could not read a word but he could read a trail in the woods as well as any man. In less than a mile from the camp they found a black boy of sixteen or seventeen years lying among the palmettos. He was bleeding from his abdomen and had collapsed. He would go no further. The white men knew that he would not last long but the young German lad tried to give him some water. He coughed it back up and looked at the men.

"Oh, le bon Dieu!" he cried softly. "Please forgive my sin."

"He will forgive you if you tell us the truth," Lazac told the boy. Then he asked, "Where are the others?"

"Others?" he looked perplexed. "Basile stabbed by white man. Toutou ran to river. I run to camp."

"And the others?"

"No others," the boys eyes began to glaze.

"No others? By le bon Dieu?" exhorted Lazac.

"No others," said the boy. "Oh, le bon Dieu. Oh, le bon. . ." His eyes glazed for good as the breath released from his body.

"Bienville will be glad to hear that there are no runaways fomenting trouble," Petit said.

"It would appear so," responded Lazac. "But our people should remain cautious."

"Do not fear, Francois Petit will remain in Nouvelle Orleans while you are gone after Indians. There will not be trouble," said the big man.

Evan could only remember the look on the faces of the De Pradels and Antoinette.

They found Petit's crew in the edge of the woods smoothing leaves over the two shallow graves they had scooped with their hatchets in the sandy earth, one for the man shot in the attack and another for Basile, who had practically run into Lazac in the darkness. They dug another for the boy. At a little distance, on the edge of the sand bar, Jacqueline Martin sat on the sand. Evan MacDonald walked up behind her.

She had nothing to say, so, despite his uneasiness, he quietly sat down near her until the men were ready to embark.

Francois Petit crossed the river above the point at Montplaisir and let the bateau float down the eastern shore past the plantation of the Jesuits to the mooring place at the Place d'Armes.

Jacqueline sat in the bow of the bateau watching the sunlight make spangles on the choppy river. The sun was warm across her shoulders, burning through her clothing It was late February, Spring was out of its bivouac and marching. She could see its advance guard green on the margins of the river. She relaxed with the warmth in her body; a kind of spring in her body, a drowsiness, an awareness that did not go deep enough to thaw the cold apprehension around her heart. The moment of lassitude passed and her shoulders were again tense.

Evan knelt beside her. Behind them the boatmen were idle while the boat floated, listening to Lazac and Petit swapping tales at the stern.

Her silence embarrassed Evan and made him fidget. She had spoken scarcely a word all morning. The way her body sagged and the profile of her face, quite wan, quite tired, induced a strange feeling in him. His one impulse as he watched was to put his arm around her.

"What is it?" he blurted. "What is it that troubles you?"

He had not meant to ask her that. But, somehow, he had to, the way his thoughts were spinning.

She turned her face up to him and he wished with all his heart that she would look away. The dread behind her dark eyes was a thing which should never be there, and a thing, above all, which was of no concern of his, whatever the bewildering emotions which plagued him now.

"Why," she began and hesitated. "Why, it is Etienne. I am worried. He was alone all the night." Then she added, "Except for Collette, but he will not allow her near him."

"Nonsense!" said Evan. "Nothing has happened to him." He was thinking that what weighed so heavily upon her was not the unlikely prospect that harm had come to Etienne during the night. He had seen enough of Etienne to know that her dread must be rather for the way the crippled man would regard her night's absence.

When she spoke it as if she had read his mind.

"He will be frantic for me," she said, twisting a fold of her skirt between her fingers. "I have never been a night away from him. Not since he came home from the Black River. He will not know what to say."

"If he sees me", reflected Evan grimly, "he will say that you have been with me."

Again, startling him, she seemed to keep pace with his thoughts, or to read them in his face. My God, he wondered, am I so guileless and transparent as that?

"He will blame Henri," she said, smiling wryly.

Evan grimaced but she shook her head.

"Poor Henri. You are as bad as Etienne. You don't understand Henri."

"I think I understand him," answered Evan.

"You never could. He is like a little child sometimes. Always he comes to me. No, I am not afraid of Henri, not really, even when he is drunk." Her eyes were on the river and she was thinking: "Always he has come to me, yet last night he ran from me, and I could have killed for the thing he said, even though it were true."

Evan moved his lips silently. Her slender shoulders drooping beneath the blue cloth, curve of her neck and the dark mass of her hair claimed his attention. He was not merely satisfied that it was he had pulled her out of the river, he was glad. The droop in her shoulders, it went to his heart. His hand moved but he did not touch her remembering the boatmen at their backs. Instead he lifted his hand and pointed.

"Look! They have the boats in the river. The boats for the army."

She raised her head. "They have been there a week now. Soon they will go, and you will go." The last words were scarcely more than a whisper which he did not hear because his mind was upon the boats.

The levee front seemed full of boats, long cypress-sided bateaux, new bateaux, smelling of tar and fresh worked lumber: old bateaux, grayed by all kinds of weather. They lay in a long line beneath the leafing willows, riding high and swinging in the muddy wash of the river. A corporal's guard of white coats watched them, with their firelocks loose on their shoulders, shambling short beats along the levee path.

Francois Petit brought his bateau in at the head of the line and laid her alongside the levee, and one of the men jumped ashore to make her fast to a cypress pile. Jacqueline did not wait until his job was done, she was over the gunwale almost as quickly as he was, and scrambling up the side of the levee. Her foot slipped, sending her upon her knees in mud and Evan caught up with her. He helped her to her feet.

On the levee top she disengaged her arm and pulled away from him.

"I must go now," she said hurriedly.

He looked away down the miry street.

"Perhaps I --"

"No, no, no!" she burst out vehemently that one of the white coats pacing near halted and stared. "You stay here –– anywhere -- but don't go with me."

She almost plunged off the levee leaving him in a foolish attitude with his hand extended to help her. At the foot she paused and looked up. Her pale face was so distressed that it shocked him.

"Don't think --" she dropped her hands helplessly. "You saved my life -- don't think I -- but --"

In his agitation he lost his sense of hers.

"It was nothing," he muttered brusquely, beginning to wish that she would go, because now Lazac and Petit and the boatmen were climbing onto the levee behind him and hearing every word.

Her dark eyes watched him, marking his impatience and then she turned without another word and hurried off, pulling up her petticoat a little so that she could go faster.

She felt their natural strength coming back into her legs, as she went up the long street at a half run. Her weakness now was all at the pit of her stomach, and it was purely a weakness of anticipation. She knew that her fears were well founded when she saw Collette huddled like a forlorn kitten on the door step.

The girl sprang up, her skirts flouncing, and ran to the fence while Jacqueline was still fumbling at the gate.

"Mother of God!" Collette panted. "Where have you been?"

Jacqueline caught her breath. "Etienne? How is he?" She had the gate open, but Collette clutched her shoulder as she tried to pass.

"Don't go in there," she cried. "That madman! He'll kill you! He's raving, I tell you. All night long. Lying there with his face like a gargoyle on Notre Dame, damn him! The names he has called you! And me, too!" She laughed shrilly. "I gave him some, myself. If he could have got out of his bed he would have murdered me. But he could not, and I had got his gun and put it in the corner out of his reach. Then I laughed at him, and he was like a mad thing, I thought he would burst a blood vessel."

Jacqueline swayed with her hands on her temples. "Oh, Collette! You should never have done so! You --"

Collette spat angrily. "That God Damn! He had no right to call people the names they don't deserve.

Besides, he is not so sick as he makes out or he would have died the way he carried on."

Jacqueline wet her dry lips. "What did he say?"

For once Collette's tongue failed her. "I would not say it to you," she muttered, looking away. "Let him tell you. I think he will."

She sat down upon the steps with her back to the door and her face was very red as Jacqueline went inside.

Etienne lay there one his bed watching over the door as a cat watches over a rat's hole. His face was the color of old bone, and his eyes, like craters, lit up with a volcanic fire when his prey came through the door.

His whole body seemed to lift at the sight of her until he sat painfully upright, his face breaking out in a great sweat at the strain. His lips drew back from his teeth.

"You --," he began and choked. "You harlot! You come back here? You dare to come back here? To my house?"

Her hands had closed the door and they remained there behind her, palms against the wood, supporting her rigid body. Her face was dead white, even to the lips.

"Etienne!" Her stiff lips barely stirred.

That she shrank back from his wrath seemed to fill him with gloating. "Hold your tongue! Don't speak to me! Adulteress! Faithless --" He cursed her with relish and incoherent vileness.

As if a spring somewhere in her had been pressed, she moved. He saw her, one instant crouched against the door, afraid of him; the next, she had crossed the narrow interval between them and stood like a threat, tense and panting.

"You shall not speak to me!" Before her stark fury he shrank, incredulous against his pillow. "My God! You ungrateful --. When I have nursed you. When I have worked my fingers to the bone for you." She ground her teeth to stop the twitching muscles in her face. Gradually, as she fought it, control returned to her and the glare faded from her eyes. She sank weakly upon the edge of the bed. For minutes she was silent, looking at him, and he was still stricken dumb from her outburst.

"Etienne, I am sorry," she said at last, tiredly, picking nervously at the bed covering. "It does no good to call you names. I know you were worried. But I could not come home. If I had tried, that girl would have killed me." She went on, speaking with no animation whatever, to tell him the events of the past night. He did not look once at her and from his expression she could not be sure that he believed her.

"This bateau," he said, when she reached that part. "Whose was it? Who was in it?"

"It belonged to a man named Petit, and there was his crew and Gaston Lazac and," she hesitated, "and Monsieur MacDonald."

The small edge of relief which had been dawning in Etienne's eyes vanished.

"MacDonald!" His voice was hoarse with horror. "You spent all night with him!"

All at once her patience was ended. She stood straight up and looked down contemptuously at him.

"No," she said, deliberately, "I did not -- but if I choose, I shall."

Her calmness broke him. His jaw sagged and his bottom lip thrust out and began to shake, violently, uncontrollably.

"I knew it," he quavered. "He is your lover. I'm nothing to you. I knew it when I saw you change. You used never to begrudge me."

"You jealous fool!" she said, stamping her foot and watching his face jerk at the vehement sound. "You're talking nonsense."

She turned her back on him, her shoulders twitching angrily, knowing that in one sense he has spoken the truth. She had changed. Never before had she begrudged him anything or spoken sharply to him. Always such vanities had been solely his prerogative. She felt a swift and wicked delight in having, for once, turned his weapons upon him. Then her moment of triumph was past as she heard his gulping sobs begin. He had disarmed her as he always would. With her head hanging, she came back to the bed. "Etienne," she said, knowing that it would be a long time before he would condescend to listen.

The High Mass was over. Dressed in their Sunday best, the inhabitants issued from the St. Louis Church into the bright February sunshine and lingered round the steps. Some, who were able to read, inspected the official notices upon the church door but most of them merely idled, enjoying the unaccustomed sun, and gossiping among themselves. They knew enough to wait, even before the white coated drummer who stood at the step's edge raised his sticks and banged his drum for attention. The town crier appeared from within the church, pulling his new brushed blue coat and loosening his stock so there would be no constriction about his throat. He shuffled his papers ostentatiously and exploded his throat clear like a pistol's report. Behind him came Bienville, Salmon and Monsieur Fleuriau, the King's Attorney-General.

The drummer ceased his beating and let his sticks hang idle. His was jaw limp in a yawn, for he had been out late the night before and had had God's own time creeping undetected back to the barracks.

The crier's high, rapid voice flowed out over the heads of the crowd, making straight swift channels of sound as he turned this way and that. His first cry had to do with a sheriff's sale of property to be held upon the Saturday next. The people only half listened, since few among them had the means to buy any property however cheaply it sold. They only stayed because it was required that they remain to hear the announcements cried.

Jacqueline Martin came out between Gustave and Therese Lambert. Gustave stopped by the door to spell out the notices fastened upon it. Therese's tongue wagged like a pendulum, a stroke to a second, but Jacqueline was not really listening. She kept rising on tiptoe, peering this way and that over people's heads. When she did see Evan MacDonald, with Gaston Lazac not twenty feet away and coming toward her, her heart turned over. She still felt free of shame. Hadn't she made up her mind this morning and come, out of piety, not expressly to see him? Why pretend that she was not glad? He had saved her life. He bowed to her and Therese as well as he could in the press of people. The sun was bright on his hair, his lean face quite clean and strong. She now felt a flutter and wished to satisfy herself that her feeling was not merely the foolish fancy of a loved starved maid. Yet she wanted to satisfy herself without thinking consciously about it. After all, she had seen him but few times. It made her feel good just to look at him without thinking. She must keep away from thinking, because then she would realize how wide the gulf between them was and utterly futile it was to think or feel the way that she had come to realize that she did.

She scarcely heard the crier as he droned on and on, nearly through with his announcements. It was the break in his voice which aroused her attention. She looked at him and saw his thin pale lips stretching to form words.

"In order that the citizens of Nouvelle Orleans be not ignorant of matters concerning their security, His Excellency the Commandant-General, the Sieur de Bienville requests me to make known to them the following activities of the military:

"Two companies for the prosecution of the war against the savages of the north will depart for Mobile next Sunday, being the company of citizen militia of Monsieur Morant, Captain, and the company of volunteers of Monsieur Lesueur, Captain. The French and Swiss troops of this garrison will follow as the boats are made ready. The people of Nouvelle Orleans are petitioned to attend the mass which will be held in behalf of the departing troops on the Sabbath next, which is the twenty-sixth day of February in this year of grace, seventeen hundred and thirty-six."

His pale lips closed over the end of his words. At his nod the drum was tapped. People began to move on, spreading and thinning into the street. But Jacqueline could not stir. The volunteers! Evan was in that company, he would go with them, only Sunday next. Now he was laughing at something Gaston had said, wholly undisturbed at the prospect of leaving within a week. She could not bear his unconcern, she felt a crazy urge to say something that would knock him out of it.

As she opened her mouth a boy came racing along the margin of the Place D'Armes. He had on a pair of breeches with a patched seat which hung almost to the bend of his knees behind, and he was yelping continually like an excited puppy.

"The soldiers! In the boats! The soldiers! At the levee!"

Gaston Lazac yelled after him. "What soldiers, gars?"

The boy's whelps diminished like an echo as he tore away. "White coats! White coats! White coats!"

207

His cry was like a cord pulling everyone to the river. The church goers who had headed for home began to drift off past the pickets of the Place D'Armes.

"Let's go," said Jacqueline eagerly, pulling at Therese's elbow. She did not want to go and be reminded either of the last time her man went to war or the danger to Evan now.

As they moved down by the Rue St.Pierre, Camille Billiot and Clementine fell in with the crowd. Camille was feeling good. He sidled beside Lazac and spoke behind his hand.

"I rooked that dumb ox Francois Petit last night. You should have seen it. He saw I held the cards but he was too stupid to know where they came from," he tittered.

"I have half of what he made from his voyage down river, now, maybe more. But don't tell Clementine, she'll be scratching after the last sol like a hen after an earthworm."

Lazac grinned lazily. "Petit will tell her himself tonight."

"Eh," said Camille blithely, "He'll be ashamed to confess himself such a fool." He broke off to look at the bateaux with soldiers disembarking. "What post is that, Gaston?"

Lazac squinted at the white coats filing along the top of the levee to the tapping of a drum.

"Fort Jean Batiste in the Natchitoches," said Lazac. "That's the captain on the left, the tall, slim one. I can not place him. It is not St. Denis." A lithe, swaggering figure, the officer, who was not a captain but a lieutenant, strode along the levee. The sunlight struck upon his bright lapel and made his buttons gleam. He spied Bienville struggling up the side of the embankment. Out came his sword. He flourished it high. His voice was clear as a bell.

"Vive le Roi!"

The people responded with a ragged cheer. "Vive le Roi!"

Not so many of them called out, but an odd sensation like a chill ran through them all. Somehow the drum and the marching men and the cheer all together stirred them, these humble, harried, struggling people upon the banks of a muddy river five thousands of miles from Versailles. Jacqueline felt the thrill as sharply as anyone. She found herself turning to look up at the flag, the golden lilies that meant France to them, drooping above the Place. Out of the corner of her eye she saw that Evan and Gustave and Therese and Clementine had all done the same. Only Gaston and Camille were more interested in the soldiers.

On the levee Bienville and the lieutenant from the Natchitoches had finished their greeting. The officer waved his hand. The sergeant barked, and the firelocks fell aslant as the men moved off toward the Qua triers dogged by urchins shrieking with enthusiasm and dancing to the drum. The drummer was a slim lad of thirteen or fourteen, the son of one of St. Denis's sergeants. The sleeves of his coat were too long. He had rolled the cuffs back upon his wrists and fastened them back with a bit of string. But his face beamed and his fingers proudly whirled the sticks.

Therese made a face. "Soldiers, do they call them. Ragbags under cocked hats!" But she blew her nose loudly.

"Ciel, I should be at home seasoning my poor soup."

Jacqueline laughed. "You old cheat! You feel like these little boys do when they beat the drum. Like I do. But then I always think 'How many will come back?' "

Evan looked at her and saw that the expression of stillness had returned to her eyes. It was as if they watched inwardly some recess of her being. Her face was half turned from him, he did not imagine that he was in her mind at all. Camille Billiot had capered a few steps after

209

the soldiers. Now he came back, grinning broadly, as delighted as any of the urchins.

"Did you see that young turkey with the drum?" he exclaimed. "His coat would have looked better on a man like me. His drum, too." He made the motions of beating a drum. "By God," he declared very pleased with himself, "but I could make a noise!"

Francois Petit leered from Camille to Clementine. "Why don't you go into the army, gars?"

Camille blinked. "I would if I had not wife," he said quickly. "Billiot! That's a name for a soldier. My brother Jean is at Fort Conde. You know Jean."

Petit filled his lip with snuff and worked it like a rabbit. "I know he stole more that ten piastres worth of pelts from me five winters ago. I know he is king of the rascals, and that he is not the only one of his name."

"So you think that?" said Camille cutting his eyes at Clementine. He decided the conversation was getting on bad ground and kept his mouth closed.

The sound of the drum was fading into the distance. Camille and Clementine moved down the levee toward their cabin. Therese pulled at Gustave and said again that she must go. Jacqueline went with them leaving Evan and Lazac leaning upon the pickets of the Place. Probably by this time Etienne and Collette were fighting like a cat and dog, she thought. But she felt no need to hurry. It was good to laze along, to be warmed by the sunlight and the sense of inner peace. She had come to mass to satisfy herself, and although she had said little and Evan had said little, she was satisfied. Now her mind was set like a mastiff's grip, it would not let go. She had always been like that.

CHAPTER XV

The feeling of war settled heavily upon Nouvelle Orleans during the last days of February. From the Commandant-General, laboring on the last of his preparations, and the Capuchin Superior of the Parish, mindful of the salvation of the men about to march into battle, down to the last debt ridden tradesman, the last strumpet, the last fisherman or fishwife under the levee, not any could escape it. All their senses became accustomed to it. They could hear it in the shuffle of leather of troops filing out to the bayou. They could see it in the dull gray glint of the sun on the firelocks. They could taste it in the scantier rations they had because of the army's requisitions or smell it in the stink of hot pitch at the Marine Forges where the last of the big bateaux were being caulked.

The battlefield might be two hundred leagues and many weeks away, but the implements of war were more in evidence every day, and the flesh and blood for carrying the battle. Not even the winter of '31, when Perier de Salvert had been mustering his Black River expedition had there been so much coming and going of men under arms, or so many big boats lying along the levee waiting to be loaded with military supplies.

In that last week of February, Bienville had more than four hundred men under arms in Nouvelle Orleans. In addition to the four regular French companies in garrison he had the company of Swiss mercenaries, the detachments from the Natchez and the Natchitoches, the two companies of citizen militia and Lesueur's newly formed volunteer corps. If he could have put this entire force into the field together with the troops at Mobile he would have been well pleased, but the circumstances of protecting the river settlements deterred him. What measures that must be taken were taken.

He detached thirty men from each of the four French companies and formed them into full companies of that complement under their captains in the garrison: De Haurterive, De Membrede, De Coustillhas, and De Benac. He drew a half-company of fifty men Swiss mercenaries under the Swiss captain, Duparc; added the men from the Natchez and Natchitoches, Morant's Militia and Lesueur's woods runners. This makeshift force gave him in round numbers three hundred men, not counting one hundred free negroes bearing no arms whom he intended to employ mainly as porters.

The rest, the remnants of the French and Swiss companies and Louis Joseph Dubreuil's militiamen, he assigned to the command of the Chevalier de Louboey for the protection of the capital. He anticipated no danger to Nouvelle Orleans itself, but there were hostile bands still roving in the wilderness north of the Tunica. The better part of wisdom was to keep this force where it could move to any part of the lower river and maintain the security of the King's domain.

As his troops were ready he had them move out. On Sunday the twenty-sixth, Morant's militia and Leseuer's volunteers made the portage to the Bayou St. Jean and embarked in six large pirogues for Mobile. Within a week they were followed by Duparc's Swiss, the men from Natchez and the Natchitoches, and a company of free negroes.

Almost every day men marched out to the Bayou and the oxen of Louis Dubreuil's teamsters leaned in their yokes and hauled the boats over the spongy road.

Saying a mass over the men and watching them as they marched away, Pere Philippe de Luxembourg, pastor of the parish, felt a heaviness in his heart. In a little while it would be time for the spring planting to begin. He had seen bad plantings and worse harvests from people who knew little of either. This season promised to be the worst of all. He wondered what manner of planting and of what manner of harvest, of blood and suffering, it would bring forth.

March came in with an unseasonable heat. The earth, rains, began to dry out. The river seemed to stretch itself like a lazy yellow snake warming in the sun, swishing higher and higher among the willows which had already begun to leaf. In the Place D'Armes the withered, gray grass gave way to green.

Work was the order of the day from Bienville himself down to the negro porters loading the boats below the Place. Bienville did not spare himself. He ate scantily because his stomach continued to trouble him, and got too little sleep, allowing himself barely four hours in twenty-four. Each morning his face seemed thinner and more stony.

He and Evan had made their peace, and Evan had again taken up residence in Bienville's house. For Bienville's part, he had driven himself so hard these last weeks that he often felt need for relaxation and companionship. Although their wills so often clashed, he was really fond of Evan, and meant to keep an eye on him. He respected Evan for confronting him, unlike those who worked behind his back to undermine everything he did in order to further their own, selfish interests. In Evan's case, he could not see Antoinette anyway, as she was at Cannes Brulees. That bone of contention was put off if not removed. They both accepted that fact and made their truce on the strength of it.

Evan had joined Jean-Paul Lesueur's company but had not gone when the bulk of the volunteers moved out to Mobile. Neither had Gaston Lazac nor Henri Martin nor, for that matter, Lesueur himself. The veteran scouts and woods runners of Lesueur's corps comprised an elite group subject to few restrictions. All the captain asked was that all of them be at Mobile when Bienville's army was ready to move. He did not care the least how they got there or what day, as long as they got there in time.

On the third of March, Bienville sat with Evan on the belvedere of his house looking out over the leafing clumps of willows lay the quiet river. Bienville sat low in his chair, a weary brooding figure. He was almost ready now and, far from bringing him relief, that fact weighed upon his mind. His bateaux would be filled that night. God knew they had been hard to get. Only a half dozen had come from Castilloux and the other contractors. He had hired the rest from settlers at a rate of thirteen livres ten sols for each day he had them in use. He could hear the negroes chanting as they worked and the sound lulled him until he caught himself at the point of dozing.

Tomorrow, Sunday, after he had dispatched the bateaux down the river, he would go himself along the Sound and along the coast to Mobile, and for him there would be memory in every mile.

Since 1699, save for his eight years of exile in Paris, he had lived at one point or another along this strange paradox of a coast. Barren and fertile, wind whipped, fever haunted, which was at once a window upon paradise and the doorstep of hell. Old Fort Louis, Fort Conde, the two Biloxis, Nouvelle Orleans. Names which lingered in his memory like the throb of Indian drums; landmarks along the bitter, thankless road he had followed in cutting to a pattern the formless ambitions for an empire overseas of the monarchs he had served. Biloxi had taken Sauvolle. Fort Louis had taken De Tonti. Havana, which was not far from this coast, had taken his own brother, D'Iberville.

Yet he was glad he had spent his life along it. He felt that his labors were not fruitless. D'Iberville had said more than thirty five years ago that the Protestant country, England, whose pioneers along the Atlantic seaboard, would soon push inland for the valley of the Mississippi, would in a hundred years occupy the whole of America unless opposed by a persistence equal to their own.He had tried without deviating to furnish that persistence. Time alone could tell whether he had been successful. He, himself, would not live to know. He eyed Evan across the veranda. Perhaps this young man would remain to continue the struggle.

Yes, tomorrow he would go to Mobile after he had knelt in the parish church and asked the help of his God. His lips moved: "Almighty God, look upon the desires of our humble hearts and stretch forth thy helping arm to be our defense against all our enemies."

The Mobile River, dirty and green tinged with the tidewater of the bay, flowed between the main shore and the finger of land which tapered to a sandbar opposite Fort Conde. At midmorning the sentry walking the parapet above the fort could overlook the island and Polecat Bay beyond, which was invisible form the riverfront, and beyond that the marshy mouths of the Tensas River. Looking from his height across the tangle of inlets there were many points of land thrusting out into the dirty, dim bay until the sight of them was swallowed up in the distance. Below the fort the bay itself broadened into a sweep of water which ran seaward to the horizon and to east and west was confined by the vague blue lines of the mainland shores.

The sentry eased his firelock upon his shoulder and glanced down at the boats lying at anchor by the wharf which extended across the miry ground between the fort and the river. He saw the long pirogue in which the Commandant-General, the Sieur de Bienville, had arrived less than an hour ago. There was the captain of Bienville's boat crew, a bear of a man, squatting on the wharf and talking with a couple of voyageurs who had just come in from the Alabamas.

Diron D'Artaguette's house was in the third square north of the fort, a pleasantly situated house, facing southward, of pine lumber whitened by lime wash, with a high pitched roof and a small gallery at the front. At its back was an extensive garden in which slaves were already at work breaking ground for the spring planting.

Bienville and D'Artaguette had retired to the post commander's office at the southwest corner of his house. Along the street the oak trees were beginning to sprout new leaves and an Indian who came along beneath them shuffled through the dead leaves being pushed aside by the new. The Indian was a Choctaw, with a French blanket on his back and he was heading back into the town. Back toward the trail to his own country, the pine country to the north, thought Bienville. He watched the Indian's back receding and decided that he must be a brave from the Yowanni town.

He flinched his shoulder and spoke over it without looking around. "Yes, monsieur, when I got to Dauphine there were no mortars on the King's vessel."

D'Artaguette caressed the knuckles of his left hand and said nothing. He was a well built man, taller than

Bienville and much thicker through the body. Bienville could remember when he had been hard and energetic. Now his posture was not so upright and his face was puffy. But his arrogant eyes had not changed.

Bienville, nervous as a cat, roved back to the table. "The hold was full of salt provisions!" he said querulously. "Do they expect me to reduce the fortified positions with salt beef and biscuits?"

"Perhaps the Chickasaw towns are not so well fortified as we have been led to believe," said D'Artaguette mildly enough, but with an overtone of derision. "It may be a tale of the Choctaws to justify their own cowardice and, yes, treachery, too! I am expecting Tarascon from the Yowannis this morning. He should be able to tell us something."

"I do not like it," said Bienville. "I am almost tempted to turn back, but it would cost me the confidence of the Choctaw Nation. I do have two more mortars on one of the Bateaux and your brother will have two as well. Either might be enough."

D'Artaguette said acidly, "They are dogs, treacherous, lying, they have vilified and threatened me. You heard Mingo Chitto order me to hold my tongue. You heard him, monsieur, and said nothing in reproof. It was only in your interest that I kept silent."

Bienville watched the window. "You don't understand them," he said, shaking his head. "They will fight for me. Our prospects are good enough, yet if your brother, the Chevalier, is able to join his Illinois forces with mine."

He looked directly at D'Artaguette now. "He is a good soldier, the Chevalier."

Diron D'Artaguette's harsh, petulant face softened.

"Pierre will make a great leader for France." His pride and affection were evident in his voice. "You know, monsieur, he is younger but we were always very close. I regard him more as a son than a brother."

For a moment he and Bienville were almost back upon that plane of friendship which had been theirs years ago. They sat, silent, not looking at each other, and gradually each became more acutely conscious of the bitterness which had come between them. The moment had passed, and in the one which succeeded they drew farther apart than before.

While they still sat, each immersed in his own reflections, D'Artaguette's secretary entered with the information that Tarascon had arrived.

217

D'Artaguette mumbled. Tarascon, his trader in the Choctaw towns, must have been hiding behind the door, because he came in as soon as D'Artaguette spoke.

He was like a furtive animal, his eyes shifting and his beak of a nose quivering as if it smelled danger, his hair was long and matted and his hunting shirt of limbourg cloth, once blue, was so stiff with filth that it could have stood alone. The room was suddenly filled with the ripe odor of the man.

When he saw Bienville his fluid eyes slithered away and he scrubbed the back of his hand across his mouth uncertainly, scuffing up his bristly whiskers which were almost as greasy as his shirt.

D'Artaguette said harshly, "Well, Tarascon!"

Tarascon hesitated, his eyes retuning covertly to Bienville.

"I sent you word that I would come here." His voice was a swift whine. "It is my trade, m'sieur'. The Chiefs."

"Such matters can wait," D'Artaguette said preemptively. "The Commandant-General wishes to know what you have seen this time."

Bienville fixed Tarascon with his cold eyes. "You know the Yowanni town? You have been in the north of the Nation recently?"

Tarascon nodded. "Yes, Excellency, Conch, Yanabi, Coweh Chitto."

"Was there any news of the fort which I had built at the Tascaloosas?"

"It was not built at the Tascaloosas," said Tarascon. "They went higher, some fifteen leagues, to the white bluff at the mouth of the Coffin Maker's Creek."

Bienville stared at him. "Why was that done? Why has Monsieur D'Artaguette had no knowledge of it?"

"I do not know, Excellency." Mingo Chitto said that it was a better place for a fort because it was nearer his village and was between the two paths which the English use in coming to the Choctaws. They have called the camp Tombekbe."

"Did you go there yourself?"

"No, m'sieu'. I did not go there because M'sieu' de Lusser does not like me. But I went as far as the lodge of the old coffin maker who lives on the creek. He said that the soldiers had been in the woods felling timber to build themselves lodges and a stockade fence. When I was at the Yowanni town I saw the two brick masons, Condamine and Bourguinon, who were going to the camp they call Tombekbe. They ate in the chief's lodge and the next day went with a warrior to Coweh Chitto."

Bienville's forehead furrowed in a frown. "You have no more news of Captain de Lusser?"

Tarascon shook his greasy head. "That is all I know, m'sieu'."

"All right, then, what else?"

"It is nothing, Excellency. Only my trade," said Tarascon plaintively. "The chiefs received so many presents at their last council here that they will not take my trade goods in reasonable trade, but try to drive bargains which would ruin me. I have told them, m'sieu that next year their gifts will not be so many; that it is only on account of the war against the Chickasaws that we have been so generous with them. But they will not believe me and say that they have received these gifts because it is their due. They even went so far as to tell me that they no longer trusted me nor M'sieu' D'Artaguette, whose habit it was to misuse them, they said, so that they gave all their skins for very few goods and got no presents at all."

D'Artaguette sat rigid and white faced. "Are you mad, man?"

Tarascon stared at him stupidly. "It is what they say, m'sieu', but it is all a Choctaw lie. It is also a lie when they say the goods of the English are better than mine and may be got for less." He smiled deprecatingly. "I tell you all this, Excellency, not because there is any truth in it, but because they will tell it to you, and I wish you to have the right of the matter."

"Do not bother to deny that you have cheated them, Master Tarascon," Bienville said coolly. "If you had traded fairly they would never have allowed the English into their country."

Tarascon muttered sullenly. "The fault is not mine. They went to the English of their own will. They are as thick in the Chickasaw country, those Englishmen, as buzzards around a dead buck. Soon they will spread to the territory of the Choctaws, which is my territory, and then my trade will be ruined for good. Excellency, they must be stopped!"

Bienville ignored his appeal. "How many Englishmen do you think are among the Chickasaws?"

"But God knows. It is said that they have come from Carolina with seventy pack horses loaded mostly with munitions of war." He added dryly, "They call themselves traders and they wear the dress of men who run in the woods, but all of them are no traders nor yet woods runners. There are English soldiers in buckskin directing the Chickasaws in making forts of all their towns."

Bienville drew a harsh breath. "So! And why did Lieutenant Ducoder see none of this?"

"Lieutenant Ducoder saw nothing," said Tarascon, "because they kept him shut in a lodge, and when he escaped it was by night. If he had anything to tell you it was what he had heard, not what he had seen. Besides, most of the Englishmen did not come in until after Lieutenant Ducoder was gone." He threw out his hands. "But, m'sieu', what does it matter if they are there or not, if I am to lose my trade anyway?"

"Damn your trade!" said Bienville with sudden savagery. "Get out! Va t'ens!"

He watched Tarascon, eyes bright with fear, back to the door, get it open without turning, and slide through. It seemed that bad news was pyramiding upon bad news.

He said, as if speaking to himself, "We must rely, I suppose, upon our God. The English, it is well known, are the heretics and the Chickasaws heathen." But his tone was odd and badly lacking in conviction.

D'Artaguette burst out with a groan of disgust. "I should have marched two years ago. There were no English among the savages then."

Chapter XVI

Evan MacDonald did not go with Bienville when the Governor departed for Mobile on the fourth of March. Hebert filled his usual position so Evan decided to stay back with Gaston Lazac and Lesueur until Major de Noyan had enough boats to bring over the four remaining companies at the capital. The militia company of Leseuer's volunteers had preceded Bienville by way of the lakes. The fleet of bateaux loaded with salt meat, flour, rice, and a small quantity of powder went down the river on the third. They were to take on the gunpowder from the magazine at La Belize, along with two mortars, and then proceed to Mobile by the sea route.

Day after day Salmon gave Major De Noyan the same story: he was combing the river above and below the settlement but he had yet to accumulate enough boats fit to carry four companies of soldiers with their arms and paraphernalia through the open water of the lakes and the sound. De Noyan felt sorry for the earnest, agitated little man, and irritated too, though he knew the fault was not Salmon's. It was not until the eleventh that he had his boats; six long pirogues and a clumsy, leaky bateau. He immediately made arrangements to have them hauled to the bayou on the twelfth, and to have his troops follow them out on the morning of the thirteenth.

It poured rain the night of the eleventh, a wild black roaring March flood. Dawn broke under a ragged pale sky. The high March wind whipped the low level of Nouvelle Orleans, rattling the trees, snatching away men's hats and billowing women's petticoats over their heads in the streets and dooryards. The road to the bayou was a quagmire. Louis Joseph Dubrueil sent a slave gang ahead of the teams of oxen moving the boats to corduroy the softest places in saplings cut from the timber on either side of the track. But the saplings frequently broke and mired under the loads. The slaves had to do as much pushing on the cart wheels as they did reinforcing the road. The teamsters bogged to their knees, sweated and made the air blue with oaths and used their goads freely. The bull whips cracked in the wind like musket fire.

Evan and Gaston Lazac, heading into the swamp at midmorning, passed the struggling procession and Lazac grinned at the goings on.

"There's men going to fight Indians," he said contemptuously. "An army is a hell of a specimen in the woods. It's got so much tied onto its tail it can't whip anybody and when it gets whipped it can't get itself away. Me, when I travel, gars, I mean to travel. Coming or going, it don't matter."

The whole scene made Evan gloomy. It seemed to him that De Noyan had taken an eternity to get his men moved, and he was sick of waiting. He had never been so oppressed by restlessness, by the intolerableness of inaction. The emptiness of Bienville's house appalled him. He had moved in with Gaston Lazac, for Henri Martin had accompanied Bienville to Mobile, and spent most of his time rambling and hunting in the swamp.

He had waited in Nouvelle Orleans after Bienville had gone until this last minute in the hope that Antoinette might return from Cannes Brulees. But the week passed and she did not come. His spirits fell and he tried to lift them with a mixture of rum and cynicism. Lazac shared the rum with him but not the cynicism. He was irrepressibly cheerful, which added to Evan's disgust. Still, nothing seemed to help. He told himself morosely a dozen times a day that he did not care if she never came at all.

He wished he had gone with Bienville. At least his time in Mobile would have been occupied. Mobile was on the frontier, there would be Indians there, and the bustle of Bienville's army. Nouvelle Orleans was dead, like a dead crawfish in its fortress of mud. It smelled, too. It was just a dirty, ugly town. There was no adventure in it. He did not blame Antoinette for staying away and he said again, furiously, that he hoped she stayed until she grew moss like the damned queer trees they had in this country. But, for all that, he had given a half real piece to a boy, the son of a smelter named Dannay, in the Rue de Bourbon, to watch and let him know when Antoine Castilloux returned to his house in Nouvelle Orleans, with the promise of another if the information were relayed promptly. Still he had no real hope. De Noyan would move next morning and he would go with him, without having seen her, into battle without her blessing. He felt that his life would not be worth much without that.

He and Lazac returned to the settlement in the afternoon, a little grumpy because they only had four ducks from a day's hunting. The negroes were still busy getting the last boat, the heavy bateau, over the road. The wagon had sunk to the hubs on one side and the bateau tilted dangerously. Evan and Lazac went past without stopping and crossed the shallow weedy ditch into the town. The first thing Evan saw as they turned down the Rue Conde was the Dannay boy throwing sticks at a lean pig which rooted in the street. The boy spied him at the same instant, dropped his sticks and flung up his hands. He began running wildly in a circle.

"Hey! M'sieu'!" he yelped. "Hey, m'sieu'! M'sieu'!

His words had the odd intonation of pig calling. Evan wondered momentarily whether the boy was addressing him or the pig, which rooted on unconcerned. But his heart leaped. Surely such excitement meant something out of the ordinary. He leaned, steadying his hands on his firelock as the boy came tearing up like a colt kicking up his heels at every jump.

"Hey, m'sieu'!" cried the boy, with a radiant face. "She has come! In the chaise, splashing mud, with the round man, her father, and the puny other one."

Evan frowned. Where had the boy got the idea it was Antoinette he wished to keep track of? He had told him only to watch for Castilloux's return. But it made no difference; his frown cleared instantly. Antoinette was back! It must be a kind Providence which caused such a thing to happen on the eve of his departure.

The boy was waiting expectantly. Evan looked around and saw the four green headed ducks dangling from Lazac's big paw. He snatched them out of Lazac's fingers before Lazac knew what he was about, and thrust them at the boy. Then he fished a half real piece from his pouch and gave the boy that, too. Lazac gaped at him, and the boy's eyes bugged out at the unanticipated generosity.

"You're a fine boy," said Evan gaily. "Take those birds to your mother and eat all you can and grow strong, so the next time the army goes out you can fight Indians too. But first I want you to do this for me. You hang around M'sieu' Castilloux's until you get a glimpse of the lady alone, if it takes you until dark. You tell her that I will see her tonight. Tell her this will be the last time, I am marching with the army tomorrow. Compris?"

The boy nodded. He clutched the ducks and the sol together against his dirty blouse. Lazac found his voice at last. "Ventre Sainte Gris!" He roared. "What will we eat?"

225

"I don't feel like eating," said Evan lightly. "I'm not going to your house anyway. I'm going to the Sieur de Bienville's and get on some proper clothes."

The orange trees which made a high hedge around Antoine Castilloux's house caught the moonlight among their leaves and dulled it. Evan edged deeper in to the shadow. He had been waiting many minutes now and the wind was cutting through his coat. He felt as nervous and shaky as the brittle orange leaves. Still Antoinette did not come.

He knew that the little Dannay boy had seen her because he had brought back word that she would meet Evan by the hedge. Moving a little out of the shadow he glued his eyes to the doors on this side of the house. But he was not prepared when she did appear. She had slipped down an outside stairway on the opposite side of the house and come round the corner in the shadows. He saw her when she stepped into the moonlight. The sight of her cloaked and hooded figure in the milky moonlight completely unnerved him. His hands dangled uselessly against the orange leaves. When she walked toward him, he started to lift them a dry thorn raked across the knuckles of his left hand, slicing them deeply, but he was unaware of it.

"Antoinette," he whispered hoarsely.

Her face was a still transparency in the moonlight as she lifted it. Her eyes were wide and clouded.

"The little boy said. . . Evan, Evan , are you really going? Tomorrow?"

"I'm with Lesueur. I, I must go."

"You want to go," she said pettishly, looking away.

He caught both her hands and squeezed them until she twisted her mouth. "Yes," he said. "Yes, but I'll come back."

She looked up at him strangely. "Will you? Will you? But it might be too late."

His fingers tightened on hers. "What do you mean?"

"I don't know. Oh, Evan, you're hurting my hands. I don't know." Her voice faltered a little. "Waiting is a horrible thing. Waiting, waiting, waiting! This awful place depresses me until I think that I will go mad."

He put his arm around her tenderly and pulled her head against his shoulder. She rested it there quietly.

"Did you miss me?" he asked her.

"Yes," she whispered. "It is so deadly dull here and out there. I don't know which is worse. There was nothing but desolate, frost bitten fields, arpent upon arpent with the dirty river on one side and the black swamp on the other. Nobody to look at but those brute slaves, if one can call them people, and father and Edouard."

"When I come back we'll make our own home," he said eagerly. "That will not be dull."

She said tonelessly, "I could never live in this place."

"But perhaps you could, in time. Or, if not, we could go back to France." In his eagerness he ignored facts which might prevent his ever returning to France, even in the unlikely event that he should ever want to. He thought with the confidence of desire. "But of course she will learn to love it here, as I do. Time will take care of that. We'll let it grow gradually."

She burrowed her forehead closer against his coat. "I must go now," she said, but she did not move.

He held her tighter, as if he could never let her go, and felt the impact of that awfulness of waiting which she had expressed before. In a little while he must let her go. In a little while he would be away from her upon a day which would be the beginning of an endless chain of days of loneliness and waiting. That loneliness and waiting loomed infinitely larger than any danger and hardship which might lie ahead of him. Its imminence seized him and shook him savagely. She felt the increasing pressure of his arms and for a heart beat her whole body responded, clung closer to his. His breath became labored and loud, his brain rocked in a dark storm. She knew what was coming and her own passion passed like a flash. She jerked her head off his shoulder and began pushing hard against his chest. His arms were like steel, his eyes were glazed, riveted upon her eyes.

"Evan!" she said sharply, "Let me go!"

The changing inflection of her voice had the power to move him. She felt his hands on her body relax. He shut his eyes tightly and shook his head.

"I must go now, Evan," she went on more softly.

"Father will be missing me."

He tried to protest but something went wrong with his throat or his tongue. He could only keep shaking his head.

She lifted her mouth. He bent his head dumbly. He would have locked her to him again but she twisted away and slipped out of his arms.

"Good bye." she murmured. "And the Blessed Virgin watch you, Evan."

He could not respond in words. He watched her moving like a shadow across the grass. Once she turned and threw him a kiss. Then she rounded the corner of the house which might have been the end of the world.

He rubbed the knuckles of his left hand feverishly and for the first time felt the blood which had dried on them.

He waited by the hedge a long time before walking. He simply plodded, ignoring where he went, without destination or purpose. It never occurred to him to go home and get some sleep against tomorrow. He simply felt like walking awhile and he turned corners at random, often doubling on his tracks. At last he came to the levee and walked upriver under it, feeling the wetness of the wind off the water, his hands bulging his coat pockets and his eyes fixed on the mud beneath his feet. So it was that passed the Place D'Armes without seeing it and at the corner above walked full tilt into Jacqueline Martin before he had an inkling she was anywhere nearer than home and abed as she should have been. He lost his balance from the collision and, regaining it, came out of his fog feeling foolish at first, and then annoyed.

"Madame Martin!" he said sharply, "What is wrong with you? Why didn't you move? I could have injured you!"

She had given a brief startled cry when he had bumped into her, but now she was calm again. He could see her clearly in the moonlight. She had her blue handkerchief tied round her dark hair and Etienne's old army coat across her shoulders.

"I was looking the other way," she said hesitantly, staring at him so intently that he had to turn his eyes away disconcerted.

"But what brings you here? Alone, a woman, after dark."

"I am looking for Collette," she said hurriedly. "I can't find her. She has been gone since before dark. I don't know where on earth she could have gone, and I am worried."

"Gone?" he said stupidly. "Gone where?"

"I don't know," she repeated patiently. "She's never done it before. She's always been so satisfied, so pleased. I'm afraid she may have gotten into some trouble."

Evan thought disgustedly that is may well have come to that. She was bred of a line of sluts, it was bound to crop out in her sooner or later.

He said aloud, "Well, you can't find her this way. Come, I shall take you home, madame. The dampness of this river air is the very devil."

Her eyes were large and dark and utterly still. The moon reflected in them with an odd brilliance. She took his arm docilely and turned with him to walk back into the town.

"But m'sieu', what of Collette?" she asked presently.

"We have come from opposite parts of the town and neither of us has seen her. Where else can we look? She can be found in the morning. There is nothing to be done tonight," he said. "I am concerned for her but must I also be concerned for you as well? Two women alone in the town has much more danger involved than just one."

He added almost defensively, "I am sure that your husband would be most distraught if he though anything had happened to you. You will find her in the morning."

She shook her head but said nothing, and they walked on silently until they reached the pickets sagging around her house. The night was still except for the wind in the dead weeds and willow and cane and brush, and the high sound of the frogs in the marsh behind them.

She stopped outside the pickets. "Don't make a noise, please," she warned him. "I left Etienne sleeping."

"You will rest now, madame," he told her, "until morning. I will make a turn around town and look for Collette but do not fear, she will returned unharmed."

She drew a long, harsh breath. "No," her voice had a sort of muted violence. "I was lying -- no, I was not lying to you, not about Collette. She is gone, that is true. But that is not what had me out of my wits. Oh, Holy Mother, it was not that! I knew I couldn't find her."

He was completely at sea. "But madame, but.."

230

There were sharp lines of anguish in her face. She looked frighteningly pale and almost old.

She moved her lips stiffly. "You are going away. You are going to die!" The words came out with great difficulty as if behind her taut lips her teeth were locked. "Die! I have seen it -- the way they kill! Drawn like a chicken, and spitted! Oh, God."

Her face twitched in a spasm. She put her hands over it and moaned threw her fingers. "I'll never see you again."

He was mute, as paralyzed from head to foot as if he had been struck by lightning. She put her hands upon his rigid arms above the elbows. Her fingers were like claws digging into the muscles of his arms, but he scarcely felt the pain.

"I had to walk," she said intensely. "I could not stay in that house. I had to walk or go mad. You think that I am a slut, I know. An unfaith woman. A shameless slut. I don't care if you do. Or if I am. I would rather be that alive than dead."

He found his own tongue at last to halt the onrush of hers. "Madame," he started.

"Be still!" she said fiercely. "I am dead! I have been for years. An old, dead, decaying woman. Without a man, and I ache for one. And then you come into my house, the best thing my poor eyes have ever seen!" Her lips were open, he could hear her panting. "My children should be your children! If God would give me that, I'd never ask another thing!"

While he watched her as a charmed bird watches a snake, racking his brain for something to say, her entire appearance altered. Her face softened. It was pale but the harsh lines ironed themselves smooth in an instant. The blaze in her eyes ebbed to a glow. Her right hand moved from his arm and touched his cheek. Her fingers were no longer hard like claws but soft as willow buds.

Almost without his knowledge his own hands came up and clasped her shoulders gently. In a recess of his mind the realization came that he could have this woman now, as only a little while ago he had longed to have Antoinette! It flashed in his mind and flashed away, ungrasped. He held her tenderly without pressing her to him, yet feeling close to her, almost wrapped with her, in a half dream in which there was no conscious passion. Since childhood he had yearned for and sought comfort and satisfaction in a number of things: his father's affection, adventure, this new land, and Antoinette. Here for the first time was another being who yearned for and sought comfort in him. It was an earthshaking thought and made this woman something of a rarity. He put his fingers up and absently mindedly stroked her dark hair where it showed under her handkerchief.

She rested against him for a long, long time, breathing deeply, regularly, as if she were asleep. Presently her head stirred, after a little she lifted it and drew back from his embrace. Her face was quiet, passionless, peaceful. His eyes never left her. The dream was slow to dissolve. There was a cathedral-like quality in the silence which enveloped them.

She held his hands for a minute and then dropped them. "Thank you. I can rest now." That was all she said. He had expected her to tell him goodbye or to kiss him, but she slipped through the gate before he could move, and did not look back. For the second time in less than an hour a woman was leaving him and he was standing like a straw headed fool. She went through the door and closed it upon the darkened interior of the cabin. He heard the scrape of wood on wood. In the silence he was conscious of the rasping of the frogs, louder, more discordant than ever. Back in the swamp an owl screamed and the sound struck him to the marrow.

CHAPTER XVII

A cock began to crow in one of the yards on the Rue de Bourbon. Soon the voices of other stirring fowls were raised in the thin gray dawn. The air was yet chill and wet. There was not even a stain of pink in the sky beyond the river. By the time the crowing of the cocks had subsided, across the misty extent of the esplanade a bugle began to grieve.

The white coated sentry had slung his firelock upon his back. His cheeks puffed wind as he sent out a second blast of the reveille. He could hear the soldiers begin to stir in their blankets, and he felt thankful that he was not one of those who had been detached from the garrison for duty in the coming campaign. There were men among those, he reflected, who even seemed to look forward to the expedition with pleasure, as if it were some kind of festivity. Let them have it. He had no stomach for tramping in the woods on the track of a pack of brute Indians. Ma foi, life in the garrison was bad enough but upon that expedition there would be no women nor much wine, but doubtless a great deal of sickness and death. He was glad to stay here. The last echoes of his blast died away in the mists on the river as the men began to emerge into the Place D Armes.

Wiping the cobwebs of sleep from their eyes, they commenced, to the profane bawling of their sergeants, to form ranks. There were four companies of them: those of Courtilhas, Petit Deliviliers, Contrecoeur, and Marets. A slovenly unsoldierly lot they were, with Corporals Broussard and Muldoon of Contrecouer's company standing out like sore thumbs by contrast. Major de Noyan, with Aide-Major McCarty at his side, walked onto the esplanade for a final inspection of his troops. His boots and his buttons gleamed. His hair was greased and powdered.

He made his inspection without comment. For the deficiencies that were so flagrantly evident in his troops it was too late to remedy. To the captains he gave the order to make ready immediately for the march.

Within the hour Noyan's four companies of regulars were marching through the ramparts upon the road to the Bayou St. Jean. There were augmented by a company of negroes under the command of Simon, a free mulatto. These were loaded with the supplies. Also there was a detachment of perhaps a score of volunteers who brought up the rear of the column.

Evan and Lazac marched with Major de Noyan at the head of the column. As they passed through the gate in the ramparts, a large crowd of colonists stood to cheer them off. It was a great spectacle for the Latin heart that loved a parade. But some of the women cried as the ranks passed by and the drums rolled. These were the wives and mistresses of the regular soldiers, for Bienville would not take any married colonists in his militia.

Evan saw Jacqueline there and started to lift his hand to her but caught himself as he thought better of the impulse. There were no tears in her eyes but her face was strained with suppressed emotion. She had Madame Lambert beside her and wondered for a moment why Collette was not there. But he forgot it, for Jacqueline's dark eyes followed him, and the look of them filled his thoughts. He looked away but did not stop thinking that there was that in her eyes which made him uncertain of himself, and there was no room for uncertainty when a man went off to war.

The throb of the drums became a remembered sound and the morning sun popping up from beyond the river sent its

long red rays down the road to the bayou in the wake of the white uniformed column. Jacqueline and Therese Lambert walked homeward beneath the rampart.

"Ah, Holy Mother," said Therese, "I've seen them march away like that before. And you have too, ma chere. It's been twelve years since I watched Gustave march off to the first war against the Natchez where he lost his eye. It's been six since you saw Etienne go. Sooner or later, a man is bound to march or to fight and leave his woman behind. He is not thinking of her then, nor does he want to be bothered by her tears. They are all alike until they learn the hard lesson."

"Do they ever learn?" asked Jacqueline bitterly.

"Sometimes they do and sometimes they don't," said Madame Lambert sagely. "It depends on the man. Gustave had to lose an eye to learn better. But some of them are smarter than Gustave and find out quicker." She stopped to look closely at Jacqueline, went on kindly, "Don't grieve, Jacqueline, he'll come back as firm as he is this minute."

Jacqueline evinced no surprise, "Perhaps. That is what is important, non? I pray god he will be unhurt. But even when he does return my life will go on as it has gone on before."

Therese wagged her head. "Under the circumstances Jacqueline, it might be as well if he didn't come back at all."

Jacqueline bit her lip in a pain that was almost physical as the image which the other woman's words produced in her mind.

"No!" she cried, "No, it will be hell for me to go on seeing him, I know, but he mustn't die! It couldn't happen!"

"It's none of my affair," said Therese Lambert, frowning, "and I can't say that I blame you for wanting an entire man. But in the eyes of the Church Etienne is your husband and will be until the day he dies."

Jacqueline smiled thinly. "Don't worry about me losing my virtue," she assured her.

"The vows I took at marriage may not mean as much now as they did then but they still mean something. Anyway, even if I wanted to, I couldn't leave Etienne. He doesn't love me anymore, if he ever really did, now he could not survive without me."

She reflected, bitterly, that she might have amended her statement by saying that her virtue was further insured by the fact that Evan did not want her but her humiliation was great enough as matters stood without making it an item of public knowledge.

Madame Lambert took her hand and patted it in a maternal fashion. "You're a brave girl, my dear, and sensible. I never worry about you doing the wrong thing. I wish my young girl was sure to grow up into a woman like you. But there's so much going on in this town, against the will of God, mind you, that she can't help but notice. It makes me afraid what she'll be when she gets a little older. I try to tell her what is right but I've seen too many girls, well raised, go wrong out here. I hope you're keeping an eye on that girl who is staying with you."

Jacqueline started. "Collette? I'd forgotten about her. I wonder where she can be?"

"Eh?" said Madame Therese. "She must have been watching the men go off. She liked that tall soldier, Broussard. She would not miss seeing him leave."

Jacqueline said anxiously, "I didn't see her. I remember now. She was not at the house when I left. I thought she must have gone to see Rene off. But I didn't see her. Poor child, she was distraught because he was going. I hope nothing has happened to her. Maybe she has already gone back to the house."

But the house was empty, save for Etienne who was in a black sulk because he had been left alone.

There were ten long pirogues tied up to the bayou back where the road from Nouvelle Orleans met it a hundred paces below the shack of Papa Jules Froissart. They were substantial craft, thirty feet long, well hewn out of poplar logs. The mists between the tree lined bayou banks partly obscured them and the two men who squatted near the edge of the stream listening to the roll of the drum coming closer to them down the bayou road. One of these was the sentry who stood guard over the boats. The other was a wizened little man who jumped up as the head of the column swung into view. It was Camille Billiot.

As Major de Noyan gave the command for the men to fall out and make ready to embark. Billiot rushed up to him where he was standing with Evan and Lazac and the captains of the four regular companies. Billiot was waving his arms and his eyes were wild.

"Monsieur le Major, I wish to enlist. I, Camille Billiot, wish to enlist. Oui, it is so."

Noyan turned with a frown of annoyance at the interruption. But Gaston Lazac let out let out a shout of laughter.

"It is so," squealed Billiot. "I, Camille Billiot, am a brave man. Un grand soldat. I wish to kill the red man. Pouf! He is dead!"

Noyan stood like a ramrod in the face of this tempest of gesticulation. His dark eyes snapped with anger.

"Get to the rear," he ordered angrily. "This is an army on the march. We do no recruiting now."

The dismay on Camille Billiot's thin face was ludicrous. "Oh, Mon Dieu," he gibbered, "Oh, le nom du Dieu! But I must go! It is my life if I do not go!"

Aide-Major Macarty-Mactigue started to laugh. Noyan's mouth opened for a blast to silence Billiot but Lazac interposed.

"Let him go along, Major," he said. "He knows the woods. He may come in handy."

Noyan shook his head and waved Billiot toward the line of boats. "Take the tenth boat with the rest of the volunteers. Allez vous en!"

Gaston Lazac fell in beside Camille Billiot as he turned to obey the order. Billiot was effusively grateful, trying to throw his arms about Lazac and kiss him, but he was too short and Lazac was too broad. He stood straight up, out of Camille's reach, and grinned at him.

"Grand merci, mon ami!" babbled Billiot. "You have saved my life. Someday, by the grace of le bon Dieu, I will do the same for you."

Lazac chuckled. "My life won't be worth a mangy possum hide the day you have to save it, Camille. But, listen, what in the name of God put it into your head to come along with us?"

Camille looked cautiously around at the men who were clambering into the boats.

"Tell me, my friend," he said, "Francois Petit is not one of these?"

"Petit? God, no! What makes..?" Lazac stopped and clapped Billiot on the back with an open hand. "Voila! So that's how the land lays, eh?"

Billiot was distressed. A frown made a furrow just above his thin nose.

"Not so loud, my friend," he whispered. "It is enough that you should know, without telling the others. Look! I weep for humiliation. How could the God be so unfeeling as to bring these things upon me, Camille Billiot? How could my own wife treat me so?"

Lazac lighting his pipe, looked sympathetic. "What's the trouble?"

Billiot's hand jerked out as it he were about to clutch something.

"Trouble? Helas! The world is full of trouble. At the risk of my life I might return to my house on the river. So I do not return. Non. What do I do? I become a wanderer. I roam the woods, I fight the Indian. I am a hero. When I return they will see what it is to face the wrath of Camille Billiot."

He stretched out a skinny arm and hooked his fingers before Lazac's nose.

"See. The fury of the devil possesses me. Last night when I returned home from my fishing lines in the river I was tired. I wished to go to bed and sleep. But my bed was full so that I could find no room."

"My wife, Clementine, femme de mauvais vie that she is, was sharing my bed with Francois Petit. I was astonished. Such brazen goings on in my own house. I opened my mouth to rain curses upon them. But before I could speak, they sprang at me. I had thought them asleep, but, non. Francois Petit, that great hairy man, made at me to tear me limb from limb. Clementine seized my hatchet from the wall. But I did not wait, non. After I left them I began to think of all the men who were going off to kill the red man. It had been for the sake of Clementine that I had remained, oui. Now, Clementine no longer needs me. So, I am here. I have waited all night. Voila!"

Lazac was not one to conceal his mirth out of regard for Billiot's feelings. He howled, leaning over to slap his thigh while the echoes of his laughter clapped against the trees and rolled across the bayou. A group of musketeers of Maret's company, who were slouching near their boat, turned to look at the big Canadian.

"Eh, mon vieux," called out one, "tell us the joke so that we may laugh, too."

Lazac stopped laughing.

"Mind your own business, you damned Parisian," he said. The soldier's weak jaw slackened, but he seemed of no mind to take issue with the big woodsman.

Billiot hung back as he and Lazac neared the ranks of the volunteers beside the last boat. His liquid eyes darted from one face to another. Then he sighed and smiled.

"Ah, you are right my friend. Francois Petit is not one of them." He pushed forward his narrow chest. "I did not think that great coward would dare to follow Camille Billiot upon the path of danger."

An hour after the sunrise Noyan's procession of pirogues issued from the sluggish reaches of the Bayou St. Jean into the open waters of Lake Pontchartrain. Upon their right hand, then, was the semi-inundated lake shore which the bayou drained; a wasteland of shallow, coffee colored waters with only an occasional rib of dry land, a steaming half world, lost to the sun, and grown over in fan like dwarf palmettos and gaunt cypress trees. All through the morning the line of boats moved eastward with the lake shore upon their right.

There was a stiff wind blowing from west to east which tattered the banks of fog and, being at the backs of the rowers, made the work lighter and the speed greater. The lake was running high in great coming waves, gray as dishwater. The pirogues fanned out upon the lake, each crew watching out for itself as they rode from crest to trough, where they were drenched in spray, and back to crest again. Continuously there was the danger of taking a camber at the wrong angle which would be tantamount to disaster. And, also continuously, they could hear the waves cracking upon the drift littered beaches of some point of land.

At noon they beached their pirogues at Pointe Aux Herbes for a meal of biscuit and salt meat washed down with a little wine. Midway of the afternoon they entered the rapid narrows of the Rigolets which marked the passage between Lake Pontchartrain and Lake Bourne. Evan, who was in the lead boat with Major de Noyan and Macarty-Mactigue took one of the paddles as the none too robust soldiers who were wielding them were becoming tired. He felt a relief to be at work, for he had been sitting on the seat of his breeches all through the day, getting uncomfortably drenched by the flying spray, and thinking nothing but unpleasant thoughts in which both Antoinette Castilloux and Jacqueline Martin played a prominent part.

At dusk they entered the channel between Goose Island and the point of land at the mouth of the Riviere aux Perles. De Noyan, cupping his hands to his mouth, called out orders to put ashore, and the call went strangely hushed on the water, from boat to boat until it had reached the farthest extremity of the line. The pirogues ran toward a wooded shore, making a gentle succession of whispering sounds as they scraped upon the sandy beach. The tired soldiers piled out into the shallow water and dragged their craft to high dry ground. They then scattered out in details to fetch firewood. When the first fire was built Major de Noyan, who was talking to his adjutant, Sieur de Juzan, and Macarty-Mactigue, called Evan into the light of it and instructed him to take down his official record of the day. After that was done to his satisfaction, he dismissed Evan and went back into his discussion with McCarty of some kind of military tactics which, in order to more forcefully drive home his point, he was diagramming with a bit of twig in the loose sand between his feet.

Evan walked down the line of campfires which stretched like a string of burning beads along the open space between the beach and the pine woods which covered the higher ground. Each company had built its own fire, and the men squatted about it munching on their salt meat and talking among themselves, between bites, in a vein that aroused a good deal of cackling laughter. Evan skirted these fires which were surrounded by regular soldiers in their shoddy white uniforms. He saw Rene and Muldoon among those of Contrecouer's company and lifted his hand, but did not stop. He brought up at the last fire of all, well back in the shadow of the pines, where the volunteers were gathered.

He saw that Gaston Lazac had arrived there ahead of him and was standing above the seated men, telling them in no complimentary terms to give him a drink in the name of hospitality. He was standing directly behind Camille Billiot and when Camille did not heed his request, he thrust his moccasined toe beneath Camille's narrow tail and, with a sudden tensing of his leg muscles, pitched him forward on his nose in the sand.

Billiot jumped up, spitting sand. He shook his fist at Lazac.

"Gaston Lazac, it is a good thing for you that you are my friend, or you would learn what it is to trifle with Camille Billiot."

Lazac grinned and unscrewed the canteen which he held in his left hand.

"Here, Camille," he said, proffering the canteen. "This will square things. You see how big a heart I have? If you don't give me a drink, I'll give you one. But," he added cautioning, "If you take too big a drink I'll scrub your nose in the sand again."

He took the canteen from Billiot and passed it to Evan.

"Is this a pretty lot of Indian fighters?" he said in disgust. "Hunched around this fire like a bunch of sick kittens. They're even too stingy to give a man a drink when he asks for it. I just tried them out. Look at that one over there. He hasn't said a word since I've been here. Just sits there with his head tucked down. I reckon he's scared to death."

Evan looked in the direction that Lazac's blunt finger pointed. The figure that he saw, drawn back in the shadows was slight. It looked like a boy. There was something vaguely familiar about it. The clothes. He had seen them before. His mouth dropped open.

"My God!" he said. "It can't be!"

In a half dozen strides he had covered the intervening space and was towering sternly over the boy like figure. It seemed to shrink from him.

"Look at me, you!" he commanded.

For a moment it appeared that the other was not going to obey. Then, in a kind of resignation, the head came slowly up.

"My God!" he said again.

Lazac was standing behind him. He let his breath out with a whoosh.

Evan looked angrily down into Collette's sullen face. No wonder the clothes had looked so familiar. They were the ones she had worn on the long ocean voyage.

He cast a quick glance over his shoulder at the men about the campfire. They seemed not interested and had returned to their meal.

"Come here," he told Collette, brusquely. With

Lazac they walked a little way toward the pines.

"What are you doing here?" demanded Evan, when they were out of earshot of the campfire. "Where in the name of God do you think you're going!"

"I know where I'm going." said Colette, with a surprising show of dignity. "I'm going wherever Rene goes."

"You're wrong about that," declared Evan. "I'm responsible for you leaving your family in Paris and I'll be damned if I'll stand for you trying any such harebrained escapade as that. You're going back to Nouvelle Orleans."

Collette's face was still white but her smile was a trifle mocking.

"How?" she responded. "Do you think Major de Noyan will allow one of his pirogues to go all the way back to Nouvelle Orleans just to carry one woman? He has barely enough pirogues to transport his troops and supplies as it is."

Evan stared at her. "You're right," he muttered, grudgingly. "But I'll get you back one way or another. Or I'll find someone to leave you with in Mobile. One thing is for certain. You are not going on this campaign."

Her eyes were running over with tears. "I am!" she said, fiercely. "Whatever you say, I'm going with Rene. If he's in danger then I want to be there, and not you nor anyone else can stop me!"

Her entire body was as tight as a drawn bow string quivering as she stood and glared at him. Evan dropped his hands helplessly.

He turned to Lazac. "What do you think I ought to do?"

Lazac shrugged. "It's a hell of a mess. One thing I wouldn't do, though, is leave her among that bunch of roosters." He jerked his thumb toward the group of volunteers who by now were full of liquor and had begun to sing a bawdy song.

"The best think I can think of is to take her in the boat with you. Let Bienville decide her fate when we reach Mobile."

The sun behind the low brick fort was dull red like a scrap of limbourg cloth hanging above the smudge of pine woods. To the men in the pirogues entering the river mouth and hugging the swamp on the western shore, the fort itself seemed to squat in a marsh. The tawny flood of the river surging past to enter the bay backed over the low ground right up against the slope of the glacis. A wooden wharf ran from the covered way across the glacis and out to deep water. As the sun dropped into the pines and the shadows grayed on the river the wharf looked like a hundred legged water bug crawling out to meet the pirogues.

Evan, in the lead pirogue, shifted his aching body and gulped at the sight of the little fort and rocked up giddily as the boat rocked, moving closer. His muscles were stiff. His clothing, his skin, the inside of his mouth, and nostrils, and throat were crusted with salt. He felt like a herring salted and dried for packing, and he knew that every man in every boat was bound to feel the same. This was the twenty-second of March. They had been traveling for ten days, hammered by contrary winds the entire length of the sound. The entire line dragged like a sick and broken backed eel.

Collette leaned from the thwart behind Evan and pulled at his sleeve. He looked back and saw her salt cracked lips moving. He guessed she was trying to ask him if this was Fort Conde and he nodded. She had stood the wracking journey better than he had expected. She was a resilient little devil, but still he felt sorry for her. He wondered if Bienville would let her go on with the army. As he had anticipated, it had been impossible to conceal Collette's sex. But Major de Noyan had not seemed concerned. He had merely taken precaution, in the interest of discipline, of moving her into the lead boat to keep her away from the soldiers. It was not the first time, he said, that a woman had gone with an army in some capacity, not was it likely to be the last.

In the dusk which masked the harsh outlines of the fort the head of a file of white coats was issuing from the covered way. Guard of honor, thought Evan wryly. Guard of honor for as seasick and rag tailed a rabble as ever called themselves soldiers of the line. The first pirogue scrubbed the piling and the voyageur captain heaved up a rope to the negro wharf hands who made her fast. Evan watched the seat of Major de Noyan's breeches as he got a hand from above and scrambled up.

It was already pitch dark and lanterns had been lit on the head of the pilings when the last boat, which carried De Benac's company, tied up and the men, dragging themselves like cripples, came ashore.

The men from Nouvelle Orleans camped on the bare ridge above the hospital among a pox of pine stumps where the high ground had been cut over for a depth of several arpents from the river. They made themselves shelters out of old planks, poles and drift logs and pine branches which they had to cut back in the woods. They added to this with sail cloth and any odds and ends that they could lay their hands on. The weather, typical of March, was changeable and they suffered it: rain and sun in a kind of rotation, and almost always a high wind. Before they had been on the ridge a week most of them had colds or fevers or aches in their bones.

These soldiers, who were called a mob a dozen times a day by their officers, and were accused of having no sense of military order, had nevertheless laid out their camp in a kind of pattern. The shelters, usually built and occupied by two men, were in fairly straight rows by company, with ways for walking between which might have been called streets.

Collette stayed with Rene in a hut in the second row which was De Hauterive's. She and Rene had built the hut together and she was very proud of it. When it rained it leaked in only half-a-dozen places instead of the two or three dozen which was common to most. Collette felt happier than at any time in her life for a number of reasons. She was with Rene, of course. But hadn't she stood up to the Commandant General himself and stated her case with only a word or two of support from Evan? That was something of which to be proud.

She didn't know exactly why the Sieur de Bienville had let her have her way, but she would always be grateful. He had seemed so tired and stern, and yet almost amused, asking her many questions, all, seemingly, with his tongue in his cheek. Could she handle a firelock, could she beat a drum? Other things, that she could not remember now, all to which she had shaken her head. He was a kind man, she had decided, and let it go with that.

But in his headquarters located in his old house below the fort, Bienville scarcely felt so kindly. A thousand problems, large and petty, had descended upon him from the moment he set foot in Mobile until the arrival of De Noyan. That even had by no means brought an end to them but rather had increased them by the addition of more than one hundred and fifty men to be sheltered and fed. Besides, the men camped above the hospital he now had others billeted all over the town. The barracks on the ridge overlooking the fort were jammed. He had even moved men into the fort itself which normally held only the guard on duty. Day after day his reserves of wheat flour and rice dwindled as this enforced idleness ate up time and provisions with impartial veracity.

The big boats that had been sent through the mouth of the Mississippi River straggled in by twos and threes. Some suffered considerable damage to their cargoes while others had fought through virtually intact. He was relieved to find that the gunpowder which had been taken on at La Belize was in usable condition. One of the big boats carrying a cargo of rice, more precious than diamonds as his stocks were being depleted, had not shown up at all. The voyageurs on the other boats had not seen her since they left the passes of the Mississippi. In their opinion she had foundered in heavy seas and was lost.

Then, too, there was the inevitable friction between the newly arrived soldiers and the inhabitants of the town, which literally rubbed the hides off many. All wanted salving, a task which required the patience of Job. Every day men came to him to complain that the townspeople stole from them or made them sleep on hard, bare floors, or were rude and unfriendly. And every day townspeople came likewise to claim that the soldiers stole from them, or tried to get them out of their own beds, or seduced their daughters or wives.

He had taken Evan MacDonald in with him again, and out of it had arisen an incident which had proven almost a diversion. Evan had brought in a bedraggled girl who wanted to go with a corporal in De Hauterive's company. It had pleased him to have his joke with Evan who had come and remained all through the interview in an agony of embarrassment. Bienville had relished his talk with the girl.

It was the old problem of women following an army. He realized that even the slightest misstep on his part could roust the sanctimonious quarters which made a profession of howling for his head. Years ago when he had commanded old Biloxi, where there had been no white women, he had let his soldiers run in the woods after Indian girls, and those same quarters had called that loose.

It gave him a sardonic delight to bait them with actions of which he knew they would disapprove. There was no harm in the girl's going with her man, so long as it established no precedent. He wanted no pack of women following his army for reasons of supply as well as discipline. Still, the girl wore masculine clothing, and so long as she did, she was a male as far as he was concerned. He would not make her femininity official, and he anticipated no complaint from the men. So he had let her go, and had his laugh on Evan MacDonald.

On the morning of the twenty-eighth the lookout on the parapet of the fort sighted the long overdue bateau from Nouvelle Orleans laboring up the bay shore. He yelled down the information and presently a pirogue came back within an hour with the heavier vessel in tow. The bateau rode like a drifting log, with the choppy river water almost over her sides. When Bienville come down to inspect her he marveled that she had ever got through at all. Her cypress siding had been staved in on the aft portside almost to the stern and her stern oar was a splintered wreck of which nothing remained but the tiller. It was a miracle that she had lost none of her crew. Half her cargo of rice had been lost outright in the Gulf, the rest was, for the most part, so sodden through with brine as to be rendered unfit for use. But also on that boat were two mortars which the crew had thrown over to keep the bateau from sinking. When he walked slowly back with Diron D'Artaguette to D'Artaguette's house, Bienville's large head was bowed.

The loss of so much rice was a calamity of the first order. He had counted heavily on that rice to feed his men up the river as far as Captain de Lusser's fort. It would have to be replaced somehow. Men must eat. He said as much to D'Artaguette.

"Make biscuits," said D'Artaguette, shortly. "You have wheat flour."

Bienville did not lift his head. "Not too much of that," he said mildly. "No, it would take too long to bake enough biscuits. I can't wait for that. We'll use what biscuits we have on hand at present. That will diminish our reserve of bread, but it's the best we can do. In the meantime, I'll have Captain de Lusser bake more. Find as many bakers as you are able and send them to me."

"And your mortars?" Diron D'Artaguette inquired.

"Your brother will have mortars with him," responded Bienville. "Hopefully, they should take care of any need that we should have. It is the provisions that most concern me."

Within the hour he had started his bakers for De Lusser's fort with orders to Captain de Lusser to build ovens and make into biscuits all the flour he had on hand. They were to go through Choctaw country with a guide from the Yowanni town. He had three bakers, the regular two from Fort Conde, and man named Camille Billiot who had come from Nouvelle Orleans with Lesueur's volunteers and had knowledge of baking. The man seemed anxious to go. He said his brother, who had been stationed at Fort Conde, was now with De Lusser at Fort Tombekbe.

At dark of the thirty first of March, the eve of Easter Sunday, Bienville's army lay encamped inside the fort, in the barracks outside, and in the motley shelters along the river ridge. It had been a day as hot as summer. Along the slope of the ridge the river had washed up a quantity of small fish and they had died quickly in the heat of the sun. The stink of them crawled up the ridge and among the soldiers. The soldiers grumbled and cursed, partly at the stink but more at the order which kept them out of the sutler's canteen that night. They had been issued fresh powder and ball during the day. All the boats at the river front had been fully loaded, and the word had gone around that they would march tomorrow which was Easter Sunday. Going off to war on a holy day was said by some to be a sin but to most of them the sin was that by Bienville's order the sutler's canteen was dark and there was so little liquor among them that they could not forget the prospects of the campaign ahead.

At his headquarters Bienville prepared himself for bed. For him it was the eve of a battle whose consequences were perhaps beyond the comprehension of any save himself in this somnolent French settlement beside the quiet river. He looked from his window at the town and saw the candle lights of Mobile wink out one by one, like minutes marking off the hour of destiny of an infant nation.

Chapter XVIII

Toward dawn a white fog crawled in from the bay and thickened in the mouth of the river, forming a belt of cold vapor like a blindfold on the water and the surrounding land. The low point opposite Fort Conde vanished and the river between flowed toward the bay with a misty gurgling but invisible under the misty blanket. On the fort itself the sentries, circling the parapet to meet each other as they made their rounds, shivered in their thin coats and rubbed their eyes, partly because of sleepiness and partly in an unconscious effort to wipe away the cobwebs of the fog which rendered them practically sightless. When they peered outside the parapet, the fog swam under their noses like a clammy sea. Even the earth on the glacis was scarcely discernible, and the pirogues and bateaux for the army which lined the wharf were entirely concealed. When they looked within the works they saw gray mounds in the well of the yard, a leveling by the fog of magazine and officer's quarters and barracks where the men lay sleeping. They felt as useless, almost, as those sleeping men. They could not see each other and one, who was young and had a lively fancy, began to imagine that he and his comrade were bodiless, mere sounds in the grayness, a scuffing of shoe leather on wet brick, a click and rattle of firelock and accoutrements.

While the fog still lay thickly on the river and the town and masked the breaking of dawn eastward beyond the Tensas marshes, the first trumpet blared inside the fort. The sound rolled across the narrow yard, struck against the ramparts and recoiled upon itself. Confined by the small space, its echoing and re-echoing rang as noisily as if a score of trumpets were blowing. The imaginative young sentry eased his firelock upon his shoulder and, looking toward the invisible east, crossed himself without conscious thought. It was Easter morning.

It was only then that the first cock crowed in the town.

The men had been formed into Mass, kneeling by companies under the April-green oaks which bordered the level, beaten esplanade. The tops of the oaks were cobwebbed with streamers of fog, breaking and rising. Black robed priests hurried through the service almost fleeing from rank to rank; from white coated French to red coated Swiss, from piebald militia to volunteers in buckskin, to negroes chanting in their rags; giving them absolution and a cry for peace upon the threshold of destruction.

Evan knelt in the forward rank of Lesueur's volunteers next to Gaston Lazac, his ears half hearing the droning priest. He was mindful enough of his shortcomings without calling them up for the benefit of the priest. He began hastily to enumerate the more recent and painful ones, with a rebuttal for each. He had not sorrowed at his father's passing, but that had been a mercy. He had, perhaps, done Raoul a bad turn, but that had been deserved. The two men at Simon's public house who might well be in their graves, he had to answer for that one. It was a weight upon his conscience. His relations with Collette, not for her sake, but as it bore upon Antoinette and Rene, but that had only happened once.

He had an odd sense of guilt in the matter of Jacqueline Martin, who was another man's wife, but surely that was no fault of his. He had given her no encouragement. She had her own reasons for feeling as she did, he supposed, and she was a damned attractive woman, too. For a little, in the midst of his repenting, he lingered upon her as she had been that last night. Then his humility returned. He felt doubly anxious to come safely through the battle ahead, not only for the purpose of fulfilling his desires but also to set right all these things, if that might be done.

He felt better at once and glanced sidelong at Gaston Lazac. Lazac's face was bowed, immobile. He wondered what Lazac might be repenting and decided that in the short interval at his disposal Lazac had not time, even, to pick and choose but must grab a handful here and a handful there. He grinned covertly at the thought. For Lazac to unburden himself of all his sins would certainly require a dozen priests and as much time as Bienville had allotted for the entire campaign.

Before he had finished his meditations the priests were done. The men were rising in the ranks and being moved off toward the river. The sun swam in the cloud islanded sky, striking the colors at the heads of the companies as they marched off the esplanade.

Lesueur's volunteers were the last to go, unaccustomedly silent as the solemnity of the Mass lingered in their consciences.

By the time they passed the line of oak trees and halted near the head of the wharf they had regained their usual spirits. Nearly every man took a bite off of his black twist, filled his cheek, and began to talk at the same time. They had profane comments for the soldiers moving in a double file through the throng of townspeople. The drums were going at a good rate and the files were stepping smartly along to the wharf's end and filling the pirogues.

As soon as a pirogue was filled it would cast off, pull upstream a short way and stand offshore, backing water. Nearer the fort, the bateaux lay with their cargoes under canvas. Evan saw the negroes dropping from the wharfside onto them. He nudged Lazac and pointed.

Lazac grunted and spat a brown stream. "The catfish will have their bellies full of meat before we reach the Oktibbeha," he said. "And half our supplies in the bargain, if they like the taste of 'em."

"What makes you say that?" asked Evan.

"Look on the wharf." said Lazac nodding in that direction.

There Evan saw the bateaumen who had brought the heavy boats to Mobile. They were lounging about on the wharf watching the voyageur captains manning the big bateaux with the negroes who knew as much about handling boats as the corbeaux, which was Lazac's name for the priests, knew about heaven.

"The cowards," Lazac spit out more tobacco juice with contempt. "They are afraid of working on the river in high water and with the threat of the Chickasaws. They have all quit. Les couchons."

Jean Paul Lesueur, a splendid figure of a man in a green dyed hunting shirt, came along the wharf with immense strides, scattering the people like poultry and shouting for his volunteers. When he had rounded them up, he loaded them into two of the scant handful of pirogues which still lay beside the wharf. As they pulled out and fell into the lengthening line the negroes who had not been impressed as bateaumen filled a third pirogue and the bateaux followed them. The green hands on board seemed to Evan to manage each one more clumsy than the one before. The oars might have been have been picks or hoes the way they handled them.

The pirogue which was to carry Bienville remained rocking idly at the end of its mooring rope. He stood among the bright coats of his staff and the sober cloth of the priests, half obscured from Evan's view by a restless movement of the crowd.

Presently the broad ruddy face of Aide-Major Macarty-Mactigue appeared at the wharf's edge. He did not look back but began to climb down at once. Major de Noyan, Major de Beauchamp of the garrison at Fort Conde, and De Juzan, his adjutant, were just behind him. Already the priests had quietly descended and seated themselves upon the forward thwarts. Evan could see one of them, his pale face bent, his fingers upon his rosary. Above their heads Bienville and Diron D'Artaguette indulging in the formalities of leave taking, had the stiffness of figures of a pantomime.

When Bienville had joined his officers, the pirogue under the big lilied banner slid on the yellow river, passed the end of the wharf and turned upstream broadside to the brick ramparts of the fort. Bienville stood up in the stern and unsheathed his sword. The colors in the other boats dipped. Bienville's voice was not loud but flowed clearly over the water. "Vive le Roi!"

The fringe of the crowd took up the cry, it rolled back like wind into the press, a zealous, meaningless, almost wordless shout. In the fort the gunners behind the casemates thrust matches to touch holes. The volley crashed, rumbled, echoed under the spreading smoke of the the guns. Gulls overhead wheeled and screamed in a frenzy. As the sound of the cannonade fired, the entire line of boats began to inch ahead, rowing for the slack water by the western shore. Bienville sat down quickly on the stern thwart as if his legs would no longer hold him up. He turned his head and watched the first of his boats come on, fighting heavy pull of the current and trying to turn inshore. As they came he counted them. Thirty pirogues, thirty bateaux, ill handed and bearing an ill assorted collection to be called an army.

However, it was his army. He felt strangely apprehensive and strangely proud.

Near its mouth the river broadened into a yellow tide, lazy by comparison with its bluff walled torrent higher upstream, and moved into the grassy marshland which separated it from the Tensas. Inlet, bayou, and bay became gorged with the flood. The marshes sank under it and sopped it like a sponge. The western shore was more swamp than marsh, broken now and then by a low outcropping of yellow bluff and tilting into higher ground with the shadow of pinewoods against the far sky. This low ground was flooded like the marshes across the river. The tops of willows and sycamores shook in the sunlight above the yellow level of the water. Ragged topped cypress marked an occasional creek mouth. All of that Easter Sunday, Bienville's boats hugged this western shore, butting through the drift which eddied off the main current, and avoiding as much as possible the frontal thrust of the river.

The shore along which the boats passed was a lush jungle bursting with leaf and flower. Evan, used to the sullen, ice guarded retreat of the highland winters, found this swift green Southern spring startling and strangely disturbing. The forest seemed oppressive, hot as the sun was hot. Feverish. Its very greenness menaced him. Ahead of them the river appeared to issue out of it. They were being drawn upstream into a green throat which would devour them. It was all alien to him. He had no measure by which to value it. Even his scout with Lazac up the Mississippi to the Natchez district had been in a winter forest, not a tropical jungle like this.

The sun grew hotter as the day wore on. By early afternoon it was almost like summer. Gaston Lazac was the first to strip off his hunting shirt and bare his immense hairy chest. But it was not long before Evan and the rest of the volunteers had made themselves more comfortable. In the boats ahead the soldiers sweated in their coats. Clouds banked steadily in the west. Late in the afternoon the sun dropped into them and the air turned sultry.

Just after sunset Bienville stood up in the lead pirogue and gave the signal to halt. The boats moved into the easy water under a low yellow bluff. Green willow tops bobbed and swayed above a submerged sandbar. By the time dark had fallen the boats were tied up securely among the willows and the men were making their camp on the bluff.

As fires sprang up along the bluff Bienville prowled down the line of his boats. All were accounted for, their cargoes in good order. He had come seven leagues without losing any. But as he looked toward the west he could see that the clouds had banked deeper in dark iron gray masses. Lightning pulsed against them like the reflection of distant fires.

On the second day the army embarked in a fine drizzle which had commenced before dawn. The men were wet before they could get into the boats and there was no shelter on the river. The wind was in the southeast, and the thin rain drove against their backs, seeking out the crevice between their collars and their necks, trickling clammily between their shoulder blades. Before an hour had passed Evan was thoroughly disgusted. It did not make him happier when Lazac cocked an eye at the weather and called it an all day rain, the beginning of a spring storm.

Time went by slowly without sight of the sun to measure it, the rain increased, and the wind blew gradually stronger and stronger. Clouds drove over steadily from the southeast, gray, tattered, and swift in passage. Westward toward the Choctaw country they formed a solid wall like pennants. The rain came in a long slant, made arrow like by the hard, flat drive of the wind. In the intervals between the gusts it fell almost straight down. Now and then the force of the wind tore the driving clouds apart so that a strange pale light filtered through. But, for the most part, light and atmosphere were alike, laden with wind whipped moisture which soaked the army to its long since sodden skin.

That night they camped on another low bluff and Evan slept in the rain above a ravine which roared all night pouring its flood into the larger flood of the river.

To Evan the third, the fourth, and many succeeding days were indistinguishable from the second, cut of the same pattern of gray rain ruffling the yellow river: of incessant rowing with the wet oars twisting the flesh from his palms; of his wet clothes scrubbing sores on his body; of working, eating, sleeping, living in an earthbound purgatory of rain. It seemed it never stopped raining.

Day after day as they rowed past bluffs wooded with hardwood and pine and flats thick laced in willows, cottonwood and sycamore, the clouds went with them, tattered and dingy, ashen and powder gray. At night they blotted out the stars.

Evan took a cold in the head and hoped that by drinking as much rum as he could hold he might keep it from going into his chest. He envied Lazac and Henri Martin who were inured to this kind of weather. But even those two and the other tough woods runners cursed at it. Among the soldiers, the weaker ones sickened from being always wet and cold, but there was no place for them to lie except, moaning and groaning, in the pirogues under the feet of the stronger. There was no shelter by day or night. All the tarpaulins and sailcloth were needed to protect the provisions from the rain. The soldiers who were not sick grumbled and cursed and threatened endlessly to desert. But the wilderness terrified them more than the rain and the river. A catamount's high, bloodcurdling wail back in the timber was enough to decide them against precipitate action.

Daily the task of pulling the boats upstream became more difficult. Numberless bayous, creeks and tributary rivers poured a tremendous volume of water into the river until it wallowed in the valley, spreading and convulsing like a huge yellow snake which had swallowed more than it could comfortably digest. Bienville lived in the fear that his boats would be smashed, his men and provisions lost, by the big trees which came driving down on the flood. On the thirteenth a pirogue rammed a drift log and two men of De Coustilhas company were thrown out and drowned before they could be reached. He thanked God that no more were lost. With each camp that was made he could breathe that much easier.

After the fifteenth, the rains became intermittent, although most days were cloudy. The river did not spare them. It rose higher, hemmed in by the bluffs, its depth enormous, its current terrific. Every man, except the those too ill, took his turn upon the oars and labored in relays, until bones and muscles fused in one mass of aching. Behind the pirogues the bateaux struggled clumsily, scraping the bluffs, often being hauled ahead by lines put about willows under the bank. The negroes had grown into old hands on the bateaux and, to their credit, they had not lost one.

Evan was so exhausted, so sick from the endless torture of fighting the river, so wretched from the swarms of mosquitoes, that he could not sleep at night. He could only toss and ache, tormented by weird fantasies in which people flickered about always in a kind of shadow, yet strangely self-illuminated like fireflies: his father, Raoul, Rene, Collette, Antoinette, Etienne, and Jacqueline. But they moved so quickly and interchanged so suddenly with one another that they made no sense.

Once or twice he summoned the energy to hobble as far as De Hauterive's company to see how Collette was faring. Her face, which used to be round, was pinched, terribly drawn, but he got the impression she was standing it as well or better than he was. She told him that Rene would not let her row and fed her from his own rations. Irritated and feverish with his own exhaustion he wondered if that were the truth or she was simply dramatizing to prove that Rene loved her. He looked at Rene. The beard covering his jaws scarcely hid their gauntness. But then, they had always been gaunt.

On the night of the twentieth, they camped on top of a white, chalky bluff below the mouth of the Tascaloosas which, upon reembarking, they passed on the morning of the twenty-first. The gravel shoals at the mouth of the Tascaloosas were thirty feet under the surging yellow-brown flood. Above it the river grew narrower and the bluffs steeper as the valley closed in. The boats barely crawled on the margin of the roaring river. At mid afternoon of the twenty third, Evan was rowing with his head down and his eyes upon his feet, as it seemed he had been rowing since time began. Suddenly before his face Gaston Lazac heaved himself up from the stern thwart where he had been sitting with Jean Paul Lesueur. Evan eased on his oar and turned his eyes up. Lazac's vast bare chest, like a wine cask which had sprouted hair, blocked his vision. Behind Lazac's shoulders was the deep blue of the sky. Under his left arm as he raised it and pointed, appeared the green rim of the valley downriver. Lesueur, like Evan, was staring at him.

"There's the white bluffs," said Lazac. "The mouth of the Coffin Maker's Creek is pretty well up in the bend. Maybe a quarter of a league."

Lesueur nodded. As he looked ahead the leading pirogues were already beneath the lower bluffs. Bienville's boat was concealed by the wooded curve of the eastern shore.

Evan pulled with a feverish revival of strength. His tongue kept licking across his hot, cracked lips. All he could think of was De Lusser's fort -- Tombekbe – Tombekbe. The name of it kept beating against his brain like a hammer of hope. A little while and they would all be able to rest, lie down, wallow in heavenly unconsciousness. A little while and they would be able to sleep under roofs again, out of the weather, away from the swarming mosquitoes. There would be fresh baked bread, not water sodden glue, and game, fresh killed in the woods. He knew that would not last long, that in a few days they would be on the move again. But his whole soul was set upon that promise of respite--Tombekbe. He smelled it, as a man dying of thirst smells water, and it gave him a strength on the oars which had had not believed in him.

The boat moved so slowly beside the wooded shore! Now they were in the bend. Out of the tail of his eye he saw the blue white bluff. It hung above the boats, not higher than fifteen or twenty feet, topped by cedars and oaks. When he cut his eyes across the river he saw that the overflow had covered the lower eastern bank and was eddying in yellow flood through the timber. The river swung in a great bend like a scythe between the western bluffs and the wooded eastern shore. The boats worked their way slowly, clinging to the cedar topped bluffs. Evan seated on the oar, growing angered because Lesueur and Lazac kept pointing at things he could not see. He knew when they spotted De Lusser's fort above the bluffs, but it was invisible to him.

After an eternity of pulling his oar, lifting it, pulling it, he saw Lazac move his stern oar hard to the right. The pirogue swung into a break in the white bluff where the yellow flood of the river backed. It was the mouth of the Etomba-Igaby, the Coffin Maker's Creek. The creek itself was lost by the backwater from the river eddying into its mouth. As the pirogue moved into the relatively easy water of the creek mouth, Evan saw the other boats lining a high bluff tangled in trees and vines. Bienville, De Noyan, and Macarty-Mactigue were almost at the top of the bluff, climbing on a steep path, pulling themselves up with the aid of the vines and saplings.

Evan's knees were water as he tried to climb, but Gaston Lazac was behind, shoving him. The knowledge that there were houses and beds and bread and meat on the top of the bluff hardened his muscles. Many of the white coated French were on the bluff above him, scrambling among the trees, weighted with their packs and firelocks, sliding upon knees, digging with their fingers in the soft mud. Glancing downward he saw other French soldiers and all of the Swiss still in their boats.

From the lip of the bluff westward and northwestward the woods had been cleared, forming a miniature desolate, muddy plain not more than one hundred yards square. The creek and river faces of the fort were protected so far as was apparent by the sheerness of the bluffs but a palisade of sharpened cedar logs covered the timber side, making an oblique angle between the white bluff and the thickly grown creek bank. Evan halted and stared unbelievingly, all his hope nourished energy seeping away. Crawling over the rim of the bluff he had had his eyes cast high, expecting imposing bastions. What he actually saw first was the height of the stockade, as if it guarded emptiness and only the Fleur de Lis on a cedar pole in the middle of the parade. Between him and the stockade was a scattering of huts and lean-tos, built out of logs and poles and roofed with bark and leaves. Bienville and his staff were grouped near the flagpole talking with a French officer who must be Captain de Lusser.

Evan felt something in his throat choking him, and wondered whether it was his heart or his stomach. Both were deathly sick. He saw a little man running toward him, a little man with the look of a particularly miserable weasel, and he recognized Camille Billiot.

Evan knew his head was spinning. Camille seemed to gyrate past him and he was reaching out his hand to stop him when he realized what he was doing. His ears roared and he heard Camille squalling at Lazac.

"You say they have Jean?" bellowed Lazac, repeating something Camille has said.

"In irons. Under guard. With a sergeant." Camille's words, though not loud, thundered in Evans ears. His knees buckled and he felt Lazac's big arm under his shoulders.

Chapter XIX

The Choctaw chiefs began to arrive at the fort three days after Bienville's army. The first to come was Alibamon Mingo with Sieur de Lery from the Village of Concha. De Lery had reported that several villages which had set out on the march had gone home because of a rumor in the Choctaw nation that the French from the north, meaning D'Artaguette, were going to make peace with the Chickasaws and then, in company with them, attack the Choctaws. Bienville cursed the Choctaws and then sent De Lery to tell them not to be so timid.

For the next three days Bienville had no time for anything except meeting the Choctaw chiefs as each made his appearance, and listening to the interminable harangues which each one took it upon himself to make. The name of the Choctaw tribe meant, 'pleasing voice', and every Choctaw chief seemed in love with the sound of his own voice. Bienville had to listen patiently to their boasts of prowess, to their protestations of undying fidelity to the French, to their demands for munitions, vermilion, and supplies. He answered each of them in turn, saying that he had made it clear before that each tribe was to furnish its own provisions, but that he would have powder, bullets, and vermilion distributed among them as he had promised.

Soulier Rouge, the recalcitrant chief of the Cushtushas, arrived with the Great Chief of the Nation. After the Great Chief had spoken, Soulier Rouge made his harangue. He declared his love for the French; a declaration which Bienville heard without enthusiasm, but also without comment, as he realized it was no time to reproach the influential chief of Cushtusha with past treachery to the French cause. Beneath his coating of dirt, which was a characteristic of the Choctaws, Soulier Rouge carried himself proudly. He was arrogant, sensitive, and it was better not to antagonize him at the time when his attitude might mean the difference between success and failure for the French.

Mingo Chitto, the Great Chief, stepped forward to Bienville as Soulier Rouge wound down to hasten an end to the meeting.

"Since the last moon changed," he said, "a band of my young men has come back from the north. They saw there a great French trail. They believed that it was made by people of the north going to join the Chickasaws. What does my father know of this trail?"

"This is no news which the Chief brings. The chief of the French people of the north is under orders from me to bring his young men and Indian allies and join us in attacking our enemies, the Chickasaw. If he has made this trail which has alarmed the chief then it is because the runner I sent to delay his march had not yet reached him. Have no fear. If he is there ahead of us, we shall have word from him."

Whether his explanation or show of scorn convinced them he did not know. He ended the meeting by telling the Great Chief that when all the chiefs had arrived a general conference would be held, in which his plan for war would be discussed. They accepted his words and took their leave in a ceremonious manner.

When they were gone, he let his shoulders slump tiredly and shot a worried glance at Lesueur, who had sat silently through the parley smoking his pipe.

"First De Lery, then the young men who came this morning," he said, almost to himself. "Now Mingo Chitto

I would say he is the most level headed of the chiefs. It may not be all talk. Something is up concerning D'Artaguette. What do you think, Jean Paul."

Lesueur caressed his under lip with the stem of his pipe. "A man might do a lot of thinking and guessing and never know if he was right or wrong. Maybe this runner never reached D'Artaguette. Maybe D'Artaguette was not able to hold his Indians. Maybe its all Choctaw talk. Me, I could give you an opinion, but I'm for finding out. It is about fifty leagues to the Chickasaw plains. A scout could cover the distance, take a good look around, and meet us on the Oktibbeha without trouble."

"Good, I will send Martin," responded Bienville. "He and Lazac are the best woodsmen I have and I wish to keep Lazac with me. He has more uses than Martin. I may need him for some unforeseen problem when we reach the Chickasaw country."

"That is true, but Henri Martin has never been in that part of the land north of the Oktibbeha," Lesueur replied. "Lazac was there two years ago and probably before. He could see more and make much better time and this knowledge could prove indispensable."

"You are right," said Bienville with a resigned sigh. "Speed in getting this news is of the greatest importance and the scout may have to find us as well. I will send Lazac tomorrow. Hopefully, he will meet us at the Oktibbeha in ten days."

Evan did not see the Great Chief arrive. For two days he had fought the fever from a pallet on the floor in De Lusser's cabin where they had put him.

When the fever broke he slept uneasily. As he awoke he felt as weak as a kitten with a sense of being hollowed out. He heard a creaking of the door and turned his head rustily. The yellow needle of sunlight through the opening door hurt his eyes. Gaston Lazac's large figure filled the doorway and blocked the sun. He pushed closed the door and knelt down beside the pallet. When he saw Evan's eyes were open his beard split in a grin.

"Feeling better?" he asked.

Evan could only answer by raising and lowering his chin, which seemed the limit of his powers.

"You have grunted like a bull alligator for the past two days," said Lazac. "And flopped like a hooked eel. I had to put that blanket around you a hundred times."

A wave of feeble anger stirred words in Evan. "That damned blanket! It was you smothering me. If I could I would have sent you and that blanket to hell."

"Maybe," he chuckled, "but I minded you like a baby. I am good at baby-minding, no? I have a notion to take it up as a business when we return to Nouvelle Orleans."

The joke went flat. Evans throat was on fire and his tongue a chip. Too much so to make asking what age and sex of babies Lazac intended on minding worthwhile.

"This is a hell of a place to call a fort, the stockade is not a fit fence for a pea patch," Lazac continued, "and the men are sleeping in the mud that is called a parade."

Evan raised himself on an elbow with great difficulty as if trying to look out the window.

Lazac went on, "Bienville has sent all the men into the timber to get logs to build more cabins and secure the stockade. You wouldn't believe it," he said, pulling a black twist out of his shirt and taking a large bite, "but he actually wanted me to work. And I did, too, as a favor to him, until I had to come see how you were coming along."

The chunk, chunk, chunk of the axes in the woods came measured and clear into the room. Evan had been hearing the sound since he awakened but until now thought it was inside his head.

A rusty lizard scurried across the dirt floor and Lazac missed him with a hurried brown stream as he slipped through a crack in the wall. "I saw old Camille," he said, and Evan remembered seeing Camille as they reached the fort. "Bienville has been giving the bakers the devil. There was only one oven and they had not baked enough biscuit to keep this mob eating for two days. They've three ovens now and baking furiously."

It seemed to Evan that he could smell bread baking, the odor of dough, and the heat of an open oven, tumbled from his brain to his stomach and turned it queasy. He lay back with dull eyes trying not to think of the hot bread which he now wanted so badly, and which he was sure would kill him if he ate it right then.

"You saw Camille?" he mumbled. "His brother...what?"

Lazac's blunt fingers dug in the floor making an odd design which he studied before he replied. "They're going to try Jean and another man before a court martial in a day or two. But it won't make any difference," he said seriously. "They will be executed." He paused, thinking, then, "A lot of funny things happen around a place like this one. The woods and the rain kind of get into a man's head if he don't watch out. Bad eating. Bad bowels. The fever. Like I said, this is a hell of a fort."

Even the irrepressible Lazac seemed sobered. Evan closed his eyes and thought of the rain and the river and the endless days, the woods closing in. Yes, they got into man's head and perhaps into his soul. He felt an unbelievable weight of weariness come over him and fell asleep.

It was two more days before he could leave the cabin. The face of the encampment had changed. The once barren ground inside the stockade had mushroomed with shelters and more cabins were going up. A wall was being erected along the creek bank and the rest of the stockade walls were reinforced and backed by planks.

The fever had left Evan in a state of depression. So far the expedition seemed a ghastly struggle far from the adventure that he had anticipated. The Indians were not the strutting warriors he had pictured. They looked shiftless and dirty. He began to share Lazac's opinion of the Choctaws as fighters and Bienville's concern about the French troops. Only his confidence in Bienville's ability to salvage the campaign gave him any confidence at all.

Camille Billiot was heart broken because his brother, Jean, had turned out to be a traitor. He would not be consoled even by Gaston Lazac's offer of a drink.

"I am disgraced," he moaned, with his head in his hands. "How could Jean treat me so! I have tried to see him but they will not let me. Mutiny! They say he has plotted mutiny! What will they do?"

Gaston stared at the ground and shook his head. He knew, of course what the punishment was but he had not the heart to say it. Yet the feeling persisted that he could not have informed Camille more plainly than if he had put it in words. Camille lowered his own head and said no more.

That afternoon the command was called to assemble in the fort to watch the execution of the mutineers who had been tried and sentenced the day before. Two scaffolds had been hastily erected in the midst of what passed as a parade ground for the fort. Every soldier would have a clear view of the execution. The gallows were makeshift contraptions of pine poles with a short rope hung from the center. The French troops had erected one scaffold for Jean Billiot. The other had been built by the Swiss contingent as one of their number, Sergeant Montfort, had been found guilty of the same offense.

The companies made a hollow square around the execution site with the Choctaws squatting in front of a gnarled cedar tree to the northwest of the scaffold to witness this demonstration of French justice.

Bienville and his staff marched out in full military discipline to the front of the assembly. He wished to impress upon both his troops and the Choctaw allies the severity of treason during a military campaign and the equal severity and sureness of the punishment. When Bienville had assumed his place before the troops Aide Major Macarty-Mactigue stepped forward and unrolled a large piece of paper.

"In accordance with the laws and in the name of Louis XV, King of France and ruler of New France and La Louisiane, the traitors Charles Montfort and Jean Billiot have been sentenced to death. This sentence will now be executed."

A drum roll commenced and the Aide-Major nodded a predetermined command and stepped back into ranks with the other officers.

Standing between Evan and Gaston Lazac, Camille Billiot screwed up his weathered face as two white coated guards escorted Jean across the parade ground in front of the troops and Indians and over to the gallows. Jean walked steadily with his head level but with apprehension upon his face. Two red coated Swiss escorted Montfort, who turned his head to his erstwhile comrades. He gave them a resigned smile then faced the gibbet.

Camille regarded the scaffold. "I am no carpenter," Camille whispered, "but I could build better than that. A gust of wind will blow it down."

He thought to himself that Jean did not show any fear as he stepped upon the bench below the rope. Still he must be afraid. No man could face certain death without fear in his soul, whatever his face showed. They said that Jean had plotted to murder Captain Lusser and the lieutenant named Grondel and run away to the Chickasaws. He could certainly believe it. Jean had always been wild as the devil, looking out for no one but himself. He wished that he had the nerve to threaten French officers and flee to the savages. Ventre Sainte Gris, if he did, what a fling he would make among those Indians. Those lithe young women. No Clementine to brow beat him. No work. Only hunting, fishing, using his women and being used by them. He sighed. He envied Jean the daring nerve which might have gotten him there. But he did not envy him the rope which the sergeant was tying around his neck.

He closed his eyes and kept them closed a long time. He heard the command from the lieutenant and then the collective breath of the army and knew that the sentence had been carried out. The air was still. Even the creatures in the woods seemed to sense the gravity of what had just occurred and were silent. Only the rush of the swollen creek could be heard. When Camille opened his eyes at last the murky light seemed brilliant, harsh and cruel. The form swinging up against a tumbled sky, the tail of its uniform coat gently flapping in the wet breeze, was not a human being at all. The other object, not far from it, jerked in slight spasms at the knees as it dangled from its short length of rope.

Men shuffled uneasily in the ranks of the Swiss and the French. Some stood with stiff faces, some with twisted faces in open consternation. Others showed a tear in their hard eyes while others paled in the sickness that was felt by all. The shadow of the gallows cooled whatever intentions were in their minds. The Choctaws smoked their pipes and nodded their heads.

There was not a word spoken after the company commanders dismissed the ranks and the men walked away.

Gaston Lazac put his hand on Camille's shoulder. Evan closed his eyes and shook his head as his nightmare seemed to continue.

Bienville held his war council with the assembled Choctaw chiefs on the first of May. A fire of cedar logs burned in the middle of the council square and the chiefs sat around it, sweating in the heat as they passed the calumet. Over the fire an earthen pot bubbled with the Black Drink of the Choctaws. In the shadows behind the chiefs sat the warriors who had accompanied each to the fort. Evan and Gaston Lazac sat just behind the company commanders beside Bienville and his aides.

"The Governor will have a hard time this night," Gaston whispered, almost inaudibly to Evan. "The chiefs will speak pompously, as is their custom in dealing with us, but each has his own interests and will follow us only as far as those interests go. They will not lose face in front of the others, however. The Choctaws have a great sense of pride, though it is different from ours."

Bienville arose to open the council. His face in the firelight looked as dark and saturnine as any of the Indians.

"Listen well, my brothers of the Choctaw Nation," he began, speaking in their own language. "We are gathered here for the purpose of discussing how to put an end, once and for all, to the menace which the Chickasaw Nation holds for both of our nations. We, the chiefs and warriors of the great French king, have come many leagues to join our Choctaw brothers in making war upon our common enemy. The chiefs of the Choctaw have assembled here at my request, in order that I may make known my plan of war. If any of my brothers wishes to speak before I give my plan, he has the liberty to do so."

The Great Chief of the Choctaw, Mingo Chitto, arose and stepped gravely into the light of the council fire, facing Bienville.

"Chahta holata imataha chito anki achukma," he said. "You are the big supporting holahta of the Choctaw and my good father. I, Mingo Chitto, Great Chief of the Choctaw Nation, speak for my people. We have given our word to the French. The Great Spirit has spoken to us and has said that no good can come to us from the English. He has told us that the French are our friends. We have listened to the Great Spirit, Abi Inki, and we believe, for you, our good father, have never done us harm. I speak for my people and for myself, even though but two winters past I was forced to go naked because by brother Diron, who is the French mingo at Mobile, would not give me a coat as he has promised."

"My father, the Chickasaws are the enemies of the Choctaws even as they are the enemies of the French. For many years we have been at war. For many years they have stolen our cattle and our women. They speak with the tongues of lying dogs and their hearts are black. For every Choctaw scalp that the Chickasaws have taken we will take ten. For the death of my son who was lost at the village of Chukafalaya last year I will deal death among the Chickasaws."

"My father, I have said my say. The chiefs of the Choctaw nation await the unfolding of your plan."

Bienville, who had remained cross legged in the Indian fashion, his eyes intent on the chief as he spoke, now looked around the circle of dark stolid faces. The chiefs were painted for war; daubed in vermilion, white clay, and indelible ink across the cheek bones and the naked, greasy chest. Paint circled their arms. Each band could be identified by the covering of his pouch. Alibamon Mingo and the Great Chief, with the other chiefs and mingoes of the Bougue Chitto and Turkey Creek bands, had bullet and powder pouches of dried gourds with otter skins shrunk over them. Soulier Rouge and the other chiefs of the Moklasha bands had their pouches covered with fox hide.

In the smoking heat the smell of the Indians was thick enough to cut. Soulier Rouge and his chiefs were a particularly mangy looking lot, even dirtier than the other Choctaws. There was something which struck Evan as ludicrous in the contrast of their dignified faces and the fact that every few minutes they had to scratch some portion of their bodies.

Gaston Lazac told him, nodding his head toward the Indians:

"That flea-bitten bastard is Soulier Rouge. He's head man at the Cushtusha town. That means 'place of fleas.' That is why he's scratching. Bienville will have to watch him. He's treacherous as a moccasin snake."

As the Great Chief resumed his seat and Bienville's eye passed around the circle, none of the chiefs moved except Alibamon Mingo. Raw boned and tall for a Choctaw, he stepped into the spot which the Great Chief had vacated. His black eyes rested unblinkingly upon Bienville's face.

"My father. I speak. You know me."

Bienville, who out of courtesy to the Choctaw had been smoking their pipe, took it from his lips.

"Speak, chief of the people of the great canes."

The Choctaw spoke well, with a resonant voice.

"I am of the great race of Ingulasha, who are in alliance with the other great race of Imoklasha, whose chieftains and mingoes are here," he began, sweeping his right arm in a gesture which included the entire circle. "For the race of the Inguslasha I say that we are ready to make war on the Chickasaws and the English. You, my father, know how to take such talk. Holauba! Holauba! Feena! It is a real lie! When the Frenchmen first came among us, I took them by the hand and I have ever remained firm to my engagements, and in return all my wants and those of my warriors and my wives and my children have been bountifully supplied. I have seen the English come among us, with promises of abundance. I have talked with them, but remembering my pledges to the French, I would have none of their things. I have taken the guns and the powder of the French. The English tell me that the English guns and powder are better. They tell me that if I take them the hearts of our hunters will be rejoiced through the land and the nakedness of our women will be covered."

"But I turned them away, for there was one thing which concerned me, and that was the behavior of the English traders toward our women. I have been told that wherever the English go they cause disturbances for they live under no government, and pay no respect either to wisdom or station. And I know this, by the witness of my own eyes, that when the traders sent for a basket of bread and the generous Choctaw sent his wife to supply their wants, instead of taking the bread out of the basket the traders put their hands upon the breasts of the wife. That conduct is not to be admitted, for the maxim of our language is that death is preferable to disgrace. So I bade my people not to take the things of the English."

"That is the word that I would speak to the chiefs of the Choctaws. The French have not broken their word to us. We shall not break our word to them. My father, and my brothers, I have spoken."

When Alibamon Mingo had stepped back into the circle, Bienville, again on his feet, confronted the Choctaws. He knew well from long experience the Choctaw weakness for fine words and eloquent protestations. He did not allow himself to feel too enthusiastic over the words of the Great Chief and Alibamon Mingo.

"I have heard you out, my brothers of the Choctaws, now you shall hear me out. This is my plan of war. From here, we, the French of Mobile and Nouvelle Orleans, together with the Choctaws east and west, will move against our enemies, the Natchez and the Chickasaws. We will be joined in the battle by the people of the north, and by the tribes of the Illinois, the Cahokias, the Kaskaskias, the Michigamias, the Arkansas and the Iroquois. How can our enemies stand against such as these?"

"Listen well. Return to your towns. When fourteen suns have passed, be with your warriors upon the banks of the Octibia, the little river which is the boundary between your country and that of the Chickasaw people. I will meet you there. Send two of your warriors with me, so that if I arrive sooner than you, I shall be able to send them to you. When all your warriors have arrived, we shall go together up the river to the new portage which is nine leagues from the towns of the Chickasaws. From there we shall march to join with the French people of the north. That is my plan of war. Have you anything to say, chiefs of the Choctaw nation?"

The Great Chief spoke for the Choctaws, "My father, your plan is good. With our warriors we will meet you upon the Octibia when fourteen suns have passed. We depart at once for our villages when we have taken the war drink of our people."

As he squatted again in his place, one of the lesser chiefs sprang up lithely and strode to the earthen pot which swung above the council fire. The liquid in the pot, made of the leaves of the yaupon, was black and thick, boiling and spewing out little hot flecks. The chief, naked except for his buck-she-ah-ma, and horribly painted, seized the gourd which hung at the side of the pot. There was a tenseness, a touch of melodrama in his motions. With a quick twist of his wrist he dipped the gourd into the bubbling liquid and lifted it out, foaming and running over. Carefully he held the brimming gourd before him as he walked slowly to the Great Chief.

He presented the gourd to the Great Chief, drawing out his breath in a long note which he held longer than seemed humanly possible. While the Great Chief accepted the gourd and drank of the scalding liquid, the Indian who had proffered it repeated his musical note, but in a different key, extending it until Evan's ears rang with the shrill of it. The Great Chief finished his drinking before the note had ended and returned the gourd to the Choctaw who then refilled it and proceeded to follow the same ritual with each of the chiefs.

He nudged Lazac. "Why do they do it?" he whispered.

Lazac grunted. "They say it's a custom. But I can tell you they are drinking tonight to get up the courage to go home. A Choctaw is scared of the woods after dark. He thinks a bad spirit will get him if he's out alone. He thinks that if he follows a woman into the woods at night he won't come back."

The gourd refilled again and again, passed slowly around the circle of Choctaws. The ceremony went on monotonously. The smell of the drink grew overpowering. Evan could stand it no longer. He slipped quietly away and walked along the bluff overlooking the river. The cool night air eased the pain in his head. He stayed a long time watching the dim waters. When he returned at last to De Lusser's cabin, the council fire was only a bed of embers. The Choctaws had gone home.

CHAPTER XX

The rains which fell upon Bienville's army all the way up the river and at Camp Tombekbe were not confined to the Indian country. In Nouvelle Orleans and the surrounding lower Mississippi River, April had been uncommonly wet. The habitants looked up with grateful eyes to the clearing skies which began with May. Their fields and their gardens were choked with grass and weeds. Now that the fields were drying they were busy cultivating and replanting the damaged acres. They were too fully occupied to give much thought to the army which had marched away six weeks before. No word had come from it since it left Mobile. By now it must be deep in the heart of the Indian country. Many of them had friends or sons or brothers or husbands with Bienville. For these they said Mass regularly. But they were not greatly worried. Soon, they said, the savages in the north will be wiped out and the men would come marching back.

Antoine Castilloux had spent most of that rainy April at Cannes Brulees and he was thoroughly sick of it. Just as the season of transplanting the young tobacco had begun Gerard Mallot, his overseer, had taken to his bed and remained there with a distemper of the chest. Castilloux had come post haste to the country, leaving Antoinette and the Baron de Laval to the comparative comforts of the Chevalier de

Pradel's house in Nouvelle Orleans. Each time he hoisted his great carcass into the saddle and rode through the fields Castilloux wished that he had remained there himself. He had the negroes whipped regularly, but even that seemed to do no good. He had to admit that it was the weather and sickness among the slaves rather than any shirking on their part which had caused the tobacco to be in such a deplorable state. The water which stood in the fields prevented cultivation. Earthworms were cutting the young plants. By the time Gerard Mallot was up and about Castilloux was fairly ill himself from furious helplessness and the unaccustomed exertion of the past few weeks. In a savage mood he returned to Nouvelle Orleans and gathered Antoinette and the Baron from the care of De Pradel.

He marked that Antoinette seemed blooming in health and De Laval more peaked than ever. All the way home in Castilloux's berline the Baron was in a state of intense agitation. His lips trembled even when he pressed them ightly together. He dropped dejectedly upon a chair in Castilloux's salon while Antoinette ran up the steep stairs to her room on the half floor above. No sooner had the sound of her feet on the stair ceased than De Laval burst into a flood of excited, almost incoherent speech. Castilloux, pulling at his heavy lips, sat down to hear him out.

Antoinette tarried in her room only long enough to toss her cloak upon the bed. Halfway down the stairs the unusual vigor of De Laval's voice arrested her. She put her fingers upon the stair rail and furrowed her brows. What was wrong with Edouard? He had been morose as a bear for days, and scarcely opened his mouth. Now he was speaking so fast the words all ran together. And then he said so clearly it made her jump, "Mademoiselle Castilloux."

She could not resist tiptoeing to the foot of the stairs and putting her ear against the heavy dark curtain which hung between the salon and the narrow little hallway. She was afraid to peek through the folds of the curtain lest they see her. But when her father's voice rumbled she could visualize him slouching indolently, his eyelids drooping, a trick of his when angry. And she heard De Laval's nervous fingers drumming the arm of his chair.

"I repeat it again and again and again!" De Laval's voice was choked and shrill. "You have deceived me, deceived me grossly! I shall not forgive you!"

Castilloux growled out. "Monsieur, I pray you to speak more calmly. You have vilified my daughter and myself with such incoherence. I am entirely at sea. Now you charge deception on my part. Speak out man. Say what you mean."

Antoinette gasped. Her father's bluntness measured the extent of his anger. Always he had handled Edouard with velvet gloves.

"What," cried De Laval, "What could be more deceitful than the lies you have told me? As to your means: you are no more, monsieur, than a gueux revetu, a beggar grown rich. Rich in arrogance, not in purse. And you lied to me! To me! You have dragged me here to this foul country! This wilderness! This morass! You shall get me out of it! I starve. The food revolts me. The unspeakable insects devour me! Good God! Shall I never go home to civilization! If I remain here another fortnight I shall go home in a box. Of that I am sure. And my blood will be upon your hands!"

Antoinette's head whirled from trying to keep up with the hysterical rapidity of his speech. She could imagine her father still slumped, watching him, waiting for him to be done.

"We have gone over this before, monsieur," he said. "It is true that I brought you here for a purpose. And that purpose was to convince you of the mutual advantages which might come from your marriage to my daughter. I see now that you have not been convinced."

She could feel De Laval's effort to calm himself. He spoke hesitantly and with great care. "Under the circumstances, Monsieur Castilloux, it scarcely warrants consideration. I have no doubt that Mademoiselle Castilloux possesses, ah, qualities. Intelligence, beauty. But she has never been, ah, quite born."

"And my means are not sufficient to make up for it?" purred Castilloux.

"Indeed, no."

Antoinette's fingers tightened on the curtain. The arrogant little beast!

"Then it is settled," said Castilloux. "And since you cannot abide in Louisiana, Monsieur le Baron, how shall you return to France?"

She caught the hysterical apprehension in De Laval's voice. "Monsieur! Is that the game you play?"

"It is no game," said Castilloux firmly. "I am a man of business."

"You...you think .." stammered De Laval, "you think that I could not return to France without your help?"

"I have no doubt that you could return--eventually. In a box perhaps. The words are your own. Do you care to wait that long?"

There was a stark frenzy in the drumming of De Laval's fingers. Antoinette smiled tightly. Waves of heat and chill ran alternately over her body; fury at De Laval, pride at her father's cleverness in handling him.

De Laval sighed deeply. "Very well, monsieur, I throw myself upon your mercy."

Castilloux moved in his chair. It was his only sign of triumph. "Good. You shall be married and return to France upon the Gironde."

She could hear De Laval breathing as if he had been running. "Would it not be better, monsieur," he ventured after a minute, "Ah, more fitting to the occasion and my station, if we were married in

France?"   Castilloux chuckled unmirthfully. "As I have said before, Pere Philippe is perfectly qualified to perform the ceremony. You know, my dear Baron, a bird in the hand--"

In a second Antoinette was flying tiptoe up the stairs, holding her skirt so that she would not stumble and make a noise. The door closed softly behind her. She dropped upon her bed not minding if she rumpled the carelessly flung cloak.

The Baronne de Laval! The Baronne de Laval! Oh, God! Versailles, and all that went with it! At last! Even marriage to Edouard, the puny puppy, could not dim the glory of that! Versailles! Old Pere Philippe, how she loved him who was to give her what she had dreamed of!

The curtain blew in at the window making a shadow across her bright, exultant face. And with it a shadow dropped over her heart. Evan MacDonald. He was young and strong and handsome. Everything De Laval was not. She must admit that her body ached for such a young man. He shared the memories of their youth. These were ties that she shared with no one else.

Ah, he would never come back! Out there somewhere in the wilderness, being butchered by savages, she had no doubt. Never come back to look for her in a place where she was not to be found. She would find other strong men at the court of the king. Men of true wealth and power. Had she promised him? No, it was not really a promise; and yet, though her slender fingers touched her eyelids she could still see him standing straight and expectant, and the light and the eager life going out of his eyes. She rolled her face and clenched her fists. He would never come back. Never. And she would not be sorry. It was her own life to live. In the chance that he lived he would forget. She knew he must forget, and hoped that he never would.

The Gironde still swung on her anchor below the Place d'Armes and Captain Villiers, required to sleep aboard each night, still came ashore each morning to have a sociable breakfast with Monsieur Salmon. He had held up his voyage to France awaiting word from Bienville and any urgent reports to the Duke de Maurepas.

In the meantime, by way of diversion, he had found time to attend the wedding of Antoinette Castilloux at the Church of St. Louis. A lovely child, he told himself, almost wishing himself in the Baron de Laval's shoes. Too bad the groom appeared in such a state of disrepair, spiritually as well as physically. To the captain's keen nautical eye he looked as if he had come through a long voyage and heavy seas. He badly needed a turn in dry dock for refitting and to have the barnacles scraped off his hull.

But as he thought again, when it was all over and he was drinking sweet wine with Monsieur Salmon, the bride was quite the loveliest he had seen in many a day. Like the sunshine itself which blessed the occasion, fresh as the tender green willows under the levee. She was fair game for any young buck and the buck who had got her was young, even though he scarcely looked it.

Thinking of Evan MacDonald, he wondered if the girl had not displayed bad taste, but he could easily understand why she had chosen as she did. She had always seemed quite fond of Evan, so he had watched her as closely as he might throughout the ceremony. He must confess, however, that his romantic investigations were rewarded by no sign of a tear. She was a self-contained young woman, remarkably like her father in some ways. It was hard to say what she might be thinking. He felt sorry for Evan, losing such a morsel, but not too sorry. He had been young himself once and had known these failures in love. It was by no means a mortal sickness. As soon as the inspiration of the malady was removed from the proximity of the patient he usually recovered, and speedily, as well.

The wedding over, time hung heavily and he was really becoming impatient when on the nineteenth of May a pirogue from Mobile reached the landing on the Bayou St. Jean. The voyageur in charge of it came on foot to Salmon's house bringing letters from Bienville at the Camp of Tombekbe. There were three letters: for Captain Villiers, for Monsieur Salmon, and a bulkier communication addressed to the Comte de Maurepas. The Captain's letter contained only an inquiry into his health, a statement of Bienville's own, an apology for detaining him so long, and the hope of a speedy voyage. From Salmon he gathered details of the inclement weather in the Indian country, the sickness of the army, and the shortage of supplies. What disturbed them both was Bienville's fear that the Chevalier D'Artaguette's Illinois army had already encountered the Chickasaws. Salmon fairly wrung his hands over this news and spent the rest of that day speculating upon any number of dire eventualities.

Within three days Captain Villiers had the Gironde laden. Her papers were cleared by Monsieur de Livaudais, the Captain of the Port, and she was ready to sail. The townspeople came in force to see her off, and the Chevalier de Louboey brought a guard of honor. It was a bright morning when she weighed anchor and steered down the current. Captain Villiers stood on the sunny quarterdeck with the Baron and Baronne de Laval. Gradually the reflection in the willows on the water faded. The cabins shrank into a uniformity with the swamp. The steeple of the church stood up for awhile and when they dropped below the bend that, too, was lost.

The Captain's quizzical eyes regarded the Baronne de Laval.

"Madame la Baronne," he murmured softly, "Are you not sorry to be leaving this country?"

Her eyes were on the water. He thought she was not going to answer at all. "No, monsieur," she said at last. "It is not healthy. It is full of bugs, and broken hearts. I will forget it."

Etienne was in a grumbling mood that morning. It was a habit with him when he first awakened but this time Jacqueline sensed a real tantrum coming.

For awhile it was only a querulous whine which pricked her nerves like a constant needle.

"Open the window," he said at last. "Open the door, for God's sake, woman, I'm smothering. How can you stand it?"

She threw them both wide and let the sunshine flood in. Ah, that was better. It looked like a human habitation now, and not like a hole in the ground or a tree hollow where animals live. She would have opened them long ago, but ordinarily Etienne preferred the gloom.

As the bright light struck his eyes he squinted painfully. Then his tongue lashed at her.

"What are you doing? Do you want to put my eyes out? How could I know the sun was so bright? You stand there with your mouth buttoned like a fool. My eyes! Shut them. Quick! I can't see!"

She shut the door and window obediently and went back to the pot on the fire to fetch his breakfast. It was steaming when she brought it to him and held the bowl while he dipped the spoon.

"Watch now," she warned him, "it's hot."

Obstinately he popped the spoonful of sagamity into his mouth. His facial muscles twisted in a remarkable grimace. She knew the stuff was burning him, that he wanted to howl with pain and could not because his mouth as full. He looked so funny! She bit her lip to keep from laughing. He spat the whole mouthful on the floor and, flying into a towering rage, snatched the bowl from her fingers and hurled it halfway across the room. The impulse of laughter died in her. By the time she had the mess cleaned up she was shaking all over and ready to cry. Etienne had turned his face toward the wall. He had gone dumb. No amount of coaxing would make him speak or eat when she brought him another full bowl. She dumped the sagamity back into the pot and slumped on the bench. Her own appetite was gone. The very idea of food made her sick.

When Therese Lambert popped her round face in at the door Jacqueline could have wept with relief.

Therese was sweating as if she had been running. "Vite!" She exclaimed. "Vite child! The Gironde will be away. Don't you want to see her go?" She cut her eyes at Etienne, speechless by the wall. "What's wrong with him now?"

"Nothing," said Jacqueline, shortly. She picked up her blue fichu without a word to Etienne. He had heard Therese plainly, but stubbornly refused to move.

Therese wanted to hurry, but Jacqueline preferred to lag with the breeze of the river like a dash of water in her face. They did both by turns, with Therese grumbling every step.

"Is he sick or sulking?" she asked, getting back to the subject of Etienne.

Jacqueline smiled tightly. "He hasn't seen Papa Jules this week," she said. "I have been keeping a close watch."

"So that's it!"

"I don't know which is worse," said Jacqueline listlessly, "To let him have the rum or to keep it form him. He is thirsty enough now to be ugly. But when he is full he's uglier still. He is always flinging about, hurting himself and threatening me."

They hurried past the Place D'Armes and scrambled up the levee in time to see the Gironde with the hands on the capstan hauling up the anchor. Therese plowed into the crowd with Jacqueline at her heels until she found a place which suited her. The white spread of canvas hung over the water with the sun striking it, and Jacqueline's heart leapt. There were figures on the ship's quarterdeck. She recognized Captain de Villiers. The other two she knew by hearsay. The slender girl was Antoine Castilloux's daughter, the gentleman beside her was her husband, the Baron de Laval. It had not entered her head that she would see this girl. She had not ever wanted to see her.

Seeing her brought back Evan, real as life, and that hurt. She had not thought of him lately. She had not wanted to, for one thing, and Etienne's constant bedevilment of her was an unfailing preventative for unwanted thought. Now, looking at that bright haired girl in her damask dress and silken shawl, she remembered painfully everything that Collette had ever told her about Evan MacDonald and Antoinette Castilloux. And Collette had told her a great deal before here sharp eyes had seen Jacqueline's own yearning for Evan. Yes, with Etienne lying there listening, and his eyes seeing things too. Poor little Collette! Old Jules Froissart had told her how Collette had gone with Bienville's army. Collette was resourceful, God knew, but an army is an army.

The sail and the ship, the yellow river water, and the shimmering willows were like parts of a dream. Therese shook her shoulder.

"Wake up, chick," laughed Therese.

The ship was far down, dropping into the bend. They stayed and watched it out go of sight and then followed the crowd back past the Place d'Armes. Therese trotted straight home to get Gustave's dinner, leaving Jacqueline make her way as slowly as she desired. She wanted to take forever, savoring the clean air. It did not change matters at all that Antoinette Castilloux was now another man's wife. She was also another man's wife.

As soon as she came in sight of the house she knew that she could expect trouble. Old Jules Froissart popped his head out of the door like a squirrel peeping from a hollow branch. As she hurried through the gate he got down to the ground as quickly as his old legs would allow him and hobbled toward the hole in the fence where the pickets were down.

She yelled at him. "Papa Jules!"

For a moment it seemed that he would not stop. Then his old back straightened. He faced around slowly and waited until she came up to him.

"Papa Jules! she accused him, breathlessly, "what have you been up to?"

He scrubbed his mouth furiously, shaking his head. His eyes stared everywhere except at her. A flood of anger and panic swept over her. She put out her hand toward his arm, then drew it back.

"Papa Jules!" Fury shook the softness out of her voice and turned it harsh. "I have told you. Mother of God! I have told you a hundred times."

Still he squirmed like a schoolboy, caressing his mouth insanely and shaking his head. The sight of his white queue dancing behind his neck shattered the last shred of her self control.

"Get out!" she screamed. "You old idiot! You old, miserable, murdering idiot! Get out! Get out!"

She kept on screaming at him after he had turned tail like a decrepit old dog and hobbled away. There were tears of rage in her eyes, her whole body was twitching in a spasm, she chewed her lips brutally to stop screaming. Unclenching her fingers she pressed them upon her short gown. Under the cloth her thighs were trembling like poplar leaves.

From the house Etienne began to sing suddenly, an incoherent, wordless bawl. She ran for the steps, almost fell flat getting up them. He sat high in the bed propped against the wall, looking straight at her as she burst through the door. A gray earthen jug was cuddled up to his chest. God knows how much he has drunk already, she thought, but I must get it from him. The rum was in his face. He eyes glittered. When she paused, he grinned at her and waved one hand mockingly.

"Heh! There you are, madame. Did you see MacDonald?"

His voice was thick, horribly thick, almost unintelligible.

She had heard it many more times than she could remember, yet it always turned her cold.

"No," he was muttering. "No. He would not be there. Would he, madame? Only his mistress. She was his mistress, madame! I heard the little wench say so, a dozen times. Now she has married and quit him. Now you hope you shall be his mistress, madame? I think you have been playing the harlot all along."

Some drunken fancy passed in his mind. His voice leaped at her. "Where is he madame?"

Foolishly she tried to still her shaking legs with her shaking hands, but it was not use.

"Where is he, madame? Is his bed as hard as mine? Tell me, woman, and I shall make you both lie in it until the devil has you!"

Her body would not stop shaking but she could still control her voice.

"Give me the jug, Etienne!" she said sharply. "Give it to me!"

He folded his arms and winked at her like a cunning animal. "No, you don't," he said. Suddenly he removed one hand from the jug and reached under the blanket. He came out holding a knife. It was an old hunting knife that Henri had given her to draw fowl and cut up game when he or Gaston Lazac would bring it to them.

"Look, madame," he said. "I told Old Jules that I needed to trim my nails. But I shall kill you with it, madame. And your lover, too, when he comes looking for you."

At his words her trembling stopped. She felt cold, clearheaded, deliberate. He had threatened her before, but this was the first time he had his hands on a real weapon. She backed toward the door, reached out without turning and felt behind it for Etienne's old firelock in the place she always kept it, leaning against the wall. It was neither loaded nor primed, but Etienne would not know that. He was having a splendid time balancing the knife as if he were about to throw it. She was not afraid. From the cramped position he was in, he could scarcely hit the wall, much less her slight figure.

When she pulled the firelock out in front of her his look of gloating faded. His cheeks changed color and became almost muddy.

"Give me the jug, Etienne," she said quietly. "You have had enough."

His amazement sobered him slightly. His words came out more distinctly.

"You...You... You'd kill me," he whispered, unbelievingly. "Murder me so that you could have your lover in my bed. In my bed!"

He screamed at the last. His shoulders convulsed. The knife flickered dully, glanced upon the door frame and spun into the sunlight.

She flinched involuntarily and raised the unloaded gun halfway into firing position. Etienne's empty fingers hung before his eyes. His intentness as he stared at them was almost pitiful. He looked cornered, bereft of his weapon, utterly conscious at once of his infirmity and his unendurable desire to kill her.

In helpless rage he snatched his hand down. His elbow struck the unstoppered jug which leaned against his body. The jug fell over, teetering on the edge of the bed. His frantic fingers snatched its side and toppled it irretrievably on to the floor where it lay rocking slightly and gurgling out its contents.

He screamed, a sound so turgid, so violent, that it clawed the flesh from Jacqueline's nerves and left them quivering. She had heard such a sound once before. At Fort Rosalie when the Indians were running amok and one of them had driven his hatchet into a horse's neck and the animal screamed in the pain of death. Etienne's face was as gray clay with a revolting sweat oozing out of it, and his mouth worked as if his jaws had disjointed.

With a violent effort which she did not dream was possible he hurled his body up and over the edge of the bed. But his crippled legs pulled his torso back short and he fell headfirst from the bed tremendously hard. His head hit squarely on the hard fired earthen jug. Blood began to flow from his temple. Jacqueline, dumb and frozen by the door, heard the distinct crack and stared in shock.

Etienne lay as he had fallen. His head slid from the jug and his cheek flattened in a puddle of rum and blood. Jacqueline's regained her senses. She kneeled by him and raised hid shoulders. His eyes were glazed, unseeing. His head lolled like a cattail brush when the stalk had been broken. She had known it since she heard the cracking sound but now she said it aloud.

"He's dead. Oh, Holy Mary! He's dead." She began to weep.

CHAPTER XXI

The army reached the Oktibbeha on May the nineteenth. The warmth of late spring was welcome but much more welcome was an end of the rain. This proved to be a mixed blessing as the river level was dropped and the expedition had been slowed by the men having to disembark from the boats and drag them across sandbars and clay bottoms. There was still not enough food to ensure a long campaign unless they could find sufficient provisions in the Chickasaw towns that would be taken.

The Choctaw had arrived at the rendezvous a day earlier and had set up their own camp. Bienville was disappointed when he saw the camp. There were scarcely six hundred warriors in the whole camp, far fewer than they had promised. As soon as he entered their camp he could see that many had a mind to abandon the warpath. The chiefs were discouraged and some wished to abandon the warpath. Bienville talked to the chiefs, saying to each one that his warriors alone could annihilate the Choctaws.

This seemed to give them some heart.

He spent a good part of the morning trying to hire some of them to carry sacks of powder and bullets which the negroes were unable to carry.

None of the chiefs liked the idea, but Soulier Rouge, particularly, was insulted.

"No," he said, "the warriors of Cushtusha are not burden-bearers. That is squaw's work"

"Soldiers and bearers are already overloaded," said Bienville. "Are you better than they?"

Soulier Rouge ignored the question. "The Choctaw carries that with which he fights. No more."

Bienville glared at him. If he had not had his long experience with Indians he would have dropped his policy of coddling them, then and there. But he held his temper and looked around at the other chiefs.

"We have loaded our boats with provisions for war," he told them, "and brought them many leagues for our allies the Choctaw to use to defeat our common enemy. We do not have the men to carry all that we will need."

It was the Great Chief who broke the deadlock, and he was followed by Alibamon Mingo.

"We have brought no squaws to carry our burdens. If the warriors of the French, who are our allies, are willing to carry loads other than their weapons of war, the warriors of Couechitto will not refuse to do likewise."

Alibamon Mingo lifted his hand. "The Great Chief speaks true. The warriors of Concha will help their French brothers."

Bienville was mollified. He spoke no further to Soulier Rouge, but began the distribution of the sacks of powder and bullets among the villages which were willing to carry them. Soulier Rouge sullenly withdrew and took no part in this transaction There were other villages which withdrew with him. He had great influence and represented a strong opinion in the Choctaw Nation. They all stood aside, disapproving the actions of Concha and Couechitto. Bienville could feel the weight of their displeasure and it made him uneasy but he ignored them.

The army ate in camp and marched an hour past noon. The French and Swiss soldiers were at full pack, having drawn provisions for twelve days. They marched out across the gummy lowlands, picking their way through the willow brakes and scaring up water moccasins and frogs at every step. Infinitesimal birds flitted ahead of them above the thigh high saw grass. Then they came out of the bottoms and went up into the wooded rolling country, turning to the northwestward with the sun dropping down on their left flank. The Choctaws strung out on either side of the white men, guarding the wings. Two hundred yards in front of the main column moved the buckskin scouts under Le Sueur, acting as advance guard. Behind the main column came the negro porters, lurching under their burdens, and last of all came the Swiss under Duparc, forming the rear guard.

Henri Martin, who was acting as one of Le Sueur's scouts, was with the advance guard. He knew more of the country than any man but Gaston Lazac, including Le Sueur himself. Two hundred yards behind them, at the head of the column, Bienville trudged along. With him, in a cluster of bright coats, walked Aide-Major Macarty-Mactigue, Major de Noyan, his aide, Sieur de Juzan, and then Evan MacDonald. The drums hung noiselessly from the drummer's shoulders. The men moved silently, without talk, with only the sound of their feet slipping in the troublesome clay of the hillsides, making only a muffled curse here and there, and shifting their packs on tired backs.

The hills rolled on covered with hardwood and pine, making marching slow. The wind changed to the west and great masses of silver clouds towered against the sky.

They made camp at sunset in a grove of white oak trees, having come six miles. Already the clouds had turned black so that the sun was lost behind them. The light was sultry and failing as the companies fell out and hastily began setting up tents to keep the provisions dry. There was a grumble of thunder around the horizon and lightning flared against the dead black curtain of storm clouds.

The soldiers ate without enthusiasm around their little fires, under threat of the storm. When that was done, each man wrapped himself in his blanket with no other protection against the weather, for all the canvas had been used to cover the provisions and munitions.

Collette crawled into Rene's blanket and huddled beside him. Her body ached so, and the fever which she ran intermittently made her head so light that she had little hope of sleep. She pressed close to Rene and her very weariness, mixed with the thick odor of their combined garments, seemed to act as an opiate and she fell into a fitful sleep. Around them the other sleepers stirred and muttered in their blankets. The night was black, broken only by the dim fires that marked the sentries paths, and the sudden pale glare of lightning against the overcast. Minute by minute the thunder seemed to encroach upon the peace of the camp.

Evan was sleeping with the officers in a marquee. He was shocked into wakefulness by the first volley of the storm. It came on a swift torrent of wind in the trees.

The dark split open with jagged lightning, filling the woods with white fire. The trees were suddenly in a hard clarity, black on white, losing their verdance as if they were carved out of the night. In that explosive second of light, their tops tossed like waves and the huddled sleepers beneath them looked like boughs which had been blown down. Then hard on the lightning flash broke a clap of thunder which brought the entire camp awake.

Before they could shake their brief sleep from their heads, the rain swept over them, pelting them like shot. A great gust of wind bent the oaks almost to earth and sent small branches driving across the open space between them. The soldiers blundered in the dark like blind men. The lightning, which flared so rapidly that it seemed at times like one continuous flash, only served to confuse them and making the intervals of succeeding darkness only that much more black. The camp was a tumult of yelling men, with their voices torn away and lost on the wind.

Bienville, hastily dragging on his breeches, burst out of the officers marquee. He was shoeless in his hurry. His first thought was for his stacked provisions, pegged down under canvas. In the glare of the lightning he could see the loose canvas belly in the wind and strain against the pegs. He yelled orders to the men who were milling about in front of the marquee. The rain came in sheets so that he could not distinguish one man from another, but he laid his hand upon a sergeant of one of the French companies, and, bawling in the intervals between the gusts of wind, succeeded in getting a detail together to keep the coverings from being torn from the stacked provisions. Already several of the pegs had been ripped up by the force of the gale, and swinging on the loose ends of the mooring ropes they became deadly missiles in the dark.

In the stabbing illumination of the lightning the campground began to take on the aspect of a shambles. Broken branches littered the glade, blankets which the soldiers in their disorder had left lying on the ground had been lifted by the wind and blown into the woods. A man could not stand in the open, the fury of the wind and rain was so great. The men took cover as best they could in the woods. None of the big oaks around the glade had fallen, but sometimes in a lull of the wind they could hear trees off in the woods crashing.

There was no more sleep all night. At times the wind died down and the rain slackened to a drizzling mist, but every time the storm came back to drench the bedraggled army, to blind it with lightning and deafen it with thunder. The Choctaws raised a great howling in their camp and tried to fire their muskets at the sky. In most cases they failed miserably because the powder in the pan had been wet by the rain. They declared that Eloha, the lightning, and Rowah, the thunder, were at war in the heavens. Some of them fired their guns to help Ishytohoolo Eloha, and others merely in contempt of heaven, to show that they were warriors and not afraid to die. When their guns would not discharge they howled defiance at the elements.

The storm had passed by dawn, but the day broke gray with a ground fog rising from the wet earth. Evan ventured out from beneath a tree at the edge of the glade and looked around. It was a miracle, he thought, that nobody had been killed by lightning or by a falling branch. But they were all there, soaked to the skin, with their clothes plastered against their bodies and stupid from terror and a lack of sleep. Each company began to form ranks and fill out as the sergeants moved about in the gray light. There was Bienville checking out the provisions. His clothes were heavy on his body, worry was written on his face. He drew his the back of his hand across his brow.

Macarty-Mactigue stepped up to receive the order of the day. He maintained his military demeanor but his appearance was anything but martial. His face was even redder than usual. His clothes were as besotten as any in the camp and his sodden coat stretched below his knees. His hose was torn and the buckles on his shoes lost in masses of mud. He had lost his hat during the night and now had thrust his snarled and soggy wig in a pocket so that his closely cropped hair was plastered on head like a scallop.

The captains assembled their men, called the muster roll and brought the expedition to order.

Macarty-Mactigue addressed them.

297

"All muskets must be cleaned and made ready for action. New powder will be issued to all troops. All muskets must be primed and loaded. Then be prepared to march within the hour."

The captains issued the orders and in a minute the men had broken ranks and were hurrying about the glade seeking the weapons which they had laid down the night before. Bienville looked at the confusion of the camp and shook his big head.

Evan dropped down beside Henri Martin who as sitting calmly on a downed oak limb munching on a hunk of saltmeat. He had taken his hunting shirt off and it lay folded on the limb beside him.

"Better get your gun clean," Evan said wearily. "Bienville's orders."

Henri gave him a surly look but said nothing until he had swallowed his mouthful.

"You don't think a real woods runner would let a little shower like that spoil his powder, do you?" he said as he unfolded his long leather shirt and revealed his gun and powder lying snug and dry inside.

He looked at Evan coldly. "A man like you will be lucky to live to see the end of this campaign," he said as he turned away.

The woods were strewn with the debris of the storm. Wind falls constantly broke the continuity of their march. The soldiers were groggy from having no sleep the night before and stumbled and slid on the wet clay. Before they had gone two miles they had to cross a bayou which ran in torrent between cane-grown banks. The cane was so thick that the Canadiens and the Choctaws had to use their tomahawks to cut a path through to the edge of the stream. The yellow water ran like a millrace, breast high on the short Frenchmen.

There was manifest reluctance in the way that they stepped into the stream but they were more afraid of being left behind in the hostile woods than than they were of the water. They staggered through, holding their muskets high. The stream was, in actuality, not much more than a deep cut ditch, ten yards across. Several of the men were swept off their feet in the swift water but grabbed quickly by some Choctaws who had moved down stream for that very event. Rene crossed, slipping on the slimy bottom but not falling, with one arm hugging Collette closely against his side. She hung close to him with her thin, fevered face looking up at him.

After fording the bayou they marched three miles across difficult wooded country until they struck another narrow, cane grown stream which they crossed more easily. The army toiled painfully through the heavy woods and camped at noon on the side of a hill. There was nothing but tangled woods before them and behind them. They seemed to be a thousand miles from the Chickasaw prairies rather than the fifteen that Bienville estimated.

In the middle of the afternoon they came down into a low bottom between the rolling hills. For the better part of an hour they struggled across it, knee deep in razor edged saw grass, Sometimes they were ankle deep in water the color of diluted rum, and always sludging in putrid mud. The stink of the mud did not bother them, for they were used to the smell of themselves, but the feel of it sucking at each foot as if reluctant to part with it irritated them. Their feet became lumps of mud as the plodded along. Clouds of mosquitoes surrounded the white men, shunning the Choctaws who were greased with evil smelling bear oil. The Frenchmen, made desperate by the vicious attacks of the mosquitoes, bent down as they walked and scooped up the stinking mud, plastering their faces, their hands, and all parts exposed through their tattered clothing. Evan smeared a handful of the stuff on his face where he had been bitten. He saw Bienville do the same. The fastidious French officers remained aloof at first but, maddened by the insects, one by one they fell from grace and availed themselves of the mud. Like an immense, aimless course of mud turtles they crawled on across the low ground until they reached the banks of the third and last stream of the day.

It was a broader stream than the other two, running brimful and twenty yards across. The willows and canes which grew down into the water were not so thick that the army could not worm its way through. They strung out at the edge of the water and cast dubious eyes at it. The Choctaws were no swimmers, waved their arms at it and talked among themselves.

The Sieur de Lery came up to Bienville.

"The chiefs say it is too dangerous to cross," he said. "They say camp here until it runs down."

Bienville exploded in a snort. "My God, camp here in all these mosquitoes and snakes and God knows what? What do they think we are, frogs? Tell them we're crossing now.

Tell them the French will go first and prove there is no danger."

He spied Henri Martin. "Cross the stream, Martin. You are not a big man. After they see you cross they will be shamed and unable to refuse to follow."

Henri handed his musket and powder horn to the man next to him and plunged at once into the stream. The water boiled over his waist, but he stood firm with his legs brace against the current. He turned his head and grinned through the matted mud of his beard and waded across. The ease with which he did it must have impressed the Choctaws, because they began sliding off the bank into the stream. They wanted to get across before the Frenchmen so that they could boast that they had not been afraid.

Bienville followed Henri Martin, wading across unaided with Evan beside him. The water came almost to Bienville's shoulder, but his wiry little body stood off the current. He and Evan stood dripping water beside Lazac and watched the head of the French column plunge in.

They came across more slowly than before. The water was swifter and deeper, and the men were nearly exhausted from the days march. Each man seemed to require an interminable length of time to place his feet, and they floundered in the water, advancing almost by inches. There was such an expression of relief on the face of each one as he pulled himself out on the bank that Evan could have laughed.

Contrecouer's was the last company of the main body to cross. Rene, with his arm about Colette, waded into the stream. Looking down at her he saw that she was about to drop. It seemed that his arm was all that held her up. She could only droop her head forward and twist her neck so that her head rested against one shoulder. His arm tightened about her and he went forward carefully, feeling with his feet on the slimy bottom.

About halfway across it happened. Something, Rene didn't know quite what it was, a rolling lump of clay or a piece of gravel, was under his foot and lost his balance. He lurched wildly in the stream and Colette's limp body fell away from him, slipping out of the circle of his arm. She was gone before he knew it. He screamed instinctively seeing his empty arm and the ripple where she had gone beneath the surface. He dropped his musket and dove frenziedly after her, coming up sputtering and empty handed. The stream had swept her down. One of the Choctaws placed below the crossing as before grabbed her and pulled her to the farther bank. She was dead.

They dragged her body up the bank and lay her amongst the cane. Rene, with the help of Evan and Henri, worked desperately over her while the rest of the army completed crossing. Rene would not believe she was dead. He kept trying to revive her, even after Henri Martin stood up shaking his head. Evan watched Rene in dumb pity. He was crying as he frantically worked on her. He kept talking unintelligibly to her through his sobs. Bienville came over bringing the army surgeon,

Dr. Dumont. The surgeon, a dumpy little man with a hard face and thin eyes, pushed Rene aside and bent over Collette. He straightened up immediately and shrugged his shoulders. Rene had again taken possession of Collette's body and was blubbering against her drowned hair.

Bienville looked back toward the ford. The last the Swiss rear guard were wading out of the stream. He turned back to Rene.

"Corporal Broussard, join your company. We will resume the march."

Rene stared up at him, but beyond that gave him no impression that he had heard.

"Corporal Broussard, join your company." Said Bienville again. He added in a gentler voice, "You can do no more for her. The girl is dead."

Rene's naturally bony face was so thin now that it seemed like a death's head. His eyes burned in it.

"I'll take her with me," he said hoarsely. "She's mine. I'll take her with me."

"Bienville's lined face was troubled. "Take him to his company, Martin," he said. "We'll bury the girl here."

"No!" cried Rene wildly. But Henri Martin grabbed him by the arm and Corporal Muldoon grabbed him by the shoulders. He struggled but there was no strength in his body. Evan took hold of his other arm and they propelled him away from the stream. He cursed them steadily as they took him to the company.

Bienville detailed a squad of porters to bury Collette and watched them until they had scooped out a shallow grave in the mud beside the stream and covered her over. He then went back to his troops. Walking up past Contrecoeur's company to the head of the column, he saw Rene Broussard standing in his position like a post, his eyes staring straight ahead. Bienville sighed heavily, feeling the weight of the march all at once.

They struck open prairie land before dusk and began to skirt it keeping the column in the shelter of the woods. When the scouts found a spring at the foot of a ridge on the prairie's edge, they went into camp. They were about six mile's from the nearest Chickasaw towns.

Corporal Muldoon and Henri Martin were trying to cheer up Rene Broussard with a full canteen. They were succeeding admirably in cheering themselves but Rene sat with his head in his hands, either shaking his head at every offer of a drink or ignoring it entirely. Muldoon got up as Evan came over to them and slapped his rump which was numb from squatting on his heels.

"What am I to do?" he complained spreading his hands in the direction of Rene. "He won't drink. What can I do?"

"Henri nodded. He took the canteen out of Muldoon's hand and with one motion offered it to Rene and then passed it to his own lips.

"The Governor wants you," Evan said to Henri Martin.

Henri's expression changed. He took a last swig from the canteen, looked irritably at Evan and went with him back to the command tent.

Soulier Rouge was standing in the center of Bienville's tent when they reached it. Behind him were four of his warriors, streaked with blue and vermilion for war. Facing the Choctaws were Bienville and De Noyan. Bienville looked away from Soulier Rouge as Henri Martin pulled open the tent flap.

"Sit down," Bienville directed. "I've sent for the Sieur de Lery and the Sieur Monbrun."

At that moment De Lery, tall and quick, almost as dark as an Indian, came in followed by the shorter, heavier Monbrun. They quickly came to attention.

Bienville came to the point, "Soulier Rouge wants to make a scout ahead of us tonight to see how the land lies. I've given him my consent and I've detailed you, De Lery, and you Monbrun, to go with him. The purpose of this scout is to determine if the enemy has wind of us and to see if there is any trace of D'Artaguette or his scouts. Report back to camp before daylight." He spoke in French which the Choctaws did not understand. "Watch Soulier Rouge and see that he pulls no tricks. Martin, you scout to the west and see if you can find any sign of D'Artaguette if he is in the country. But be back as soon after daybreak as possible. Find D'Artaguette. I don't need to tell you how to go about it."

Long before the scouts returned, Bienville knew they would bring bad news of some description.

About midnight the camp had been startled into wakefulness by a sound of gunshots. This created a great commotion among the Choctaws, who began to revive all their old rumors and suspicions of French duplicity. They began to talk among themselves that Bienville had sent De Lery with Soulier Rouge in order to have the chief's head knocked in, and of a letter to the Chickasaws to notify them of Bienville's arrival. Bienville went among them himself to quiet them, but the alarm had spread among them to such an extent that they began to talk of abandoning the expedition entirely. Only their fear of the dark made them put off until daylight their determination to desert in a body.

At daybreak, when the Choctaws had worked themselves to the verge of panic, the scouts came in.

De Lery was bloody from thorn scratches and boiling with rage.

"By God," he exclaimed, "they know we're coming now! And it's the work of that filthy swine!" He pointed at Soulier Rouge who, a hero among the Choctaws, was strutting before his warriors.

"We sighted a Chickasaw camp westward. The two of us spent nearly an hour working our way onto the ridge overlooking it. It was a Chickasaw hunting camp. There must have been fifteen warriors in it. They didn't know we were within a thousand miles. Before I could stop him, Soulier Rouge put a bullet in the middle of the camp. He didn't hit anybody, but they jumped up like all the devils in hell and went after their guns. We left and they didn't chase us, not out of the light of their camp fire. But they know we are in the country. And," he said, almost as an after thought, "we didn't see hair, hide, or track of D'Artaguette."

Chapter XXII

Bienville's tent loomed like a gigantic mushroom in the edge of the woods. Around it the soldiers ate their breakfast, sitting hunched over the ashes of the dead campfires. The sun was rising and throwing long red rays through the woods when the Great Chief of the Choctaw Nation came up among the Frenchman and made his way to Bienville's tent.

"My father," he said, "my people would like to hear what village you intend to attack first."

Bienville felt too tired for the argument that he knew was coming.

"Tell the chiefs and warriors of the Choctaw that I have orders from the King of France to go first against the Natchez who were the authors of this war and the tribe of which we owe our troubles."

"The Choctaw understands the white father's wish to punish the Natchez," the Chief said gravely, "but he wishes that the village called Chukafalaya might be attacked first. It is the village nearest on the prairie. It is the village that has given more trouble to the Choctaws than all the others. At that village I have lost a son and an uncle."

Bienville shook his head. "My orders from the King tell me to attack the village of the Natchez first.."

The Great Chief was persistent. "My warriors have used all the provisions which they brought with them. They can go no farther without more provisions. There are many provisions in the village of Chukafalaya. The chiefs of the Choctaws are eager to take them."

The obstinacy of the chief disturbed Bienville. He knew the character of the Choctaws. If he allowed them to attack Chukafalaya first and capture the booty in the village they would abandon the expedition then and there and strike out for home, since it was an old custom of theirs to run as soon as they had struck a blow. He decided to compromise.

"Your plan to seize the provisions at Chukafalaya is good," he told the Great Chief. "This is what I will do. When the village of the Natchez has been taken we will all return and attack Chukafalaya. Is that good?"

The Great Chief was not enthusiastic, but after some further parley he agreed and went off to join his warriors. He promised to send his scouts ahead to guide the army to the large prairie where the Council House of the Chickasaws and the village of the Natchez were situated.

Shortly after the meeting Henri Martin entered the camp. He reported immediately to Bienville.

"I have seen no sign of D'Artaguette," he reported, "but I encountered a Chickasaw runner about an hour before dawn. I had to kill him so I could not get any information from him. But he seemed to be taking a message from one of the towns to another. I suspect that the Chickasaw know of our presence and are planning to come together at some place."

This news did nothing for the uneasy feeling that was growing in Bienville but he ordered the little army to move. The sky was cloudless and the wet clothes of the soldiers dried stiffly on their backs in the hot morning sun. The ground in the woods was covered with ripe wild strawberries. The soldiers stooped and plucked the berries, eating them until their faces were smeared with red. Their feet and ankles looked bloody from the fruit which they crushed underfoot. It was a beautiful stretch of country of forest and lush prairie through which they marched until noon behind the Choctaw guides. The Choctaws led them in a circuitous route, with the purpose, they said, of avoiding the first villages in order to surprise the Natchez beyond.

The sun was directly overhead when they debouched upon a small prairie not more than a mile in width. It spread out before them in undulating folds as green as a velvet coat thrown carelessly upon the ground. The enclosing woods made a ring of darker green around it. The army halted in the edge of the woods, standing at ease, and looking out across the prairie. The sky overhead was as blue as deep water and a hush like that of the Sabbath lay over the land. The Indian cattle, grazing heads down in the tall grass of the slopes, seemed unmindful of the proximity of the hostile army. Clearly outlined on a green ridge which crossed the prairie from east to west, were the cabins and stockades of the Chickasaws, drab and inoffensive in appearance, like a huddle of mud dauber nests in the sunshine.

The Choctaw scouts came back to tell Bienville that there were no streams further on to cross. He ordered the army to march along the wood which bordered the Chickasaw villages. He could see their disposition clearly from there. There were three villages strung along the narrow ridge in the shape of a triangle so that every approach to the crest was guarded by one at least one of them. Each village was a cluster of cabins, some round, some square, about a stockade and a log fort. The apparent strength of the fortifications disquieted Bienville. He called the Great Chief and asked the names of the villages.

The Great Chief indicated each with his arm. "That upon the eastern end of the ridge is Apeony, this one nearest us Ackia, and that one upon the farther side of the ridge is Chukafalaya. We should be able to take that one quickly, and the others. There will be much loot in them."

Bienville knew then that the Choctaw had tricked him. He called a council of his officers and the chiefs at once, wishing to heaven that Gaston Lazac would get back with some news of D'Artaguette.

Rene Broussard was still possessed of a black grief. Evan and Patrick Muldoon tried their best to bring him out of it, telling him that he had done all he could, even that there were plenty of other women in the world. It was of no use. He was sunk into a bottomless pit of self-reproach.

"It was my fault," he kept saying. "I killed her as dead as if I had shot her. The poor little thing. Why couldn't I have treated her better? Why couldn't I tell her how I really felt about her? She was too good for me. Holy Mary, I am no good. I killed her." Then he would groan and twist his head between his hands and go on talking to himself. "Why did she follow me? If I had married her she'd have stayed behind and waited for me. It's all my fault. O le Bon Dieu, have mercy on her soul." Then he cried.

Evan clapped him on the shoulder. He was feeling sorry enough about Collette's death himself without Rene making it worse.

"Rene, my friend. Collette was dear to me, also," he said, "but right now we must put this aside. We have work ahead of us this day." He pointed toward the prairie and the Chickasaw forts. "After we finish our business today, you and I will go back and say goodbye to her by ourselves."

Rene looked straight ahead and then turned his face to Evan. "Yes," he said quietly, "if it wasn't for those bastards we wouldn't be up here in this God-forsaken wilderness, and Collette would still be alive. I'll kill them all."

"Now, that's the attitude," approved Corporal Muldoon. "But don't take chances, my friend."

Gaston Lazac, dripping mud from his hips down, and hot as a fox on the run, walked into the middle of Bienville's council. He dropped the butt of his flintlock between his feet and crossed his arms on the muzzle, facing Bienville.

"Hell," he remarked, "I had to travel to catch up with you. I found your boats and have tracked you from there. But this is not the Natchez prairie. That's beyond, with the Chickasaw Council House."

Bienville turned a sour glance at the Choctaws. The Great Chief and Alibamon Mingo looked sheepish beneath the grime which coated their faces, but Soulier Rouge and his faction stared back, their eyes unblinking, lusterless as chips of coal.

"The Choctaws have made up their minds to attack these villages," said Bienville. "Their scouts led us here after promising to guide us to the Natchez prairie."

Lazac grunted and swung about to look across the prairie toward the Chickasaw forts. The council had assembled beneath a large black oak on the crest of a wooded ridge. As they looked out over the prairie they saw a party of Choctaw warriors come out of the woods farther down the ridge where the Indians had made camp. There were a dozen warriors, fantastically painted and feathered. They went crouched over, seeking concealment in the tall grasses. The Frenchmen on the ridge could see that they were following an Indian path up the slope toward the fort call Ackia. A cow grazing near the path lifted up its head to stare stolidly at them. But they were Indians and the cow was not alarmed. It resumed its feeding. Suddenly the Choctaws, whooped, once raggedly, then in unison, and ran toward the fort, discharging their muskets as they ran.

"The infernal fools!" ejaculated Bienville.

There was a volley from the fort, and the Choctaws turned tail and made off, scattering through the long grass, without any of them being hit. They halted out of musket range, at the foot of the ridge, and hooted and howled, waving their guns above their heads.

Bienville, forgetting his position, swore like a woodsrunner. The skirmish created an uproar among the chiefs. They began to clamor for an immediate attack. Some of the French officers joined them.

"Let us attack these towns now, sir," exclaimed the Chevalier de Contrecoeur. They're guarded by nothing but flimsy picket fences. We can storm them in no time.

It would be folly to leave them to threaten our rear while we go on and attack the Natchez."

Bienville looked harassed in the face of the clamor for assault on the Chickasaw forts. He turned to Lazac.

"What news have you of D'Artaguette?"

Lazac shook his head. "I went as far as the Coonewa. I saw no sign of him. He hasn't showed east of the Chickasaw Fields. You'll have to make your plans without counting on him."

Bienville's face hardened. His mission was to wipe out the Natchez. He had made up his mind to stick with it when Major de Noyan spoke up.

"That settles it, sir," said de Noyan, earnestly. "We can't count on help from D'Artaguette. We have to go it alone. There's no alternative but to take these forts and seize the provisions in them. Then there will be time to move against the Natchez. Remember these men are tired and hungry, many of them are ill. They won't go much farther."

Bienville frowned in the agony of irresolution. He had a great respect for his nephew Jean's opinion. He rose to his feet quickly. If they wanted to fight here, he would let them fight here. There was no choice, anyway. The Choctaws had worked themselves to such a pitch that they would desert him if he balked now.

His voice was sharp, giving orders: "Very well, we will attack in an hour. The village of Ackia will be assaulted first. I will give my orders to Major de Noyan who will be in command of the attacking force. All officers will now join their companies. And I ask all the chiefs to hold their warriors ready to attack with us on one hour."

The Choctaws, pleased as children that he had given into them, clustered around him protesting their allegiance. He let them talk and when they had gone off to join their warriors he walked to the edge of the ridge and surveyed the situation of the Chickasaw forts. Major de Noyan and Gaston Lazac stood beside him.

"Look," said Bienville, pointing. "Everything is heavily fortified. They have stockades around each of those cabins protecting the fort. We can't reduce fortifications like that without artillery. The mortars that we lost in route to Mobile were to be used in just such a case. It would not have been so bad if D'Artaguette had made it here with his mortars. But this changes all our strategy. We will have to rely on our grenades, but I do not think they will have much impact on roofs protected by mud and thatch."

"The cabins that protect the approaches to the forts also have stockades," he continued. "We will have to reduce them before we can try to breach the fortifications of the village by force of assault."

"I have never seen Indians build forts like that," said Gaston Lazac. "Not without the English." He looked pensively across the plain then exclaimed, "Jesus! Look there!"

Above the fort which the Choctaws called Apeony a flag was being run up. The Frenchmen stared. It was an English flag. The slow breeze made it flap and then hang idle from the staff. Men were moving under the flag inside the stockade. White men, they could tell, by their clothes. Their faces were indistinguishable at a distance.

"Englishmen," said Bienville, in a tight voice. "That explains the fortifications. I was afraid of this."

Lazac started to say something but he was interrupted by Evan MacDonald who walking up quickly. He saluted. His heart was hammering.

"I ask you permission, sir, to go forward with Major de Noyan."

"Go on," said Bienville. He was thinking of something else. "One more won't matter."

The sun crawled across the western curve of the sky while De Noyan was forming his column in the edge of the woods about four hundred yards from the main stockade of Ackia. He had drawn, at Bienville's orders, the company of grenadiers, which included Muldoon and Rene, under the command of D'Hauterive, a detachment of fifteen men from each of the eight French companies under Sieur de Juzan, along with sixty Swiss under De Lusser, and forty-five volunteers and militiamen under Le Sueur.

The time of the assault was at hand. The column stood tensely in ranks, waiting. The command went down the line, "Look to your firelocks."

The grenadiers knelt in five ranks at the head of the column. They had been issued one grenade apiece, and a slow-match for lighting it. Each one bent his head busily engaged in firing his slow-match from the lock of his gun. One by one the matches caught and smoldered. The grenadiers slung their muskets on their shoulders and stood up in ranks. There was an uneasy scuffing of feet. Bienville stepped out into the open in full view of the fort of Ackia, but well out of musket range. He lifted his sword as a signal to the Choctaws.

A trumpet blew the advance. De Noyan's sword stabbed savagely at the air. In excitement his lips drew back from his teeth.

"Vive le Roi!" he cried. "Forward march!"

Evan, standing in ranks with the volunteers at the foot of the column, felt his heart leap and his knees turn to water.

The drummers on the flanks lifted their sticks and let them fall. Their drumming was a ruffle of minor thunder. the Fleur-de-Lis at the head of the column was a pale alien flower in the heart of the the green Chickasaw wilderness.

The Frenchmen began to march. The column advanced down the slope through the thinning trees and the pink and white flowers which dotted the earth. Negroes carrying mantelets twenty feet long, made of woven ropes, protected the head of the column. Behind the mantelets came De Noyan and then the grenadiers in five ranks, ten deep, at intervals of five yards, with D'Hauterive, walking on the right flank. Behind the grenadiers marched the Swiss in six ranks, and then came De Juzan's corps from the eight French companies. The column extended well over a hundred yards, so that the volunteers and militiamen at the foot were still in the shelter of the trees when the grenadiers began to cross the little stream which cut through at the foot of the ridge. It was nothing but a sticky, muddy ditch closed in by willows which gave the French concealment as they crossed. But they were not yet in musket range of the fort.

On the French right the Choctaws had come out of the woods and were moving warily up the slope of the ridge on either side of the Indian path. As the head of the French column sloshed across the ditch and swung right between the willows and the slope of the ridge leading to the fort, the Choctaws crouched where they were and waited.

The grass between the ditch and fort had been cut. It looked like pasture and Evan heard Lazac's voice in his ear, "The English must have cut the grass to help protect the fort. The Chickasaw burn it in the fall when it is dry, but they never cut it. The don't have scythes."

The head of the French column had almost reached the declivity upon the southwestern slope of the ridge up which Bienville had decided to make the attack, and the foot of the column was brushing through the willows at the ditch. There had been no fire from the fort which could be seen above the brow of the ridge, the pointed ends of the stockade biting into the blue sky like a row of uneven teeth. The soldiers moved steadily, holding ranks, and looking almost military in the bright sunshine in spite of their unkempt appearance and ragged clothes.

The negroes with the mantelets entered the declivity. The column turned right again at the command and faced the fort, one hundred and fifty yards away. The declivity in which they stood ran straight toward the fort with a half dozen or more stockaded cabins guarding it on both the left and the right. De Noyan drew in his stomach and his eyes narrowed. They would have to run the gauntlet of these outposts before they could come within effective range of the fort.

The negroes halted uncertainly, letting their mantelets sag to the ground. They rolled their eyes in the direction of De Noyan. He barked at them and they jumped to attention and stumbled forward again dragging their burdens between them.

"Vive le Roi!" shouted De Noyan.

The cry went raggedly through the column, "Vive, le Roi!"

The drums on the flanks throbbed. Still the Chickasaws held their fire. There was no sound from the Choctaws on the other side of the ridge. The grenadiers stepped out a little, feeling cocksure and jaunty. There would be little resistance and the women in the Chickasaw town would be theirs after two months of marching. Behind them the Swiss and French began to close ranks swiftly until one man was pushing on another. Sweat poured from their faces and their bodies were hot. At the foot of the column just circling the bulge of the ridge Le Sueur's volunteers, a good many of whom had experienced Indian fighting, came in a loose mass, looking to the right and left to get the lay of the land.

There was a stab of orange flame from the nearest cabin, a little mushroom of black smoke spewing out into the still air. Then an uneven volley was discharged from the cabins at the advancing column. A big negro was hit and dropped down like a stone. He began to thrash about and cry out in pain. The other bearers dropped the mantelets and ran in fear, some to the right, some to the left and others straight back through the oncoming ranks creating a moment of confusion before the flat of the sergeant's swords restored order.

The sporadic firing from the fort continued. On the other side of the ridge a great howling went up from the Choctaws, punctuated by gunshots as they discharged their muskets into the air.

De Noyan yelled, "Avant!" and started trotting toward the fort, looking back over his shoulder. The grenadiers, nervously fumbling their grenades, broke into a shambling trot. The Swiss and French behind them lunged forward, clipping on their bayonets. The volunteers broke ranks, half following Le Sueur to the right and the others circling to the left behind Gaston Lazac, intent upon circling the cabins and taking the fort from the flanks and the rear. They did not go far before the Sieur de Juzan, his face contorted with excitement and self-importance, caught the movement and bawled at Le Sueur to get his men back in line.

"The French under my command will attack the fort," he shouted. "Captain le Sueur, keep your volunteers in position until further orders!"

Le Sueur, raging, complied with the order.

Evan heard Lazac muttering, "That little polecat. He wants to have the glory. He'll have his belly full soon."

Evan could see the grenadiers already caught in the crossfire from the fortified cabins. They began to hurl their grenades. There was a loud explosion inside one of the small stockades and black smoke came up out of it and spread like a tree. He saw the Chevalier de Contrecoeur hit and collapse like an empty sack in front of one of the cabins. Rene Broussard and Patrick Muldoon, running side by side, stepped over his body and plunged into the village. Already three of the cabins were afire and thick smoke all but made the fort invisible to men in the rear ranks.

A ripple of flame, low, almost on a level with the ground, ran across the front of the Chickasaw stockade. The Chickasaws inside the fort were lying on their bellies and pouring a withering fire upon the attackers through ports cut even with the ground. Bullets sang about the knees of the charging soldiers until they seemed to be running knee deep in a swarm of bees.

The sudden, concentrated fire was too much for them. Everywhere they went down, tumbling like nine pins. All in range went down, whether hit or not, burrowing for safety against the scant shelter of the rising ground. The dead and badly wounded went down spreading in unpremeditated positions, but the unhurt, who were wise, dropped flat.

One fellow in a white uniform went down crouching just in front of Evan, with his knees drawn under him and his rump sticking up above the level of his shoulders. A ball creased his buttock and he dropped flat with a yelp of pain.

The fire from the fort and the uncaptured cabins was vicious. It had taken all the fight out of De Lusser's Swiss and De Juzan's French corps. There was no longer any semblance of order in the column.

Scrambling along the ground and running full tilt, they took to the cover of the burning cabins. No manner of threats, entreaties, boots, or flats of officer's swords availed to make them come out into the open and reform the column. The wind blew the smoke from the cabins like a pall over the battlefield. Evan and Lazac, coming up through it with Le Sueur and his volunteers to join De Noyan, passed the soldiers crouched behind the cabins.

"The white coats turned yellow," said Lazac, contemptuously.

They passed De Juzan, coming back from De Noyan to rally the troops from behind the cabins. A moment later he was dead. He fell in the midst of the panicky soldiers, many of whom bolted altogether and left the field.

When the volunteers joined De Noyan in the center of the village there was no one but the officers and a few grenadiers. He had been wounded in the thigh and was bleeding freely, although he was trying to stop the flow of blood with a strip torn from his shirt. Henri Martin was the first to come to his aid. He tried to raise the major to his feet when he dropped with a musket ball through his head.

De Noyan looked at Le Sueur, his face gray. They were all under heavy fire.

Le Sueur shouted above the rattle of musketry, "We can't hold this position and we can't advance. We've got to retreat. The soldiers won't fight."

De Noyan, shaken by loss of blood tried to respond. "We've lost so many officers," he said, "De Lusser is dead!"

"You have to get behind the shelter," said Le Sueur sharply. "Here, Gaston, help him behind one of these cabins."

The group of officers who had held their position in the center of the village under severe fire began to withdraw toward the flaming cabins. At the first movement of retreat a yell went up inside the Chickasaw fort. A gate in the log wall swung open and a party sallied out, bent on scalping those who had fallen close to the walls of the stockade. A few were still alive and the Chickasaw would tomahawk them in the head before taking their scalps. One man struggled to rise and fend off his attackers. It was the Swiss lieutenant Grondel.

Gaston Lazac raced back to the man's aide. Before he knew what he was doing Evan was right behind him.

Grondel had buried his sword in a Chickasaw and was fending off a second with an empty musket. Lazac was on the man and drove his hunting knife into the Indian's kidney but several more Chickasaws rushed to the scene.

Evan pulled up and shot the warrior nearest to Lazac. Lazac grabbed the next brave by the wrists as he tried to bring his tomahawk down and threw him aside like a rag doll breaking the Chickasaw's arm in the process. He lifted Grondel under one arm as two more Chickasaws came upon him. Evan stepped in just in time, clubbing at the Indians with his spent musket. He knocked one down with the musket butt but the second was inside the reach of the musket and he dropped it as the warrior turned on him.

The rough housing and fighting he had done with his Scottish kinsmen now came to his defense. He pulled a knife from its sheath on his lower leg just in time to fend off an attack by a tomahawk. The blade diverted the weapon from crushing his skull but it still glanced off the side of his head. His arm dropped and he ripped at the belly of the Indian, who fell in a pool of blood, the knife still in him. Evan went to his knees with his head ringing, only to find Grondel's sword, which he wrested from the dead Chickasaw's body and slashed like a claymore at two new foes.

A breeze had come up, sweeping the smoke from the burning cabins over them in an acrid cloud and the Chickasaws stepped back.

It was stifling but afforded a screen for Evan and Gaston to escape. Lazac dragged the injured Grondel back through the smoke with Evan behind him carrying only the sword.

Le Sueur took control. "We've got to get out of here," he said. "Those devils will be on us like crows on a hawk's tail in moments."

Two men helped Grondel while Gaston Lazac carried De Noyan behind one of the burning cabins. The scattered volunteers, at Le Sueur's command, kept what fire they could upon the main stockade.

De Noyan grabbed Evan by the shirt and, haltingly, said, "Go to the Sieur de Bienville and report our situation. Tell him that if he does not send reinforcements or have the retreat sounded at once all our officers will be dead. Tell him I cannot have myself carried off or the men will flee and the Chickasaws will cut us all down." He groaned, holding his thigh between his hands.

Evan ducked out from behind the cabin. A burning roof fell in with a roar. He saw the rafters of it outlined in the flame as it collapsed. He coughed the smoke from his lungs and started to run. Somewhere off in the smoke a man cursed without stopping, repeating over and over the same blasphemies with a childish sort of horror. His voice lifted and faded. His words were indistinct, then stopped altogether and Evan knew that he was dead.

He came out of the rolling smoke at the foot of the ridge. As he crossed the ditch he could see the Chickasaws still howling and prancing in the safety of the stockade. He cursed them. Bienville, his face a study in anguish, met him on the slope.

"My God," he said, "what is it?"

Evan gasped, the smoke still in his eyes and his lungs. He got out his report from De Noyan.

320

Bienville seemed to age as he listened. His eyes had told him that the column had been mauled. But hearing De Noyan's report brought home the full extent of the debacle.

He cleared his throat when Evan had finished. "Tell Captain Beauchamp to take eighty men to cover the retreat of the our remaining forces before the stockade and to take and additional fifty men to help carry off our dead and wounded."

He stood there on the hillside watching Beauchamp's force march out to cover the retreat. At that moment the Choctaws, perhaps emboldened by the new show of French force, began to run up the slope of the ridge, firing their muskets as they ran. The Chickasaws returned the fire with a sharp volley from the stockade. Some of the Choctaw warriors fell, clawing in the prairie grass. The rest scattered like a flushed covey of quail and sought shelter in the woods. Bienville was too disgusted to curse them as they disappeared.

He saw with satisfaction that Beauchamp had appeared in time to prevent a sortie from the stockade against the demoralized troops scattered about the cabins. But the Chickasaws kept up a hot fire all the time Beauchamp was evacuating the wounded from the village. The soldiers who had taken refuge among the cabins heard Beauchamp's drums beating the retreat and immediately departed without order, reaching the camp on the opposite ridge long before Beauchamp drew off with the remnants of De Noyan's original command.

Bienville and Evan went among them as they marched back into the camp. Bienville, walking beside the men who carried De Noyan, gripped his nephew's shoulder hard.

There were tears in his eyes. He was thinking of De Noyan and those hurt worse still. For the moment, in his mind, all the blame for the lost battle was his.

Evan found Patrick Muldoon. He had been shot through the lung. When he opened his mouth the blood came out and dripped down his chin. There was no hope for him.

Evan knelt beside him. The man's broad Irish face accepted what was bound to come. He asked for no sympathy. Feebly he crossed himself.

He spat blood. "Get me the father," he managed.

Evan turned. He saw Brother Crucy among the wounded and called to him.

"Where is Rene Broussard?" Evan asked Muldoon.

It required a prodigious effort for the Irishman to speak. "I don't know. He wanted to take the fort single-handed. He killed eight before I was hit," he said with an effort at a smile. "Jesus, Mary --" he said, before the blood came up in this throat and choked him.

Brother Crucy touched Evan's shoulder and bent over Muldoon with his cross. Evan rose and walked away. Rene, he thought, must have been left on the field. He was nowhere among the men who had come back.

He looked back at the fort. There was no more firing. It was strange how peaceful the little valley between the ridges had grown is so short a space of time. He saw the cattle which had fled at the sound of gunfire beginning to venture back to their feeding in the lush prairie grass. The wind which had sprung up died and the smoke from the burning cabins towered in undulating columns unbelievably high -- black funeral plumes above French blood and French defeat.

Chapter XXIII

The French were stupefied by defeat. They gripped their guns and waited while a thin darkness settled in the woods. The world was pale and gray and full of nothing for a man to set his mind upon to keep from thinking of the Chickasaws. There was not much talking. Each man had his own thoughts; some looking backward into a past which had held no terror like the present; some thinking of the possibly greater terror ahead of them; some thinking of nothing at all.

Evan sat with his knees drawn up, his hands dangling between them. His head felt full of some kind of fumes which hindered his mental processes. Every now and then he would duck his head it as if expecting the movement to help it clear. But his light headedness persisted and his face grew hot. It seemed as if the fever were coming back. His body ached and his head was sore. He kept wondering what had become of Rene; and then it penetrated the mist in his brain that all his friends must be dead. Collette was dead. Henri Martin was dead. Muldoon was dead. Rene must be dead. Perhaps Lazac and Camille Billiot were dead as well. He couldn't remember the last time that he had seen them. He tried to remember. Was it since the battle?

He shook his head. He didn't know. He thought what a queer thing it was that so many people could be erased so easily.

The man in front of him, a soldier whose white uniform coat had split in a great gap across the shoulders, wet his lips and spoke tentatively.

"My bowels," he said, "They don't act naturally. How about yours, friend?"

Evan stared at him dully, trying to remember what he had said.

"It was those Indians," the soldier went on. "What right have they got to ask a civilized man to fight savages like that? My stomach was running water the minute I laid eyes on them. Christ in heaven," he said, "we're all going to be killed. What kind of damned country is this, anyway? We come a thousand miles with nothing to eat but what gives us scurvy and flux. And then they let us be butchered by Indians!"

Gaston Lazac walked up behind Evan. "You're in a hell of a mess, son," he said to the soldier. "But the Commandant-General will get you out of it. The Sieur de Bienville has never failed his men yet."

The sky was gray as iron with a smudge of rust in the east where the sun hung below the horizon waiting to rise. The army had sat at the ready deep into the night but the Chickasaws plainly did not think themselves strong enough to attack such a force in the open. The sentries paced along the slope. They looked eastward with a kind of forlorn hope at the sight of the sun, which, while they watched slid up and perched upon the top of the far woods. Behind the sentries on the ridge the camp was awake as the greater part of it had been through the night. There was a sound of groaning from the wounded and a muttering from men grown desperate with exhaustion, hunger, and terror.

As the sun, shining now like a burnished copper piece, climbed up, it threw long russet shadows through the woods. The thin morning mist which had hidden the opposite ridge and the Chickasaw forts began to break and drift away in streamers. The fort of Ackia stood out suddenly in the clear morning sunlight and the French sentries were frozen with horror at the sight they saw. Behind them a rippling echo of their consternation went through the French camp.

The points of the Chickasaw stockade were bedecked with a grisly ornamentation. Heads, arms, legs, and bodies of men were hung from the top of the palisade. They were the dismembered bodies of the officers and men who had been taken, dead or wounded, by the Chickasaws after the French retirement.

In the hubbub which arose in the camp Evan rolled over where he lay and looked around. The fever had left him during the night and his head no longer rang. He was now trembling in a cold sweat but his head was clear enough so that he grasped the significance of what he saw. He felt his insides retch emptily.

"Rene," he thought, "Rene is one of them."

It started a train of thought. Rene and Collette. Both dead. Both dead and gone. What was it they had been looking for in this country? Freedom and the right to live? Crazily he felt like laughing, but the sound would not come. His throat was too dry. His mouth and throat ached, and tasted horribly. Poor Rene. What a way to die! Chopped up like a quarter of beef! He wondered if Rene had been dead before they cut him up.

There was a stir among the French officers. Several of them came crowding around Bienville hotly demanding that something be done about their mutilated comrades on the Ackia stockade.

Bienville's face was gray with strain and fatigue. "Gentlemen, there is nothing we can do. I share your horror of such barbarity, but, I repeat, there is nothing we can do."

Courtilhas, the leader of the belligerent bloc, said angrily: "Those are our fellow officers, sirs. We would be blackguards and cowards if we were to allow them to suffer such indignity. I propose an immediate assault on the fort for the purpose of rescuing the remains of our comrades. French chivalry will countenance no other action."

There was a murmur of assent among the officers around him. Only Beauchamp and Macarty-Mactigue among the unwounded officers seemed inclined to a course of caution.

"Gentlemen," said Bienville, harshly, "You talk like fools. Don't you realize that we're whipped? Don't you realize that there is nothing in God's name we can do but run home as fast as we can with our tails between our legs? We have shown we cannot storm the fort. We have no artillery. We are burdened with wounded. Our provisions are almost gone. Our Choctaws can be expected to desert us at any moment, leaving us to the mercy of a hostile wilderness. Unless we march, and march quickly, the river will he fallen so low that we will unable to move our boats. Gentlemen, whatever our emotions, we must face the facts. Our duty lies with those men who are now alive, not those who are dead. I am prepared to accept all responsibility. I ask you to obey my orders. As soon as we can make the wounded ready for travel we will march back to our boats."

His fierce old eyes stared them down. The group dispersed, some of them seeing the wisdom of Bienville's reasoning, but others, yet unconvinced, grumbling among themselves and casting black looks at the fort on the opposite ridge. From the three Chickasaw villages the only sign of life was the thin stalks of blue smoke rising from their cooking fires.

The French camp became a beehive of activity. Among the soldiers, employment of any kind became a refuge from the dead terror which held them. Through the long, hot morning, still dreading every moment to hear the war whoop and see the Chickasaws boil out of their forts, they sweated, improvising stretchers to carry the wounded and getting their baggage together for the march.   An hour past noon the trumpet blew. The drums beat with the final show of bravado, and the men began to march southeastward down the ridge. They went in two columns, bent beneath the weight of their baggage and their wounded. At the foot of the ridge the Choctaws joined them.

Evan lurched as he walked, but no one noticed, for half the army was staggering. His head throbbed and throbbed. He kept his eyes fixed on the back of the man ahead of him, and exercised a great deal of care in placing his feet on the ground. It seemed so far away. He didn't know if it was from the blow he had taken on the head or if the fever was returning.

The army went so slowly under its own weight that it took the entire afternoon to cover four miles. Bienville called a halt where a little bayou cut through the woods, giving them water. The soldiers put down their wounded and their guns, and sprawled upon the ground. The officers had trouble getting enough of them to stir and go down to the bayou for water to drink and mix with the cold meal from their pouches. They ate the gummy, unseasoned porridge apathetically, and sprawled again.

The Choctaws had grown impatient with the slowness of the army's march. Soulier Rouge and his adherents were bitter in their talk. They kept saying to the other chiefs that Bienville was moving so slowly that the Chickasaws might still overtake them unless they abandoned the French and pushed ahead. Seeing what was going on among them, Bienville called up the chiefs as soon as he had made camp.

The Choctaw chiefs came in a body into the coppered circle of light that marked Bienville's campfire. Soulier Rouge carried himself insolently. He had seen these Frenchmen bodily beaten by the Chickasaws, and he had lost all respect for them.

It was to the Great Chief that Bienville addressed himself.

"Listen well, Great Chief of the Choctaw Nation. It has been told to me that the Choctaws are talking among themselves of deserting us and going at once to their own country."

The Great Chief looked at Soulier Rouge, and the chief of Cushtusha pushed himself forward.

"I will speak," he said, loudly. "It is I who say that the Choctaws should leave the French. The French are squaws, not warriors. They have been beaten in battle. Now they travel like tortoises upon the march. It was not the Choctaws who brought the French into this country. Let the French get themselves out of it."

Bienville held his temper with an effort. Again he spoke to the Great Chief, ignoring Soulier Rouge to that chief's annoyance.

"The Choctaws cannot break their alliance with the French at this time," he said. "Our troubles are your troubles. It was to please the Choctaws that I attacked the Chickasaw fort, since it had been my plan to go against the Natchez. We have given aid to the Choctaws in their need. We expect the Choctaws to aid us. We are friends.

The Great Chief was moved. "That is so," he admitted. "But the French wounded are delaying our march too much. We must make more haste."

"My men are loaded with more than they can carry," said Bienville. "If the Choctaws would help us carry our wounded we could be able to make more speed."

"No!" exploded Soulier Rouge.

The Great Chief hesitated. His eyes swept the circle of the chiefs. When they stopped on Alibamon Mingo, the chief of Concha came forward.

"My warriors will carry my brother, De Noyan," he said.

His words were like a spark. Other chiefs came forward, joining Alibamon Mingo and the Great Chief in promising to help the French carry their wounded.

Soulier Rouge shouldered into the group to face the Great Chief. His eyes were malevolent.

"You are the Great Chief of the Choctaw Nation," he said scornfully. "The white, Diron, at Mobile called you a woman. He is right. Nothing but a woman would carry the Frenchman's loads."

The Great Chief's body grew rigid with fury. His hand dropped swift as a rattlesnake to his belt and snatched out his snaphance pistol. Before he could level it at Soulier Rouge, Bienville jumped forward and knocked down his arm.

"No!" he said sternly, "there will be no killing here."

Soulier Rouge turned on his heel and left them, walking with an erect, contemptuous carriage. The Great Chief stood, his pistol dangling, glaring after him.

The old dreams came back to Evan in even worse nightmare form than they did before. He tossed and turned in his blanket, with the sweat pouring out of his body until he was drenched. All the while his mouth was so dry that it seemed to crack when he breathed. Shadow-shapes chased him in his dreams. Things and people he had known. Sometimes they were indistinct. Sometimes they were clear and spoke to him.

For a little while he dreamed of his father as he had been long ago. He was walking in the Highlands for some reason. But it quickly faded. There was now cool, spring water. Delicious water. He could smell it and it intoxicated him. Then he saw it bubbling out of a mossy bank. It seemed he began to crawl toward it but there was something in the way. It was Antoinette. She stood between him and the water, laughing at him. He tried to scream at her but could not, and only blubbered, clutching at her skirt. She laughed again and disappeared, taking the water with her.

He tossed about some more, coming half-awake, and shivering with the chill of his body. Sleep came and went in fits, and the dreams with it. His delirium mounted. He dreamed briefly of Jacqueline and Etienne and again came that maddening sense of the nearness of water. But it was to Etienne that Jacqueline gave the water. She seemed a great way off, and when he tried to call to her to bring him some of the water she could not hear him. So he tried to go to her but woke before he got there.

Then it made no difference whether he was asleep or awake. He had no sense of reality. He was taken with an obsession. Rene was not dead after all. He had been taken by the Indians and was still alive. It was Evan's fault that Rene had come to Louisiana, so Evan must rescue him from the Chickasaws. The more he thought of it the stronger the conviction grew. It was strange how clear it all seemed now. He simply had to go and get Rene away from the Chickasaws. He lay here on his back, alternately shivering with the chill and burning with the fever, thinking out what he was going to do.

He had a hard time of it when he tried to get up. His knees were so weak that they kept dropping him back on the blanket. He tried over and over without success. Then he managed to get upon his hands and knees. He remained in that position for a long time with his head hanging down between his braced arms. When the giddiness stopped he began to crawl slowly and painfully out among the sleeping soldiers. He tried his best to keep from disturbing them, but now and then he brushed against a sleeper and the man stirred and cursed. But they were sunk in such a leaden stupor that no one awoke. After an interminable crawl he was out of the limits of the camp and alone in the moon dappled woods. There was not a sign or a sound of a sentry. They had fallen asleep on the watch.

Once in the woods he began to feel more confident. Nobody could stop him now from going to save Rene. He caught hold of a low branch and with a good deal of struggling pulled himself erect. He had to hold tight to the tree and rest from that exertion. Then he started out through the woods paying not the least attention to direction. His legs did strange things under him at first but, little by little, his strength increased with his determination and he got along well enough, supporting himself, when he tired, against a tree.

The moon was high in the cloudless sky, throwing confusing shadows in the woods. He walked suddenly over the lip of a ravine and tumbled to his knees, sliding half-way down to the bottom. He scrambled up quickly and lurched on. Low branches whipped hard across his face, stinging and bringing blood. He did not hesitate. He had to find Rene.

Gaston Lazac discovered at daylight that Evan was gone. He found Evan's blanket empty and his hat lying beside it where he had left it. He thought at first that he might have gone off among the soldiers bivouacked among the trees. He walked through the waking camp calling for Evan, but got no answer. That worried him. Bienville heard him and called him to find out what the trouble was.

"He was sick with fever when we made camp last night," said Lazac anxiously. "Maybe he went out of his head during the night."

"It's possible," admitted Bienville. "Take a good look around the camp. He might have crawled off and gone to sleep somewhere."

Lazac went back to the blanket and made a cast around it. He found the track where Evan had crawled away during the night. He followed the scuffling marks through the leaves and dirt until he got into the open woods. Then he came back to Bienville.

"He left the camp altogether," he said. "He must have been crazy. I want to go after him."

Bienville looked unhappy. "We cannot wait for you, Gaston. I've got to get these men to the boats as fast as I can march them. The river is falling."

"I know," said Lazac steadily. "I don't want you to wait for me. Whether I find him or not, I'll hit across country to Scanapa and the Choctaw territory." He hitched his musket under his arm. "I'll be going."

Bienville gripped his shoulder. "Good luck, Gaston. I hope to God you find the boy. He is a fine lad."

"I wish you could have seen him in the battle," answered Lazac. "He was like a veteran. He saved both De Noyan and me as he encountered and killed several Chickasaw braves. There is much more to him than even we ever guessed."

Bienville nodded his head, "I wish to God I could wait for him or send a party to find him, but I have my duty to these men. If anyone can get him through this country and back to Nouvelle Orleans it is you. God be with you, old comrade."

He stood looking after Lazac until he was out of sight. The big woods runner followed the evidence of Evan's trail out into the woods. It was an easy trail as it cut back into the big timber. But Evan had a good start. If Evan was able to travel he might have a difficult time catching him. He saw that the trail led south. He wondered where Evan thought he was going.

CHAPTER XXIV

The sun was hot on Nouvelle Orleans. The willows along the levee were shimmering green-gold masses in the breeze off the river. Shadows of houses and trees were bold blocks along the ground. The river was falling. Already the mud outside the levee was cracking in the heat.

It was Sunday, May the twenty-seventh, and a bell was tolling the hour.

Edme Gatien Salmon, Commissaire-Ordonnateur of the Province of Louisiana, sat, checking over the list of requisitions which he intended to send to Paris by the next ship. He worked conscientiously, his long upper lip drawn down tight, his mind intent upon his work. He was a studious man who worshiped efficiency. The avariciousness of his predecessors in office outraged his sense of duty. He had no thought of personal gain but was a born clerk obsessed with the notion of doing his job well. It was for this reason that he admired Bienville, whose method of governing he considered efficient.

He found his concentration upon his task suddenly disrupted by the rising tide of excited voices which seemed to come from the levee upon which his house fronted. For a minute he endeavored to ignore it and go on with the business at hand. At length in exasperation he put down his quill, but carefully, so that it would not splotch his papers, and went out upon the gallery.

There was a growing crowd of men and women on the levee. A man stood in the middle of the crowd trying, at the same time, to answer their questions and to force his way out of the ring with which they enclosed him. The man was dressed like a woodsman in a ragged, filthy hunting shirt and leggings which had seen hard travel. His face was thin and almost lost in a wild tangle of beard. With a nervous start Salmon recognized him. It was Jules Dubuisson, the scout that Bienville had sent to the Illinois with Captain Leblanc.

In a fit of sudden excitement and apprehension, Salmon leaned over the gallery railing and waved to attract Dubuisson's attention.

"Hey, my good fellow, come up here!"

Dubuisson stared up at him, his eyes red rimmed beneath bushy brows. He started to say something, then paused and took off his bedraggled coonskin cap in a belated salute to the Intendant.

"I wanted to see you," he said, huskily.

The jabbering crowd at Salmon's plaintive insistence opened and let the scout come through. There was an anxiety in them which reflected the tense exhaustion in Dubuisson's face, and the rising ripple of sound that went through them intensified it.

Salmon did not wait for the scout to come up. He ran down the stairs at the gallery's end. Catching Dubuisson by the arm, he dragged him in through the door in the wall. They went upstairs together, the woodsman so weary that he walked with a heavier step than the Intendant.

In his office Salmon pushed Dubuisson into a chair and reached for a decanter. He handed a glass of brandy to the exhausted man and stood back. This was a situation which he could not put down in neat rows of figures. It flustered him where the most complicated arithmetical problem would have left him calm.

"What is it, man?" he exclaimed, excitedly. "What is the news? Why are you back here alone?"

Dubuisson bolted the brandy and sighed. He wiped his hand across his mouth.

Salmon refilled the glass.

"D'Artaguette led his men into a trap," he said. "He must be dead by now and the others, too."

Salmon, stunned, could only reply, "What?"

Dubuisson drained the glass again and looked hopefully at the bottle. Salmon ignored it.

"They wiped us out. Our damned Indians stampeded before even they smelled smoke. They're probably running yet. I hope they run to hell. There must have been a thousand Chickasaws and God knows how many English."

"English?" repeated Salmon, as if things wouldn't come straight in his mind. "The entire army was massacred? Bienville, too?!"

"God knows," said Dubuisson. "We didn't see Bienville. He never got there and D'Artaguette wouldn't wait." He leaned forward, his eyes on the bottle and his tongue wetting his lips.

Salmon said sharply, "Why in God's name did D'Artaguette not wait? He had his orders."

"I'll tell you," said Dubuisson, taking his time. He was piqued with Salmon's watchfulness over the bottle.

"D'Artaguette made his plans on the orders Leblanc brought him. We came back down river with him and got to the Chickasaw bluffs in the beginning of March. D'Artaguette had thirty soldiers from the garrison at Fort Chartres, along with near one hundred woods runners, voyageurs, and volunteers from the settlements. He had practically all the Kaskaskias. He was waiting for Monchervaux to come in the with the Michigamias and the Cahokias from the Illinois confederacy and for De Vincennes to bring the Indians from the Wabash. It was more than a week before De Vincennes arrived with his Indians. He had also brought about forty Iroquois with him. We waited several more days but no one else arrived so we started a slow march hoping that Monchervaux would soon catch up, and Grandpre, who was bringing in the Arkansas. Neither of them ever caught up with us."

"The second day out on the march, the Tunica runner, Chiki, joined us with a letter from Bienville. D'Artaguette called a council of his officers and the chiefs. There was a hell of a pow-wow. D'Artaguette said that Bienville could not join them before the end of April. The chiefs said they couldn't wait that long, their supplies were running out. All his officers said to damn the delay and go ahead and fight. I think that he knew better but there was nothing he could do."

Salmon shook his head, dreading that what he knew must come next. He relented with the decanter and handed it to Dubuisson who emptied the contents into the glass and drank half of it.

"Well," he said wiping his mouth again, "we tried to take a town -- and they trapped us. The whole damned tribe of the Chickasaws, it looked like, led by Englishmen. We never had a chance. All the Indians except the Iroquois ran like rabbits. If it hadn't been for them, I would have been killed, too. They held the Chickasaws while we cut our way out. Captain Leblanc was killed before we got out. I don't know whether D'Artaguette was killed or captured, but we never saw him any more. What little was left of us retreated as fast as we could. Two days later we met Monchervaux with a hundred and seventy Indians and fifteen Frenchmen. He turned around with us and went back toward the river. We were attacked by a large band of Chickasaws but fought them off. They had a number of blacks with them. Undoubtedly they are escaped slaves from as far south as here. We took a gold Fleur-de-Lis off the neck of one big young black who was killed in the fight."

He finished the glass of brandy.

"We made our way back to the river. I had been hit in the thigh and could hardly walk. I spent some time in one of the settlements and returned here as soon as I could to bring the news. That's it. God knows what happened to the other army."

Salmon's sallow face was gray, his thin fingers trembled. He reached over and pulled at Dubuisson's hunting shirt, shaking him.

"Ciel, man," he blurted out, "if they have destroyed our other army what are we going to do? The Indians will be down upon us!" He stood in agonized indecision. "Tell me man, what can I do?"

Dubuisson looked at him wearily, "You can get me another bottle."

The news spread like fever from one end of the settlement to the other, spawning contradictory rumors as it circulated. Dames, always alert for bad news, seized avidly upon calamity and shrieked it to their sister gossips. Men looking into wine cups or mugs of rum believed what was said across the table, and what was said was not governed by any law of logic. Bienville and D'Artaguette, the tale ran, had been massacred by untold thousands of Chickasaws and the entire English army of Carolina operating together. The Choctaws had turned treacherously upon the French and joined the enemy. All of these savages had taken up the hatchet and this immense force was racing southward with the express purpose of sweeping the French into the sea. The valley of the Mississippi was on fire. There was nothing to squelch it. Nouvelle Orleans and all the settlements along the coast and the river were doomed. The cold touch of panic ran through the settlement and the people remembered the days of terror after the Natchez massacre.

Therese Lambert brought the news to Jacqueline. The practical madame was for once perturbed. She had seen Jules Dubuisson, and thought it entirely likely, from what he had said, that Bienville's army had been trapped in the same manner as D'Artaguette's. But she passed lightly over it in telling Jacqueline, saying that it was nothing but idle talk. She had wanted to be the first to tell Jacqueline before some fool gossip, eager to impart bad news, made it look as if Bienville's army had also been massacred.

"Don't let it worry you," she admonished Jacqueline. "It all happened two months ago. Bienville's army had time to get news of it and keep out of trouble."

Jacqueline shook her head. They could hear the bell on the Church of St. Louis ringing the faithful to worship. The news would have spread within the cathedral walls. There would be paternosters and Ave Marias for the unknown and unnamed men who had died in battle against the savages.

Jacqueline's hand was on Therese's arm. Her voice was almost a whisper.

"Let's go. I feel like praying."

Father Raphael's voice droned above the heads of the congregation like summer thunder pregnant with the threat of a storm.

"Lamb of God, Who takest away the sins of the world..."

And like the echo of his voice, far off and almost forgotten echo, the hum of the congregation: "Spare us O Lord!"

"Lamb of God, Who takest away the sins of the world..."

"Graciously, hear us, O Lord!"

Jacqueline, beside Therese Lambert, heard it as in a dream. Instinctively she whispered her on responses. "Hear me, O God! Bienville is beaten. The Indians are butchering the French just as I saw them do at Fort Rosalie. Where is Evan? Oh, God, where is Evan?"

"Lamb of God, Who takest away the sins of the world,..."

"Have mercy upon us!"

Her shoulders twisted in helpless despair. "Have mercy on him. O, God, what good is worship of You to us, if You let your people be slaughtered and violated by heathen savages who have no notion of You? What good is Your religion to me, if You have taken away the only thing on earth I ever really wanted?"

"Jesus, meek and humble of Heart."

"Make our heart like unto thine."

Her own heart was cold, like a lump of clay in her breast. It hurt her. Her brain was numb with thinking. Thinking, "Evan. He's dead, He won't come back."

Father Raphael's voice lifted, "Let us pray."

Evan's knees were in the moist sand, his body leaned forward so that his hands sank out of sight up the wrist in it. His neck thrust out and he almost drowned himself in it. The water clear and shallow as he peered into it, pausing for breath between gulps. Minnows flirted past this nose, seeming by reason of the shadow which followed them across the sandy floor of the creek to be double the number they actually were. Their swift, darting movements made his head start to ache again.

The water was good, but it had a foreign taste in his sore, sour mouth, and it hurt his throat going down. Then it made him remember how empty he was. His stomach had contracted to the size of his fist, and his whole body was sick. God, he thought heavily, why doesn't a thing like this have an ending somewhere? Get it over with. What's the use of struggling? You don't get further if you struggle than if you don't. It's nothing but an added torture.

He stared at the water and thought how easy it would be to put his face down and keep it down until he drowned.

A tree had fallen upon the opposite bank of the stream. It lay half in and half out of the water and formed a screen between Evan and the other bank. The dead twigs of it were thick and matted, like his unkempt hair which he pushed back from his eyes when it obstructed his vision. He stared at the tree dully at first, still toying with the notion of pushing his face into the water. Then his eyes began to focus. The foliage beyond the tree stirred. It might have been no more than the breeze. But a trace of cunning came back into Evan's mind. A minute before he had wanted to die and be out of his misery; now he was alert against anything that might threaten him and determined to elude it. He reasoned that whatever it was across the stream it could not see him for the branches of the dead tree. Slowly foot by foot he began to retreat from the edge of the stream, backing toward the woods behind him.

The foliage was pushed aside and a man came through. It was Gaston Lazac. He had his flintlock in his left hand and he stood there blinking in the hot sunlight, looking first up and then down the stream.

At first sight of him Evan felt a quick surge of relief. But the fever had left his head full of muddled impressions. Seeing Lazac made him remember why he was in the woods. He was looking for Rene. He had forgotten that for a while and just wandered. Now it came back to him. He peered feverishly at Lazac and as he peered he became suspicious. Lazac wanted to keep him from finding Rene. He began again to edge backward toward the woods.

Lazac stepped into the stream and started to circle the fallen tree. Then he saw Evan scuttling frantically now for cover. For a second he stopped dead still with the clear water bubbling over his moccasins and brought up his gun. Then he saw that it was a white man and not an

Indian. He yelled out at Evan and started to run, splashing water in a high fountain around him.

He was surprised that Evan did not stop. He yelled again, thinking perhaps Evan didn't know who it was. With the sound of the second yell, Evan looked full at him, jumped to his feet and plunged in staggering, headlong flight into the brush. At that Lazac decided that he was mad and let out after him with the speed of a scared deer.

He overtook Evan before they had gone twenty yards, with the bushes whipping behind them as they passed. Evan tried to dodge the down bearing bulk of Lazac, and stumbled, falling, scrambling among the moldy leaves at the foot of an oak tree. Lazac, blowing out his breath, stood over him.

"Wait," he said, "its nobody but me."

But Evan clambered shakily to his feet. Lazac's big hand closed on his arm a moment before he was off again. He twisted like and eel, pulling the huge woods runner off balance, so that they fell together in the leaves. Lazac straddled his chest and held him still.

"Jesus," he panted, "don't you know me?"

He was watching Evan closely as he fumbled at his canteen. Unscrewing the top he waved it in front of Evan's face.

"Drink this. It'll make you as good as new in no time."

The smell of the rum seemed to overpower Evan. He relaxed, closing his eyes, and let Lazac pour the fiery stuff down his throat. It choked him and he began to cough.

Lazac took the canteen away from Evan's lips and took a drink himself. He swallowed and spat.

Evan opened his eyes. "I was looking for Rene," he said, wearily.

"You won't find him," said Lazac. "He's dead."

Evan stared at him, turning that over in his head. It still didn't come clear.

Lazac explained, putting his hand on Evan's forehead.

"You've got fever. Rene's been dead for days. You just thought he was alive."

It was queer how the liquor cleared up some of the muddle in Evan's head. He began to remember. It was too much to think. He let his eyes droop shut and his head loll. He could hear Lazac's voice droning as if it were miles away and fading ever farther.

"Listen," Lazac was saying, "we'll wait here awhile until you get a little strength back in you. Then we'll hit south into Choctaw country. I'll aim for Scanapa. You need somebody to work on that fever, even if it is only a Choctaw shaman."

They lay there in the woods and Evan, under the influence of the liquor, fell into a doze. The sunlight sifted down to them from the interlacing upper branches like a shower of golden dust. As the sun slid westward the shadow crawled longer and longer across the leaf strewn forest floor. A stillness hung in the woods, as real as the lengthening shadows.

CHAPTER XXV

It was never thereafter clear to Evan what trail they followed to Scanapa after Gaston Lazac found him in the woods south of the Chickasaw towns. All he ever learned of it was what Lazac told him when he began to shake off the fever. They had been a week on the trail, and most of the time, Lazac said, Evan had been so weak that he had to be carried, like a quarter of venison, across the brawny shoulder of the woods runner.

But he remembered the Choctaw village; the cabin in which he had been confined, the logs of its walls, as big as his leg, and fastened together with lianas. He remembered the fleas which leapt up at his bed from the dirt floor, the stink of it in the heat which had descended upon them. He remembered the drastic remedies of the shaman who could not decide whether Evan was afflicted with the heat sickness, pale abeka, or the little people's sickness, iyaganaca abeka, and consequently treated him for both, dosing him with a purgative brewed from the root of the huckleberry, and plastered him with poultices of flag and the bark of the young cottonwood.

They were eight days in the Choctaw village in which time Evan's fever left him and his strength returned, either as a result of the shaman's ministrations or in spite of them.

When they left Scanapa, instead of traveling southeast to Fort Tombekbe, Lazac struck out southwest toward the Choctaw town of Boucfouca and the headwaters of the Riviere aux Perles beyond it. They reached the great river after three days and spent two days more in shaping a pirogue from a cypress log.

They sweated in the heat, hacking and charring the log. A hot blanket had fallen on the Choctaw country. A sweat drawing, strength sapping heat that Evan had never experienced. It was the sentient personality of this subtropical land coming to life. It was the very breath of the South, so far removed from his Scottish Highlands, which was the breath of the north. It was the humid heat which made green things grow like magic, which turned the cleared land to thicket, the thicket to jungle almost as a man watched. The line of green treetops turned hazy in it. Great masses of clouds, cottony, sterile, billowed up, their sides shimmering like silver in the sun.

Lazac seemed not to mind the sun, working with his hunting shirt off, his great brown back turning black in the heat. But the white glare made Evan's unacclimated brains reel if he stayed too long in the sun. Often he had to find the shade of a tree and lie there broiling while the sickness passed from his head. His clothes were saturated. His body reeking with crusted sweat when at the end of the day he and Lazac stripped and washed in the river.

But, oddly enough, in spite of the smothering heat and the strain which labor imposed upon his still weak body, he felt a sense of peace. The woods were peaceful, cool, deep and green in their shade. The river, sparkling in the sun, was peaceful. The agony of battle, of privation on the march, or defeat, was over. He was going home. He did not know when he had come to think of this land as home. Surely before the march he had regarded it as a medium for his adventuring. A sort of chessboard upon which he could carry out his romantic ideas to his heart's content. Always there had been in the back of his mind no thought of settling here. Always he had believed, that when his appetite for romance was filled, he would go back to the Highlands, or to France. Here, suddenly, this land was home to him. He did not inquire into his change of heart. He was content with it, as a man wandering on a winter's night is content with the sight of a lighted window.

So, on a morning in mid June, they went down the river, their pirogue breaking through the mist which rose when the sun struck the stream. Evan sat in the bow, flip-paddling as he had learned and pushing the boat off the snags which infested the river. Lazac's big bulk weighted down the stern as he stroked steadily.

Behind Evan were the blood and smoke and defeat of Ackia. But down river with him trooped the memories: the shreds and vestiges of dissolving illusions; the echoes of battle. The swift roar and yellow menace of the Tombekbe flood. The chants of bateauxmen. The pitiful scarecrows from the French garrisons. The rain, rain, rain, and the wet, cold camps. The clouds of mosquitoes. The scurvy, the flux, and the fever. All the small, protracted miseries of the march, somehow they overshadowed the brief, bitter episode of the defeat.

He felt no sense of defeat. Rather, passing through mile on mile of wilderness, he realized the futility and insignificance of such struggles as the recent campaign, except insofar as they were a measure of human endurance. That was the answer. The rewards went to he who endured. That was the adventure he had sought. The imperishable adventure which did not pass, but grew steadily day by day down through the years.

Fourteen days later they were at the portage of the Bayou St. John. Papa Jules Froissart sat in the shade on his doorstep scraping at a melon with his hunting-knife. He had raised it in the patch beside his hut.

Hospitably he greeted Evan and Lazac, as if he had seen them yesterday, and invited them to help themselves to a melon. Lazac stepped into the patch to fetch two, while Evan sat down in the shade with Papa Jules. The old man was in one of his more lucid moods.

"Where have you and Gaston been, my son?" he asked Evan.

It amused Evan a little, remembering all the fanfare of the army's departure. Now Papa Jules did not know, or had forgotten, where they had gone.

"We went with the army. They left us up in the north."

Papa Jules's pale eyes regarded him. His mouth worked on the melon, "Eh? Oh, yes, the army. I am old. The army. I forget. They came two weeks since. They were beaten. They should have known better. I could have told them. But no one listens to Jules Froissart."

Once before, when the old man had said that it was futile for the French and Indians to fight, he had thought him crazy. Now he was not so sure.

"The Sieur de Bienville," he asked Papa Jean, "has he returned with the army?"

The old man munched away on his melon for so long that Evan thought he was not going to reply.

"Oui," he said, at last. "He was with them." He cackled. "He looked as old as I do. He looked old and ill. But he is a good man. I spoke to him, and he spoke to me while the men were marching up from the boats. The men were ragged. Their shoes were worn out. Some of them fell when they tried to walk. Ah, poor men. There were not so many of them as when they went off to their foolish war."

Evan shut his eyes for a moment. He could see them, staggering and slipping holding to each other, using their muskets for crutches as so many of them had done on that frightful march from the portage to

Ackia. The undersized sans culottes which the government in Paris had foisted on Bienville in the guise of soldiers.

Lazac hunched his head forward, taking careful aim as he spat at a dragonfly which had alighted on a nearby stem of grass. He missed.

Over his shoulder he asked Papa Jules, "Did Bienville ever learn what happened to D'Artaguette's army?"

"The man from the north? He was killed and his army dispersed. There was a panic in the town when they heard the news. They believed that Bienville had been massacred too. They said that the Indians were coming. But I was not afraid. I know that they are not fools."

Evan pitched the rind of his melon into the bayou and got up, nudging Lazac with his toe.

"Our thanks to you, Papa Jules, for the melons," he said. "Now we must be on our way into the town."

Papa Jules broke into his cackling laugh. "Yes, you must be on your way. You have no time for an old man like Jules Froissart. The young stallion must run to the mare in season. Eh, eh, it is well."

"The girl, Jacqueline, will be waiting for you. She is no longer bound," he said. "The half-man is dead."

Evan had begun to turn brick red, but at Papa Jules's last words the color ran out of his face.

"What?"

Lazac, every bit as startled, blew out his breath.

"Etienne is dead? Jesus, what happened to him?"

Evan did not listen to Papa Jules's reply. He was startled at the extent of his agitation. Thoughts clustered in his brain like hiving bees. Thoughts which had not been there before. If Etienne were dead, then...

She had been Etienne's wife and could not be taken seriously. But if Etienne were dead, then... She was a woman, as she had been for

347

that moment in his arms. Yes, a desirable woman. One, whoever her next husband might be, any man would be fortunate to get. His memory went back over the month since the defeat at Ackia. That month in which he had shed his illusions like a snake's skin in the springtime. They had not gone painfully, but had died by merging into his maturing sense of reality. He remembered working, shaping the pirogue from the cypress log. That had been pleasant, his first act of construction in this new land, as if it were only a beginning, a shaping of his own life from rough timber. Since then he had really loved this land, and it came to him that he had known all along that Jacqueline was a symbol of all that was worthwhile in it.

But there was one illusion left to him. It clung like a leech after all reason for it had gone.

My God, he argued with himself, half appalled at the trend of his thinking, I'm in love with Antoinette. I can't get out of that so easily. He had a duty to himself to honor his love for Antoinette.

Shaved and washed and once more respectable in clean linen, Evan left Bienville's house in the cool of late afternoon to walk to Castilloux's. As he had been dressing to call on Antoinette he had been of half a mind not to go at all. The more thought he gave it, the less enthusiastic he was about it.

In some way, Antoinette was jumbled in his head with those jumbled illusions of life. He wondered why in the name of heaven he was going through with it. There must be some trait of Gaelic stubbornness in him which made him go ahead. He had started out by being in love with Antoinette Castilloux, but since his days in the Choctaw village he had barely thought of her.

He toiled in his memory of the days on the return journey to Nouvelle Orleans. When had she entered his mind? Not while he was making the bateau. Not in the journey down the river. He closed his eyes and tried to see her in his mind's eye. He remembered the blond hair, the blue eyes, and the beautiful face but he could no longer see them. He told himself that she had been his first love. He could not let it end without seeing her and talking to her. He had been through much but being with her might bring it all back. He must see he her or he would always wonder.

Bienville had been glad to see him, but had not seemed greatly surprised. Indeed, it appeared that he was too bitter or dazed to be greatly pleased or surprised at anything. Papa Jean had been right. Bienville had aged startlingly since the campaign. All the time he had talked to Evan he had dwelt upon the plans which he was drawing up for a second expedition. A campaign of vengeance. Shortly, he had sent Evan away, saying that he had to be at work. Evan had gone, leaving him there with his chin propped on his hand, brooding above his empty desk. That, as much as anything else, strengthened Evan's yearning to get back to the reality and simplicity of living as he had known it in the Highlands, and as it had come to him again in the wooded heart of the Choctaw country.

He turned into the Rue de Bourbon, which was drying to dust in the hot weather and saw Castilloux's house, white in the late golden light of the afternoon. Castilloux sat upon the gallery enjoying the breeze. He rose heavily in some surprise when his eyes alighted on Evan.

Antoine Castilloux leaned on the rail as Evan stopped in the street below, not asking him to come in.

"Well, my young friend?" he said in his thick voice.

His discourtesy made Evan bold. "Monsieur, I'd like to see Antoinette, if you please," he said bluntly.

Castilloux's eyes, half hidden in their folds of flesh, were amused. His voice sneered faintly.

"Antoinette? La Baronne de Laval, to you sir," he said with considerable unction. "She sailed with her husband some six weeks ago upon the Gironde. Neither she nor the Baron de Laval cared to remain any longer in this country. If I ever had any doubts of their wisdom in doing so, sir, I have none now. The criminal incompetence of your master, the Sieur de Bienville, has brought this colony to a pass where neither the lives of its persons nor their enterprises are safe. I am surprised that you have the gall to show your face again after taking part in such a sorry military fiasco."

Castilloux's voice rose toward the end of his tirade. Evan found himself smiling broadly at the man. All at once he felt relief bubbling out him in a kind of malicious joy. Antoinette and De Laval hastening off to the French Court. Only weeks ago it would have seemed stark tragedy, now it was only ridiculous. As he looked up at the bulbous man pouting on his veranda at the endangerment to some of his profits, Evan thought of that tired, old man, Bienville, sharing the hardships with his soldiers.

For an instant he imagined that he saw Antoinette standing beside her father, as if father and daughter were, in a way, inseparable. The aura of divinity had disappeared. He saw her merely as the daughter of Antoine Castilloux, and the thought was not pleasant.

He could not help but let out a laugh. A laugh of relief, contempt, and pity that was not lost on Castilloux. He turned without a word and walked away. Castilloux stood quite still watching him go, leaning forward upon the rail, his thick lips pouting, his pig-eyes contemplating the unlooked for response from Evan. Then he shrugged, which caused his belly to jerk forward, and, turning, went into the house and shut the door.

Evan had not yet seen Jacqueline Martin. He went now in the direction of her cabin with haste and decision. It was almost night, shadows began scurrying like rats under the picket fences along the streets and hiding behind the corners of houses. He heard a woman's voice calling stridently for a truant offspring. Here and there an early candle made a blob of light against the obscure bulb of a house.

Jacqueline's house was dark when he reached it, a forlorn little coop perched above a miniature jungle of reeds and grass. He felt a sense of outrage that she should have to live there. The door opened readily under his hand, but the house was empty. Involuntarily he called her name, thinking she might be in the cubbyhole which had been Collette's. But there was only a echo. For an instant he felt a sense of desolation. Then his anxious heart was reassured as he saw the smolderingly coals on the hearth. He went outside again and seated himself on the bottom step, waiting for her to come.

Presently, he saw her coming through the gloom. Her body made a slender, straight shadow, the heavy wooden bucket braced against her hip. Evan sprang to his feet to take it from her. She stopped dead, recognizing him, her breath a short, quiet gasp in the dark. Her rigid arm holding the bucket shook and there was a flat splash of water hitting the earth as the bucket tipped. Evan snatched it from her before she let it go entirely, stooped to set it decisively on the ground, then stood straight before her. Now that he was face to face with her his tongue stuck to the roof of his mouth.

After her first start of surprise she stood quietly as if waiting for him to move or speak. When he did neither it was she who broke the taut, straining, silence.

"Gaston told me that you had come back." Her words came with difficulty as if impeded by tears.

Her voice shattered his indecision. His hands, which had been dangling limp, seized hers and pulled her to him. His right arm circled the small of her back, braced there like a bar, straining to hold her

351

closer against his chest. He felt the swift response flow from her like a wave and ripple through his body. Her own hands came up, feeling his face. Her fingers gently traced their way over his cheek and his lips. She burrowed her face into the hollow of his shoulder and began to cry. He held her closer, with a great feeling of protectiveness.

"Darling," he whispered against her hair.

She stopped crying as suddenly as she had started, and looked up into his face, tears beading her lashes.

"I was waiting for you to come," she murmured. "I --" she did not finish because the movement of her lips enticed Evan so that he could not help but cover them with his own.

Her mouth under his filled him with a swift hot passion. His arms became a veritable vice, crushing her until she slid her face aside and, half laughing, told him that he was about to break her back. He was instantly contrite and, lifting her bodily, carried her up the steps into the cabin. He was surprised how light she felt in his arms.

He dropped her on the bunk which had been Etienne's and sat beside her. Laughing gently she pushed him away as he tried to kiss her again, and sat up.

"You are taking advantage of me when I am only a poor weak widow woman," she chided him. "Coming into my house when I am alone and trying to share my bed. Shame on you."

Her teasing disconcerted him.

"I -- I'm sorry," he stammered. "I lost my head."

She laughed then, with a rich sound that made his heart glad. "No, you're not one bit sorry. You had better not be. If you were, I'd send you out of here."

It was pitch dark in the cabin. She leaned toward him until he could feel her warm breath on his cheek.

"Oh, my darling, I've been living in hell. When the news came that the northern army had been massacred, I was sure that the same had happened to you. Then Bienville came back; I rushed to the rampart gate to watch them come. They seemed to pass me endlessly, the ragged, sick men. But you were not there. I asked Captain Le Sueur and he told me that you had dropped out of the march and that Gaston had gone back to look for you. From the look of his face I could tell that he thought it was of no use. I could have killed them all for not waiting for you. But I knew then that you were dead. I knew that the Chickasaws had found you and had tortured you horribly before they killed you. I've had nightmares about it ever since. Only God knows why I haven't gone out of my mind."

A deep humility that she should feel so about him overwhelmed him so that he could not speak.

She sighed. "Poor little Collette. Gaston told me about her and her Rene. I didn't know where she had gone. I wish there had been something that I could have done for her. She tried so hard. And poor Henri. He was so tormented."

Evan patted her shoulder. "Don't grieve. It's all in the past. That is over and done. It's what's in the future that counts. Rene and Collette came to this country to build new lives and a new world. Henri loved this country. They would all want us to do what they wished to do."

For a second she held her breath. Was he also thinking about what was in the past for him? Was he thinking about Antoinette? She would not ask him. Rather, she would let that die a natural death and hopefully it was already extinct. Now that he had come to her she was full of confidence. He belonged to her and she wondered why she had ever doubted that things would turn out right.

She repeated his words: "Yes, it's what's before us that counts."

He blurted out, "How soon will you marry me?"

She smiled and again tears started into her eyes. "There's no reason in waiting. Etienne is dead, and I'm glad for his own sake and for my own. The sooner I find my happiness the better."

His arms went about her and she clung to him. "I'll do my best," he said, huskily as the emotion choked him. "I'll do my best to make you happy and keep you well. I know now what it is that I want besides you. I want land and a home of our own. Land that I can clear and a house that I can build with my own hands. Nothing is worth having unless you work for it. I'm just beginning to understand what this country holds for a man who will work or it. I'll get land, one way or the other. Then there's nothing that can hold us back."

They held each other, wrapped in their dreams, while several minutes passed. Then Jacqueline gently slipped out of his embrace and stood up.

"I'm starved to death," she announced as if it were something to be delighted about. "It's funny. Until tonight I've had no thought of food at all, and now I'm starving."

She went over and poked the coals on the hearth until they glowed sullenly.

"You must be hungry, too," she told Evan, who couldn't take his eyes off of her. "I'll fix some sagamity for us." She looked around a bit wildly. "Where's the water? What did I do with the water? I can't make sagamity without water to boil the grits."

They laughed together as they went outside to find the forgotten bucket of water in the darkness.

Chapter XXVI

Evan went in to see Bienville the next morning. If anyone could advise him in obtaining land it would be the Governor. He was well aware that he had no money so perhaps he might have to provide some service to the colony. He was prepared to do whatever it took, from serving as Hebert's assistant to any other task, so long as he got the opportunity to acquire his own land in due time.

"Land?" Bienville echoed him at the request. "For what do you want land?"

Evan said, steadily, "I want to settle on it. You see, sir, I'm getting married."

"Eh, married?" Bienville peered at him over his reading glasses. "Married to whom?"

"Jacqueline Martin," said Evan, as if that explained everything.

Bienville made a low humming sound. "Martin? Oh yes, I know the woman. A good woman, from all I know," he said dryly. "Gaston Lazac thinks highly of her. You could do worse, lad."

"Thank you, sir," said Evan, beginning to think that his plans were better known to some others than to himself.

"Well, let's see. It was land you wanted, eh? Land to settle on. So, you desire to be in my employment no longer, eh?"

Evan felt uncomfortable. "I'm sorry sir. It isn't that I don't appreciate all you've done for me but..."

Bienville cut him off. "Bah! Don't apologize. You'd be a fool if you did otherwise. Do you think I wish to bury you in secretarial work when you're eager to accomplish something on your own?" He reached for a roll of cloth backed paper tied about with a red ribbon that was lying on the top of his desk. Untying the ribbon, he spread the roll across the desk. It was a chart of his personal grants along the river. Evan stepped close and looked over Bienville's shoulder.

"I have land of my own, enough to spare," said Bienville. "Once I thought it was important to acquire much land. That was a mistake. It is far better for the colony to have land for many men, than to have all the land for a few." He seemed to be talking more for his own benefit than for Evan's. His thin forefinger traced across the chart, stopping finally at a point beyond that which was marked, "Cannes Brulees."

"Here is an excellent tract, uncleared but diked against the river. I can give you this tract of ten arpents fronting on the river by fifty arpents in depth. Is that satisfactory?"

Evan had trouble with his voice, "I, uh, perfectly, sir."

"Good. I am vested with authority by His Majesty the King to grant lands at my discretion. I will grant you absolute title to this piece of land on the following conditions which I will have drawn up for you to sign. First, the title is absolute only if you cultivate the land for two consecutive years. It is also subject to possible royal dues, to furnish timber for forts, to repair ships and other public works, and the land may be taken over at any time for the purpose of erecting fortifications if such are necessary. This is the right of the King in eminent domain. You understand me, this is no seigneurie, but a freehold."

Evan laughed. "It's good enough for me. I'm afraid I wouldn't make a good seigneur, anyway."

"I suppose not," said Bienville, so dryly that Evan would not be positive that it was a compliment or not. "I'll have this deed drawn up and sent over to Monsieur Henri, the clerk of the Superior Council, to be executed and registered." He stood up and put both his hands on Evan's shoulders, holding him in a half embrace. It was the nearest the undemonstrative Bienville ever came to an open show of affection. "Good luck to you, lad. It does my heart good to see you taking your future in your own hands."

But he did not let Evan go, holding him awhile in talk, although Evan was in a fever to go back to Jacqueline and tell her about his astounding good fortune.

"You have made an impression and made friends in this colony," Bienville said. "Gaston Lazac has told me of your conduct during the battle. So has Major de Noyan and Captain de Lesueur. These men all have a high regard for you. These are not men who speak lightly."

He then turned toward the window. Evan knew that he was not finished, however. He felt that Bienville was eager to talk to someone, and he thought he knew why. Bienville was utterly alone now. His enemies had used his defeat to his discredit until even the common people were beginning to lose confidence in him. There was talk in the streets that Bienville had sacrificed the security of the settlements in an attempt to gain prestige. Evan suspected what was going on in Bienville's mind and his suspicions were confirmed as Bienville spoke again.

"You hear what people say," he said. "They blame me for what's happened, don't they?"

357

"It was not you fault, sir," Evan replied stoutly. "No man could have done more. If you had had troops worth their salt, you would have won.'

"So," said Bienville, reflectively. "But they talk. The little people. I don't care about the Castillouxs or the De Pradels. But it hurts me to have the little working people, the shopkeepers, the settlers, the woods runners, think that I have failed them." He walked back to his window, stood for a moment with his hands locked behind him, looking out, then turned back into the room.

"Evan," he said, "sometimes I don't know. I feel like a sailor whose ship has gone down under him. I'm swimming now for the shore, but the tide is running out. God knows it's no new feeling. I've been swimming against the tide for close to forty years. But now I'm old, and the shore seems farther off, and I don't know how much longer I'll be able to keep above the water. There are things that make a man feel that he has failed. D'Artaguette at Mobile blamed me for his brother's death. He was taken, you know, by the Chickasaws and burned alive. I don't blame D'Artaguette. He loved his brother. It was not my fault, yet I was to blame. The same is true of the entire campaign."

"It was ill luck," maintained Evan.

"Perhaps that's the answer," said Bienville. "Although it might seem to some to be a convenient way of shirking responsibility. When I was young, I paid no attention to the thing they call Fate. Indeed, I damned it. I could make my own fate. Now, I'm not so sure. Things seem to happen beyond my control. Perhaps my critics are correct, and I have lost my hold on things. At any rate, I'm not too optimistic about another expedition, but it must be done. For myself, I'd like to follow the example of your friend, Billiot. He left us at the Tohomes Village on the Mobile River. He said there was too much trouble in a white man's town. He thought life was simpler and better among the savages. So he took up with an Indian woman and stayed there. I don't envy him the squaw, but I envy him the peace."

Evan could not think of anything to say.

Bienville had seated himself at his desk. "Go on about your business, lad," he told Evan. "Don't mind me. My tongue is loose at both ends these days. I'll keep you here in talk, if you don't mind, until neither us will get anything done. Give my warm regards to your wife-to-be."

Evan left him there at his desk. Once he had been a hero to Evan. Now, he was even more, an old tired man who had given his best days in the service of his people. How could any man do more with his life than that.

Evan had gone about halfway to Jacqueline's when he heard Gaston Lazac yell to him. The big woods runner caught up to him and they walked along together.

"Why don't you tell me things?" asked Lazac. "You didn't tell me you and Jacqueline were going to be married. What kind of way is that to treat a man?"

Evan grinned at him. "I didn't know myself until last night. And I haven't seen you since. But you, you scoundrel, I think that you have known for some time."

Lazac looked a little guilty but did not address that. "Jacqueline seemed sort of pleased," he went on with his teasing. "Though God knows why a woman would want a man who is so shamed-faced he won't even tell his friends about it."

"Don't worry," said Evan. I'll let you witness for me when the priest marries us. And we'll break a bottle of brandy to celebrate."

Lazac snorted. "Jesus, I'd come anyway. Seems like everybody but me is taking a wife. Did you hear about Camille Billiot?" He began to bellow with laughter. "I knew he'd never come back and stand up to Clementine!"

They reached the cabin and there was Jacqueline in the door, watching them. The sight of her made Evans throat tight. She ran down the step and slipped unashamedly into his arms as Lazac looked on.

When they had completed their greeting, Evan began to tell her eagerly about the land. She looked up at him, her eyes opening wider and wider and shimmering like dark, deep pools when the sun is in them. When he had finished she hugged him again, fiercely, but did not speak.

Lazac broke into the scene which made him uncomfortable.

"So Bienville granted you some land, eh? Well, damn me if I ever could understand why any sensible man would want to scratch in the ground, but I'll do you a favor, just as a sort of wedding present. Listen!" he said loudly, because they did not appear to be paying attention, "I'll help you clear the land. That's fair as any man could want. But I won't help you farm it."

Evan turned his head without letting go of Jacqueline. She was looking past his shoulder and laughing at Lazac.

"Thank you so much for your kindness, Gaston. But what will we do if you don't farm our land for us.

They all laughed but Evan understood the true friendship of both Bienville and Gaston Lazac and was thankful.

Evan walked up the path toward his cabin silently looking over the cleared land and contemplating his life. Gaston Lazac had helped him clear the land in the hot months of July and August. It was good land, his grant; well watered, with a good spread of flat farming land on the river and a belt of cypress for timber near the back. Most of the river front had been grown over in canes. He had burned it off, which had saved him the trouble of having to clear with the axe. He liked the look of the land when it had been cleared. Between now and December he would grub out the cane and stubble and then plant it to tobacco for the market and corn for his own use. December, he had discovered, was the earliest month to plant tobacco, then spring for the corn. In the meantime he would have to buy meal.

Jacqueline had helped the two men put up the cabin. They were proud of it. It was built of red cypress logs which he and Lazac had cut in the swamp and skidded out themselves. It was hard work, but it had been worth it. Jacqueline had plastered the chinks between the logs with clay to keep out the weather. Returning now from the river after having seen Lazac off in his pirogue to Nouvelle Orleans, he looked proudly at the square bulk of the cabin. The sun was at his back and the flat rays of it turned the entire cabin as ruddy as the brick chimney on the north end. Passing the chimney, Evan rubbed his hand across it. His fingers came off tinged with red dust, for the sandy clay along the river made bricks so soft that they could be ground to powder if you rubbed them together. But it was a substantial chimney, and he had made it.

Inside he found Jacqueline, hot faced, bending over the fire to stir a pot of sagamity. She turned her face enough to smile at him. He walked past her and patted he shoulder. The heavy smell of grease in the cooking pot sat well on his empty stomach. He took his seat on the bed and sat contentedly watching Jacqueline at her chores.

This was home, as completely as if there was no other world outside of it. He had heard no word from Nouvelle Orleans in a month. He could go much longer without word and not be disappointed. Idly he wondered how many months or years it would take Bienville to prepare his new expedition. Now, he was not really concerned. The drums might roll, the troops and the tribes might march to new heights of vainglory and sweep like a prairie fire over the Indian country. The honor of France as represented in Chickasaw scalps might be of paramount importance in the valley of the Mississippi but he did not believe it. In place of his old illusion of romance he now had a half philosophic faith in the future of this land. That it was in the hands of the settlers. But its final evolution would not be sped nor made more sure by futile heroics. It would be made in a long series of days by men like himself, who would spend their lives building homes for their families. It was the accumulation of these lives and these families that would be the history and the future of this great land, not the echo of drums and muskets.

Like Bienville, he realized, he would not see the fruition of this land, the story was too vast. His lot would be to add a chapter to that which Bienville had started. Bienville was the father of this new land. His generation would serve as the midwives to bring it through its infancy. He had been fortunate to see the latter stages of the birth of this new world, now he would take part in the formation of its character. He would help teach it to stand on its own legs and take its first steps. If he were so fortunate, he would see his children begin to write their own chapter as they helped it grow in strength and vitality. It would not be an easy task at any stage but that was what made it worthwhile.

He had come to this land seeking adventure but had become a part of an adventure for the generations. Let Antoinette return to the staleness of France. Let Raoul devise his machinations to advance in business and society Theirs was an old world. A world that was cut into a pattern that could only be altered at the seams. This world was a virgin bolt of cloth. It could be made into anything imaginable and each person could be that tailor. He smiled contentedly to himself.

He had sprawled upon the bed, staring up at the rafters; now Jacqueline's voice calling him to eat cut through his thoughts. He looked at her admiringly across the table. She was so full of vitality after a hard day. "Come," she said, "the supper is ready and we must soon get to bed." She smiled. "Tomorrow we have so much to do."

THE END

Printed in the United States
88912LV00003B/112-114/A

9 781425 989491